Shadow Music

by

Elisabeth Rose

Shadow Music

Cover Art by *Abigail Owen*

The Wild Rose Press, Inc.
PO Box 708
Adams Basin, NY 14410-0708
Visit us at www.thewildrosepress.com

Publishing History
First Mainstream Paranormal Edition, 2019
Print ISBN 978-1-5092-2503-3
Digital ISBN 978-1-5092-2504-0

Published in the United States of America

Her fingers closed on a page…*a roar of voices, a deafening, clamorous burst of music, an overpowering scent of roses in hot night air…*

An electric shock shot through her hand and right up her arm, forcing an involuntary cry from her throat. Her fingers wouldn't respond, wouldn't release their grip on the paper. Something, some force, compelled her to remove the page from the box, trembling and suddenly clammy skinned in the heat of the day. The sound faded, the scent of roses replaced by stale tobacco smell as the stall holder bent down beside her.

"What's that you've got, love? Are you all right?" His curious face peered at her from under his wide-brimmed straw hat.

"Look," she whispered, unable to drag her eyes from the music in her shaking hand—a piece of manuscript, double paged. At the top was "Shadow Music" and "Violin" in elegant, looping old fashioned script, handwritten, as were the notes. In a different hand, scrawled in frantic haste across one corner with the last letters straggling into a thin line were the only other words.

This way madness lies.

Praise for Elisabeth Rose

Dedication

As always, to my family
Colin, Carla, Nick, and Paige

It is said that when the heart cracks it cracks with no sound but when it breaks it wreaks havoc with earthquake, thunder, and lightning.

Chapter One

Sydney, Australia, 1998

"Are you interested in music? Sheet music?" The stallholder pointed to three overflowing cardboard boxes on the grass beside his trestle table.

Nina paused in her browsing, a well thumbed copy of *Persuasion* in her hand, her eyes seeking *Emma*. Why would he ask her that? She glanced up with a puzzled smile.

The bushy grey beard parted to reveal a wide gap between two front teeth as he grinned. "You look like a musical girl."

"Do I? I am, I suppose." If you could call working in a CD shop being musical, which was as close as she came to music making nowadays.

"What do you play? Piano?" Encouraged, he bent and shoved one of the boxes forward.

"Violin. Rusty violin." She looked at the three crammed boxes. Music? She hadn't bought music for years. She was a listener now, a listener and a seller, hadn't picked up her violin more than twice in the last year although when she was at school she'd practised rigorously and according to her teacher, had talent. Wasted now. "I work in a music shop in North Sydney."

"There's some violin stuff in there, I'm sure." He

regarded her with such an expectant, hopeful expression she gave in. What did it matter to her on this lazy, sunny Saturday afternoon? He was a volunteer at the St Andrews church fete; he had good reason to try his best to offload the stock.

Nina handed over *Persuasion* and two dollars, squatted down with her purchase tucked under her arm in a brown paper bag and began riffling through the sheets crammed into the first box, pulling the occasional piece out for a better look. She had no intention of buying music, should be heading home to vacuum clean but she'd already disappointed him by taking only one book.

Her fingers closed on a page…*a roar of voices, a deafening, clamorous burst of music, an overpowering scent of roses in hot night air…*

An electric shock shot through her hand and right up her arm, forcing an involuntary cry from her throat. Her fingers wouldn't respond, wouldn't release their grip on the paper. Something, some force, compelled her to remove the page from the box, trembling and suddenly clammy skinned in the heat of the day. The sound faded, the scent of roses replaced by stale tobacco smell as the stall holder bent down beside her.

"What's that you've got, love? Are you all right?" His curious face peered at her from under his wide brimmed straw hat.

"Look," she whispered, unable to drag her eyes from the music in her shaking hand—a piece of manuscript, double paged. At the top was "Shadow Music" and "Violin" in elegant, looping old fashioned script, handwritten, as were the notes. In a different hand, scrawled in frantic haste across one corner with the last letters straggling into a thin line were the only other words.

This way madness lies.

Nina stared, fascinated, enthralled, bewildered, overwhelmed. The paper had attached itself to her hand the way a small child will hold on, desperate to be included, not to be left behind, lost. Almost alive.

"Put it back." His voice burst forth loudly, harsh and vehement. Nina's gaze whipped toward his enraged face, mottled now with deep red patches above the grey beard.

"No! I want it." Her reply shot back startling them both even more than his outburst. And as she said the words the idea formed in her mind that not only did she want the music she had to have the music no matter what. "How much?"

"I don't think you should take it." Uncertain now. The unexpected forcefulness faded. His skin resumed a more normal colour.

"I want it." Nina glared at him until he grudgingly produced another brown paper bag.

"Fifty cents," he muttered.

After a second's hesitation Nina handed him the page—reluctantly because she overwhelmingly didn't want to let it slip from her grasp. Only because she knew he was going to give it straight back was she able to release her hold on it—or its hold on her. He slid the sheet of manuscript inside the bag while Nina rummaged frantically in her purse for coins.

"Where did it come from?" Her hand reached for the bag as he took the money.

"I've no idea." He turned his back.

"Thanks," she muttered. Go home, find her violin.

Play. Now.

Dark, towering storm clouds built up rapidly during Nina's three-block walk home from St Andrews. Her feet increased their pace and she told herself the urgency was to avoid the inevitable onslaught of rain and hail, nothing to do with the paper bag clutched in both hands against her body, protected against the rising wind and the first big drops of rain.

She let herself into the tiny terrace house with a sigh of relief. Wind howled about the eaves, buffeting the screen door at the back. Hailstones clattered against the roof. Shivering and hurrying with nervous fumbling fingers, she made sure windows and doors were securely fastened then went to the spare room to pull her violin from the top shelf in the cupboard. A folding music stand lay next to it. She set it up, annoyed by the stiffness in the hinges and the stubborn tightness of the screws.

She undid the clasps of the violin case, lifted the lid. Her violin lay gleaming and ready in its blue plush bed. She placed a standing lamp so light pooled onto the music stand and carefully, reverently, removed the sheet of manuscript from the bag. No electric shock now, no sound, no rose perfume but it seemed to quiver in her hand. That would be her imagination.

Something scraped against the window in the wind, rain lashed down, thunder rumbled. Nina lifted her bow and tested the strings for tuning, adjusted the pegs. Began to play.

The melody was extraordinarily beautiful. Tears began streaming down her cheeks and she had to blink rapidly to see the notes as they blurred in front of her eyes but she didn't stop playing. The haunting phrases flowed from beneath her fingers and bow and echoed around the empty house, filling every corner with yearning and sorrow and love.

The wind lent itself to the music, becoming part of the sighing and sobbing of the violin, rising and falling as the melody rose and fell, now quiet now building in intensity to a climax then falling away to a whisper. She played as if in a dream, as she had never played before, drawing on resources of feeling and emotion she didn't know she had. As she reached the end of the first section, the phone rang loud and shrill, startling her so that her concentration broke momentarily and she faltered, her bow jerking from the strings.

"Bugger!" She tried to ignore the incessant ringing, standing with teeth gritted until the caller gave up after an endless time. She raised her bow and continued. Now the notes were harder to read. Not only was the manuscript faded in places but the second section comprised cadenza-like runs and trills swooping and soaring over the whole range of the violin, and the marking indicated the music should be played freely, fast, with passion. Faster than she could manage.

Stopping and starting, she stumbled through to the end but the overwhelming compulsion to keep playing she'd experienced in the first section had faded.

She went back to the beginning. Again that haunting melody brought tears to her eyes and with them a terrible sense of loss. Again she had to keep playing. And again and again, the first section, over and over. When she started the melody for the tenth time the thought "enough" crept into her brain.

But she couldn't stop. Each time she reached the end of the first part something compelled her to start again. The music forced her to keep playing. The same unnerving compulsion she'd had to take the music from the box at the fete.

"I must be mad." The sound of her voice startled her and her scratchy, sore eyes flashed to the words scrawled at the top of the page. Is this what they meant? Was it a warning?

Nina flexed her aching arms and neck. Her fingertips had gone numb from the pressure on the fingerboard. She was out of practice, she was exhausted. She desperately wanted to stop playing. When she reached the difficult second section the next time she forced herself to attempt it. She made mistakes; it was too hard for her—the power diminished.

She lowered her shaking bow and quickly put her violin into its case, snapping the catches to seal it in. Her cheeks were wet but this time with tears of relief. Weak and trembling, she extended a hand to take the music from the stand. To take it and tear it up, destroy it, throw it away, but her fingers stopped inches from the surface and a curious reluctance to touch it made her arm drop to her side.

"I'll do it tomorrow," she muttered and snapped off the lamp, hurried from the room, closed the door firmly behind her.

Still dazed, boiling the jug in the kitchen for a cup of tea, Nina's gaze strayed to the clock. After midnight! No wonder her arms ached. She'd been playing for hours. Playing the same page of music. Her stomach growled and complained. She'd forgotten to eat.

She heated tomato soup from a can, then, clutching her steaming mug in both hands, tottered across to the couch. Curling up at one end, she rested her head on the crocheted throw rug Gran had made. For as long as she could remember it had been somewhere in the house—sometimes on the spare bed, sometimes over Gran's knees when she sat in the garden, sometimes as now, draped over the back of the couch.

Nina put out a shaky hand and pulled it down, spreading it over her feet and legs. Reassuringly normal, crocheted squares of brightly coloured wool, memories of Gran, strong and vibrant, no nonsense Gran, competent, good humoured, reliable. Sane.

Not like her granddaughter. Nina blinked back tears. But Gran was long dead and no help at all.

The melody soared through her mind as she lay in bed in the darkness listening to the rain, but gradually the soothing normalcy of her bed and the sounds of water running in the gutters and dripping from the eaves brought her back from the edge of insanity. Be analytical she told herself. Be rational. When was it written? Sometime in the late nineteenth century? Definitely romantic—influenced by Rachmaninov, Tchaikovsky, Brahms? Either someone from the original era or a more modern composer writing in that style. Somehow though, she doubted that.

It wasn't just that the manuscript itself was very old because it was—or at least the paper had yellowed and the ink turned brownish. In remarkably good condition despite its age, no tears or creases—but the handwriting at the top was faded and the florid looping script had the look of a bygone era. Perhaps she could have it checked by an expert. Carbon dated. Did they do that with paper or just fossils? And where would she have it done? The university? What else would they find?

Were there Ghostbusters in Sydney?

She shifted restlessly and turned over. She'd left her book behind at the second-hand stall, hadn't even noticed till now. Her tired brain wandered and in its wanderings finally drifted into sleep.

He spoke to her in her dreams. He said, "Mira is not dead. She will live again. You must play for me. You must play."

Nina cried out, "I can't. I'm not good enough. I can't."

The melody rose strongly. She heard it played, not by herself but by someone else, someone far better, someone passionate and strong. The perfume of roses filled the air.

The dream violinist played the second section perfectly. A wild, gypsy style dance, full of runs and trills and flourishes. Faster than she could ever hope to play. He was improvising, not reading the notes. He played from the heart, from the soul, pouring out his emotions in the tumultuous music, his violin sobbing and sighing, singing and soaring. It was thrilling and hypnotic and she wanted it to go on forever. Then the music stopped and his voice came to her quite clearly, full of sadness and despair, pleading.

"Play. The music will bring her to me. My melody has the key to life."

And she woke with his words still in her ears and an unbearable sense of loss.

Sunlight streamed in through the crack between the curtains—strong, full sun, not early morning. Nina lay sprawled across the double bed. Her sheets were twisted and half on the floor, her head still rested on the pillow but she'd dragged the pillow to the side of the bed and jammed it against the wall in her sleep.

Only one thing remained from the dream. His voice. Insistent, urging, pleading with her to play. Play what? She sat up slowly as realisation dawned and snippets of the melody came skipping into her mind. Memories of last night's torment came flooding back. He wanted her to play that music.

"I can't," she said aloud. "I can't. I won't!"

She swung her legs over the side of the bed and went to her dressing table for clean underwear. Then she stomped to the bathroom and stood under the shower for twenty minutes, eyes closed, willing herself not to think about the events of last night. When she passed the spare room door on the way back to her bedroom she averted her eyes and hardly faltered, vehemently denying to herself the effort it had taken to go past without opening the door. Without taking a look at the music still sitting on the music stand—waiting. Waiting for her to come and play it.

"It's ridiculous. Mad. Crazy," she muttered to herself as she pulled on baggy cotton pants and a tank top. "I'm imagining it."

She collected the Sunday paper from the corner shop and read it as she ate fruit and yoghurt for brunch, sitting at her little outdoor table under her one tree in the back garden. The fluffy white cat from next door was already sunning himself on the red brick path and looked up lazily as she settled down.

"Hello, Soda." She held out her hand to him but as usual he ignored her, preferring to stretch his front legs out and yawn widely before closing his eyes again. "Lazy thing."

An advertisement for a chamber concert caught her eye. The Australian Chamber Orchestra was performing Vivaldi's "Four Seasons" at the University next Friday night with the orchestra's leader playing the violin part.

"I'll go to that, Soda," she said. "Want to come?"

She lazed through the rest of Sunday. Did some Tai Chi practice, cleaned the bathroom, did a load of washing and hung it out, sat in the garden with Soda and read a book, wished she hadn't left *Persuasion* at the fete…didn't open the spare room door.

Later that afternoon Gordon phoned to invite her out. She was in two minds about him. They'd dated a couple of times but it was clear their interests weren't in synch. He liked football, she didn't. He liked action movies with lots of explosions and shooting, she didn't. He liked hanging out with his mates and their girls, she didn't. But he had a taut, fit sportsman's body and an irresistible, slow sexy smile.

Nina went to bed early. She had work in the morning. She slept peacefully, untroubled by dreams of any sort.

The music store where Nina worked was the largest in North Sydney. She travelled by ferry across the harbour and then if she felt energetic and was early enough walked the few blocks up the steep streets to the centre or more usually caught the shuttle bus.

Riding the ferry at the beginning and end of each day, gazing out across the water as the little boat ploughed its way toward the magnificent arching Sydney Harbour Bridge was one of the best parts of her job. Sydney Harbour had to be the most beautiful harbour in the world, although she hadn't travelled out of Australia, and had only images from TV and movies with which to compare it. Ships of all sizes and shapes manoeuvred up and down the waterway. Large container ships bound for Europe and Asia, oil tankers, yachts, harbour police, passenger vessels heading off to cruise the Pacific islands. Nina watched them all and daydreamed about going too one day, but only to visit. She'd always come back to Australia.

This Monday Nina had other things on her mind. Yesterday she had successfully put it out of her thoughts, the music, but it crept back in when she began to relax her vigilance. The door to the spare room remained closed and at the moment she had no intention of opening it. She would have to eventually, she knew that. But not yet.

On the ferry coming home after a typical, normal, rather dull Monday she told herself she was being ridiculous. It was a piece of paper, nothing more. The door remained closed.

It stayed closed all week. She had no reason to go in there, often went for days without going in there. She didn't play her violin every day anyway. She didn't need anything from the room.

On Tuesday she went to a movie with Gordon, on Wednesday she visited her sister, Thursday she went out with friends from work to celebrate someone's birthday. Friday she went to the chamber music concert. Gordon didn't want to go and was annoyed that she didn't want to go out with his friends to someone's housewarming party.

"I don't understand you, Nina! I'd rather be with you than by myself. It's Friday night for Christ's sake. How will it look when I turn up without my woman and say you wanted to go to some poncy orchestra thing instead."

"Come with me then," she'd said.

"I thought you wanted to be with me."

"Just because I want to go to a concert doesn't mean I don't want to be with you!"

"You should prefer to be with me."

"That works both ways, Gordon."

"I'm not sitting through some bloody boring concert!"

"I'm sorry."

"Barbara was right about you. You are Miss Perfect. Too refined for the likes of us. I'm just a plumber."

"That's ridiculous" Barbara clearly had an eye for Gordon and wouldn't miss the chance to take a swipe at Nina.

"Oh, yeah? Playing the violin. University degree. Looking like an inscrutable Chinese Buddha all the time. Lighten up, Nina!"

"Goodbye, Gordon," she said stiffly and hung up.

She went to hear Vivaldi's "Four Seasons" and it was wonderful. She'd forgotten the impact a live performance could have, the immediacy and total immersion in the music at the moment it was produced. The concert venue was perfect for the size of the group, resonant and vibrant, the performers expert and dedicated. Nina sat enthralled and let the crisp, clear string sounds wash over her. The leader of the chamber orchestra played the solo violin part and he conducted as well, using his whole body and his violin to communicate with the other players. They played as one, perfectly in tune literally and metaphorically.

Nina went home in a taxi, her spirit still dancing in

the heights to which Vivaldi and the chamber players had lifted her. She dumped her handbag and jacket in the bedroom as she came in, kicked off her high heels and slipped on scuffs, went to the spare room, opened the door without hesitation and unpacked her violin. The music waited patiently for her on the music stand. This time she knew what to expect. She also knew how to control the power. A little. Her hand trembled slightly as she lifted her bow and tucked her violin under her chin.

The music responded and again she felt some other force lifting her, pushing her to keep playing. The beautiful melody captivated her once more and the tremendous sorrow she'd heard in the dream voice flooded into her body and out into the sound she produced.

Her violin throbbed beneath her hands. It came alive and breathed the music with her. She reached the difficult section and made a better attempt this time, buoyed by the faint memory of the dream. Somehow she knew how it ought to go now but still didn't have the ability.

"I'll have to practise!" she muttered in frustration. "Technique. I need better technique!"

Still the music drew her to keep playing. She played this time because she wanted to. She wanted to get it right. At midnight her neighbour thumped on the communal wall and she forced herself to stop playing and shut the violin in its case for the night.

Again that night he came to her in her sleep, pleading, demanding. "Play for me. You must play. It's the only way."

The violin sounded, rich and full, played by a

master. Other instruments sounded faintly. A flute, a guitar, a cello.

"Why?" she asked in her dream. "Why must I play?"

"So she will live." His voice rose to a desperate cry on the last word and the music swelled around him.

When she awoke on Saturday morning she remembered the dream clearly. She remembered the tone and quality of his voice and the way he played the music, the way he shaped the phrases, the nuances. She knew there were other musicians in the group. At least three.

Nina went by bus to her regular Saturday morning Tai Chi class. She needed the calming exercises and familiar routine more than ever. Never had she had such a mess in her head as since she'd bought that piece of music.

They went through the usual joint loosening exercises and then prepared for the meditation. From over a year of practice her breathing slowed naturally and her body relaxed, becoming heavy as the tension drained away. This practice was done in a standing posture and as Nina slowly raised her arms into the position known as "embracing the tree," her thoughts strayed to Gordon and the fight they'd had. She allowed the images to slip into her mind and out again, refocussing her attention on a point in the centre of her body.

The melody crept into her mind, singing through her head, strong and vibrant. She let it flow. Her instructor repeatedly assured them that meditation was not about forcing the mind to conform but about gently returning the awareness to the body's centre when the thoughts wandered.

"Mira is not dead."

Nina's eyes flew open and her involuntary cry of surprise broke the silence. An uncomfortable rush of heat surged through her body and the music faded. If she hadn't recognised the voice from her dream she would have sworn someone in the class had spoken. Her classmates continued their practice with closed eyes but Nina went to the back of the room and sat down, whole body trembling, too afraid to close her eyes and open her mind again.

At the end of the meditation she rejoined the group. Brett, the instructor looked at her.

"Was there a problem, Nina?"

"I'm sorry, everyone." Her cheeks pulsed with heat. Their puzzled smiles and murmured reassurances did nothing to console her.

"Come and talk to me later," he said.

Nina nodded. What she could possibly say to him?

The lesson continued. Nina went through the motions physically but without the mindfulness of her usual practice and it was with trepidation she approached Brett at the end of the class. A slim, compact, middle-aged man, sincere and dedicated to the art of Tai Chi, Nina knew he would listen to her with respect and offer any advice he could but she also knew he wasn't a psychiatrist and couldn't be expected to understand the supernatural either. Her recent experiences seemed to fall into one or other of the two areas.

"What happened?" He studied her through round, wire-framed spectacles.

"I'm not sure. I heard a voice. I thought someone

spoke to me. You didn't, did you?" Nina asked with a little laugh which sounded forced even to her ears.

He shook his head. "People experience all sorts of bizarre things in this practice. Do you practise much at home?"

"Yes. I try to do some every day."

"You'll go through different stages. I can see that you're beginning to relax more now in the movements but there is still a long way to go. It's like peeling away the layers of an onion. There is always more to go, more tension to release. For all of us, me included."

"I understand that and normally I can get into it really well. It's just that today…"

"Do you have any emotional problems at the moment? Stress?"

"I had a fight with my boyfriend." It sounded trite and petty but he nodded.

"That could be troubling you. The mind is an extraordinary thing. It likes to replay things over and over when we'd rather forget them. Meditation is the best way of giving it a rest from itself."

"It wasn't his voice though."

"Do you know who it was?"

"No." That was certainly the truth. "Thanks." Nina smiled and walked with Brett to the door.

"Talk to me any time if you need help."

"I will. Thanks again."

As soon as she got home she went to the spare room and, deliberately averting her eyes from the music, opened the wardrobe and searched through her pile of violin music. Scales and technical exercises, that's what she needed. She tossed them onto the floor as she found them. All the books she'd slogged through as a child and hated.

Nina sat crosslegged on the floor with her messy pile and sorted, discarding some as too basic and finishing with a half a dozen she thought would be useful. Then she got up and opened her violin case. The doorbell rang.

"Bugger," she muttered, considered ignoring it but didn't.

"Hello, Nina darling."

"Hi. Come in, Florence." Nina stepped back out of the way, smiling. Florence from next door was always good value. "How are you?" A dose of reality draped in silver and gold jewellery and too much makeup.

"Oh, the usual. Back's playing up again and the waterworks need a bit of attention." She laughed cheerfully. "Bloody pain in the neck, getting old."

"Cuppa?" asked Nina as they headed down the narrow hallway.

"Never say no to a cuppa. Or to a bit of the other." She winked lewdly at Nina who thought Florence's days of "the other" were probably long gone.

Florence made herself comfortable on the couch as Nina filled the electric jug.

"How's that good-looking Gordon?"

"We had a fight." She'd learnt it was pointless prevaricating with Florence.

"You'll make up. Just let him make the first move. Don't let him see you want him back." Florence patted her improbably dyed red hair with a be-ringed hand. "That's the secret. I remember when I was working in Bangkok, at the most plush hotel, there was *the* most gorgeous man. He came to my show every night and hung around afterward. Brought flowers and champagne, the works…we had a fling. My darling, was he good in bed!" Florence rolled her eyes heavenward and clutched a hand to her substantial bosom. "I absolutely adored him but he was extremely jealous. Silly man. He could see how popular I was. My God, I was the toast of the town, everyone came to hear me sing. Everyone! I told him I didn't want to see him until he could behave himself. I nearly died of grief but I had to do it!"

"What did he do?" This was a new tale from Florence's lurid past. Embellished or true? Who knew?

"He disappeared. I thought he may have committed suicide, one nearly did you know. Over me."

"Heavens! Had he?"

"No, no. He was just sulking, silly man…but he came to his senses, realised he couldn't boss me around and keep me away from people. Especially in my profession. What did he expect? I would sing with a bag on my head and wearing overalls…or give it up? For him? I tell you, men need to know where they stand with you!"

"So what happened?" Nina handed Florence her tea. Black with two sugars in a proper cup with a saucer.

"Thank you, darling." Florence rested the saucer on her black, satin-clad knee. "He couldn't stay away. Four days he lasted and then he came back with red roses and a diamond ring. He wanted to marry me but of course I said no. There were plenty more where he came from and not nearly so jealous, too." She chuckled throatily and winked a heavily mascaraed eye at Nina again

"I doubt whether Gordon wants to marry me."

"Do you want to marry him?"

"No! But…"

"He's got a great body and knows how to use it," finished Florence with great satisfaction. Nina blushed and nodded, giggling.

Florence continued with great but probably misplaced confidence. "There's got to be more than that for the long haul…but in the meantime…make hay while the sun shines, I say. He'll come round. If he doesn't realise what he's got then he's a fool and doesn't deserve you."

She crossed her legs and exhaled loudly. "Now, darling. I know how it is to be a musician. God knows I sang for nearly sixty years of my life. I know that sometimes you get carried away with what you're doing and forget everything else but please, darling, not at one in the morning. I used to be up all night singing at one time in my life. In Berlin I did two shows per night. The first at eleven-thirty the second at two. I got so used to being up all night I hardly knew what the sun looked like. But now? Now I need my sleep."

Nina grimaced and began apologising. Florence held up her hand, flashing a fistful of chunky jewels set in silver.

"No need to apologise, darling, just so as you know. I love to hear you play, you're very good. Any other time. In fact you don't practise nearly enough!"

"I was about to do some, actually, when you came."

"I'll go then." Florence heaved herself up and then, steadying herself with one hand on the back of the couch, she ran her fingers over the crocheted rug. "Poor dear old Mrs. Lee. She adored you grandchildren.

Always came in to tell me when you were coming to visit, Elsie did. I miss her. We lived side by side for twenty years. She was here when I moved in. Of course she was older than me. Fitter though. Looked after herself better."

"Didn't spend her youth in nightclubs," suggested Nina. Gran probably hadn't set foot in one.

"I had to. I was a singer and not an opera singer either!" Florence laughed uproariously as she headed toward the front door. Nina held it open for her then watched as she carefully stepped down the three steps to the path, her gaudy, hot pink shirt flapping over the black satin pedal pusher pants. Florence turned.

"Bye bye darling. Take care. Thanks for the tea."

"Bye Florence. Look after yourself." Nina closed the door and went straight to the spare room.

She began with tone exercises then moved on to scales. Strangely, she was able to take the page of music off the stand and put it on the bed, replacing it with her study books. It didn't seem to object at all. Did it know what she was doing? She shook her head and shuddered. Talk about madness!

Next came technique building exercises, studies that she'd prepared for the endless round of exams in her later years as a student. The plan was that she would practise every day and then try the manuscript next Saturday with her regained technique. Pleased with herself and her newly designed regime, Nina put away her violin with no trouble at all. Of course it would take months of practice to be anywhere near good enough to play that piece at all well.

Her stomach growled. She'd skipped lunch what with Florence coming in and then practising for what?

Three hours? Nina stared at the clock, horrified. She must have been at work that long. No wonder she felt weak and light headed.

She cooked herself spaghetti and meatballs with a green salad, even pouring herself a half glass of red from the bottle she kept mainly for cooking although a previous boyfriend had recommended the label. She doubted whether Gordon drank anything other than beer. An evening in front of the TV, followed by an early night. She had practice to do tomorrow—Tai Chi and violin.

****

During a quiet period at work on Monday, Nina went to the world music section and pulled out CDs of gypsy music from Eastern Europe, the Middle East, Spain, and France. She listened to several tracks through headphones, disturbed every now and again by customers, but heard nothing that resembled the music on her sheet. Sometimes there would be a phrase or a flashing violin part and her interest would be quickened, but it never developed into what she wanted to hear.

Guitars featured prominently but she hadn't heard the dream guitar strongly enough. Not yet anyway. Still, listening to this type of music gave her a feel for the style. Some of them certainly played with the same sense of abandon that her dream violinist did. She bought a couple to take home.

Workmate Rolly looked at her curiously as she rang up her purchases at the end of the day.

"Since when have you been into gypsy music? I thought classical was more your thing."

"I like all sorts of things. I'm interested in the

violin playing. Have you heard any of this stuff?" Nina showed him the covers of the CDs.

"No. We could play it in the shop tomorrow."

Nina laughed. "Wouldn't Alistair love that! And Tien."

"I'd rather gypsies than the middle of the road pap he has on all day downstairs."

"You can but try." Nina put her new purchases into her bag.

"Coming for a drink? We're all going to Mojave. Probably have dinner as well, later."

Nina shook her head. "No, thanks. I've things to do at home."

For once the ferry trip seemed to take forever. She sat impatiently watching the far shore edging closer and willing the passengers to get on and off quickly at the intervening stops. Finally she dashed up her street, put the key in the door and dumped her bag as she kicked off her street shoes. She pulled one of the CDs out and put it on as she changed, then threw together an omelette and salad for dinner, eating slumped on the couch as she listened.

The music they played was similar in some ways, very passionate but not as romantic, more folk oriented. The Spanish music was exciting and she liked it very much in its own right, but it was not like her dream man's playing at all. He seemed to be unique. Her page was obviously an original composition drawing on all sorts of sources. It had more classical lines, particularly in the first slow, melodic section.

Nina switched off the CD player. Time to get to work. Time to practise.

All week she followed the same routine. She got up

earlier than usual to do her Tai Chi practice before work. After that she showered, had breakfast and caught the ferry. Each evening she arrived home at about six—sometimes later if she stopped off at the shops to buy groceries—cooked a quick meal, ate, then settled down to practise. She put in two hours every night, setting her alarm and making sure to finish by nine-thirty so as not to bother Florence or Dirk on the other side. Florence maintained old Dirk was as deaf as a post and drunk most of the time as well and Nina hardly saw him, but she still didn't want to upset anybody.

She slept soundly and had no more dreams or recurrences of the incident at Tai Chi. By Thursday her tone had filled out, her intonation and finger dexterity were markedly better, and she fell in love with her violin all over again. The nightly sessions became addictive.

When the phone rang on Thursday just as she finished clearing away the dinner dishes, eager to practise, she snatched it up.

"Yes," she snapped.

"Hey Babe. What's happening?"

"Oh! Gordon." Her shoulders slumped. He hadn't entered her head since that last abrasive phone call.

"Miss me?"

"Oh, um…" Her violin waited in the spare room.

"Well?"

"I've been busy. At work and…practising."

"I missed you, Babe. Missed you…a lot." He lowered his voice. "I can be over there in half an hour."

Nina hesitated. Why should he expect to pick straight up where he left off, as if she would be panting for him? Especially after what he'd said to her.

Her hesitation was just a bit too long. "There are plenty of others, Nina."

Florence's words echoed in her mind.

"Yes," she said. "There are, Gordon."

"What does that mean?"

"It works both ways."

An arctic silence. Then, "If you're waiting for an apology, it's not going to happen."

"I'm not. I don't expect one."

"Well, that's that. It's been…You're a real bitch, Nina." He slammed the phone down.

Nina stood blankly for a few minutes then slowly replaced the receiver. He wasn't as tough as he made out. Just as Florence had said, none of them were. She sighed. Gordon's hurt feelings would have to fend for themselves.

She almost ran to the spare room. Today was Thursday. She had practice to do. On Saturday she would try the music again.

Chapter Two

Saturday, lunchtime. She'd made herself wait until after Tai Chi. Nina opened her violin case with shaking hands. The music watched her take up the violin. It waited for her to lift her bow.

"I'm going mad." A strangled little laugh accompanied the words.

This time she heard the difference immediately. And she heard the voice. His voice. The voice from her dreams.

"Mira. Play for Mira. She is my life. My love."

She wasn't expecting that, so close, so loud in her ears. The bow jerked from the strings. The voice stopped but the music beckoned. She started again, wary but determined, excited. The voice was real, not just in her dreams. He talked all the way through— strong, masculine, deeply resonant—an English accent! Not "proper" like the Queen but well spoken with some sort of regional tinge.

The second section still defeated her, but she set herself to work on a few bars at a time. The voice faded as she struggled but she knew he was there, encouraging her, willing her on.

"I can't play anymore. I'm sorry. I need a rest." She lowered her bow and stretched her arms and back. She sensed an acceptance of her physical limitations, that he knew she was doing her best, was committed, was willing, that she would continue.

After a tea break and a hastily made and gobbled sandwich, Nina went back to practise. She made herself work on technical exercises. Her fingers wouldn't move fast enough for some of the runs, and the chord patterns were odd and unfamiliar. She needed to improve her intonation as well.

"You've got a lot of work to do, Nina," she said. The phone rang but she ignored it completely. She'd forgotten to switch it to answer after Gordon's call. The second time it happened she ran through to the living room, waited for it to stop, then pressed the "answer" button. "No more telephone," she declared to the empty house. Or maybe to the voice in her head.

Later she stopped to use the toilet. And she was hungry again. It dawned on her that the house was almost in darkness. She'd been playing all afternoon. The kitchen clock said 7:35. Nina gripped the kitchen bench and closed her eyes. What was happening to her? This truly was madness!

"This way madness." She'd been staring at that page all afternoon and the handwritten words had barely registered. Now they crashed home.

Was she mad? *Talking to yourself out loud is the first sign of madness.* That's what they'd taunted each other with as children. Especially as they'd had poor slow-witted George from down the street who muttered and mumbled to himself all the time, as an example. But he really was mad or at least slightly touched in the head. Harmless though.

She closed her mouth abruptly. Put on some music, no not music, the TV, the radio, anything with real people. Nina switched on the television. Voices,

American accents. Banal, mindless, perfect. And she'd make herself a decent dinner. Stirfry vegetables with rice. As she ate she tried to watch the television but her mind insisted on wandering sneakily back to the spare room, her violin, the music, his voice.

That voice—so sad. Heartbroken. *He loves Mira so much and she's dead.* She must be but he won't accept it. Tears sprang to her eyes. What a tragedy. Who were they, these people torn apart by death, striving to come together again? For Nina had no doubt now that the man wanted to be with Mira more than anything and somehow he wanted her to help. But how? What could she do? Play that music? What would that achieve?

On the TV people argued about something and left the room, slamming doors. She flicked to another channel. People sat behind a desk talking about politics. She flicked again. Dancing. Part of her desperately wanted to go back to the spare room and play, to hear his voice. The rational part of her said no.

She listened to the rational part. For now. The thought of where the other would lead terrified her. She stayed glued to the couch wrapped in Gran's rug.

Someone pounded on the front door. The bell shrilled. She sat up abruptly, startled, the hair on her neck straining. She crept down the hallway and slipped the chain on.

"Who's there?"

"Nina? Babe. It's me."

Gordon. Nina rested her head on the door. What to do? He wouldn't leave unless she spoke to him, she knew that much. She opened the door reluctantly.

"Babe. Let me in. Please, sweetheart." Drunk. Not falling down drunk but pretty far gone. He peered at her through the crack the chain left.

"Babe. The chain. You've locked me out! Why Babe? I love you. Nina? Hear me? I love you."

"How did you get here? You didn't drive, did you?" She couldn't see his car. Hadn't heard it drive up. She always heard him coming with that throaty exhaust.

"Steve drove me."

Nina liked Steve best of all that crowd.

"Where is he?"

"In the car…Babe, let me in…I want to talk to you…Please, sweetheart." He only managed short bursts of coherent thought with gaps in between.

"Get Steve."

"Nina. Come on. I won't hurt you. I love you. Babe." Wheedling now, leaning against the door frame.

"Get Steve."

He turned and stumbled a few lurching paces down her front steps, waving an arm in the direction of the street, a vague beckoning gesture. A car door slammed. Seconds later Steve appeared and they had a muttered conversation. Steve came up the steps.

"Nina? Hi. Sorry about this. He's desperate. He wants to see you." He gave her a frustrated shrug. "He's not violent. He won't hurt you, I promise. Just talk to him for a few minutes."

Nina drew a deep breath. Steve was sober. Despite his faults, Gordon would never hit or physically harm her. She slipped the chain off and opened the door.

"Will you stay please, Steve?"

"I don't know. I don't want to get involved in this." Steve started backing away. Gordon passed him on the steps.

"Steve, please?"

"Come in, mate, if that's what she wants," Gordon said.

Nina stepped back to let them pass. She closed the door and followed them to the living room. Gordon slumped onto the couch in an untidy sprawl of arms and long legs.

"What do you want?"

"I want you back, Babe." He held out his hand toward her, and when she didn't move, let it fall. His mouth twisted into that smile she loved. Damn it! Her body was so weak. "Remember last time? Here? On this couch?"

She did remember. He narrowed his eyes and the smile widened. He knew her weakness. So did she.

Steve said, "I'll go. He won't hurt you, Nina. I'm sure. He'll probably go to sleep soon."

"Thanks for coming in." She flashed him a tight smile.

"See you." He beat a hasty retreat.

Nina studied Gordon, hands on hips. He grinned back at her, knew he'd won.

"Want some coffee?"

"Nope."

"I'm not giving you more beer."

"Don't want beer. Come here." His voice thickened with lust.

Nina moved closer and knelt by the couch. She searched his face, stared deeply into his eyes. Who was this man? Did she really want him? Did she even like him? They had nothing in common apart from lust. Gordon returned her gaze as well as he was able and stretched one arm out to snake around her neck. He drew her close and kissed her, pulling her up onto his lap and holding her tightly pressed against his body. Nina gave up and abandoned herself to his embrace and the insistence of her own suddenly flaring desire.

****

Gordon woke next morning in Nina's bed with a splitting headache and someone drilling into his ears with a high-pitched, whining machine. He groaned and pulled the pillow over his head, trying to block out the sound, lying motionless to minimise the pain. Dimly through the mists of his gigantic hangover, it dawned on him that the sound was that of a violin. Nina played the violin although he'd never heard her. Wasn't interested in that sort of music at all. It must be her.

Bloody hell! What was she doing playing at this hour of the morning? He dragged himself into a sitting position and propped his head on his hands as the room dipped and swayed. His throat felt like sandpaper. Five minutes later he attempted to stand and managed to stagger to the door, leaning on it to steady himself as he negotiated the corner. It *was* Nina. In the spare room right next to the bedroom. Loud! Jesus Christ!

"Give it a rest, Babe," he croaked.

Nina's head whipped around. Her expression changed from one of surprise to complete anger.

"Get out!" She spat the words at him like a snake, dripping with venom.

"It's early, Babe. My head's gunna burst if you keep that up."

He stood half naked and defenceless in the hallway watching her through the open door. She looked different and it wasn't because he was hung over. He hadn't had a chance to look at her properly last night, not from a distance, unclouded by lust and alcohol, but now he saw how her cheeks and hipbones stood out, her arms sticklike. She'd lost the serenity and air of mystery that attracted him to her in the first place. A disturbing, unsettling intensity hovered about her and he'd never heard her speak like that before, to anyone.

"It's eleven in the morning Gordon, not dawn. I have practice to do."

Nina marched toward him and he thought for one horrified, uncomprehending moment she would strike him. He shrank back instinctively but she caught hold of the door and slammed it in his face. The violin began again, a strange haunting melody that put his teeth on edge and made him want to get away as far and as fast as he could.

****

Nina heard Gordon moving about the house and gritted her teeth. The shower sounded for a long time, feet padded down the hallway, then the clinking of crockery in the kitchen. He'd leave soon. She kept playing.

She still couldn't get the second part right. Three bits were beyond her and would be for a long, long time. The voice coaxed and encouraged but he couldn't help her move her fingers faster no matter how she tried. And she kept miss-pitching the top notes, sometimes flat, more often sharp.

He spoke nearly all the way through now, still pleading with her to play, insisting that Mira wasn't dead, that she would live but as she improved and her interpretation became better he said, "The Golden Dawn. It is the music. The music."

Then he said several times. "Love is the key. Love is the key to everything," in a voice so sorrowful and at the same time so hopeful tears cascaded down her cheeks again as they had done that first time. Such a profound sense of emotion, intense, heartfelt, was overwhelming and so addictive she wanted to drink from the source continually. The man who owned that voice would be passionate and strong, vibrant and determined. Very determined. Not even death could stop him in his search. She envied Mira. She wanted him to speak to her the way he must have spoken to his lost love.

Can you fall in love with a voice? Probably. People did it all the time with pop singers. Could you fall in love with a spirit?

She was able to stop now when she really wanted to. All she had to do was try to play the passages that were too difficult. His voice faded then and she could easily lay down her instrument and bow.

When she emerged from the spare room and went to the kitchen for a drink she was amazed to catch a glimpse of Gordon sitting at the outdoor table with Soda under his chair. He wasn't exactly sitting, reclining was a better word, with his feet up on the table. He had her sunglasses on and a mug of something in his hand, the newspaper spread before him. She'd forgotten he was still in the house, assumed he'd gone home.

She opened the screen door and he looked around as it slammed behind her.

"How's your head?"

Gordon stared at her, brow creased in concern. "Do you know how long you've been playing?"

Nina shrugged.

"Three hours plus whatever you did before I woke

up."

She stuck her hands into the pockets of her shorts. "So?"

"Nina, you play the same thing over and over."

"I can't get it right. That's what practising is, Gordon."

He stood up too fast, then winced as his head caught up with his body. He took two paces and put his arms around her.

"It's a bit obsessive, isn't it?"

She stood like stone within the circle of his arms. He kissed her cheek then stepped back and looked down at her. She kept her eyes averted, staring at Soda who had got up and wandered over to scratch his claws against the wooden fence dividing her from Florence.

Gordon pulled her close again and hugged her tightly. When was he going to leave? She wanted to have another try at those difficult bits. He sensed her withdrawal and let her go, pushing her away.

"Look Nina. If you don't want me to come around, if you want me to go, just say so. Although you didn't mind me last night."

Nina stared at him then, her face blank. "You came here, remember. I didn't invite you. And that was after you said and I quote, "well that's that," and finishing up with "you're a bitch.""

"You were happy enough to let me into your bed." She couldn't deny that.

"Yes, well." Nina flushed and he ran his hands over her breasts, teasing her nipples with his fingers.

"Gordon."

"What?" he said softly and didn't stop what he was doing.

"You're a bastard." She didn't want to do this now.

"Am I?" He kissed her with the expertise she couldn't resist.

He took her by the hand and led her firmly back into the house, through the living room, down the hallway toward her bedroom. As they passed the spare room, Nina paused, glanced in, saw the music beckoning, her violin waiting. Gordon turned as he felt the tug on his hand.

"No you don't," he growled, kissing her hard and maintaining the grip on her fingers.

Nina leapt back as if scalded, her eyes frantically searching the hallway. Gordon stared open mouthed.

"Babe?" Bewildered, frustrated.

She closed her eyes, then opened them slowly. Her legs trembled. She steadied herself by leaning on the wall.

"Babe? Come here." He reached out a hand but she shrank back. "What's wrong? Why are you scared of me?" Anger rising.

Nina shook her head, speechless. Tears rose and spilled down her cheeks while frustration twisted his mouth in fury.

"I don't need this! Call me when you know what you want. If ever." He charged into her bedroom, retrieved his jacket, opened the front door. He looked at her then, still huddled shaking against the wall.

"You're crazy, Nina."

The door slammed behind him.

Nina's legs gave way and she slipped to the floor, wrapping her arms around her bare legs, hugging herself tightly, sobbing in huge gasping breaths. Gordon must be right. She was crazy.

The voice had spoken to her again but this time she wasn't playing the music and she wasn't meditating. This time she'd been kissing Gordon—and the voice didn't like it.

He'd said quite clearly and distinctly in her ear, as if he stood behind her, "Not him! He's not the one."

Twenty minutes later Nina managed to struggle to her feet. She pulled the spare room door shut then stumbled to the kitchen to boil the jug. Gran's remedy. Hot sweet tea. While that was boiling she went to the bathroom and doused her face with cold water.

Clutching the mug, she went outside and sat where Gordon had been sitting, shaded from the increasingly hot sun by the overhanging branches of a tree from next door.

She needed help. This was getting out of control. But who could help? That was the big question. Who could she go to with this sort of problem? A psychiatrist seemed the obvious answer but she didn't fancy some stranger probing her innermost thoughts and feelings. At great expense so she'd heard. And they would probably put her on some sort of pills. Schizophrenia, that's what they'd say. Hearing voices? Take two of these every day. Maybe they'd be right. Maybe she was schizophrenic.

"I'm not mad!" Nina thumped her mug down. "I'll ask Brett."

But she would have to wait until next week to see him. Unless she rang him at home. He'd told her to ask if she needed help and she did. She was desperate.

His answering machine came on.

"Brett. I'm sorry to bother you. It's Nina Lee from Saturday morning class. I…could you call, please?…I have a…a…problem. It's…hard to explain. Thanks."

She hung up and then had to call back and leave her number in case he didn't have it in his class records. She pottered about half heartedly doing household chores. She hadn't dusted in weeks and the bathroom definitely needed cleaning.

The phone rang as she was putting rubber gloves on.

"Hello sweetness."

"Dad! Hello. I'm so glad you called."

"Why? Something wrong?" His voice held instant concern.

Nina swallowed. "No. I just haven't seen you for ages, that's all. Mum all right?"

"She's fine. We're leaving tomorrow."

"Oh. So soon? I thought you were going in October."

"It is October," he said. "What have you been up to Nina?" Suspiciously, only half-joking.

"I don't know, Dad. Working. Tai Chi. I've been playing my violin a lot lately." That would please them, after all the money they'd spent on lessons, not to mention the emotional strain of making her keep practising.

"Glad to hear it. I told you you'd thank us for it one day." Thank them? Not the way she was feeling at the moment.

"What made you start playing again?"

"I don't know. I found some old music at a fete. It looked interesting so I bought it. Dad, where does 'this way madness' come from?"

Her father hesitated briefly as his mind coped with the abrupt switch of topics.

"King Lear, I think. Look it up."

"King Lear. The mad king."

"Deranged by grief. Listen we're leaving early tomorrow so we won't see you before we go. We'll keep in touch. Jason will be here on his own so it would be good if you looked in occasionally to check on him and see the house is still standing. Lucy will do the same."

"Dad, he'll be fine. He's not a little kid anymore." They always treated him as if he were six instead of twenty-two.

"I know, I know. Anyway, look after yourself, sweet."

"I will Dad. Have a wonderful time. Drive safely."

"I'll put Mum on, now. Bye, we'll be back for Christmas."

Nina listened while her mother gave a rundown on the detailed instructions she'd given Jason.

"Mum, I'm not going to go over there and check on him every day."

"You don't have to. Just call him every week and visit when you can."

"All right. Now don't worry about him while you're away. Enjoy yourselves. Send me a postcard from the Top End and watch out for crocodiles." Nina grinned as her mother flapped some more and then finally hung up amidst a flurry of goodbyes.

Telling them was an option she hadn't even considered. They would have cancelled their long-awaited trip in an instant and had her booked into a shrink in no time flat.

Brett rang her that night after dinner.

"Nina? It's Brett. How can I help?"

"Thank you for calling. I don't know if you can help but I didn't know who else to ask…"

"Is it about what happened in class that time?"

"Sort of. I hear that voice quite a bit. I know that sounds crazy…but I don't think I am…crazy, I mean."

He didn't speak and she could almost hear him weighing up the odds of his having a loony on the line.

"Is it only during Chi Kung or at other times?" He wasn't giving anything away.

"Mostly when I'm playing the violin. I play violin. I bought a piece of music. Old music and I hear the voice when I play and then sometimes during Chi Kung."

"Nina…I'm not a doctor and I wouldn't presume to know exactly what is happening…have you seen a doctor?" He was tactfully avoiding saying psychiatrist, she could tell.

"No. I know what you're going to say and I understand. You think I'm imagining it. It's all in my mind."

"Nina," he interrupted, "it is all in your mind. Everything we think comes from our mind but it doesn't mean it isn't real to us. In Chi Kung we tap into our deepest thoughts and sometimes fears. The thing is to let them go. That's the hard part, letting go of things."

"It's as if he won't let go of me."

"The voice?"

"Yes." Tears choked in her throat. "He wants me to keep playing the music."

"This might seem crazy to you but I think you should see a clairvoyant."

"A clairvoyant?"

"Now you think *I'm* crazy." He laughed lightly.

"No, I don't. I hadn't thought of it that's all."

"The Chi Kung we practise is for strengthening, relaxing and healing the body as well as calming and opening the mind. It's a holistic approach, comes from martial arts training. Other systems deal only with the mind. There are a lot of forces at work here that I don't pretend to understand. The ancients knew about them. Many cultures use trance and meditation to contact the spirit world. I've read about this in relation to China. There are descriptions in the literature dating back four thousand years. There were mediums, 'wu' they were called, and emperors often consulted them. They claimed to transmit advice from the spirits. Mediums still do it now. Channelling."

"But is it true? Real?"

"Is what you're experiencing real?" he countered.

Nina sat deep in thought after her conversation with Brett. He'd been reassuring, had taken her seriously. It was true what he'd said. Psychics weren't a modern New Age fad at all. She did an online search.

There were lots of clairvoyants, many of them phone-in services but that didn't appeal to her. Psychic advice over the phone had to be a scam. She had an image of a blousy, overweight woman with her hair in rollers, painting her toenails making herself a few extra dollars from home while her small children crawled around the floor and a baby screamed in the next room.

She wanted to see someone face to face, to know who she was talking to. She didn't think what she wanted could be done over the phone, not that she really had any idea what she wanted. To be told she wasn't going mad, basically. She picked a number at random, someone called Serena close to where she lived and who gave palm, aura, and tarot readings amongst other things, past lives included.

Serena answered, sounding reassuringly calm and rational. Nina made an appointment for Monday afternoon at four. She would tell her boss she had a doctor's appointment and he couldn't fit her in any other time. Which was sort of true.

****

Monday passed abysmally slowly. Rain started during the night and poured down all day. Nina's feet were already soaked before she'd reached the end of her street on her way to the catch the morning ferry.

"Great start to the week," commented one of her fellow commuters dismally from under his black umbrella as they waited on the little dock. Nina nodded, clutching her own red umbrella with the wooden duck's head handle.

"At least the weekend was good." She looked out at the grey expanse of harbour. Their ferry appeared through the rain, ploughing toward them over the greasy, pock-marked swell.

"Yours may have been," he said. "We had six eleven-year-olds sleeping over for my daughter's birthday. Hardly slept a wink on Saturday night and then they were up at dawn running around giggling and carrying on." He heaved a sigh and then laughed. "Could have been worse I suppose. It could have rained all weekend. I think that'd be my definition of hell—stuck in a small house with a bunch of overexcited eleven-year-olds in the rain."

Nina smiled and made appropriately sympathetic noises. What would he say if she told him about her weekend? *Just the usual—practised the violin obsessively for hours, over and over on the same piece of music. Talked not only to myself but also to a voice in my head who not only talks to me but other people as well who I can't hear but know are there...acted so weirdly my boyfriend stormed out telling me I'm crazy. Made an appointment to see a psychic who will probably tell me the voice is a past life seeping through into this one...yes, just the usual old run-of-the mill weekend.*

Nina gave a snort of laughter and the man looked at her curiously as the ferry hand ran the gang plank onto the dock.

"Sorry," she said. "I was just remembering some of my birthday parties at that age. Poor Mum."

He grinned. "I know. Parents must be mad."

And not just parents. They boarded the ferry.

At work, Tien, her floor manager, sent her down to see Alistair, who regarded her suspiciously when she asked to leave early.

"Seeing the doctor? Don't look sick."

Alistair always spoke in shorthand, leaving out anything unnecessary. When she first started working in the store Nina had found him totally disconcerting but after two years she knew it was just his odd manner and not a personal attack. He lived alone and as far as any of them could tell didn't have a life outside his CD store. She knew he was horribly embarrassed by anything personal and horrified by anything remotely connected with the intricate workings of a woman's body.

Nina strove not to take advantage of this but some of the other female staff members weren't so scrupulous and rang in with "girl's trouble" excuses on a regular basis. She hated herself for fibbing to him.

"I'm not sick. It's something personal, Alistair."

He held up his pudgy hand. "Stop!"

"I'll come in on Thursday night to make it up," she offered. She hated staying for late night closing.

He nodded. "Thursday. Good."

"Thanks, Alistair." Nina smiled and was rewarded with a grin from his plump, kindly face. He fiddled with the buttons on his navy blue cardigan and then waved her away, running the other hand over his thinning, grey hair.

She went back upstairs to the department she and Rolly shared with Tien. Classical, jazz and world music. Rolly was the jazz expert, she was supposed to look after classical and Tien was their manager.

"What did he say?" asked Rolly.

"It's fine. I'm doing Thursday evening instead."

"You don't have to do that. Get a doctor's certificate."

"But I won't have one, will I?" Nina picked up the phone which had just started ringing and turned her attention to the customer enquiry. Rolly gave her a surprised glance and continued sorting a new batch of CDs, putting one or two aside for his own purchase later on.

Nina left in good time for her appointment with Madame Serena, as she dubbed her in her mind, although Serena went by the single name only. The address was in a suburban street. A housewife playing at being a psychic for a bit of pocket money? Nina began to have doubts. The fee wasn't exorbitant but still, she felt like a sucker walking up to the ordinary looking front door in the rain and ringing the bell to pay for goodness knew what hocus pocus.

The woman who opened the door reminded Nina of the middle-aged lady who did her mother's hair. Plump, dark hair rolled neatly into a bun, pastel pink blouse tucked neatly into a grey skirt. Neat black pumps on her feet. Where were the crystals and silver jewellery and the flowing robes and scarves? Perhaps this was the wrong house.

She opened her mouth to say she was sorry she'd made a mistake but the woman held out her hand and said, "I know, I'm not what you expected. I don't need to be psychic to see that." She laughed, a genuine, jolly laugh. "Put your brolly down there on the porch and come in. What a day!"

Nina did as she was told and followed Serena into a room to the right of the front door. Cream-painted, small and cosy with Australian landscapes on the walls, a polished wood cabinet against the wall and a lamp shedding warm, yellow light onto a table covered with a green cloth. The matching green patterned curtains were drawn, blocking the traffic noise and the drab, grey light from outside. Two straight-backed chairs faced each other across the table and Serena indicated Nina should sit down. Dry mouthed and with a suddenly hollow middle, she did.

"Now Nina. What can I do for you?" Serena settled herself and studied her face with an uncomfortably intense expression. "Something is troubling you, isn't it?"

She had decided not to say anything about the voice or the music. Serena should be able to tell her, if she was any good. Which Nina doubted very much.

"I'd like to know what will happen to me."

"Your future? Something specific in mind. Marriage for example? Your work? Travel?"

Nina nodded. "All of that."

If Serena saw that she was going to be in one place with no job and no prospect of marriage then her future looked pretty much as though she was in for a stretch in an institution of some sort.

Again that intense scrutiny. She nodded. "All right. Do you have a preference? Which method?" she added when Nina looked blank. "Aura, palm, cards, astrological chart?"

"Tarot cards maybe?" It was the first thing that sprang to mind.

Serena smiled. "I thought you might say the cards." She got up and took a black silk wrapped deck from the glass fronted cabinet behind her. She unwrapped them carefully and spread them before her, studying them before selecting one and putting it aside. An intricately detailed picture with a fascinating colour and design.

"That's the significator," said Serena. "It represents you, the seeker."

She scooped the remaining cards up and began to shuffle them, reversing some during the process. Serena handed her the deck.

"State your query. Or if you prefer, think it. It's the cards who will answer, not me."

Nina took the cards in her hands and thought: *What is happening to me? What will happen to me?*

Serena instructed her to cut the deck following her instructions and then reassembled it in reverse order. She put the significator down and then began laying out the cards following what was obviously a set pattern.

Some familiar pictures appeared—The Lovers. She'd seen that in a James Bond movie. The one where he tricks the psychic by having a whole deck made up of the same card.

Death. She gasped as the figure with the scythe appeared.

"It doesn't always indicate a death. The surrounding cards influence it."

Serena spoke as though she were mundanely discussing the pros and cons of a knitting pattern. When she'd laid out the appropriate number of cards, she studied them for some time before she spoke.

"There is a mystery somewhere. I'm not sure what. It isn't clear. But there is definitely a man in your life. Someone dark, tall. Young, like you. He has travelled from overseas. Love is certainly involved. And the past. Something…" A frown flitted across her benign features. "There is…trouble and…fear but great satisfaction and pleasure as well. You will be happy. You are a creative person and you must let that part of your personality shine through. You have been hiding it or subduing it. This card," she pointed to Death, "indicates a death of the old and a new beginning." Serena smiled. "See? A good fortune all told."

Nina smiled back uncertainly. Was Serena telling her everything? Somehow she thought not. "Is that all?"

"More or less. Would you like more detail? Ask a more specific question."

Gordon? What would happen there? Serena wasn't talking about him, he was a local boy, hadn't ever been overseas.

"What about a current love?"

"There is no indication at present of an enduring

relationship. Just the man from overseas. Tall, dark, and shall we assume handsome? It is not clear whether he is implicated in the love or whether it is someone else." Again she paused, frowning slightly. "He will certainly have an effect upon you. You will have to have another reading after you meet him."

"Do you think I will? Meet him?" Was this her dream man she was talking about? Impossible.

"The cards are never wrong. Take care, my dear. Follow your heart and be brave."

Nothing she said was completely false, nothing was impossible. Improbable maybe but not impossible. Had she provided answers? That remained to be seen but for now Nina paid Serena's fee with a small sense of relief. Without realising it the woman had reassured her of her sanity.

Nina picked up her red umbrella and went slowly down the steps into the rain. She still had the feeling Serena hadn't told her everything the cards had portrayed. Maybe she did that with information she thought would be too upsetting to her clients. A mystery, she said.

She was right about that. But lots of people had little mysteries in their lives, from where did I put my glasses to who stole my car. And as for the tall, dark, and handsome stranger from overseas…well that was standard gypsy fortune teller stuff.

Still, it had been interesting. Very interesting. A tall, dark, handsome foreigner was something to look forward to. Unless the cards were telling her about the voice man, the dream violinist. If it was him the fear she'd also mentioned would be all too real. Nina shivered.

The spare room door was still firmly closed when she got home. Nina went straight past into the laundry to dump her umbrella and wet shoes. She sat on the couch watching the TV news to eat dinner but Serena's words kept revolving in her head. "You are very creative. You've been stifling your talent" or words to that effect.

Was that what this was about. Her stifled creative side bursting for release?

****

For the first time he appeared to her in her dream. And he was handsome. Far more handsome than she'd imagined in her wildest fantasies, with finely chiselled features and a full, sensitive mouth. Thick dark hair curled over his collar, though not as black as her own, and his eyes were deep brown and fired with an intense passion just as she'd envisaged.

A soft white linen shirt unbuttoned at the throat and with loosely rolled sleeves was tucked into slim-fitting black pants. He held his violin in slender artistic hands, held it lovingly as a living thing. Nina yearned for him to touch her with those long, elegant fingers and to feel his embrace. She wanted to hear him speak to her with the passion he reserved for the woman Mira, wanted him with all her heart and soul.

He said, "I am Piers. I am the one you must heed. For Mira. Everything is for Mira."

"Who is Mira? Why should I?" she demanded, sick with jealousy.

"My love, my life. Listen to me. Do this for me."

Nina ached to help him. His voice swamped her senses, overpowered her so that she could think of nothing but wanting to please him. "I will, I will do

47

anything."

"You are the one, the only one. It is you I want."

Her heart expanded with love and desire as he gazed into her eyes and spoke the last words. Then he raised his violin and the music swelled up and around her and she drifted back into deeper sleep.

The scent of roses wafted on warm, summer air. She was in a garden. A beautiful, formal garden, at night. Voices babbled in the distance through the trees. A party, sounds of laughter coming from a brightly lit house. They mustn't see her here. She'd snuck away, waiting for him in her prettiest gown.

She was kissing Piers. His arms were around her and his tongue was hard and forceful in her mouth. She could feel his body against hers, chest broad, thigh muscles firm and exciting. He drew back and his dark, penetrating eyes burned into hers. She wrapped her arms tightly around him and breathed his name. "Piers, kiss me again. I love you."

He bent his head to hers and once more invaded her mouth with passion. He stopped and whispered hoarsely, "You're mine. Mine alone. Always."

"Yours," she cried. "Yes, Piers."

Nina woke heavy headed and lethargic still in the dark of night, aware she'd dreamed, aware he'd appeared to her for the first time but with one certainty pounding in her head. His name was Piers, her phantom lover. She hadn't known that before. The name suited him, exotic but somehow aristocratic at the same time.

Not everything Piers had said remained in her memory but something had changed this time. There'd been a shift in the basic order of things. It was almost as if he were transferring his love to her. Although the thought was suffocatingly exciting, thrilling to the core, she wondered why. Why would he do that when he was so devoted to his love, to Mira? Nina would never replace her, she knew that. It was an impossible idea but still the thread remained.

Was he trying to resurrect Mira's soul in her body? Succeeding? Nineteenth-century Piers must have dabbled in the occult. But he wasn't a lunatic; he was strong and passionate and sensitive and a wonderful violinist. The melody swirled in her head constantly.

A flash from the dream appeared before her eyes. His face, so handsome and intense, his eyes looking deeply into hers, his voice saying, "I love you. Only you." His hand reaching out to her, touching. So real. So exciting. She wanted to sleep, to meet him again.

They were in a glade of oaks. Hot, still sunlight filtered through the thick canopy of leaves. She lay on the grass and watched Piers above her, his face suffused with passion and love. He moved inside her hard and strong and urgent and she went with him, her whole body crying out to be closer, to enclose him and draw him into her, hold him and make him part of her. He kissed her driving his tongue deep and possessively even as he drove into her body striving for that ultimate release, that ultimate expression of his love.

Then she was lifted on her own wave of desire and she called out his name. The light faded and it was night again. The scent of roses was heavy in the air. Piers approached silently, his body a darker bulk against the moonlit leaves of the shrubs and bushes of the garden. His arms encircled her and she rested her head against his chest. Forever.

Chapter Three

Cutting Marsh, England, July 1892

Her head throbbed unbearably, every joint ached, even her skin hurt. In her lucid moments Miranda heard voices murmuring, soothing, felt water trickle down her throat and cool dampness pressed against her forehead and neck. But those moments were rare and for most of the time she inhabited a world of reeling visions, strange impressions, harsh light and unbearable noise.

She was on a small boat which pitched and tossed on the waves, smacking into the water with a crash, sending salty spray flying onto her face and dress. But looking down she saw with horror the clothing she wore was odd—loose and with sleeves which left her arms bare. And her legs, shockingly exposed in short pantaloons of a strange stiff blue fabric. Her feet were bare too, save for flimsy sandals. In public. She gripped the railings to maintain balance but the little boat suddenly ground to a screeching halt against a wooden pier and she leapt ashore and ran.

She'd never run so fast. Panting and desperate, she fled along a street suddenly unbearably hot with a searing sun burning down onto her head. Buildings crowded the roadside, unfamiliar houses with small fenced yards and pointed roofs. Strange trees lined the street. All the doors were closed, the road was deserted, she was alone. Searching.

She had to find...what? She didn't know...

"Where are you? she screamed. "Where?"

"Miranda, drink this, my dear." Her father's voice, calm, quiet and achingly familiar.

An arm supported her head to raise her, a glass was pressed to her lips. Something sweet and cold slid down her throat.

"Papa," she murmured.

"Sleep, my dear. You have a fever." His fingers touched her cheek lightly. She sighed and slipped into a fitful doze.

Someone called her name. She stood in a garden heavy with the perfume of roses.

"Ethan?"

He called again but the voice was different, deeper more commanding.

"Where are you?" she called.

But there was no reply.

Then she was running, searching for him but all the paths looked the same and the perfume of roses was overpowering, suffocating. Hot, unbearably hot. She flung her arms wide to push aside the crowding rose bushes which towered over the path and clutched at her with thorny branches.

He was gone. She knew with a certainty that filled her body with despair, heavy and immovable.

She woke with a start. Her pillow was wet and the sheet twisted uncomfortably under her body. The room was dark, the curtains drawn against the light but no sunlight showed round the edges so it must be night.

Her mother sat opposite. She was beautiful, more beautiful than Miranda could ever have imagined. She smiled and her dark eyes twinkled with kindness. She reached out a small hand and stroked Miranda's cheek.

"My beautiful child," she said.

"Mama."

Mama wore a beautifully embroidered silk robe with a high collar and wide sleeves. Gold on red in a Chinese design of dragons and flowers. Her thick black hair was smoothed from her round face into a roll and held in place with lacquered pins.

Light streaked across the floor through a crack in the curtains but this time Miranda's eyes didn't scream with pain. She turned her head as the door opened.

Mrs. Bowden came in with a wash bowl and towels. Her face lit with delight when she saw Miranda watching her.

"Thank the Lord," she cried and retreated through the door. "Doctor, come quickly. She's awake and back with us," she called then reappeared. "My goodness, you gave us all a fright, my dear."

"I'm sorry. I don't remember…"

"You wouldn't. The fever had you in its grip and if it hadn't been for the expert care of your good father we would have lost you, for sure." Mrs. Bowden placed the fresh towel and wash basin on the night stand and began straightening the bedclothes.

"Nonsense, Mrs. Bowden. She was in no real danger but you were very ill, Miranda." Her father strode to the bed and smiled down at her, his grey eyes showing the relief he couldn't truly express. He laid his palm against her forehead. "Much better. How do you feel?"

"A little hungry."

"Excellent. Some weak chicken broth, Mrs.

Bowden, please."

"Certainly. And I expect you'd like a nice, hot bath and clean clothes."

"Perhaps just a wash, Mrs. Bowden. I don't think I'm strong enough to bathe quite yet."

"Of course. I'll see to the broth."

"How long have I been ill, Papa?"

Her father pulled up a chair and sat down. "Three days. Young Ethan has enquired every day. He'll be very happy to hear the news."

Miranda pictured the sandy-haired, square-jawed face of her oldest, dearest friend and smiled. But he wasn't the one, wasn't the voice in her dream. He wasn't the one she was searching for.

"I had strange dreams," she said.

"The fever does that. It makes you imagine things, unreal, fanciful things."

"I saw Mama. She spoke to me. She was beautiful."

Sadness flitted like a passing shadow across his face. "She was but you never saw her. It is my most bitter regret I have no portrait or photographic image of her. Only in my memory does she live on."

"I know it was her. She had on a red and gold gown with big sleeves and her hair was pulled back away from her face and held with long lacquered pins."

Her father straightened with a puzzled frown. "She wore a red and gold gown the day we married. It was a traditional Chinese dress but she didn't wear Eastern dress at all after the wedding. It was her mother's. I must have mentioned it to you," he said flatly.

Miranda nodded. Perhaps he had. But she didn't remember. He didn't talk about her much at all. Too stricken with grief, Mrs. Bowden surmised when once Miranda had asked her why. Not that Mrs. Bowden would know. They'd moved to the village when Miranda was five and Tyler eight and their mother had died bringing her into the world.

But Papa was talking about her mother now and she had questions.

"Mama wasn't completely Chinese, was she?"

"No, her father was English. He met her mother in Australia on the goldfields."

"In Australia. The other side of the world." An image of hot brassy sky, strange trees…She frowned and the picture slipped from her mind's feeble grasp.

"Rest now, my dear." He stood up.

****

Ethan and his mother called a few days later, pleased with the news of Miranda's recovery. Mrs. Bowden ushered them in to the sitting room where she lay reclining against a pile of cushions on the settee.

"I'm so pleased to see you recovered, Miranda," Mrs. Broome said. "We were terribly worried. Especially Ethan."

She cast a smiling glance at her son who stood grinning down at Miranda and clutching a bouquet of fresh cut flowers. "I brought you these," he said.

Mrs. Bowden stepped forward. "I'll put them in water for her, sir. Please sit down. Tea will be ready shortly."

"Thanks, Mrs. Bowden," said Miranda.

Her visitors obeyed the command, Ethan in the chair closest to Miranda. He leaned forward.

"How are you feeling? You're very pale."

"She's not recovered properly yet, Ethan. She was

extremely ill. Of course she's pale and she won't have been eating."

Miranda and Ethan exchanged a smile. Mrs. Broome was renowned for her desire to ensure everyone ate sufficiently, an attitude which endeared her to the village as a whole.

"I'll be better in time for the Summer Ball," she said. "I'm looking forward to dancing."

"So am I." Ethan nodded. "Father has engaged an orchestra from London. They're supposed to be the toast of the town."

"How exciting."

"You must be sure to rest properly, Miranda. Especially as it's so hot this summer. Very enervating, this weather, and everything's as parched as a bone." Mrs. Broome fanned herself with a small ivory and silk fan she produced from her bag.

"Maybe that's why I dreamed of the hot sun," Miranda said. "I had strange dreams while I was ill. I imagined I was in a foreign country. And on a boat. I've never been on a boat and yet I knew exactly how it felt."

"This heat is enough to make anyone have strange dreams," said Mrs. Broome.

Mrs. Bowden brought tea and the conversation meandered on until Miranda began to droop. Mrs. Broome rose to her feet, announced they'd worn her out, and bustled Ethan out the door.

Miranda went to her bedroom and lay down. Ethan planned in his stolid, unromantic way to marry her one day. There was a long-standing understanding dating from their childhood but no actual engagement as yet. She could easily picture herself as Lady of the Manor at

Broome Hall.

When they married she would leave the doctor's small house and move into the east wing with Ethan. Mrs. Broome was almost like a mother and they would get on well together under the same roof. She would teach Miranda everything she needed to know about running a large household and how to entertain the local gentry. Her future was assured and secure.

She slept naturally, peacefully and deeply.

****

Sydney, 1998

Slowly Nina began to resent the time spent in practice, the consuming of her life. It wasn't leading anywhere. She still couldn't play the difficult bits the way Piers demonstrated each night, for she was now positive that's what he was doing, and she felt the way she had as a child, forced into going over and over a piece by a stern disciplinarian. But she couldn't stop. And she didn't know how to stop dreaming.

How could she stop the sexual thrill he produced just by looking at her with those dark passionate eyes? She wanted him to ravage her with that strong, masculine body, she wanted to feel him deep inside her and lose herself in his love, go with him to oblivion. But she always woke up, spent, exhausted, and alone.

It had become an addiction, an obsessive behaviour way out of her control. She could control the actual length of practice and what she did within that time frame but she could not put the music away, still less destroy it, and she could not go for more than a day without the overwhelming desire to play it again. Just like a true addict, she needed her fix even though she hated what it did to her.

She tried to destroy the page but again that curious reluctance stole over her as her hand reached out. It knew her intentions. Her hand dropped harmlessly and she said, "It's only a piece of paper, for goodness' sake."

One lunch time, browsing in a bookshop, she remembered her father's words concerning the quote from King Lear. "Look it up," he'd said as he always did to queries of that sort. She'd forgotten about it after he'd told her the source, concentrating exclusively on playing the music. Rather than read the whole play, a Dictionary of Quotations would be the go.

In the References section she found the book and scanned the index for phrases starting with "this." No luck. How about madness? Yes! There it was! "Madness lies, that way" p 241:29 It was "that" not "this." She flipped back to the right page and found reference 29.

"O, that way madness lies: let me shun that." King Lear

Nina stared at the entry, mouthing the chilling words. For chilling they were. She hadn't known the rest of the quote, hadn't even got the first bit right. Neither had the writer for that matter but that was small consolation. It was a warning there was absolutely no doubt about it now. And Serena had told her to take care. Take care not to follow the path to madness? Had she seen what was on the path? Was that what she was holding back?

****

The following week her older sister Lucy phoned. Nina had just cleared her messages after returning from work. There weren't many. Her parents had rung to leave a cheery update on their progress and a real estate agent left a message asking if she was interested in selling her house as there were apparently queues of people waiting to snap up property in the area. Gordon had rung once, leaving a brusque, "Turn on your mobile. Call me" which she hadn't returned. She hadn't bothered charging her mobile for weeks. She left the machine on almost all the time now, having no interest in talking to anyone. She had to play the music. She lived to hear his voice.

Lucy was lucky to catch her before she turned the answering function back on.

"Nina! Thank goodness. What's wrong with your mobile? That bloody machine's been on permanently and I refuse to talk to it. How are you?"

"Fine."

"You don't sound fine. Have you been sick? You haven't called Jason. We're both supposed to keep an eye on him, not just me, you know."

Her brother? That's right. Her parents asked her to check in on him while they were away. She'd told them he was an adult and could look after himself.

"Is he all right?"

"Yes, of course."

"Well what's your problem?"

"Nina! What's going on? Are you on drugs or something?"

"No, of course not. None of your business anyway what I do," Nina snapped, ready to hang up.

"What's up? Is it Gordon?" Lucy's voice dropped in sympathy. Nina snatched the unexpected escape route.

"We've split up."

"Oh, I'm sorry. Maybe I should come over. Bring some comfort food. I wondered why I hadn't seen you for so long. It's almost six weeks, more, since you came round."

Six weeks since she'd found that music. Amazing. She'd had no idea it was that long. A sudden rush of affection toward her sister was tempered immediately by the thought of the music waiting for her in the spare room.

"It's okay Luce, but thanks. I'm over him, really. We didn't have much in common. That was the problem."

"Sure?"

"Yes, thanks for calling. Promise I'll call Jason. I had a message from Mum and Dad, they're having a great time."

"I know. I've spoken to them a couple of times." The reprimand wasn't subtle.

"Well, I've got a few things to do. I'd better go."

"All right then. See you."

Nina bit at her lip. Lucy and she were very close. They'd shared everything growing up and had lived in this house together for eighteen months before Lucy married. She'd cut the conversation short and fobbed Lucy off with Gordon whom she hadn't given a second thought since he left her. Why hadn't she told Lucy, of all people, the truth? If she could tell anybody, Lucy was the one.

She went to practise.

****

Despite her secret addiction Nina had managed to control it enough to keep her work life unaffected, much the way she knew some heroin and cocaine addicts did. If she lost her job she'd lose any semblance of normality and it was the ferry ride each day that enabled her to reset her mind between her two lives.

The weather turned hot and humid. Sydney sweltered in the early onset of summer weather even though November was technically still spring. Nina enjoyed the early morning ferry ride even more in summer. The harbour sparkled, the sea breeze fresh and salty as they chugged across to the northern shore. The trip in the evening was just as pleasant, relaxing and refreshing after the grime and fumes of the crowded streets.

The music store, cool and inviting, attracted extra people in off the hot streets and Nina and Rolly in the upstairs section were constantly being asked to play samples tracks for people who they were sure just wanted to sit down and rest in the air-conditioning. Trade picked up at this time of the year, anyway, as Christmas approached and Tien told them not to spend too much time with obvious time wasters, those noncustomers who wanted to listen to track after track in a supposed effort to make up their minds.

Casually they began to hazard guesses at people as they came up the stairs, tossing the cryptic "TW?" accompanied by a raised eyebrow at each other and then typically, Rolly expanded this to other initials denoting personal characteristics in a childish game similar to "I spy."

"OHLL," he murmured to Nina as she passed him at the counter. Nina glanced up and saw the person, an overweight young woman with a red perspiring face, standing at the top of the stairs.

"Something something lady," she murmured back

as she searched the catalogue for a customer.

"Overheated large lady."

"That's one word not two," she said indignantly after she'd finished her search and dealt with the customer.

People appeared in a constant stream causing Tien to come out of his office and help serve for most of the afternoon.

There was a lull just before closing. With twenty minutes to go Nina couldn't wait to get home. Her feet ached and she'd had enough of dealing politely with hot and sometimes obnoxious customers. Rolly's silly game, which had helped relieve tension but which Tien's presence had scuppered, started up again but Nina couldn't concentrate and fidgeted about looking at the clock every few minutes.

"Is that clock working?" she asked Rolly.

"Yes," he said absently looking up from the list of figures he was studying. His eye fell on the customer who had just appeared at the top of the stairs.

"Here's a good one," he said quietly. "DRTDH."

Nina glanced across. The man was staring about the floor as if searching for someone amongst the four or five people browsing at the bins. He spied Nina and walked purposefully toward her. She took in his long, unkempt, curly hair, creased blue shirt and jeans, the leather jacket slung over his arm and the battered suitcase he carried.

"TW," she whispered to Rolly, playing the game. But there was something about him, something unsettling about the way he focussed on her, something almost familiar.

"Dirty and rumpled but tall, dark, and handsome,"

he whispered back.

With a shock of recognition she realised Rolly's words echoed Serena's. Thirtyish, certainly tall and his hair was dark brown. Handsome? Maybe. A gaunt face and too thin but there was something extremely attractive about him despite his dishevelled appearance.

He walked straight to the counter and put his suitcase down. Then he looked directly at Nina, right into her eyes, and began humming a melody. *The* melody. Nina froze, rigid with shock. Rolly laughed.

"Nice tune," he said. "Recognise it, Nina?"

Nina couldn't tear her eyes from the stranger's. He stopped humming and said softly, tentatively, as if confirming something, "Nina?"

Rolly's astonished gaze flicked from one to the another like someone watching tennis.

"Do you know each other?"

Nina found her voice. "No."

"No," said the man.

"Excuse me folks but…what's happening here?" Rolly asked plaintively.

"I don't know. It's that tune. I know the tune," Nina gabbled, dropping her gaze to the counter top and then just as quickly back to the stranger's face.

"What is it?" asked Rolly. "I've never heard it before."

"I think it's an original composition," the man said. "Nina is the first person I've met who recognised it."

"Am I?" Something else registered through the shock waves. "You're English."

"Yes, I arrived in Sydney yesterday."

"A traveller." Her voice came out in a whisper. Her knuckles shone white as she gripped the edge of the counter.

He lifted an eyebrow slightly. "Yes."

Tien came out of the back room. "Closing time. I'm sorry, sir. I'll have to ask you to leave. We open at nine in the morning."

The man nodded briefly to Tien. He held Nina's gaze. "I'll wait outside for you."

After he had picked up his suitcase and disappeared down the stairs, Rolly said, "Tell me you're not going to meet him."

"I am." Nothing was more certain in her life.

"Want me to come with you?"

Nina flashed him a grateful smile. "No, thanks Rolly. I'll be all right. I've been waiting for him, I think."

Rolly shook his head, frowning. "But you don't know him, you said so."

"I'll be all right," Nina said in a voice that meant no more argument.

He was waiting outside the front door. Nina came out the side entrance and walked around the corner, studying him as she came closer. His shoulders sagged in the heat, standing there with his jacket and suitcase. He looked exhausted, vulnerable, and fragile, and above all, lonely. She quickened her step and he turned.

Face to face. His eyes shone with wonder and excitement, transcending the tiredness of his body. Hers would be the same. Who was he? How had found her and how did he know that melody?

"We need to talk, don't we?" he said.

"Yes." Nina led him down toward the harbour where the fresh cool evening breeze came in off the ocean. They sat on a bench along from the wharf where her ferry came in.

"My name is Martin Leigh," he said stretching out his long legs. "I'm English, from London. Arrived yesterday." He wiped his face with his hand. "God, it's hot here. It's freezing at home."

"How did you find me? How did you know about me?" Nina wondered suddenly, hysterically, whether Serena had set her up, sent along a tall, dark, handsome foreigner…with the same surname, Lee, too. But Serena didn't know the melody.

"It's a very long story. I'd need to start right at the beginning. It's complicated." Martin seemed to wave that away. He stared at her intently. "Nina, do you have the violin part?"

"Yes, I do." It didn't occur to her to lie or prevaricate. "Why? What do you have? Are there more parts?"

A relieved, satisfied expression smoothed some of the tiredness from his face. "Yes. I've got the flute part and a cello part. I'm a flautist, a professional flautist. Do you play it, the music? Of course you must or you wouldn't know the melody."

"I can't stop playing it," said Nina softly and saw her own desperation reflected in his eyes. "But I'm not good enough. I can't get it right and he, it, makes me…keep practising."

"It's an obsession. It's like being an alcoholic, I imagine. You tell yourself no more but the next day you think one more won't hurt."

"Yes. It's exactly like that. Well, the warning is there, isn't it?" Nina laughed mirthlessly. "Fat lot of good it does."

"Warning? I don't have a warning on mine. What

does it say?"

"I looked it up. It's Shakespeare. From King Lear. It's handwritten across the top in a scrawl. Different writing to the manuscript. It says 'this way madness.' "

"O, that way madness lies; let me shun that," quoted Martin.

Nina raised her eyebrows, impressed. "You know it?"

He laughed. "Did it at school. And Macbeth. I love Shakespeare. He's so…relevant to lots of things and he puts it so well. Succinctly."

"Well he got that right."

Nina stared out across the darkening harbour at the twinkling lights of the Bridge.

"Are we mad?" she said without turning her eyes from the view.

"*Though this be madness, yet there is method in't,*" he said softly.

"King Lear?"

"Yes. He had a lot to say on the subject."

His words comforted her. Martin wasn't crazy. He was obsessed too but he was approaching it rationally and clearly like a scientist. He had a method of sorts and he would help her. He'd come half way around the world to find her and, incredibly, had succeeded.

"Follow your heart and be brave," Serena had told her as she left. Her heart told her to trust him and what choice was there?

"Come home with me, Martin." She stood up.

Chapter Four

"You know, I used to be quite normal and respectable. Well, fairly respectable anyway, as much as any musician can be."

Martin gave a short laugh as he said this and looked at Nina. She stared back with that perfect, expressionless, exotically beautiful face of hers—unblinking dark eyes, smooth, rounded cheeks, impossible to tell what she was thinking. "I play the flute, sorry, you know that."

He laughed again, nervous for some reason, sitting here in her tidy, cosy little terrace house. After all the travelling and searching and madness, he'd found her and wanted to make her understand, didn't want her to think he was some loony, eccentric English crackpot, hearing voices. But she wouldn't think that because she'd heard them too…still, a knot of nerves twisted in his belly. "I was a student at the Royal Academy. In London. It's a very famous music school." He paused.

Nina said quietly, "I know."

"Sorry, of course you do, would—know, I mean." He took a desperate sip of coffee and carefully replaced the mug, pleased not to have spilled anything down his shirt although the state it was in, no one would notice. And it smelled bad too. She hadn't commented though, despite sitting next to him on the ferry and sharing pizza for dinner in a restaurant at the local shopping centre. She'd been assessing him, he was sure. Making certain she wasn't inviting danger into her home. "Sorry," he said again. "It's just that no one's listened to me before who really understood. You can't tell anyone, can you? About this?"

Nina returned his gaze, unblinking, then looked away and shook her head slowly.

"Gordon thinks I'm crazy. He was my boyfriend."

His eyes met hers again for an instant but hers skated away, embarrassed. Shy? Not frightened, please not frightened. No, she wouldn't have met him after work, wouldn't have invited him into her home. It was the obsession. She had it too.

"My girlfriend thought I was mad," he said. "And left. Can't blame her."

Nina nodded but said nothing. She was extraordinarily beautiful. He hadn't been prepared for that. She'd taken his breath away when he saw her standing there in that shop. Not just because he'd come around the world on a seemingly insane venture to find her and had succeeded, but because when he laid eyes on her something had clicked into place.

He realised she was waiting patiently for him to continue.

"After I graduated I freelanced and then I got a job in an orchestra. Did well, had a decent apartment, girlfriend but then this...music thing happened. I lost my job and had to move to a tiny basement flat. Just a bedroom, living room, gas cooker and sink behind a curtain in the corner and a bathroom of sorts. It's always damp, even in summer it smells mouldy. Of course summer there is nothing like summer here. Or what I imagine summer will be like..."

67

Martin's voice trailed off. He was babbling, his eyelids suddenly leaden. Jet lag catching up with him, like hitting a wall. He took another sip of coffee hoping it would stave off sleep for a while longer. She made good coffee, plunger coffee with freshly ground beans. He concentrated.

"I had to teach when I lost my orchestral position. Musicians usually do teach despite their best intentions but I got work occasionally, mainly subbing when someone got sick and the odd session gig. I had enough saved up to fund this trip."

He stopped abruptly. Raving again, didn't seem to be able to stop talking, pouring out all sorts of information she wouldn't be the slightest bit interested in. It must be the relief of having found her. That combined with exhaustion. And her stunningly beautiful face. The less she said the more he raved. He had to stick to the relevant details or she'd throw him out…or call the police.

"I took up yoga years ago. That's where I learnt to meditate. Trying to stop myself worrying." He glanced at Nina and she gave the barest glimmer of a smile. Her lovely dark eyes gave nothing away.

"I found a very experienced teacher. I was lucky really. There are so many fakes around, people who'll take your money and don't know much more than you could read in a book. Charlatans. I practised with her for nearly eight years up until very recently, then she moved, went to India and she never contacted me. I think she became a recluse in a retreat somewhere."

"That's a pity."

Martin cleared his throat. "Nina…she left after…after…I played for her. She was frightened. She said I shouldn't become involved with it…with them."

That caught her attention. She shifted, tensed. "Could she hear them, too?"

"I'm not sure. She wouldn't say. She must have. Otherwise why leave so suddenly? She was very angry with me. It was extraordinary. Such rage. Against all her teachings and everything I'd learnt from her."

The shock of seeing her usually placid countenance contorted almost out of recognition by fear and horror was as vivid now as when it occurred. "She wouldn't tell me what happened. She virtually threw me out. It was horrible, really horrible. I couldn't believe what I was seeing. Perhaps she wasn't as good as I'd thought."

"Had to go to India to recharge, maybe?" Nina said.

Lost in the memory as he was, her cynical, flippant comment was like a splash of cold water. But a tiny smile played on her lips. She was trying to reassure him, play down the fear. He obliged as well as he could with a small grimace.

"Go on," she said and tucked her legs under her, settling in for the evening.

"Before that, long before, about eight months maybe, I was poking around in a secondhand music shop. You can often pick up bargains and unusual works, things that are out of print. I was after a copy of the Poulenc Flute Sonata. I'd lent mine to one of my students and of course, never got it back. Stupid. Actually it wasn't his fault. Someone nicked his music case on the tube. He never got around to buying me another copy. If he had I never would have found the piece and this wouldn't have happened."

"To you."

"You think it would have happened anyway? To someone else?"

"Don't you?"

He thought about it. "I suppose so. It had already happened to other people before and there's nothing special about me."

Nina relaxed into the cushions and rested her glossy black head on the crocheted rug spread on the back of the sofa. Her gaze never left his face. She appeared calm but he knew she must be as excited as he was. Her eyes glittered in the lamp light. She hadn't been able to share what she knew until now, either. Not fully.

"The Poulenc was there in a pile of music. Ruth, she ran the place, told me it had come in recently from a deceased estate. I bought a few other things, too. When I got home I started to run through the Sonata and that's when I found the piece. It was in between the first and second movements. Handwritten but without the other thing, the warning. It looked pretty easy and I started to doodle through the opening bars to see what it was like. That melody…it seemed to leap off the page."

Nina sat forward now, untucked her legs, listening intently, eyes fixed on his face.

"It was mesmerising. I had to keep playing, I literally could not stop. The second part is harder and there were a few passages I stumbled on the first time. The force or compulsion or whatever it is, weakened when I made mistakes and I was able to tear my flute away from my lips and stop. I wasn't game to play the first bit again. I put my hand out to move the page off the music stand and when I touched it, it actually tingled under my fingers. I swear I could feel it like an electric shock, mild but definitely real. It was as though it was alive. I was terrified."

She nodded. "Go on." The words were a mere whisper of sound.

"I pulled the Poulenc out from underneath it and upended the music stand so that it fell on the floor, then I sort of kicked it away under my desk and left it there like a big malevolent spider waiting to bite me. But you know what it's like. The next day I decided I was being ridiculous and when I had a student I just bent down and pulled the page out cool as can be. Nothing happened. I had this vague idea that the student would protect me somehow. Don't know what she could've done. She was only twelve." He laughed but it came out as a dry, mirthless croaking.

"After that I was able to control myself a bit better. I made sure I made mistakes here and there so that the power didn't get too strong. But there was something driving me to keep playing it over and over, day after day. I had to play it every day. And then one day I finished up my practice session with the melody part alone. I'd figured out that if I played a completely wrong note at the end I could stop quite easily, also the less expression I put in the easier it was to stop. I went to my bedroom to meditate. I always did half an hour of sitting meditation every day but I'd never done it straight after playing the melody. I usually did it first thing in the morning but for some reason that day I hadn't. The tune was wafting around in my head and that was the first time he spoke to me."

"Who was it?" Nina's breathless interjection startled him. He'd almost forgotten she was there he was so wrapped in the memory of that first extraordinary experience. The voice had come into his mind so clearly he'd thought someone was in the room with him. But he knew no one was. He lived alone.

"It was a man. Young, light, English, definitely upper class, well educated, but I knew he wasn't contemporary, right from the start. Something about the way he spoke. He said, "She's dead.""

"You could tell from that? Two words?"

"No…I…I must have heard more…I may have decided later. I don't know." He tried to search a brain made mush from jet lag and no sleep. "Does it matter? I know now for sure that they're not contemporary. I think they're from the late nineteenth century—the eighteen eighties or nineties. I know there are two strong men's voices and one weaker one. The one I heard first is the flute player. His name is Jasper, the strongest, although the other is the leader, I think. Piers. His name is Piers. He's the violinist. He's very angry."

"Piers," Nina echoed faintly and then again, stronger. "I know his name…" She shook her head. "I have dreams I can't remember. About…bits and pieces…I can't remember. He told me his name. Piers. He speaks to you too? Is he angry? I think he's more sad than angry."

She had a faraway look, trying to fit the idea of anger with her own impressions.

"Sad? I suppose he could be. He always seems to be driving the other two along when I hear him, trying to convince them of something."

She still had that dreamy expression, besotted. "I only hear him clearly. Piers. But he talks to the others. He sounds desperately sad to me. He has the most wonderful voice."

"I suppose we're hearing the same voice?" Martin said, a curl of jealousy making him speak more harshly than he'd meant. That voice didn't strike him as wonderful at all. Aggressive and bullying, he disliked this Piers intensely. Jealous? Of a voice?

Nina nodded. "I'm sure we are. The violin…"

"Oh. Yes, of course. I forgot. How could I forget that?" He flopped back onto the sofa cushions, his mind whirling, wondering if they *were* both insane.

"How did you find the other part?" prompted Nina. Martin forced his brain back into gear.

"You know exactly how stunned I was when Jasper spoke to me. You must have felt the same…My eyes flew open and I lost him, of course. I tried to regain the contact but I couldn't in the normal course of meditation. I discovered I had to play the melody first or at least sing the tune in my head. Usually when you meditate you try to clear your mind or focus on one thing alone. I've been doing it for years now and my concentration is quite good—for a short span, anyway. When the tune was fresh in my mind Jasper was very clear and as I got better at it, more relaxed when he spoke, in other words, I could hear the other man, Piers, as well. The third one is very faint still. He only came through clearly when I talked Sylvia into playing with me, but that's getting ahead of myself.

"How did I find the cello part? I went back to the shop and went through the rest of the music from the deceased's estate. It never occurred to me then that Ruth might have sold more of it. It was about six weeks later. I flipped through every page of every book and there it was, stuck in "Virtuoso Exercises for the Violoncello." Same handwritten manuscript but there were initials pencilled on the top corner—S. W. Ruth let me have it for nothing. It was useless without the other parts. She also gave me the address of the person who brought it all in. It had only been there a matter of weeks before I found it. I was tremendously excited.

That same day I badgered a cellist, Sylvia, to play it through with me. I didn't tell her anything just said I'd found these parts and the melody was quite haunting and I wanted to hear it with the bass. She's a very good player but I doubted whether she would get it note perfect because the manuscript was very hard to read in places on her page. From my limited experience I thought she would probably be safe from the effects. Actually it looked as though someone had had a good go at destroying it. Failed, of course." He looked at Nina. "Have you tried?"

She nodded. "I couldn't do it."

"No. You can't. Anyway we started to play the opening and I could see Sylvia becoming hooked on it the way I had that first time. She played beautifully, so expressively, and almost as soon as we began, I heard Jasper and Piers and then the third man, an Irishman they called Michael. They were talking about a woman. They're always talking about a woman. She's dead or rather, has just died and she's very beautiful. Her name sounds like "Mirror" and I think they all loved her but Piers particularly."

"It's M-I-R-A. Short for Miranda…" She frowned. "I think that's right. I don't know how I know. Maybe I dreamed it too." She scraped at her lower lip with her teeth. "Go on."

"Sylvia got to the second section and stumbled over one of the bars. Instead of going over it, she stood up and refused to go on. "I'm not playing this anymore," she said and left. Pretty much straight away. She wouldn't speak to me after that. I'm sure she didn't hear the voices, she just hated the vibe from it."

Martin stopped. What he was going to say next would sound daft even to his own ears and goodness knew he was certainly half crazy by now. Nina waited expectantly, her face still giving nothing away but with an abnormal intensity suffusing her whole body.

"I think…that somehow, it only lets people play who it wants to. Who are sympathetic in some way."

Would Nina think he was crazy? She had a classic inscrutable look as she stood up.

"I'll make more coffee, or would you rather have tea?"

"Coffee, please, but I really need to sleep soon," he said and leant back in the chair eyes closed.

She did think he was mad. Loony old King Lear had nothing on Martin Leigh. He suddenly saw himself as she must be seeing him. And squirmed. Hair unkempt and messy and although reasonably clean, in dire need of a run-in with a barber. The tight curls which his mother assured him as a child were the envy of every woman and girl in the area and which he knew were the butt of every boy's joke, had grown thicker and less manageable the older he got. When reggae had become popular, for once his hair fitted a fashion style but now he kept it short. At least he had until a half year ago, until this obsession had overtaken him.

Since finding the music, he'd hardly given grooming a thought beyond washing regularly. His clothes were stale and smelly from travelling. It was hot here in Australia. Much hotter than he'd been prepared for, if prepared was the word to describe the haphazard shoving of clothes into a suitcase borrowed from his landlord and upstairs neighbour, the long-suffering Franz.

November in England did not prepare the traveller for November in Sydney, even if intellectually, he comprehended the change of season. Martin had thrown in underwear and four or five shirts and T shirts but neither shorts nor sandals. He would need both in the coming weeks and it wasn't even summer yet.

Would Nina think it too much if he asked to use her shower and washing machine? He needed to find somewhere to stay tonight. It was getting late. She'd know of a hostel or a cheap hotel in the area.

He heard her coming back and dragged his eyes open. She was stunning. Fresh and pretty in her cotton dress…and sparkling clean…and would smell lovely too, if he were able to get close enough to her to test his theory. She was graceful with a fascinating, exotic beauty inherited from an Asian ancestor.

She put a tray down on the coffee table. Coffee and biscuits.

He straightened up and smiled. "Could I wash, please, Nina? I'm…I need a wash," he finished awkwardly as he stumbled to his feet almost sending the tray flying. "I'm sorry."

Nina grimaced in dismay. "No, I'm sorry. I should have asked if you needed to use the bathroom. It's through there." She pointed to the doorway leading to the back of the house. "And the toilet's right next to it."

She sat down as Martin hurried out of the room. She was probably being polite and had wanted to drag him to the bathroom, no, more likely the laundry and disinfect him before he even sat down on her furniture or touched anything.

Luckily a nailbrush sat on the soap dish. He scrubbed his hands, washed and dried his face and borrowed an elastic band from a dish of hairpins and bits and pieces on the bench. Now all he needed was a shave and clean clothes but his suitcase was in the hallway by the front door and he could hardly start showering and changing clothes now. Martin sighed and went back for some of those biscuits.

Nina smiled when she saw the effort he'd made. "Feel better?"

He nodded, nervous again under that calm steady gaze from her beautiful dark eyes and the realisation that although he was convinced he'd found his soul mate, Nina probably wasn't. Nina thought she'd found a man as loony and obsessed as she was. One she hoped would help her.

"I think you're right," she said. "About the music choosing us."

He closed his eyes and swallowed what might have been a tear threatening to escape so intense was his relief but she was busy pouring coffee and didn't see his struggle for control.

She handed him a Snoopy mug and he took a chocolate-coated biscuit, chewed and swallowed. "I think they choose who will play the part the best by deterring those not suitable."

"And we're suitable." Not sceptical, just establishing a fact.

"Yes. They didn't like Sylvia even though she was a beautiful player. Why was that, I wonder?" It had puzzled him then and still puzzled him now, months later.

"She didn't like the music. Some people hate it. The stallholder I bought mine from didn't want me to have it. He got quite nasty."

"That's what I mean," interrupted Martin. "Why does it repel some people?"

"I don't know," said Nina helplessly. "But how did you know there were other parts to find?"

"Mainly from the part itself. I've got rests marked so there had to be other instruments. I just don't know how many. And I don't have the complete melody all the time. Sometimes it's a harmony line. There had to be other parts. When I found the cello part I realised there were still others missing because both cello and flute have rests in the same place."

"My part doesn't have any rests at all. It's Piers' violin part." Nina's voice shook a little as the full implications registered, as they had months ago to Martin. "It must be the main one. The most powerful. He's the only one I hear. I knew there were others because he speaks to them but I don't hear them. Not clearly. I think there's a guitar."

"Violin, flute, cello and guitar. I wonder if there are more." But if so where were they and what were they and how many?

"Martin, how did you find me? It seems so incredible that you would come to Australia to search, let alone actually track me down. Or track the music down. How did you do it? I was going mad and if you hadn't walked in today I don't know…" Her eyes filled with moisture and she pressed her lips together tightly.

He stood and moved to squat beside her chair. He took her hands in his, holding them firmly to stop the shaking. She sighed deeply and clutched his fingers, searched his face for reassurance and strength. Martin smiled. The urge to kiss her powered up from nowhere and almost overwhelmed him but he shoved it away.

"There are two of us now and we're not mad, either of us. There's a reason for what's happening. We have to find it."

Nina's mouth trembled. Tears hovered on her lids making her dark eyes luminous and childlike. He squeezed her hands and she attempted a smile. He released her and reluctantly resumed his place on the couch, picked up another biscuit at random to prevent himself reaching for her.

"I've had longer to get used to it, more than a year, and I've decided I won't have a life of my own again until this is solved."

She nodded. "It's only been a few months for me."

"You're doing really well. You still go to work." He glanced round. "Your house is clean and tidy. You're still in control. I wasn't at your stage."

She heaved in a deep shuddery breath and wiped her eyes. "Tell me the rest of the story." But she was calm now and he felt one step closer to earning her complete trust.

"After Sylvia left I didn't know what to do. I tried playing the cello part on my flute but it resisted. It really did. It was the most extraordinary sensation. It was literally as if the music didn't want to be played. So I had to give up. I considered asking another cellist but I wasn't game to make someone else have that same experience. I thought I would wait a while and try again in a few weeks' time. Then I remembered Ruth had given me the name and address of the person who had sold her the boxes of music. Did I say? There were three crates full of it. All sorts of stuff. Mostly violin, cello and piano but some flute and a little bit of guitar. That made me think too about what other instruments may have been in the group. Perhaps there was a violin part and a piano part or a guitar part.

"And there were the initials S.W. I began by reading the phone book to see how many S W's there were. Hopeless. There were hundreds. And that was assuming S.W. lived in London or was even still alive. Or even referred to a person. Then I tried the name Ruth gave me—Celia Harrow. I looked her up in the phone book and rang her to make an appointment to visit.

Apparently she's quite elderly and lives alone. She was rather reluctant to see me but seemed happy enough to talk on the phone. The boxes were her late brother's. George. He died last year and she and his widow had started going through his things, clearing stuff out. They got rid of all his music and some of hers as well. The piano pieces it turned out, had been hers. She told me she'd never been much good on the piano. George had been the musician of the family, took after their mother who came from a long line of musicians. Her father, Celia's grandfather was a professional violinist in the early 1900's but was killed in the First World War and his father had been a cellist. He was Irish."

Martin stopped and looked meaningfully at Nina. She stared back.

"Michael?" she whispered.

"I think so. And not only that. His name was West and his son's name…" Martin paused for dramatic effect. "…was Stanley."

"S.W," she breathed. Her face had gone quite pale and she flopped back onto the couch like a stringless puppet.

"Are you okay?" Martin asked anxiously.

Nina nodded. "Yes."

He smiled. "You look how I felt when she told me. I nearly dropped the phone. She was burbling on about what a musical family they'd all been and how glad she was that someone had bought some of the music who would truly appreciate it. She had no children and George's family wasn't interested. Then she asked me what I actually wanted. Why had I rung? I'd started out by telling her I'd bought some of the music and wondered where it had come from and she just took it from there with hardly any prompting. When she asked what I wanted to know specifically I floundered a bit. I could hardly ask her if her brother heard voices.

"I said, 'Did your brother play with a group? In the music there were two parts to a chamber work and I'd really like to track down the rest because it's such an interesting piece'."

"That's putting it mildly," interjected Nina with a surprising little snort of laughter.

Martin spread his hands, grinning. "What else could I say? She'd think I was crazy. I was—am—crazy but she didn't need to know."

She smiled back with such an uninhibited show of complicity his heart turned right over in his chest. He stared at her several moments too long and she dropped her gaze hastily, the smile hovering about her lips. He'd have to tread warily here, with Nina. Regardless of his own immediate certainty, she displayed no signs of seeing him as anything other than a saviour, a partner in this most bizarre of quests. He couldn't afford to frighten her with unwelcome advances.

He fell in love too easily and although women were attracted to him, before long he somehow managed to disenchant them. Maybe they sensed the basic unreliability and shied away like horses from the smoke of a fire, instinctively knowing there would be nothing but pain and anguish in that direction. He wasn't a man a woman could depend on and until now, until Nina, it hadn't really bothered him.

Evie, the latest and last in the procession had left not through natural disenchantment which would have come eventually, but as a result of this very thing they were embroiled in. She was terrified by what he had become. What he was now.

"What did she say?" Nina's question jerked him back to the present. For a moment Martin thought she meant Evie. What did Evie say?

Evie said, in amongst the tears, "Martin, you're scaring me. I think you need help…professional help…I can't cope with you like this." He stood helplessly watching her cry. Part of him, a strong part, wanted her to go, immediately, to leave him in peace with the music and his quest but another part realised that perhaps she was his remaining link to reality and sanity and that he should beg her to stay and help, to take him to a psychiatrist.

Instead he said, "Goodbye Evie."

"Martin?" Nina again. He yawned so widely his jaw ached. Tried to gather his thoughts. Celia, telephone, where was he?

Nina said, "Shall we continue tomorrow?"

"If you like. I'd better go." He had no idea where. He'd slept in a park the previous night.

"You can sleep in the spare room, if you like. Unless you have a place?"

"No. Thank you. I mean, yes, please." Inarticulate fool. Hopefully she'd realise it was exhaustion making him babble. And overwhelming relief. Thank goodness she wasn't afraid of him. She wanted him to stay.

Martin closed his eyes and rested his head on the crocheted rug. He heard Nina get up and remove the tray. She went into the kitchen and then a door opened and closed in the hallway.

He dragged himself to his feet and found her spreading a sheet on a low bed in what was obviously her room for dumping extra stuff. Her violin case lay in the corner and a music stand along with a pair of rollerblades, assorted hats, summer and winter, piled on the wardrobe, two tennis racquets propped behind the door, several large posters of the Beatles and one of Mount Fuji on the wall, a pile of papers stacked neatly on the floor under a small desk and two bookcases jam-packed with books and CDs.

Where was the music? The desk itself was clear but he had the feeling Nina had hastily stuffed things into the drawers or tossed some rubble into the wardrobe. That's what he would have done.

"I'll do that, Nina." He picked up the remaining bedding.

"It's fine. You get your bag." She expertly slipped a pillow case onto the pillow. "Perhaps you'd like to have a shower. There's a towel." She pointed to a blue striped one neatly folded on the chair by the desk. Martin took the hint.

Franz's suitcase held a pitifully small collection of his belongings. He had literally thrown any clothing in that came to hand plus the most valuable possession, his flute. He hadn't packed pyjamas but had tossed in a toothbrush and all his underwear and socks as well as an extra pair of jeans and one decent pair of black trousers and shoes. He'd been carrying his leather jacket around since he landed yesterday. His clothes looked and smelled as though he'd been sleeping in them, which he had.

Nina's shower was like standing under Niagara Falls. He helped himself to shampoo and conditioner and toothpaste and used her pink safety razor, carefully clearing the beard hairs from the blade before replacing it on the bench. A new man emerged from the bathroom but Nina had disappeared into her room.

Martin had to sit up, yawning, for a while until his hair dried enough for him to go to bed but he amused himself by looking at her books and CDs. Working in a music shop would have benefits. She had quite a selection of classical, mainly violin things of course but she obviously liked the Beatles and that whole sixties era of British pop. He did too.

Both his parents had been right into it and his father had even been to the Cavern in Liverpool and heard the Beatles before they were famous. He never tired of telling his family that as if he were personally responsible for discovering them and sending them on their way to fame and fortune. The kids used to roll their eyes and groan when he got started but they were secretly very proud and used to boast about it to their friends. "My Dad saw the Beatles before they were famous. He knew they were good. He knew they were going to be great one day."

Then his mother ran off with a man who sold used cars and the happy home fell apart at the seams. His Dad was never the same after she left and he died a sad, bitter man who never forgave her, the woman he loved with all his heart, for betraying him so publicly and humiliatingly. *"She's Leaving Home"* was the one Beatles song Martin couldn't listen to.

He gave his hair a last rub with the towel and lay down. Body and brain had had enough and he slept.

Nina had gone to work when he got up. He wondered what her work hours were. She must have been tired after the late night. She probably started at nine and he knew she finished at six. The clock in the kitchen said three in the afternoon. She hadn't left a note. Perhaps she expected him to sleep all day. Despite having only met him yesterday she had an uncanny knack of knowing what was in his mind but didn't seem perturbed by it, which put her ahead of everyone else he had encountered lately.

He poked about in the pantry cupboard and found some bread for toast. There was also a jar of the infamous vegemite which he'd heard about but never tasted. Black, thick and very salty, rather like marmite. Obviously an acquired taste.

The phone rang while Martin was eating his second slice of toast and honey, not caring to acquire a taste for vegemite just yet. He let it ring until the machine clicked on.

"Martin? Are you there?" Her husky voice sent a frisson down his spine. "Pick up the phone."

He snatched up the receiver. "Yes. Nina?" Maybe she was hoping he'd left. But he had nowhere to go

"How are you feeling? I rang earlier but you must have been still asleep." She paused. "I thought you might have left."

Hardly. She was why he'd come to Australia. "No. I'm still here. I hope that's okay. I've only just got up."

"That's fine. I'll be home about six thirty." She sounded pleased.

"Would you like me to cook dinner?"

"No, no, I'll do a stirfry when I get home." She laughed softly. "You can do the washing up afterward."

"Right you are. I'll find a bottle shop and buy some wine."

"Martin..." She lowered her voice. "It's real, isn't it?"

He swallowed hard before he answered.

"Yes," he said.

Chapter Five

They sat in the same places as the night before. She in her armchair opposite him on the couch. He wanted her to be sitting next to him so he could he feel the warmth of her body and smell the subtle freshness of her perfume but she treated him like a guest, friendly, with the distance of new acquaintances.

There was something indefinably welcoming about the house, like coming home, though he'd never even been anywhere near Australia before, let alone set foot in the place. Despite her reserve he was comfortable with her too, beyond their shared experience of the music. They'd prepared dinner together and eaten it sitting in her tiny back garden where it was cooler. They'd laughed and been amazed at the coincidence of having the same last name albeit spelt differently. Another link. As promised he'd done the dishes.

She'd changed from her work clothes into loose white cotton pants and a baggy pink shirt, sexy and cute all at the same time and he wanted to hold her and feel her body through the thin cotton of her clothes but knew he couldn't touch her or the fragile relationship would crash. They had enough emotional chaos to sort through without his unwanted advances adding to the mess.

But Nina was simply the most perfect woman he'd seen in his life. He'd thought she was yesterday at the shop but he'd been jet lagged and his nerves strung to breaking point by his quest and today, waiting for her to come home, relatively clear headed, he'd wondered if he'd imagined that snap of certainty that she was his soul mate. Too far-fetched, too romantic in the worst possible way.

But he could hardly take his eyes off her and had to avert his gaze when she glanced at him so she wasn't unnerved by the stalkerish attention. She told him as they ate she had a Chinese great grandparent on her mother's side, come to Australia in the 1850's gold rush. She'd inherited her mother's colouring and oval face shape but her features were less Asian than European. She'd inherited the best of both worlds and then some. The short bobbed hair swung against her cheeks in a glossy, black curtain and she looked at the world through dark, mysterious eyes.

Neither had mentioned the music before or during dinner. Somehow, with two involved, the pressure seemed less intense, more bearable. There was truth in the saying, "a trouble shared is a trouble halved." At least for him and he suspected, by her expression and her manner, for Nina.

Now, though, the time had come to continue his part of the story. He topped up both their glasses with the remains of the crisp, chilled Riesling he'd bought that afternoon and which had gone so well with the stirfry.

"So Celia told you about her brother, the musician," she said.

"Yes. George had played with a string quartet. He was the second violinist. She said they rehearsed together every week almost, for years. Occasionally they would have someone join them. A clarinet or flute player or pianist for example to do one of the famous quintets, and they gave concerts every now and again. They were all amateurs but Celia said they were dedicated and very good players. She gave me their names and phone numbers and I intended to ring each one and ask about the music and if I could visit to talk about it. I also managed to get George's widow's name and contact. Jessica. Celia had become quite chatty by now.

"I decided to ring Jessica first. I thought she might remember if George had said anything about it or what he had done with the other parts. I thought if he had the flute and cello parts he must have had all of them at some stage especially as it seemed to have come from an ancestor. She didn't answer the phone so I moved on to Charlie Davis the first violin. He was a tetchy old character. Quite abrupt—and when I mentioned the music he said he remembered playing it just the once. Couldn't remember where it had come from or anything else about it except in his words, "It was a horrible piece of music, too darn hard to read—handwritten— and I refused to play it. I gave it back to George and said don't ever ask me to play that tripe again."

"That would have been my part," said Nina with a laugh. "Did he mention the warning?"

"No, and I didn't know about it then so I couldn't ask him. He may have written it but it didn't sound as though he had had the part long enough to bother. He might have. We'll probably never know."

"Not much help."

"Except that he reacted the same way as Sylvia. And for someone who only saw it briefly it had a profound effect on him. That made two people and I still don't understand why."

"The music didn't like them," Nina said dismissively. "What about the others?"

"The viola player was a complete write off because there was no viola part and he knew nothing about it. They must have run through it when he wasn't there. I was getting a bit discouraged by now. I'd been on the phone for hours and hardly got anywhere but Stephen Adamson, the cellist, was the best. He invited me to his house the following day. He said the music had really intrigued him at the time but they'd only played it once and Charlie reacted with such vehemence George had collected up the parts and they never saw them again."

Martin picked up the wine and drank.

"I went to visit the next afternoon. He lives in Wimbledon. His wife had baked a cake and set out afternoon tea. I had the impression they didn't have many visitors. They're a lovely couple, both well into their seventies but fit and healthy. Edith fussed about, making sure we were comfortable. They adore each other still. She told me they'd just had their forty-ninth wedding anniversary. Quite restored my faith in love."

He said it flippantly hoping to cover the depth of feeling seeing them together had so unexpectedly unearthed. Even the memory of that loving couple brought with it a deep longing to have what they had, what his parents had missed out on and what he seemed doomed to miss out on as well. Unless Nina...

"Love is the key to everything," she said. It sounded like a quote. "My parents are coming up to their thirtieth anniversary."

Martin did a rapid calculation. She must be in her

mid to late twenties.

Nina smiled. "I'm twenty-six and my sister Lucy is twenty-eight. We have a younger brother, Jason."

"Are you psychic?"

She grinned. "No. You're obvious. But I went to see one."

"A psychic? I never thought of doing that. What did she say?"

Her smile faded. "That I'd meet a tall, dark foreigner. She assumed he'd be handsome."

He smiled again. "You did. Me. And I am."

No answering grin this time. "Yes, but at that time I thought she may mean Piers. He's tall and dark and incredibly handsome."

Again that stab of jealousy. The man was long dead but he reached out from the spirit world and ensnared Nina. For the first time the thought crashed into his mind—Piers had to be stopped.

"He's hardly likely to appear," he said.

"Except in my dreams. And in your mind." She fixed him with steady gaze. "She also said the path was troubled and there was fear involved."

"She was right about that."

"She was but I had the feeling she wasn't telling me everything. I wasn't sure…it all seemed vague. Not wrong but not exactly right, either." She tilted her head with a small shrug and exhaled. She drained her wine glass. "Maybe that's typical, what they say to everyone."

Martin said, "Anyway. Stephen said he remembered that piece because it had such a hauntingly beautiful melody. He was amazed when Charlie reacted the way he did. He would have kept playing but George collected up the parts so quickly he didn't have a chance to even finish going through it. The really interesting thing was George had asked a woman to play the flute part. They were doing a work with flute and string quartet at the time. Stephen remembered her being quite taken with it as well. Unfortunately she died of breast cancer about three years ago so I couldn't talk to her but then, we've got the flute part. Do you realise? They must have had three parts playing together, the three we've got." He emphasised the last words.

"But what about George? He was a violinist why didn't he play the violin part if Charlie hated it so much?"

"I wondered that too but not until later. It just didn't occur to me when I was talking to Stephen. You see he mentioned that there were a few other pages that George didn't hand out. He's sure there was a score and a guitar part at least. He remembered George humming along following the score as they played. He might have been singing a missing part."

"The voices would have been very strong."

"You'd think so. I needed to talk to Jessica. She must have noticed something if George was experiencing what we've been experiencing. I'd tried to ring her again the previous night but she didn't seem to be home. I kept trying every day at all different times but she didn't answer. I even rang Celia again to ask her if she knew why Jessica wasn't answering but she said as far as she knew she was still in London but could easily have gone away without telling her.

"While all this was going on I wasn't practising or working at all. The orchestra fired me, I'd forget about my students and they'd turn up for lessons suddenly and surprise me. Over a period of time they began to drift away to other teachers. I rarely got calls for subbing and when I did more and more often I would refuse. That's the kiss of death when you're a freelance. People won't call again.

I kept playing the music and I even asked another friend to play the cello part. Actually it was Sven, a double bass player. I thought if he played it on double bass he might not be affected the way Sylvia was. He wasn't. It's hard to tell with Sven what's going on most of the time because he smokes a bit of dope and he's already a bit…not exactly crazy but eccentric, I suppose. He's reliable where it counts though or I wouldn't have let him flat-sit for me now. He's not a very good reader. I think the combination of things negated the effects.

If Sven heard voices he'd think it was quite normal. He probably hears them all the time anyway. He thought the melody was "cool man"—he speaks with this funny mix of Swedish accent and American slang—and sort of improvised his own bass line."

Martin stopped as for the first time in months, something funny occurred to him. "Piers and Company probably didn't recognise their music."

Nina burst out laughing at the same moment. Martin laughed and laughed until tears ran down his cheeks and his stomach hurt. Nina, through the tears, was holding her stomach as well, laughing not because what he had said was so funny although it did conjure up a picture of three confused spirits scratching their heads and saying to each other "What's that? Is that our music?" but because they could finally joke about it.

When the laughter had subsided to the occasional

gasp, Nina said, "Want a beer?"

His wine was long gone. Martin nodded. She reappeared with two icy cold stubbies and handed him one. His first beer in Australia. He knew why they served it cold here now and why his Australian acquaintances complained about the warm beer in England.

He'd ventured outside to the bottle shop after Nina had rung that afternoon and it was hot. Baking. Humid, too. He'd wandered about, first taking careful note of her address and where he was going so as not to get lost. She lived in a terrace house and the area seemed to be undergoing gentrification, although it hadn't reached her street yet. He found the local shops where they'd eaten pizza, mostly trendy restaurants and cafes but nowhere to buy shorts or sandals. He bought Nina flowers at a greengrocer's when he was tempted in by the exotic array of fruit on display. They'd eaten fresh mango and pineapple for dessert tonight.

The fragrant pink and white blooms sat in a china jug between them on the coffee table and her dark eyes strayed to them quite frequently. Pleased.

He put his beer carefully on a coaster.

"I finally wrote to Jessica. I found her address in the phone book and got a reply a month later. She'd been away. I must have kept missing her at first because as Celia had said she was in London at the time when I tried to call but had gone abroad for three weeks shortly after. She agreed to meet me...I think she and Celia had discussed me and decided I was all right. We met in a restaurant for afternoon tea. My hair had grown quite long and I tied it back so as not to look too wild and I wore a suit. I don't always look like this."

His glance must have been anxious because Nina grinned. She didn't seem to mind how he looked but then she wasn't a seventy-year-old English lady fairly recently widowed.

"She remembered the music. George had come across it in his mother's things. They lived in George's family house and the attic was chock full of suitcases and boxes and crates—sounded like the cliché of an attic, the sort of place the Famous Five would find clues. Every now and again they would have a go at clearing some of the stuff out. Jessica said she was sure they would find some priceless antique or a Rembrandt or something but they never did. She's a terrific woman, Jessica, bags of energy and a great character. She'd been hiking up mountains in Switzerland when she was away.

Her mother-in-law was a pianist and all her music was up there, along with other bits and pieces from George and Jessica's children, who had taken up and dropped music lessons all through their childhood, apparently.

The music, our music, was in a box of his grandfather's. That's Stanley West.

It caught George's eye because it was handwritten and he thought it may have been an original composition by Stanley. Naturally he wanted to play it and took the parts along to the next rehearsal of the quartet."

"That didn't go well," Nina put in.

"No. Jessica remembered how distraught he'd been when he came home that night. He was terribly upset, she said. She couldn't understand it and he couldn't tell her why either. She said it was really peculiar and she was frightened because George was normally a calm, rational man not given to great emotional outbursts. He told her about trying to play the music and she asked him to play it for her. They were amazed by the effect it had on them both. She wanted him to keep playing it but he refused. He must have had a very strong will."

"Or he wanted to protect Jessica. Maybe he sensed it was dangerous. Maybe George wrote on the violin part!" Nina sat bolt upright, eyes shining with excitement.

"Maybe. Jessica didn't mention that either. She said he was quite adamant that the music be destroyed."

"But he couldn't."

"No, that's what she said. Something, some force, prevented him from actually tearing the paper or throwing it into the fire. He wanted Jessica to do it but she refused point blank. She told me she has no idea why she felt so strongly about preserving a piece of music that she'd only heard once but whatever the reason she suggested he separate the parts if he wanted to stop it being played. George agreed and together they put the cello and flute parts into some other music books in different boxes. That's where I found them. I'm not sure if they knew they were in with music for the same instrument. I wonder…"

"But how did I get the violin part and where's the score? And the guitar part?"

"Jessica said George split the parts, he thought irrevocably, by sending one to Australia and one to New Orleans. He sent the most powerful, the most dangerous, the violin part furthest, to Australia, but the score and the guitar parts must be important as well. She didn't know which he sent where and she was sure he'd only sent two overseas envelopes so maybe he sent the others to New Orleans. Seems unlikely though, doesn't it?"

"Sending two to the same place?"

"Yes, especially when he'd gone to so much trouble to separate the rest."

"And Jessica didn't know what happened to the guitar part and the score?"

"She had no idea."

"Did he hear the voices, did she say?"

"He wouldn't tell her. He kept insisting the music be destroyed and wouldn't rest until he was rid of it."

"He must have."

"Yes. Doesn't make sense otherwise."

Sense? What was he saying? Sense, like Elvis, had long ago left the building.

"Why did he send the music to Australia and America? And who to? He didn't just write 'Anybody, Australia' and post it, did he? Come to think of it that would have effectively got rid of it."

"You're right. It'd sit in the dead letter office forever. No. He sent it to friends and told them to get rid of it. I spoke to the friend here in Sydney, I rang him, and he said he'd shoved it in a box in the garage and forgotten about it and then a few months ago had had a clear out and sent it along to a church fete. That was after he got over his surprise at some English nutter ringing him out of the blue to ask about something that happened over twenty years ago. I'm amazed he remembered but he said it was such an odd thing George had done that it stuck in his mind and he never got a satisfactory answer from George himself. I didn't enlighten him either. He said the music arrived in a sealed envelope which George asked him not to open and he hadn't, but his son did when they were getting everything together to take to the church fete."

"Which is where I found it. Wow." Nina shook her head. "It's amazing."

"I was incredibly excited when he told me he'd handled it or at least his son had, so recently. I decided then and there to come here to find it. It didn't seem crazy at the time, it seemed the next logical step and I booked my ticket as soon as I got off the phone. He gave me his address but I didn't tell him I was coming to Sydney. I thought I'd ring when I got here and talk to the son, John."

"What about the New Orleans envelope?"

"Jessica gave me the person's name but they only had a PO box number and she had long ago lost touch with them."

"But when did you play for your yoga teacher?"

"While I was waiting for Jessica to reply. I've made it seem sort of like a detective story but you must remember that all the time the voices were there every time I played and I had this terrific compulsion to keep listening to them. It's close to eight months now but it's incredibly frustrating because I kept getting the same snippets of conversation. Jasper would say, 'She's dead, man.' Piers would yell, 'No, no. She will live.' Jasper would yell hysterically, 'Piers, she's gone.' Piers would scream, 'Mira.' And then start cursing Jasper and Michael and Jasper would say again, 'She's dead.' And it would go on like that. It still does.

I don't know if that's what my yoga teacher heard or if that's what anyone else heard—Sylvia or Charlie or George. I thought my yoga teacher might be able to

98

help me through meditation. She was more advanced at it than I am. Maybe I should have gone to a clairvoyant, too. Should go to a clairvoyant," Martin corrected.

"My Tai Chi instructor suggested it."

"I always think psychics are such frauds. There are lots of them in London, at all the street markets with their cards and their beads and scarves and all that paraphernalia. What a joke."

"Mine wasn't like that. She was very ordinary. I didn't say anything about why I'd come and she rabbited on about how I would meet the tall, dark man, a traveller and there was love involved. Also a mystery, but she couldn't say exactly. Standard stuff, I imagine. Not a word about the music or the extra voice in my head. Not that I really expected anything." Nina stopped. She stared at him with a new awareness in her face. A frown passed across her brow like a shadow but she didn't say anything.

"Nina. It's real. We both know that." Martin drank the last of his beer. "I'd booked a ticket for ten days ahead, just enough time to get organised and talk Sven into staying in my flat. I had no idea what I would do when I got here. The flight was hellish.

I felt like a zombie and it's so hot here even at night. It was sleeting in London when I left. I got the train into the city in the late afternoon and sat in that park, is it Hyde Park? Lay on the grass, actually and went to sleep with all the other odds and sods there. I didn't mean to I was trying to get my head together and work out what to do and the trees and grass and sunshine were so inviting after that plane trip. I meant to look for a cheap hotel but I woke up early in the morning, yesterday morning, and eventually found a café to have breakfast and a kind of wash. It was too early to find a hotel room so I phoned George's friend, Alan. I wasn't even sure what day it was because of the time difference."

"It's Thursday today."

"Thanks. I know now, actually, because I read your newspaper. Luckily Alan was home, he's retired, of course, and he gave me his son's number and I got onto him at work. John ran the stall all day and remembered you because you flirted with him and you were pretty."

"What? I did not. You're making that up!" Equally amused and outraged, but Martin wasn't sure at which part of his report.

"I'm not. That's what he said. He remembered you were really taken with that handwritten part and particularly the writing on it. He said he would never forget the look on your face when you touched the music, as if the page attached itself to you. You looked as if you'd finally found something you'd lost. You bought it, of course. You'd told him where you worked and there you were."

Like an angel standing behind that counter in her pale blue summer dress smiling at something her colleague had said. He knew instantly she was the one.

"And here we are. Martin, that's an amazing story. It's unbelievable."

"I know. But it's true."

Martin stared into her eyes. Brown eyes unwaveringly met his. Both knew what the next step was, fearful though it might be.

"You said earlier that you know their names and how many there are and what they talk about but…who are they and what do they want? Why choose us?" Her voice quavered on the last words. "Why are we suitable?"

"I have absolutely no idea."

He stood up and held out his hands to her. She grasped his fingers and rose to her feet. Her hands were warm, slightly moist. She looked up into his face with those beautiful dark brown eyes and he couldn't resist. He kissed her gently on the lips and she accepted the kiss for what it was, a gesture of solidarity and acknowledgment that they were in this together, even though the touch of her mouth on his nearly smashed his self restraint into tiny pieces.

"You know what we have to do, Nina?"

She nodded. "I'll get my violin."

Martin squeezed her fingers without taking his eyes from hers. "I'll get my flute."

Nina followed him to the spare room where he opened his suitcase. He withdrew a large envelope from the compartment inside the lid and produced the two parts. She opened the wardrobe where she stored her music and took the page off the top of the pile. It tingled against her fingertips, with repressed excitement this time but she handed it to him wordlessly, fighting the reluctance which almost overcame her.

Martin studied the handwritten warning across the top. She'd forgotten he'd never seen it before.

"Jessica would recognise George's handwriting," he said.

Nina gritted her teeth and almost snatched it back, unaccountably and overwhelmingly terrified he would take the music, her music, away from her.

"I won't keep it, Nina," he said calmly and began to unpack his flute.

"I'm sorry," she muttered, ashamed. If anyone understood this obsession, Martin did. She took out her violin. Her stomach churned with apprehension. Two instruments, what power may be unleashed? What danger? Martin had played two parts together and survived but he hadn't heard the violin part.

"What do you think will happen?" Despite her best efforts her voice wobbled.

"I'm not sure. I played two parts but they were the flute and cello. Your part is going to make it completely different. Piers is the leader."

"I'm not a very good player." Her violin was slippery in her fingers.

Martin was a highly trained, professional musician. What would he think of her meagre, amateurish ability? He smiled. "Piers doesn't seem to mind. He chose you to play it, didn't he?"

Nina fiddled with the tuning pegs on her instrument. It sounded ridiculous stated so plainly. She hadn't even hinted to Martin how she felt about Piers. "I don't know why he didn't pick a better violinist."

"It must be a combination of factors that coincide in you."

"We won't be able to play for very long. It's after eight thirty now, I don't want to upset Florence. She's my next door neighbour. She doesn't mind but…"

"Nina." Martin put his flute on the bed and rested his hands on her shoulders. Strength flowed into her body through his fingers. "It'll be all right. I know how to control this and so do you. I'll be here. I'll stop it if it gets too…" He hesitated, searching for the right word.

"Scary? Out of control? But Martin what if you can't?" Nina stared up at him. "It might be too powerful. Piers might…" But she didn't know what Piers was capable of.

He squeezed her shoulders. "Trust me."

She gazed into his eyes for long seconds until Martin dropped his hands and turned to pick up his flute.

"Do you have two music stands?"

"No, but I know the first section by memory," said Nina. "We can fold my part so I can read the last page. They should both fit then."

"Right." Martin arranged the music carefully. The flute part was written in the same hand as the violin but with the occasional bars rest. The second section looked far less complicated than hers.

He played a few scales to warm his flute and the lush, silvery sound flowed into the room. He was very good, far better than she would ever be. They tuned their instruments together, made some subtle adjustments. Martin drew a deep breath.

"Ready?" One last look at Nina. She nodded.

As soon as the first notes sounded the music flowed effortlessly with an instant rapport, an instinctive understanding of the other's sense of phrasing and nuance. Piers spoke almost immediately. He was pleased, and for the first time Nina heard another voice she assumed must be Jasper's. He was reluctantly agreeing to something Piers wanted him to do, something connected with Mira, of course, but all she heard were snippets as if it were a bad phone connection.

Piers said, "Aaahh. This is the way. The powers grow stronger."

Then, "Do this for me, Jasper. You must. The

music is the key. It is better now. This will work."

Jasper said, "It's madness." Then, "You have no right."

Piers answered, "For Mira. If not for me, for Mira."

Jasper. "I'll try…It's madness."

Piers. "You must."

Jasper. "Very well…She's dead…It can't work."

Piers. "Golden Dawn knows the method…"

They reached the end of the slow melody and began the difficult section. Martin had no trouble at all with the notes where Nina struggled. Piers willed her on but he faded as she reached her black spots.

"I just can't get this bit right." She dropped her bow in despair and lowered her violin as the room came back into focus.

Martin stopped abruptly. "What did you hear?" Breathless, eager.

"I heard Jasper for the first time. Piers wanted him to do something and he didn't want to but then agreed finally. Piers sounded pleased with me."

"With you?" Martin's eyebrows rose. "Does he speak to you? Personally? I thought Jasper was speaking to me at first but now I think I'm listening in, sort of an eavesdropper on their conversations." Was that a trace of envy, jealousy in his voice?

"He does in a way. I'm an eavesdropper as well but I know he knows I'm there playing for him. He encourages me to keep playing…he does speak directly, sometimes." A flush warmed her neck. She laid her violin in its case, turning away from the intensity of his gaze.

"What? What does he say?"

Nina licked her lips, closed the lid on her violin

and snapped the catches. Too intimate. Piers spoke to her. He chose her, not Martin. His love was for her. She wouldn't share those words. Something else. She turned around.

"I was with my ex boyfriend. We were in the hallway right outside the door and I wanted to come back in here and keep playing. The music seemed to beckon me…" She stopped, face burning now. Was it guilt at the prevarication or because he might assume she thought Piers was referring to him? Did she think that? Not at the time.

"Tell me, Nina." Irritated.

"Gordon was…well, he kissed me and Piers said quite distinctly, 'Not him. He's not the one'." The words tumbled out in a heap, giving him no chance to interrupt. "I was terrified. I couldn't believe it. He could have been right beside me it was so loud, close. That's when Gordon told me I was crazy and stormed out. And when I decided to ask for help." She finished in a shaky whisper.

Martin stepped forward without a word and drew her into his arms. Nina rested her head on his chest and sighed.

"I'm so glad you found me, Martin," she whispered.

"So am I."

"What did you hear?" Nina lifted her head but stayed in his arms. Nothing had felt so secure for months.

"Piers. Much the same but stronger. As if he'd gained in power. But…to me he sounds…threatening. He wanted Jasper to do something in connection with Mira but he wasn't nice about it. He said something I

105

hadn't heard before…Golden Dawn. Have you heard that?"

"Yes a couple of times. I heard it too. What is it? It sounds like a brand of butter." Nina stepped from his embrace, reluctantly. His hand slid down her back as he released his hold.

"I don't know. Do you want to play any more tonight?"

"No. It's funny, the compulsion isn't as strong with you here. Do you feel that?"

"You're right. Perhaps we've diluted it. Can we Google Golden Dawn?"

"I'm not online at home but I do have an encyclopaedia."

In the kitchen Martin started making tea while Nina searched the bookshelf for her one-volume encyclopaedia.

"There are lots of Goldens," she said. "Golden Age, Golden Hind, Golden ferret…good grief, look at that."

He read where she pointed, and snorted with laughter. "But no Golden Dawn."

"We'll have to go to a library and get on their internet."

"I can do that tomorrow while you're at work. And I need a haircut."

Nina regarded him thoughtfully. She hadn't concentrated much on his appearance before, beyond registering an instant attraction when he appeared in the shop. "I rather like your hair. Such lovely curls."

He touched hers with light fingertips. "I rather like your hair. So glossy and soft."

The gesture was more intimate than the hug or the

kiss. Those were shared through solidarity, this was on a whole different level. Personal. Did he see her as a woman apart from Shadow Music? He'd given no other sign. Would that be desirable? She'd known him about twenty-four hours, didn't know him at all, yet she trusted him with her sanity. He trusted her with his. There was no room for more. She had Piers.

"Where's a library?" He poured the tea into mugs.

"Come over to North Sydney later in the morning and we could go to the library together at lunch time." Nina sat down, this time in the armchair he had occupied the first night, cradling her mug in both hands. "I thought something more might have happened."

"We both heard other voices. Do you know a cellist?"

Nina looked up sharply. "Bring in someone else, you mean? But it's…" She wanted to say "our music" but Martin interrupted.

"Dangerous? I don't think so. The worst that will happen is the cellist hates it like Sylvia did."

"I suppose I could ask my brother. He used to play."

"We could tape him on his own and play with the recording by ourselves. Then he wouldn't be involved too much. How good is he?"

"He could have been really good but he didn't work at it. He's at Uni doing economics. Still has his cello though."

"Call him."

Nina reached for the phone and dialled. "I'm supposed to be checking up on him anyway while Mum and Dad are away."

Jason answered almost immediately. "Oh, it's you.

Are you doing your inspection?"

"Nice to talk to you, too." She laughed, catching Martin's eye. Green eyes flecked with brown, surrounded by laughter lines. First impressions proved right—kind, gentle, and calm in the face of this simmering, indefinable something. An inner strength she could rely on.

"Sorry. I'm expecting a call. I'm fine, the house is in one piece, and Ringo is still alive."

"Glad to hear it. If Mum came home to a dead cat your days would be numbered. Listen Jason, I want to ask you a favour."

"Oh, yes?"

"It's not a big one. I want you to play something for me on your cello. It's a piece of music and we want to tape it."

"Who's we?"

"A friend. Martin. You don't know him."

"Yeah, I guess. When? Can I look at the part first? How hard is it?"

"We can come over whenever suits you. I don't think you'll need to practise. It doesn't look difficult to me." Nina gave Martin a grin and he did a thumbs up. Attractive lines round his mouth when he smiled.

"How about Sunday afternoon straight after lunch 'cos I'm going somewhere at three."

"A girl?" Nina couldn't resist.

"You're as bad as Lucy. Pair of snoops."

"Well? Is it?"

"Yes. Her name's Andrea."

"See that was easy, wasn't it? Thanks, Jason. We'll be there about one."

"I'll go and find my cello."

"And dust it. See you." Nina hung up and smiled at Martin.

"Marvellous." He suddenly sounded terribly English as he continued. "Nina, is it all right if I stay with you? Do you mind? I realise I'm a total stranger who's just appeared out of the blue and I'm more than happy to go to a hotel if you'd prefer."

Something akin to panic slammed Nina in the belly.

"I don't want you to go anywhere! Since you came I've felt solid ground under my feet for the first time since I found that music. You've got to stay. Please. Unless you want to be on your own…if you do then go…but…I'd really like it if you stayed…but don't because of me…if you'd rather not…" She finished in hot confusion, breathless, wide-eyed. Maybe he didn't want to stay but didn't know how to say it.

He leant back on the couch and exhaled. "Thank you. I want to stay with you too. I'll pay my way of course," he added.

She could almost taste the relief. What would happen if he left didn't bear thinking about. But if she kept smiling at him the way she probably was, he'd get completely the wrong idea about her reasons for wanting him to stay.

"Good." A yawn caught her by surprise. "I think I'll go to bed. Good night."

"Good night. I'll stay up a while. My body clock's not right yet. What time do you leave?"

"I catch the ferry at eight-fifteen so I have to leave here by five-to at the latest. They go every hour and you get off at McMahon's Point where there's a bus or Milson's Point where you'd have to walk. Do you

109

remember where the shop is?"

Martin nodded. "Sleep tight. If I don't see you in the morning I'll come to the shop at lunchtime."

"I'll take lunch when you get there. About one."

For the first time in weeks Nina went to bed with a sense of purpose, looking forward to the next day, relieved to be found sane. Martin had brought with him a glimmer of hope that this nightmare might one day end.

"Meet me."

"Why don't you come to call?"

"No. It would not be prudent. I am not a respectable visitor for a young lady. Your father would not approve." He chuckled softly and his lips scorched hers again. A current of molten passion coursed through her body. Ethan's kiss was that of a bumbling boy compared to this man's. She would follow him anywhere, do anything he asked, anything.

The crunch of footsteps sounded on the gravel and Ethan's voice called softly, "Miranda? Are you there? Miranda."

Piers touched her cheek gently and disappeared into the blackness like a wraith. She pressed shaking hands to hot cheeks, body trembling, staring into the bushes where he'd vanished. The hot night air closed in on her, and the ground heaved beneath her feet like an animal. Ethan caught her as she stumbled, head reeling.

"Miranda! What is the matter? Are you faint? Perhaps you are still weak from your illness?"

She clutched him for support as the world regained its equilibrium.

"It's so hot, Ethan. I came out for some

air…maybe I am still recovering…"

The orchestra started up and Piers' violin soared over the other instruments with its strong, vibrant tone, speaking directly to her, she knew. The violin was his voice, reminding her, calling to her.

"Perhaps you should go home," Ethan's concerned face loomed close, peering anxiously. "Your father should examine you. The fever you had was very dangerous. We were all terrified we would lose you."

Leave here? Leave Piers? Miranda laughed. "No, no. I am perfectly well now. I am ready to dance again."

Ethan smiled albeit uncertainly, and tucked her arm in his to lead her through the rose garden to the ball room.

Chapter Six

Cutting Marsh, August 1892

The Summer Ball approached. Miranda and Mrs. Bowden had fussed and fiddled endlessly over the patterns and fabric for her new gown, much to the amusement of her father.

"I don't see why you can't wear one of your old gowns," he said but she knew he was teasing and was glad to see her happy and recovered from the fever. He didn't even grumble overly much about the expense of the pale blue watered silk and the lengths of French lace and ribbon.

"She'll need many more gowns and all manner of garments when she marries Mr. Ethan," Mrs. Bowden said, not for the first time. "She can't go to the manor wearing her old clothes."

"Ethan hasn't asked me to marry him, yet," said Miranda. Perhaps he never would; perhaps he and his parents had their sights set on a more fitting bride than the daughter of the local doctor, however much regard they may have for both her and her father. After all, the Broomes had been at Broome Hall for centuries and the family was part of the rich social fabric of the country. Broome's had married into many of the other aristocratic families over the generations and the squire was in fact an Earl although he chose not to use the title much.

But Ethan loved her, and she loved him with a certainty forged over years of friendship. Mrs. Bowden echoed her thoughts.

"He will. Everyone knows you two are meant to be together and have been since you were children. Isn't that right, Doctor?"

"Women know better than a doctor about these things," he replied. "I shall be back in time for supper, Mrs. Bowden." His laughter rang down the passageway as he went off to visit a patient on one of the outlying farms.

Mrs. Bowden's sister was an expert dressmaker in nearby Plymouth and Miranda, all couture decisions made, had gone several times to her rooms for fittings. Despite his good-natured rumbling her father had paid what Miranda considered an exorbitant sum for the new silk gown, his only proviso being she choose something demure and suitable for an innocent young woman.

"I trust you Mrs. Bowden, to keep Miranda's enthusiasm in check."

He couldn't complain about the skirt of palest blue trimmed with French lace and white ribbon, the small puff sleeves, the gently scooped neckline and the neatly fitted bodice. She'd never had a gown so elegant and beautiful. Ethan would be stunned when he saw her in it. He may just be given the push he needed to propose.

Just the thought of his expression made her laugh. She couldn't wait for the days to pass. Everyone who was anyone in the surrounding area would be there. The Squire's Summer Ball was the social occasion of the year.

Tyler was looking forward to it, too. Even her

father would attend although he maintained at dinner two nights prior to the big event he'd rather stay peacefully at home.

"Too much noise and too crowded. Everyone talking at once and musicians playing...such a racket it makes my head ache. And in this heat it will be unbearable."

"The heat wave may have broken by then," said Tyler.

"But you enjoy it, Papa," Miranda said. "You know you do."

"So long as Mrs. Meadows doesn't start telling me about her indigestion and describing her symptoms."

"Perhaps she should eat less," said Tyler.

Miranda caught his eye and giggled.

"I have tactfully and not so tactfully suggested that."

"If she corners you, Tyler or I will rescue you," said Miranda.

"Don't you worry about me, my dear. You enjoy yourself."

"I will."

"Maybe Emily Sturgess's baby will arrive three weeks early," he said hopefully.

But for Miranda the last days just would not pass fast enough.

****

The Squire, accompanied by Mrs. Broome, elegant in a deep rose red gown trimmed with dark lace and flowers around the hemline, greeted their guests at the entrance to the ballroom. Ethan hovered nearby, resplendent in a tail coat which showed off his broad shoulders to perfection. When his gaze landed on

Miranda, his face immediately relaxed into a relieved smile which turned, as she'd expected, to astonishment as his eyes travelled to her dress and her figure displayed so nicely by the new gown. Mrs. Bowden's sister had given the services of her maid Sally to do Miranda's hair earlier in the day and now soft curls piled on her head with ringlets artfully wisping her neck and cheeks, all held in place with a fancy tortoiseshell comb.

"Welcome, Doctor. Good evening, Miranda." The Squire shook her father's hand. Miranda curtsied.

"Good evening, sir."

"What a beautiful dress, my dear," said Mrs. Broome. "You do look lovely tonight."

"Should do, she's been preparing for over a month," said her father.

"Papa!" Her cheeks burned.

Their hosts laughed and turned to the next arrivals. Ethan stepped forward.

"Good evening Doctor. Hello Miranda. You look simply…"

"Lovely," supplied her father and chuckled. "Hello, Ethan. Take care of her. I see Colonel Muffat. Must have a word." He disappeared into the throng.

"You do look lovely. More than that. Exquisite," Ethan said.

"Thank you, Ethan."

He took her arm and led her through to the main ballroom. The room had been cleared of furniture save for the chairs arranged along the walls for the comfort of weary dancers or those who preferred to observe the activities. Already the large high-ceilinged room was crowded with beautifully attired people.

Miranda recognised a few faces but for the most part the guests were strangers. An attack of nerves suddenly had her in its grip. This elegant crowd was chatting to each other with an ease the upper classes managed effortlessly. The women's gowns were beautiful and far richer and more fashionable than hers despite the newness. She would appear the dowdy country girl beside them but the men, sophisticated and confident glanced her way with appreciation in their eyes which gave her ego a small boost.

"There are so many people, Ethan," she said. "I hardly know a soul even though I've lived in Cutting Marsh most of my life."

"You know my cousins, the Redpaths. Come and say hello."

Ethan nodded and smiled as he threaded his way through the throng.

Miranda had met Lucinda and Harriet Redpath on more than one occasion at Broome Hall and even though she hadn't found them particularly scintillating companions she was delighted to greet them now. Harriet wore a buttercup yellow gown which set off the deep auburn of her hair beautifully. Lucinda, an awkward, ginger-haired, pale-skinned girl wore a pink ensemble which made her look even more insipid and sickly than usual.

"Hello, Miss Templeton," they chorused, then giggled at the coincidence.

"Good evening to you both. Please, call me Miranda. I'm sure we know each other well enough by now."

The sisters tittered and exchanged glances.

Ethan said, "Miranda, I must leave you with my

cousins for a moment. I promised mother…"

"Of course you go and do your duty." Miranda smiled.

"Save me the first dance."

"I will."

"The first dance," said Harriet when he'd departed. "Whatever will Miss McCusker say?"

"Miss McCusker?"

More significant looks but no giggles this time. "Miss Valerie McCusker. She is the daughter of an American financier. Pots of money."

"And she has her eye firmly fixed on our cousin."

"Ethan?" said Miranda in astonishment. A rival for his affection had never entered her head.

"Those Americans do love a title." Lucinda smiled happily at the prospect.

"But what does Ethan think?"

"It's not really a case of what he thinks more a case of what Uncle and Aunt Broome think." Harriet pursed her lips.

"But he's never mentioned her."

"To whom?" inquired Harriet with some acerbity. "He doesn't need to mention her. We all know her."

"Oh, look, there's Cecil Arbuthnot." Lucinda and Harriet fluttered their fans and simpered. "Is he coming this way?"

Miranda gave a cursory glance about. "I couldn't say, as I don't know the gentleman."

"Fair hair, very elegant and a refined manner."

Miranda swept the crowd and spotted a blond young man chatting to an elderly couple. "He's talking to someone."

"The Percivals," whispered Lucinda, snatching a

quick look. "They're down from London."

"So is Cecil," said Harriet. "In fact most of this crowd is."

"They like to get out of London to the country in this heat."

"It's just as hot here, I imagine," said Miranda. That's why she hardly knew a soul. Why hadn't Ethan mentioned the American heiress? How familiar were they with each other?

"It is unbearable. Makes one feel as though one could do something quite mad."

Both girls giggled again.

The orchestra began warming up their instruments at the far end of the ballroom. Miranda craned her neck but couldn't see the musicians. The dancing was about to begin but where was Ethan to claim the first dance?

The orchestra launched into a rather sedate waltz. Cecil Arbuthnot approached and bore Lucinda off to the dance floor. Harriet smiled knowingly.

"He'll ask for her hand by summer's end."

"Will he?"

"Definitely. It's a very good match."

"Do they love each other?"

Harriet raised an eyebrow. "They like each other, that's more than enough."

"I couldn't marry a man I didn't love."

"I suppose you don't have to worry too much about who you marry."

"What do you mean?" Was that a slight coming from this young woman she thought of if not as a friend, then a friendly acquaintance, Ethan's cousin?

"People in our situation have an obligation to marry well whereas you…"

Miranda met the cool blue eyes and saw only disdain. A flush crept up her neck. Harriet turned away with a sociable smiled plastered on her lips as a gentleman appeared to claim her hand. He nodded briefly to Miranda.

"My dance I think, Miss Redpath?"

"Yes indeed, Mr. Taylor." Harriet inclined her head and took his hand.

Miranda, left alone, edged toward the wall where the more elderly guests had taken up positions on the chairs ready to view the proceedings and discuss who was who and who was likely to marry well. Judging by Harriet's comment she was not included in the likely brides list because no one here would regard her as a good match. Harriet as good as said she was not worthy of marrying Ethan.

She craned her neck searching for him amongst the crowd but realised this made her look quite frantic and worried as opposed to sophisticated or demure. A middle aged rather plump gentleman approached with a smile on his round face.

"May I have the pleasure of this dance, Miss Templeton?"

Miranda hesitated just a second but Ethan wasn't to be seen, this gentleman was and the first dance was half over.

"Thank you. Yes, you may."

He held out his arm and she placed her hand on it. "George Sutherland," he said. "Doctor Templeton's daughter, I believe."

"Yes, that is correct." She wanted to ask how he knew her father but they'd reached the dance floor and conversation was impossible. Couples whirled by.

Miranda's partner was competent and solid, leading her with earnest precision around the room. Lucinda danced by, smiling up into Cecil's placid face. One or two other familiar faces swirled past. Then Ethan waltzed alongside with a dark-haired young woman in a sumptuous dark blue gown. Diamonds sparkled at her throat and dripped from her ears.

His eyes locked with Miranda's and for a moment she glimpsed embarrassment but then another couple intervened and Ethan and his partner were gone.

"Who is the lady dancing with Ethan?" Miranda asked. She already knew the answer, thanks to the Redpath girls.

"Oh, she's the American, Miss Valerie McCusker. She's an awfully nice young lady. Much nicer than one would expect from an American."

"She's very beautiful." She was. And with her beauty went money and with the money went confidence.

"You are very beautiful too. If you don't mind my saying."

Miranda glanced into his face in surprise. "Thank you."

"It's my pleasure." His grip on her waist tightened slightly, uncomfortably. Fortunately the music ceased and Miranda was able to step back and follow him to the side of the room.

"Thank you, Miss Templeton."

Miranda smiled. "Thank you, Mr. Sutherland." He bowed and withdrew.

Tyler wandered by and stopped when he spied her standing alone.

"How are you enjoying yourself?"

"Very well. I've just danced the first dance. Tyler, do you know many of these people?"

"Some. One or two chaps from Oxford are here. Will and Jane Drury. You know them. And I know the Redpaths, of course. So do you."

"Harriet told me many people have come down from town."

"Yes. Excuse me, I must claim my next partner."

The orchestra began a lively polka which considerably thinned the ranks of older dancers. Miranda went searching and found Will Drury, a friend of Tyler's who had recently married Jane French a Plymouth girl whom Miranda knew.

"We have exciting news, Miranda," said Jane almost immediately. "We are expecting our first child in the New Year."

"How wonderful. Congratulations." Miranda kissed Jane's flushed cheek.

"Jane tells everyone we meet," said Will but he smiled fondly down at his wife's pink-cheeked excitement.

"So she should. It's news worth sharing."

Miranda considered the couple. Like Ethan, William was heir to an estate a few miles distant which had been in his family for generations. Jane's father was a lawyer with a legal practice in Plymouth. No one had objected to the marriage as far as Miranda knew. Was that because Jane's family was English through and through and she was the epitome of a fair-haired, creamy skinned, pink and white English girl? Would the Redpaths think differently if Miranda's mother had not been of Chinese descent?

"What a strenuous dance," said Jane as couples

bounced past. "I find I tire easily these days."

"You must be very careful, my dear."

"My father recommends plenty of exercise for patients in a similar condition to yours," said Miranda. "Perhaps walking rather than vigorous dancing. Especially the polka."

Jane smiled. "I shall make a point of taking a sedate walk every day."

The polka wound to a halt. Panting couples made for the refreshment room as the Master of Ceremonies announced an old-style country dance.

Ethan suddenly appeared before them, flushed and slightly breathless having clearly just been dancing. Greetings exchanged, he said to Miranda, "I'm so sorry. I was supposed to dance the first dance with you. Please forgive me."

Miranda, under the scrutiny of three pairs of eyes, summoned a smile. "I am sure you have a good reason, Ethan. I danced with Mr. Sutherland instead."

"Please dance with me now?" He extended his hand and Miranda took it.

The dance was an old country one involving eight pairs of dancers moving in intricate steps, changing partners and circling. Not much opportunity to speak. Miranda couldn't fail to notice Miss McCusker farther down the row in their group and couldn't fail to notice how her eyes met Ethan's more than by chance when the dance brought them together.

Harriet was absolutely correct in her observation. Miss McCusker had her mind if not her heart set on Ethan which begged the question burning in Miranda's mind. How did Ethan feel?

When the dance ended Miranda grasped Ethan

firmly by the arm and pulled him in the opposite direction to the American.

"I need some refreshment, Ethan."

"Very well. There is cordial and tea served in the side room."

He fetched her a glass and they stood in a quieter corner.

"I've never seen so many people in one place before."

"You missed the last Summer Ball, if I remember."

"Yes I'd twisted my ankle. I was so disappointed, but this year makes up for it."

Ethan drew a deep breath. "Miranda, I have something I must say to you." He glanced at the nearest people less than two yards away. "Will you come onto the terrace for some air?"

"Very well." She left her glass on a table and followed him out through tall French doors into the thick night air, heart skipping and bouncing like the feet of the polka dancers. Was this the moment she'd been waiting for?

"It's still very warm." He tugged at his coat sleeves and smoothed a hand over his chin, gestures she knew signified nerves. She knew him so well. He was working up to something momentous. Harriet and Lucinda must be wrong, he was going to propose. What else could it be to make him so nervous? Had he spoken to her father already? Was that why her father had been so cheerful when they arrived?

The heavy scent of roses wafted up from the garden. Mrs. Broome's pride and joy.

Ethan gazed into her face, light from the open doors and windows falling on his beloved features.

"Miranda, I don't know how to say this…I know you and I have always thought…at least I have…and I think you felt the same way…that we would be wed one day."

"Yes," she breathed. "We do feel the same way." A smile trembled on her lips.

"The thing is, Miranda…even though I do love you and always will, I can't marry you."

"What?" Had she heard correctly? Can't marry? "Why not?"

He licked his lips and rubbed his chin again. Understanding fell like a hammer blow. The Redpaths were right.

"Miss McCusker?"

He nodded. "I barely know her but…"

"She's a good match and I'm not," she said through the bitter tears choking in her throat.

"I'm sorry, so sorry, my darling Miranda." He took her hands in his but she pulled them away.

"Is it because of my mother?"

"Your mother? No." But he lied. She always knew when Ethan lied he was so bad at it. She swallowed the tears and forced her voice to behave. The thudding pulse in her ears slowed. She dragged in a deep breath. She would not grovel and plead.

"I hope you'll be very happy with her." Chin up she stepped back into the room leaving Ethan in the dark.

As luck would have it Harriet Redpath stood just inside the door. Had she overheard any of the exchange? Perhaps not but the gloating little twist to her lips indicated otherwise.

"My condolences, Miranda."

"Has someone died?" Miranda retorted with a tight smile.

"I'm sorry. I didn't mean to overhear but I was about to step outside for some air and there you two were."

"You already knew, didn't you? So it would come as no surprise."

Harriet replied through a smile but her words were pure acid. "I'm sure you'll make a fine wife for someone but a country doctor's daughter with foreign blood can't compete with a lady from the same social class as an Earl." A little titter of laughter indicated her amusement at the idea. "You and Ethan may have been playmates for a long time but childhood friendship holds no weight when marriages are arranged."

"Love might. Love should."

"Miranda, you have no idea how these things work, how high society works. You lead a sheltered life here in this village. You have never even travelled to London, have you?"

"No."

"And you can't ever overlook the details of your birth. That your mother was…foreign." The rouged lip curled.

"Is not Miss McCusker foreign?" asked Miranda, a spark of anger igniting at the slur on her beautiful Mama.

"Miss McCusker is of a very good family from Boston. Their roots are Scottish nobility."

There was no comeback to that except graceful withdrawal.

"Excuse me, Harriet."

Miranda turned and pushed her way through the

throng. The music had begun and couples were waltzing in the centre of the floor. Tyler had a dark-haired young woman in his arms. His sweetheart Laura Jenkins wouldn't be invited here. A farmer's daughter in this company? The doctor must be about the lowest acceptable on the social ladder, only received because of his professional standing in the community. A special case.

Furious tears forced their way to her lids but she sniffed and blinked until they'd subsided. She had Harriet to thank in an odd way for preparing her just a little for the blow Ethan had delivered. She breathed deeply, determined not to show the slightest evidence of weakness or disappointment in this company. She wasn't ashamed of her parents and she wasn't going to be looked down on by these people. People who were more than ready to call her father out in the middle of the night to take advantage of his skills. No. She wasn't going home to cry herself to sleep, she would stay and she would dance with men such as Mr. Sutherland who thought her beautiful and she would enjoy herself.

****

Sydney, 1998

Piers spoke directly to her. He said, "This is the man. You must use him. He is right, he is the one. Listen to him but remember I am the one you must heed."

Nina ached to help him. His voice swamped her senses, overpowered her so that she could think of nothing but wanting to please him. "I will. I will do anything..."

"You are the one, the only one. You are mine." Her heart swelled with love and desire as he gazed into her eyes and spoke the last words. Then he raised his violin

and the music rose up and around her blotting out everything.

Uneasiness hovered about the room when Nina woke next morning. She couldn't quite remember everything Piers had said but he said something…something to do with Martin…some purpose as yet unclear. Perhaps when they heard the cello part as well…

She crawled out of bed early, yawning. Hot again with the threat of a storm later—better take her umbrella. She transferred the essentials from her usual purse to a larger straw bag.

Martin's door was still closed when she left for the ferry. When would he wake today? Jet lag was something she hadn't had to deal with. How long did it last? She exchanged "good mornings" with the usual passengers waiting on the wharf and chatted about the weather and the chances of a storm which they all agreed was likely and would be welcome.

"It's too early to be having these temperatures," complained her companion of the birthday party weekend. "Summer is going to be murder. Sure to be bushfires."

In the shop, business was slow. Nina fidgeted about willing the time to pass faster. Yesterday she thought Martin would either have left or had been a figment of her imagination. The only thing making her believe he was real was the fact that Rolly had met him and had asked her first thing what had happened. She hadn't told him Martin was staying with her. Even Rolly would think that too odd and she would never be able to explain how she instinctively trusted a total stranger. Or why.

When she'd told Rolly she'd been waiting for Martin, it was true. She hadn't known it, of course, the words had simply popped out of her mouth—but they were true. He fitted Serena's prediction perfectly as soon as he spoke in that English accent. But Piers fitted Serena's prediction too—tall, dark, indescribably handsome and unutterably sexy, oozing charisma.

Martin was tall, dark, and handsome in a way that could grow on her, he was certainly attractive, and he had the added bonus of being real. He was thoughtful and helpful at home, knew how to wash dishes and make a cup of tea, left the toilet seat down and didn't make a mess in the bathroom. He'd brought her flowers, something Gordon had never done, he was a musician and a good one, he knew about Shakespeare and probably lots more besides…

"Wake up, Nina." Tien's voice cut into her thoughts. He had the phone in his hand and glared from the office door.

"Sorry, what did you say?"

"The customer wants to know do we have a recording of Pavarotti singing *La Bohème* in stock. Look it up for me, please."

"I don't need to. We do." She rattled off three different versions.

She loved Italian opera. Did Martin? They could go to the opera together. They wouldn't get to see Pavarotti but the home-grown singers were very good. Piers couldn't take her to the opera.

"Replace these, will you, please, and then you can go to lunch?" Tien indicated a pile of CDs on the counter. Nina glanced at the clock. An hour too early for Martin.

"Someone's coming in to meet me for lunch at about one, Tien. Okay if I go then?"

His perpetually serious face creased in a series of furrows. "I'd rather you went now but all right."

Nina went to the bins with the CDs. Tien hated his routine to be threatened by insubordinate staff. Too bad. She'd take the later lunch break and Rolly could go now. Rolly didn't care and went off down the stairs without a backward glance.

The hour passed slowly, not aided by looking at the clock every five minutes. At twelve-thirty Tien took himself off for lunch as well, unnecessarily telling her not to go until Rolly returned, which he did just ahead of an almost unrecognisable Martin.

He looked older, more aloof and more of a stranger than when he'd appeared the day before yesterday, when he actually was a complete stranger. He'd been to a barber and the very short cut emphasised the gauntness of his face but suited him much better. He carried two plastic shopping bags and was wearing a new pair of sandals and lightweight linen slacks.

"I like it," she said.

His smile was reassuringly the same. "Are you ready to go?"

Rolly studied Martin, brow creased.

"Rolly, this is Martin. You met him the other day."

"Hello."

"Thought you looked familiar. The whistling man. Did you figure out what that tune was? It's been stuck in my head for two days."

Nina caught Martin's glance. "Has it?" she said. "It's a chamber music work but we don't know who wrote it. Martin's trying to track down a recording of

129

it."

"How do *you* know it?" asked Rolly.

"Don't know, heard it somewhere, I suppose." Nina slung her tote bag over her shoulder. "Let's go Martin."

In the street, the heat and glare of the midday sun pummelled the senses. Nina jammed her sunglasses on. Martin did the same.

"You'll have to be careful of the sun." His skin had the Northern European's winter pallor.

"I wasn't prepared for an Aussie summer. I'm not used to my shoes sticking to the road in November."

"It's a bit unusual. January and February are worse but there's supposed to be a storm this afternoon. Where shall we go first? Lunch or the library?"

"I'm starving," Martin said. "Let me buy you lunch."

"Thank you. I usually have a sandwich and some fruit outside somewhere. Too hot today, probably."

They found a café with a spare table and ate salad rolls and drank ice-cold juice, chatting politely of this and that, the differences between England and Australia, Nina's desire to travel one day, the weather. Was Martin as conscious of the sudden and awkward switch to a social setting? He chatted casually, unconcerned by or unaware of her nervous glances at his newly trimmed hair, her trite responses to his questions, the self-conscious pinkness of her cheeks when he smiled, the way the corners of his eyes wrinkled in a seriously attractive manner she hadn't noticed before. Like being on a first date except for one obvious difference.

"Let's split up," suggested Martin as they entered

the cool dimness of the public library. "I'm better with paper and books and you can't tell how accurate internet info is so it'll be good to cross reference."

"I'll do a search and you try the encyclopaedias."

Fifteen minutes later he rejoined Nina, engrossed in her computer search, staring at the screen, jotting things down on a piece of paper.

"What did you find?"

"Lots. What about you?"

He pulled another chair across and peered at the screen where the words, "The Hermetic Order of the Golden Dawn" were displayed.

"That's what I found too. Have you read about them?"

"I'm in the process. They sound pretty weird, don't they? Some sort of secret society thing, like the masons only with magic."

"Yes but they were connected to the Rosicrucians."

"I don't know anything about them. What do they do?"

"They date from the Middle Ages and had all sorts of beliefs but amongst other things they seemed to be seeking an elixir of eternal life."

"The Golden Dawn was around at the turn of the twentieth century. There was a lot of interest in that sort of thing then apparently. What we call New Age stuff now. Piers must have been one of them." Nina stared at the computer screen trying to make sense of this new information.

Martin said, "You know what, Nina? Piers was seriously trying to raise Mira from the dead."

Nina looked around at the other people in the library. Everyone appeared normal as far as she could tell. No members of weird cults wearing peculiar robes, no satanic priests or priestesses. Perhaps that elderly grey-haired lady was a witch borrowing fiction from the large print section, or those teenage girls reading magazines were vampires? That man at the next computer looked decidedly odd—definitely a being from another planet checking out the local culture.

She returned her attention to Martin. He appeared quite normal as well—a neatly attired, thirty-something, good-looking Englishman, slightly pink-skinned from the sun, sitting next to her in a public library looking at a computer screen.

"You've got to be kidding." Loudly, earning a frown from the alien.

"Well, it explains what we're hearing, doesn't it?" Martin whispered.

"Does it? It doesn't explain why we're hearing them. Not to me anyway." She shoved back her chair and stood up. "I've got to get back to work."

"I'll stay here," said Martin. "It's obvious. Piers and Jasper and Michael were involved with the Golden Dawn group and tried to resurrect Mira after she died. Don't you see? We're getting some kind of psychic fallout from their experiment."

"But it's impossible! Once you're dead you're dead." That got the alien's attention. He frowned and shook his head.

Martin shifted to her chair and scrolled down to read further, intently absorbing the words on the screen.

She lowered her voice. "How could they think they could do that?"

"I don't know. I'll read up on them and report to you later." Martin glanced at her and grinned. "Meet you same time, same place this evening?"

He suddenly looked boyish and vulnerable in his enthusiasm, like Julian or Dick from the Famous Five off another quest. Nina managed a feeble smile.

"All right. See you later." She turned and left the library, stepping from the refrigerator straight into the oven. Large billowy clouds crowded the sky to the west and a hot wind had picked up. Perfect bushfire weather. Nina put her sunglasses on and strode toward the shop.

Piers trying to raise Mira from the dead? Totally mad. Piers must have been a lunatic. But he wasn't a lunatic, he was strong and passionate and sensitive and a wonderful violinist. The melody swirled in her head. Piers' version not hers. The more she thought about what Martin had said the more furious she became. No wonder Jasper was reluctant—he must have known Piers was obsessed with the woman. Perhaps he didn't want to have anything to do with resurrecting her because she was a bitch, a slut. Mira must have been some female to have enthralled Piers that way. A real femme fatale. He wasn't the sort of man to fall for a weak, spineless girl. She probably seduced him. Either that or kept him panting. Men were incredibly weak where sex was concerned.

Nina stopped abruptly, aghast at the vicious line her thoughts had taken. Why was she so angry? What on earth was going on? The hot sun beat down on her head relentlessly. Was it frying her brain? She was consumed with jealousy of a dead woman she knew nothing about and a spirit who had loved her. A spirit she was in love with? A flash from the dreams appeared before her eyes. His face, so handsome and intense, his eyes looking deeply into hers, his voice saying, "*Do this for me. Only you. You are mine."* His hand reaching out to her.

"Piers," she murmured.

Someone touched her arm.

"Are you all right? You look a bit pale and wobbly. I shouldn't stand in this sun if I were you."

Nina blinked. She'd stopped in the middle of the footpath. Frozen in place. A woman was peering at her through dark glasses.

"Oh. Thanks. I'm fine."

But the melody remained in her head with Piers smiling at her as she walked on. He'd never been with her like this before, away from the music, away from home. He'd invaded her mind, overrun her thoughts—like a new lover.

She worked through the afternoon on automatic pilot, Piers with her constantly while she served customers, checked stock, answered the phone. When Martin appeared ten minutes before closing and began browsing in the classical section, his appearance jolted her. She'd forgotten he was coming. He would interfere with Piers. He would come between them.

Storm clouds had built up into a threatening purple black mass covering the sky like a shroud. Thunder, growling and rumbling, rolled around the heavens in the intense, oven-like stillness. The little ferry bounced toward the jetty on the choppy swell. The gangplank heaved up and down alarmingly as the passengers boarded and sought seats inside under cover. Half way across the harbour the rain came bucketing down, obliterating any view of the bridge and the approaching shoreline. The ferry eventually bumped its way into the Balmain East wharf. Martin slipped his arm around

Nina and together under her red umbrella, they struggled up the hill and along the rain-washed streets for home.

For the moment Piers was silent. Martin waited impatiently while Nina poked in her bag for the key.

"Come on. We'll drown at this rate." Laughing, as he tried to shelter them from the slanting rain which lashed in under the overhang of the porch. Thunder roared all around now as the storm hit full force. Jagged bursts of lightning etched bright against the inky clouds. The door opened and they tumbled inside. Nina slammed it behind them with a whoosh of relief.

****

She emerged from her bedroom in dry clothes and joined a similarly reclad Martin on the couch where he was sipping a cold beer. He'd poured her a glass of wine rather than offering her a stubbie the way Gordon would have. He handed it to her.

"Tell me what you found." She drew her feet up under her and faced him. Piers had gone. Somewhere as they ran in the rain he'd slipped away like the water sliding down the gutters.

"There was a lot of stuff about the Golden Dawn. It started in the eighteen eighties in London and fizzled out in 1903 due to all sorts of things, not least of which was bickering amongst the members, or initiates they're called. It seems there were quite a few breakaway groups. Some dabbled in spiritualism, which the original founders frowned upon. Yeats, the poet, was a member." Martin paused. "There were quite a few artistic people drawn to their ideas. Well known, some of them. One of the things that one particular breakaway group was into was astral travelling and

135

astral projection."

"But not bringing people back to life," interjected Nina.

"Not that I read but who knows? There were so many influences from so many different sources—Rosicrucians, ancient Egyptian, witchcraft, spiritualism, the occult, ancient Celtic beliefs, Christianity, druids, eastern mysticism, you name it…"

"Piers didn't manage to do it, did he? Or he wouldn't still be trying." Nina took a sip of wine and gave Martin a triumphant look as if to say, "answer that".

"I don't think he is still trying. I think we're getting a sort of late signal, like radio waves that are still going on endlessly into outer space. You know? They say if you go far enough and fast enough into deep space you could pick up the first TV broadcast as it happened the first time. Maybe they were into astral projection and he got stuck or something."

"So? Where does that leave us? Why the compulsion to keep playing?" How could Martin disregard the last eight insane months of his life? "You came half way round the world because of this, this…cosmic fallout, Martin. Remember? Have you forgotten what you told me just two nights ago?"

Martin sighed and stared at his beer bottle. He bit his lip. "Maybe I just want to believe that's what it is. Now that I've met you…you said yourself the compulsion isn't as strong…maybe it's fading…I don't know. It just seemed to make such perfect logical sense when I read that today, it all seemed to fit."

"But it doesn't!" The anger shocked her, coming so abruptly and fiercely rising up like milk on the boil. "It doesn't make any kind of sense. Don't you want to play the three parts together? Don't you want to finish this? You can't just read that stuff and then say, 'Oh, well that explains that'. "

Martin stood up, face blank. "I don't want to argue with you, Nina." He walked across the room toward the hallway. "I'm going to do some yoga. I haven't done anything since I arrived."

Nina's anger faded as abruptly as it had risen. "I'm sorry. I'll get dinner ready. It won't take long."

"Give me forty minutes?" Distant and polite.

"Of course."

Nina pottered about in the kitchen putting together spaghetti with meatballs and making Greek salad. The storm still raged but with no windows on either of the side walls, the occupants of the terraces were shut off from the full effects of the elements. She usually found the evidence of storms in her front and back gardens in the form of leaves and small branches and flattened flower beds. Sometimes if the wind blew the wrong way, water would come in under her back door onto the laundry floor.

When the tomato sauce was bubbling, the meatballs were cooked and waiting, and the spaghetti had just entered the boiling water, Nina went to have a quick look out the backdoor. A small puddle had formed where she expected to find it but there didn't seem to be more water coming in. The worst of the cloudburst was over and rain fell in a steady curtain. She took the mop from its place by the washing machine and began cleaning up, widening her sweeps, backing toward the kitchen as she went.

"Nina. Nina…something just happened." Hoarse

and unnatural.

"My God, Martin, you scared the hell out of me!" She dropped the mop and whipped around at the sound of his voice. But his face stunned her, drained the anger away in an instant, so pale and shocked. "What's wrong?" An icy cold tremor ran down her spine.

"Tell me." She led him to the living room and sat him down while she ran to get a glass of water. Her hand trembled as she handed him the glass. He drank deeply and carefully placed the tumbler on the coffee table. His hand shook and that sent a frisson of fear through her.

"Piers spoke to me."

Nina blinked. Was that all? "He speaks to me all the time."

"He told me I have to get the other parts," went on Martin as if she hadn't spoken. "Nina, I was meditating and he appeared quite clearly and spoke to me. He's never done that before. He's…extraordinary. So powerful…" His voice trailed off.

And sexy and handsome and passionate. "I know."

Martin suddenly grasped her hands so tightly her fingers were crushed. "But Nina. When I opened my eyes he was still there…standing in the room."

"What?!"

"He was standing there as clearly as you are sitting here with me."

Freefalling in the deep space of lunacy, Nina clutched at reality as it receded into the distance. "That's impossible. He's dead. We don't even know if he ever even existed. It's impossible."

"He was there. Only for a few seconds but he was there." Adamant. Certain.

Chapter Seven

Nina stared at him as her world disintegrated. In all of this, Martin was her rock. She relied on his rational mind and his ability to guide her through this craziness without losing his way.

"But you were saying you thought it was getting weaker, the radio signal thing." Desperate for reassurance.

"I haven't done any meditation since I've been here." That sounded more like the man she knew, already at work trying to figure out what had happened and why. "And I hadn't ever heard the violin part before. That was in my head quite strongly when he appeared. Do you meditate?" he asked her suddenly.

He relaxed his grip on her hands but didn't let them go, just held her fingers, lightly now, comforting. Her heart rate slowed, mind began functioning.

"I used to when I started Tai Chi but I got too scared to do it because Piers spoke to me…" She broke off and met Martin's gaze. "What if we both did at the same time?"

"I don't know whether I'm up for that again tonight," he said with a cautious smile. "Or any time soon."

"What was it, do you think? Did he look…I don't know…real?"

"He was real."

"No. Solid. Substantial or was he like an image, you know, in a movie?"

"He looked…" Martin frowned. "Filmy, I suppose. Not completely solid but it wasn't an after image, if that's what you're thinking. He was definitely there in the room."

"I believe you." Nina squeezed his fingers. "It's just so…" She cast about wildly for a big enough word to encompass the whole experience. There wasn't one. "You conjured him up."

"He's a very handsome man. Great charisma. Even in that brief flash, I could see that."

A little worm of jealousy squirmed in her belly that Piers had appeared to Martin instead of her. "I'd really like to see him," she murmured. *Not just in my dreams.*

"What I would really like is dinner. I'm starving and it smells really good." He gave her a disarmingly boyish grin. The worm stopped squirming. Nina leant forward and gave him a light kiss on the newly shaved cheek.

"Coming right up." She jumped to her feet.

As they ate, Nina said, "Did Piers tell you where to get the other parts?"

Martin shook his head, mouth full of salad. He swallowed and began twirling the last of his spaghetti onto his fork.

"George sent the other parts to New Orleans, remember?"

"You're not going there, are you?"

"Why not? It's no crazier than coming to Sydney. I've got an around the world ticket valid for a year. New Orleans rather appeals to me. The music will be great if nothing else."

She stared at him, appetite gone.

"When would you go?"

Martin eyed her speculatively before he answered. "Not until we've played with the cello part. I'm on a tourist visa so I'll have to leave Australia in a few months anyway."

"Oh, of course." She toyed with the food on her plate then got up to clear the table.

"We don't know what's going to happen on Sunday." Martin stood as well, picking up the empty salad bowl and taking it to the kitchen. He turned on the taps and began to fill the sink.

"I thought you said you thought it was losing its power, whatever 'it' is."

He scrubbed their plates and stacked them on the draining rack. "And I thought you got mad at me because I said I knew what was happening. I was wrong. Whatever is happening isn't getting weaker, it's waiting for us to get stronger. Piers is trying to get us ready for something. Here, dry these dishes."

"Us?" Nina picked up the tea towel and stood twisting it between her fingers.

"We seem to have been selected."

"But what for?" Her voice rose. It was all so damned frustrating.

"I don't know but I think we have to keep on until we find out. We can't walk away from it, can we?" He placed the last saucepan on the rack.

"Even if we want to." Softly, voice barely working. "I'm scared, Martin."

"So am I after tonight. I'd got used to the other things but…seeing him. Wow. I don't want to try that again. He gazed into the sink full of dirty water.

"There's one good thing, though."

"Is there?" She couldn't see it.

"We're in this together, aren't we?" He let the water out of the sink and dried his hands, turned to her.

"But what happens to me when you leave?" Tears trembled on her eyelashes. She wiped them away quickly with the tea towel.

"When *we* leave. When *we* leave. I'm not going anywhere without you." Martin put his hand on her cheek, eyes locked on hers for a long moment. Then he bent his head and kissed her. He tasted of spaghetti sauce and salad dressing. Nina closed her eyes and let him deepen the kiss. His hand slid around the back of her neck and she wrapped her arms around his narrow body as he held her and part of her enjoyed the sensation while another part suddenly and powerfully wished she were being kissed by Piers.

Martin disengaged himself gently and sighed. "I'm sorry," he murmured. "You have a boyfriend. You still...I shouldn't kiss you." His arms slid from her body.

Her eyes opened slowly. Had he sensed what she was thinking? Impossible. Piers hadn't intervened either which meant—what? He approved? He must because the last time she'd been kissed...Hazel eyes regarded her, waiting for a response. She didn't want to hurt him, the last thing she wanted was some sort of barrier between them.

"I don't have a boyfriend and I didn't mind."

"No, but it's not quite the same thing as...well...you don't..." He trailed off in confusion.

"I hadn't thought of you in that way before, Martin, that's all." The wrong thing to say. As soon as she said it she knew, but she couldn't mention Piers, even to Martin, especially to Martin. Not now if that's how he felt.

He turned away into the living room and flopped onto the couch. "Exactly! That's why, Nina. Just leave it. I'm sorry. I won't kiss you again."

"What, never?" She strode across and sat next to him. "Isn't that a bit extreme?"

He glanced at her and she tried to hide the grin but couldn't. He smiled and then his expression changed as he reached for her hand and played with her fingers as he spoke.

"I always rush into relationships and then end up stuffing them up somehow. I don't want that to happen with you." His tone changed, more businesslike. "Anyway, forget it, we've other things to sort out."

"New Orleans?" Nina sat up straighter. "Are you seriously going to go?"

He nodded. "Why not? But you'd have to come too. I don't think I could handle it on my own any more. Could you?"

She met his gaze. "No. I'd love to go with you but I don't know whether I can. I don't have a passport, for a start. How much would it cost? Plus there's my job. How long would we be away?"

"None of those things are insurmountable obstacles except maybe money."

"I've saved quite a bit. I've always wanted to travel." It was possible, depending exactly how much it would cost. There was no reason why she couldn't go with him. She could take leave from the shop. She could get a passport.

"I think we're both crazy."

143

"Does that mean you'll come?"

She threw her arms wide. "Why not? I've known you all of two days, some people I've known for years and I wouldn't share a taxi with them, but why not go round the world with you—a virtual stranger." Nina shook her head in amazement.

"Do I seem like a stranger to you?" Disappointment flooded his voice.

"No, you don't." She gazed into his face. Hazel eyes stared back at her with complete openness and she had the same instinctive trust in him that she'd had when they sat on the bench that first strange, hot night, gazing out over the brightly shining lights of Sydney Harbour. She gripped his fingers tightly. "You don't," she repeated hoarsely because her throat had gone dry all of a sudden.

"I won't let you down, I promise," he whispered.

"I know you won't," she whispered back. But she couldn't tell him how Piers spoke to her in her dreams and how she wanted him to love her the way he loved the woman Mira. She couldn't tell him of the uneasy feeling she had sometimes that Piers was manipulating him through his affection for her and that in some undefinable way, in the future, she might let Martin down.

****

Piers stood by her bed. Was she dreaming? She must be. But when she opened and closed her eyes several times and sat up, he was still there, looking down at her with an expression of such love, she held out her arms to him. He disappeared. She lay back shocked and suddenly frightened. Had that been real? It couldn't have been him.

****

Cutting Marsh, Summer Ball, 1892

Love at first staggering sight. Such a thunderclap went off in her head, such a shock of recognition as his smouldering dark eyes met hers she faltered in the dance and looked around blankly to see if anyone else had heard the noise. But the other guests whirled on unaffected.

He was playing the violin. She was dancing with a tall gangly friend of Tyler's who had trouble with the steps of the waltz. She hadn't noticed the musicians before, hadn't been close enough to see them through the crowds. But this man was extraordinary, tall, browned by the sun, dashing, mysterious. Out of place on the small stage with the other musicians, larger than life.

His gaze bored into her as she stumbled through the dance steps and the temptation to keep staring at him became irresistible. Did she know him? No. Impossible to forget that face.

"Who is that violin player?" she asked.

"De Crespigny. He is supposed to be a brilliant musician, making a name for himself in London. Squire Broome thought it quite a coup to engage him for the dance, Ethan said. Can't say as I understand why. He seems barely adequate to me."

When the orchestra took a break she made some excuse to her partner who seemed inclined to linger, and slipped between chattering guests and out through the side doors, conscious of those dark eyes following her every move. Moments after, he came upon her waiting, excited and breathless with anticipation in the rose garden.

Light from the brightly glowing windows of the Hall fell across his face as he approached, shoes crunching softly on the gravel path. The scent of the roses hung heavy in the hot night air. Miranda gazed, enthralled by the strong, clean-shaven features, unusual in these days of flourishing mustachios, his full, sensuous lips and thick dark hair. Elegant in evening dress he had an air of caged strength and danger, like a leopard or a black panther. She had seen pictures of these animals and they made her shiver with the same sense of excitement and fascinated apprehension.

"What is your name, most beautiful one?" He took her hand in his and her fingers folded naturally into their embrace. The brush of his lips on her palm pulsed through her body so she could barely draw breath.

"Miranda Templeton. You are Mr. de Crespigny?"

"Yes, Piers de Crespigny, late of Jamaica. Musician extraordinaire at your service." He let go her hands and executed a courtly bow which made her laugh and released some of the tension held so tightly in her chest. "You are very forward for a young lady, Miss Templeton. Inviting me with your glance to a tryst in the garden at night." The dark eyes regarded her accompanied by a stern frown.

Miranda lifted her chin and said primly, "Sir, I could not know I would come across you in the garden."

"Even worse. Shame on you. Is young Mr. Broome your intended?"

She couldn't tell this man the truth. "We have an understanding. He is very nice and I love him," she retorted even as her insides melted away under the heat of his slow gathering smile. He leaned closer, lowered his voice to a purring, intoxicating whisper, and his body arched over her in the darkness.

"Apple pie is nice. Dogs are nice. Do you want a nice husband or a man who will transport you with desire, who will overwhelm your senses, who will love you as you have never been loved nor will ever be loved again? Will love you through time itself."

Miranda swallowed, shocked from her exciting little fantasy play by the sudden intensity of his tone, the change from light-hearted flirting. The reality of her situation crashed in. Alone in the dark with a stranger, an employee, a man she had encouraged and who radiated such strength and determination she would be powerless against him if he chose to take advantage. If he chose to press his lips elsewhere than her hand, if he recognised the hot turmoil in her body and knew the cause.

She raised her chin, glad the darkness hid her trembling, and forced a coolness to her voice completely at odds with the storm of conflicting desire and apprehension. "Are you saying you would be that man?"

Piers pulled her closer until she felt the hard warmth of his body through the silk of her dress. He bent his head and murmured, "Yes," just before his lips closed over hers.

The heavy perfume of roses overwhelmed her. All sound ceased. Time passed her by. She had always been in his arms, would always be in his arms. She knew him. She'd never seen him before. Had she?

"Who are you?" she whispered, hypnotised, shaken to her core, when he freed her mouth from his.

"I am your destiny. You are mine. I have searched

for you and now we are found," he said. "We will be together again. You must come away with me."

The roar of voices and laughter from the hall became suddenly loud again. Miranda pulled away abruptly. "I can't do that!"

This was madness. She glanced around with quick frantic movements, but their position was obscured by leafy lilacs and a climbing yellow rose on a trellis over the path. The murmuring voices and light footsteps sounded of other couples strolling in the night air but no one came their way. His fingers grasped her shoulders with firm, possessive strength. She didn't want to break free. Couldn't.

"Meet me tomorrow," he said.

"Why don't you come to call?" Would she lose him if she proved difficult? Something told her no. Something in the way he spoke, the way he looked at her, as if he'd found what he'd been seeking.

"No. It wouldn't be prudent. You are almost an engaged woman, remember?" He chuckled softly and kissed her again. Sealing his ownership. He knew she wouldn't argue. Miranda shivered under the touch of his lips. Ethan's kiss was that of a bumbling boy compared to this man's.

The crunch of footsteps sounded on the gravel. Ethan's voice called softly, "Miranda? Are you there? Miranda."

Piers touched her cheek gently and disappeared silently into the blackness. Miranda held shaking hands to her scorching face. The ground seemed to heave beneath her feet. She opened her eyes wide in alarm and flung out an arm. Ethan caught her as she stumbled, head whirling. Cloying rose perfume clung in her nostrils.

"Miranda, what's the matter? Are you faint? Perhaps you're still weak from your illness."

She clutched his solid arm gratefully as the world regained its equilibrium.

"It's so hot, Ethan. I came out for some air…maybe I am still recovering…"

The orchestra began, Piers' violin climbing over the other instruments with its strong, vibrant tone speaking directly to her, the violin his voice, reminding her…

Ethan's arm encircled her shoulders, heavy with sympathy. "Your father should examine you. The fever you had was very dangerous. We were terrified we would lose you."

Miranda forced a smile. His was the wrong arm, his was the wrong scent, he was the wrong man. There was no other man and never would be. "No, no. I'm perfectly well now. I'm ready to dance again. You should rejoin Miss McCusker."

She drew away, moving toward the house and the light. Strangely, the thought of Ethan with Miss McCusker didn't bother her at all anymore.

Ethan caught up and tucked her arm in his. "Miranda, I saw you leave the ballroom and came to find you because I thought you'd be upset and I wanted to say how sorry I am and how…" He paused, preventing her from walking on.

She tore her attention away from Piers' violin. Thank goodness he hadn't come upon her a few moments earlier. What was he trying to say beyond an apology? "Ethan, I know your position. Harriet was kind enough to inform me."

"Harriet? What did she tell you?"

"That someone in your situation in society couldn't possibly marry someone in mine."

"Harriet is spiteful."

He didn't deny the truth of her remark. Miranda refrained from comment. It was all irrelevant now. She truly didn't care.

Another couple rounded the corner in the path giving her an excuse to resume walking. Ethan went with her but she barely noticed because her heart flew, soul soared to combine with the music. With Piers.

She had no further opportunity to speak to him and when her father found her and announced he was tired and ready to leave she had no choice but to obey even though the Ball was far from over.

****

As far as anyone knew Piers left Cutting Marsh with the other musicians and had not returned. With a sagging heart Miranda thought the same so her astonishment was acute when a note addressed in elegant sloping script arrived for her the next day. She'd spent the intervening hours wondering if the whole encounter had been a dream or a hallucination brought about by the extreme temperatures and the aftermath of her illness.

Piers wrote for her to meet him in the grove of oaks off the Plymouth road. She was to make sure she was unobserved. He would wait each afternoon for the next three days from two in the afternoon onward.

What girl could resist? A smile crept to her lips.

****

Sydney, 1998

Nina went to Tai Chi the next morning while

150

Martin stayed home and cleaned up the leaves and branches strewn about the garden. He did some washing for them both and when Nina returned she found lunch prepared and the outdoor table set for three while a Mozart piano concerto played softly on the stereo. Over breakfast Martin had suggested they should give themselves a break from the music and Piers and the whole unwieldy, mind shattering problem until Jason had played the cello part for them.

"Let's be normal for a day. Show me the sights of Sydney."

Nina had nodded in relieved agreement. Strangely, Piers had left her alone the previous night and she'd slept deeply and soundly, undisturbed by visions or dreams. Maybe he was satisfied with them because they'd decided to continue the search for the missing parts and had taken steps to play the cello part.

"Who's coming to lunch?" Three place settings? Who did Martin know in Sydney apart from her? "You haven't conjured up Piers, have you?" she said with a snort of laughter.

Martin burst out laughing. "No, I only know you here. Florence. Is that all right?" He added a grimace of belated concern.

"Of course. How did you meet her?"

"I was out the front sweeping and she came out. What a character! She started giving me the third degree but she was putty in my hands when she found out I play the flute."

"You seem to have a way with the older ladies, don't you?" Nina grinned. "Celia, Jessica, and now Florence."

"Florence would give those other two a heart

attack. They're both very proper English gentlewomen."

"Like you."

"I'm not a proper English gentlewoman! Not old either."

"No, you're a proper English gentleman." Nina stretched up on tip toes and kissed him on the cheek. "It makes a lovely change. Like to go to the beach later? After Florence goes?"

"Love to. Can we go to Bondi?"

Nina sighed. "All right, Mr. Tourist. Or we could get the ferry across to Manly. That's a good beach. You can watch beach volleyball there, too."

"No, I must see the famous Bondi Beach."

Florence burst in with typical panache wearing a large floaty leopard print shirt and white slacks and regaled them with stories of her life in London. She'd sung at all the top nightclubs and plenty of the others. Martin was able to field most of her questions regarding musicians and venues still operating.

"I lived in Chelsea in a house like the one in *Mary Poppins* or was it Henry Higgins' house in *My Fair Lady*? Anyway I had a house and a maid. I had to have a maid—there was absolutely no way I could fend for myself in those days. My life was completely crazy, upside down, a whirlwind. If she hadn't fed me properly I would have lived on champagne and chocolates, smoked salmon and caviar. That's what my admirers expected me to eat all the time. That's what they brought and what they ordered when we went out after the show. None of them realised they all did the same thing. None of them realised there were others."

She laughed uproariously and winked at Martin.

"You men are very easy to fool when you're in love. Too gullible." She looked shrewdly from Martin to Nina but to Nina's relief said nothing more.

Martin poured her more wine then took their empty plates inside, shaking his head at Nina as she attempted to help.

"Where did you find that gorgeous, gorgeous man, my darling?" asked Florence in a stage whisper, grasping Nina by the arm. "When you've finished with him, toss him over the fence. I don't mind leftovers."

"Florence, you're a shocker! I met him at the shop."

"And he swept you off your feet as you sold him a CD. How wonderfully romantic."

"Something like that." He'd certainly stunned her. "He needed a place to stay and he seemed nice." That sounded awful put into bald, plain words, as if she'd picked him up off the street and brought him home on a sudden mutual sexual attraction. Women were raped and murdered by men that way. No one could ever understand what was really happening, why she trusted him so much. "Florence, do you really like him? I mean not just…you know, you're not just saying that?"

"Darling." Florence became serious briefly. "I've met a lot of people and I mean a lot, and I've known a lot of men and I mean a lot, and I'm a pretty shrewd judge of character. He's all right, this one. He adores you, I can tell you that straight off but I don't know whether that's what you want to hear, is it?"

"Not really. I sort of knew that. I don't know how I feel yet. He's attractive…"

"He certainly is. I've always had a soft spot for that very "proper" English sort of accent and that reserve usually goes with hidden depths of passion, if you can unearth it through the good manners." She chuckled lasciviously, then patted Nina's arm fondly. "And he can be trusted. He'll do his best for you. I'll lay my reputation as an expert on that."

"An expert on what?" Martin reappeared with a bowl of grapes, cherries, and sliced mango and pineapple.

"What do you think? Men, of course." Florence cackled as Martin looked uncertainly from one to the other.

"You could at least discuss me so that I can listen in," he said in disgust.

"Where's the fun in that?" asked Nina. "Anyway what makes you think we were discussing you?"

"They all think that, darling." Florence neatly speared a juicy slice of mango with her fork.

"Weren't you?" Martin looked at Nina, eyebrow lifted. Florence was right about the accent. What about the hidden passion? Come to think of it he did kiss well—perhaps she should give him another go?

"Yes," she admitted. Could he read her mind? Hot cheeks would be a giveaway. He seemed to be on her wave length on lots of things.

"Good report I hope, Florence."

"Listen to him, would you?" Florence filled her mouth with fresh, juicy fruit and wiped her chin with a paper napkin. "I was just telling Nina when she gets tired of you to wash you off and send you over to me."

Martin gave an audible gasp of surprise and Nina and Florence nearly fell off their chairs laughing.

"My heavens, Florence." Martin laughed incredulously. "You must have been something else in your day."

"My day isn't over yet, young Martin. Come up and see me sometime," she said in a passable imitation of Mae West, complete with sexy wink from heavily made up eye lashes.

"I think I'll organise coffee." He leapt to his feet and retreated to the accompaniment of their laughter.

****

Later, as they strolled barefoot in shorts along Bondi Beach just at the water's edge, dodging swimmers and children playing in the shallows, carrying their sandals and letting the incoming waves wash around their ankles, Nina said, "Were you serious about going to America? Wanting me to come?" She'd thought about it a lot the night before, in bed and the more she thought the more exciting and possible it became.

"I thought we weren't going to talk about any of that today?" said Martin casually. "This is the most relaxed I've been since I found that blasted music. Eight months, it's been."

"Me too," said Nina in surprise. It was true. She'd been wound up like a watch spring, gradually getting tighter and tighter as the weeks passed. "More like three months though. I don't know how you survived."

"No wonder this beach is so famous." Martin stopped and gazed around at the perfectly curved golden stretch of sand with low rocky headlands at either end and houses and shops separated from the beach by grass, walkway and road and the magnificent old Pavilion. Swimmers and surfers skimmed and splashed in the sparkling blue waves while the less energetic lazed under coloured umbrellas.

"There are beaches like this all up and down the coast. Don't know why this one is famous," said Nina. "I prefer some of the others for swimming. Not as many tourists and it can be pretty rough here at night. Do you know, Japanese tourists come here, get photographed and then jump back on the bus all in about five minutes? Some of them even get married here in the full white wedding gear. That takes a bit longer—ten minutes."

"I'm not a beach connoisseur like you." Martin laughed and kicked water at her. Nina responded in kind and they ended up running and laughing and splashing until she called truce and they sat on a bench in the late afternoon sun to dry their clothes, gazing out at the endlessly rolling breakers and watching the surf board riders barrelling in toward them and then paddling back out to try again.

"I could live here," said Martin. "It's a fantastic place."

"Yes, it is."

"I had no idea what I'd find when I got on that plane at Heathrow, when was it? Last Tuesday? Monday? Less than a week and here I am sitting in the sun at Bondi Beach—with wet clothes thanks to you."

"You started it."

Nina brushed sand from her legs. Gordon didn't like the beach and they'd never been swimming or surfing together. In fact they'd never spent such a pleasant, aimless day together with or without ending up in bed somewhere along the line. Gordon had disappeared completely from her life and she hadn't missed him at all. It had been a totally physical relationship, she'd known that at the time but it was still mildly surprising that he'd faded so completely and quickly from her thoughts.

"Like to go out to dinner tonight?" asked Martin. "Get dressed up and go dancing or something?" He spoke casually but Nina heard an underlying tension and it had nothing to do with the music or their quest for Piers.

"Do you like dancing?" she asked mildly, teasing gently.

"Not particularly but I thought you might. I'd like to take you out. Somewhere special. You've been so good to me, letting me stay and everything. Would you like that?" Very proper, formal Martin made an appearance and all memories of Gordon were plunged into the archives.

"I'd love that. And Martin I wanted you to stay as much for me as for you. I think I would've gone really crazy if you hadn't shown up."

"Remember what we said," Martin said softly, gripping her hand. "It's our day off."

Nina smiled. "Sorry. There are some really good restaurants in the city right near the bridge overlooking the harbour or there's that one by the wharf at McMahon's Point."

"You choose."

"Let's go into the city then. Circular Quay is lovely at night."

And so they did. Nina dressed with great care in a slim fitting, short, white dress which set off the golden tan of her skin and was rewarded by a stunned look and then a low whistle of admiration from Martin. He was wearing black slacks and a silvery grey shirt and tie and looked very distinguished. Just as she'd thought, the hot, hairy, dishevelled, desperate and exhausted man wasn't the true Martin. He was the sensitive, confident, strong and reliable one who emerged from the jet lag and bizarre unreality of the last months.

But Florence's comment about the passion underlying the perfect manners teased at her relentlessly through dinner, while they danced and afterward as they strolled hand in hand along the seawall at Circular Quay. Maybe it was the wine, maybe it was the relief of sharing the secret, maybe it was the enjoyment of a glamorous night out unlike anything she'd experienced recently or even not so recently. Maybe it was Martin himself. Nina wanted to do some exploring. She wanted him to kiss her again, just to see if it was as good as she thought.

They caught a taxi home.

Nina closed the door behind them and followed Martin to the living room. He stopped and turned as she reached him and without a word she walked into his arms. He looked down at her upturned face, his hands resting lightly on her waist and for a terrible moment Nina thought he was going to push her away.

Instead he said softly, "Nina, I didn't take you out tonight to make you feel you owed me something—to seduce you."

"I know." Her tongue slid slowly over her lower lip, her arms around his neck.

"I don't want you to do anything you'll regret." His lips came closer.

"I know."

Nina closed her eyes as he touched her mouth gently with his and it was as good as she'd thought. Better. Much more sensitive and loving than Gordon, not so much force and lust, although there was definitely lust creeping in now. On both their parts. Both his arms were around her and his firm torso, slim and wiry, was warm against her body. Roving hands sent tingles of delight up and down her whole body. Tongues intertwined, fingers gently massaged her breasts teasing her nipples erect.

"Martin," she managed to breath in between kisses and pants of delight.

"Mmm," he murmured into her neck where he nibbled and kissed.

"I thought you weren't going to…ever…kiss me…again."

"I'll stop then, shall I?" He did momentarily and Nina grabbed his head between her hands.

"No!"

He continued where he'd left off, murmuring in broken phrases, "You're so gorgeous, Nina. Perfect. I wanted to do this when I first set eyes on you."

Nina couldn't reply for some time and by then it was too late as they'd been edging toward her room and Martin expertly unzipped her dress. It slipped to the floor at their feet in a silky shimmer and she stepped out of it and concentrated on undoing his belt and buttons and sliding his pants and shirt off. She lay back on the bed and opened her arms to him. Florence was convincingly proven right.

Later, Martin pulled the covers over them both and lay with his arms around her, holding her close. His heart beat steadily under her ear and she sighed with deep satisfaction. He kissed the top of her head.

"What?" he asked softly. "Regrets?"

"No, stupid." Nina stretched up and kissed his lips.

"Serena the psychic told me there would be pleasure and satisfaction in my future."

"Really?" Martin shifted so that he could look her in the face. "What else?"

Nina chuckled. "She said that there would be a tall, dark and handsome man from overseas and that love was involved."

"She got that right," he said in a self-satisfied voice and stroked her cheek gently.

"Perhaps I should see her again. She said I should after you appeared."

"Do you want to?"

"I don't know."

Nina shifted so that her head was on the pillow and he turned and settled more comfortably. She closed her eyes, her breathing slowed.

The scent of roses wafted on warm, summer air. She was in a garden. A beautiful garden, at night. There were voices in the distance through the trees. A party, sounds of laughter coming from a brightly lit house. They mustn't see her here. She was waiting...

She was kissing Piers. His arms were around her and his tongue was hard and forceful in her mouth. She could feel his body against hers. His chest was broad and his stomach and thigh muscles firm and exciting under her roving hands. He drew back and his dark, penetrating eyes burned into hers. She wrapped her arms tightly around him and breathed his name. "Piers. Piers kiss me again. I love you."

He bent his head to hers and once more devoured her mouth with passionate kisses.

He stopped and whispered hoarsely, "You're mine. Mine alone. Always."

"Yours. Yes, Piers."

Then they were in a glade of trees. Hot, bright light filtered through the thick canopy of leaves. She lay back on the grass and watched Piers above her, his face suffused by passion and love. For her. He moved inside her hard and strong and urgent and she went with him, her whole body crying out to be closer, to enclose him and draw him into the depths of her, hold him and make him part of her. He bent his head and kissed her mouth, driving his tongue deep and hard even as he drove deeper into her body, striving for that ultimate release, that ultimate expression of his love. Then she was lifted on her own wave of desire and she called out his name.

The light faded and it was night again. The scent of roses was heavy in the air. Piers approached silently, his body a darker bulk against the moonlit leaves of the shrubs and bushes of the garden. His arms enclosed her and she rested her head against his chest. "Piers," she said. "Piers. I love you."

He began pummelling her shoulder. Nina struggled to free herself as the pummelling became uncomfortable and her eyes flew open, closing again quickly against the harshness of the light and the confusion in her mind. She breathed deeply as she struggled to the surface of sleep and opened her eyes again to the familiarity of her bedroom.

The bedside light cast a soft yellow glow over Martin's worried face. His hand lay heavy on her shoulder.

"Nina? Nina, wake up."

Nina blinked and strained to adapt herself to this other reality. Piers had gone. Martin was in his place. Martin with an anxious face. Martin with whom she had just made love. Or had it been Piers?

"Martin?" She stared about the room. Her room. Her bedroom.

"Nina what were you dreaming? Can you remember?"

"Piers. I was dreaming about Piers. It was so real." She touched his cheek gently. He was real. His beard stubble prickled her fingers. Piers' face was smooth…

"You cried out his name. What did he say? What did he want?"

"I can't remember. It was Piers—so real." The taste of him, the feel of him. "I could smell roses. It was hot, really hot. We were—somewhere—in a garden. There were trees."

Martin drew her to him and she snuggled into the comfort of his embrace. He stretched out an arm and turned off the light then began kissing and caressing her gently. Nina responded with increasing ardour and as her passion increased so did the memory of Piers' body under her hands and the feel of his mouth on hers. It was all she could do not to cry out his name as she reached her climax.

****

Martin knocked on the Lee family front door at one-thirty the next day. Nina had brought a portable cassette recorder to record the playing and Martin had the cello part in the envelope. They'd decided after a short discussion over breakfast not to bring their own instruments so as not to be tempted to play along when Jason recorded his part.

"I hope he's remembered we're coming," said Nina irritably as they waited on the front step. "He's probably still in bed."

She thumped the brass dolphin-shaped knocker again with more force than Martin and this time they heard footsteps and an outline appeared through the frosted glass panel on the door.

"Hello," he said cheerily and stuck out his hand to Martin as Nina introduced them and then strode on into the house leaving them to greet each other on the doorstep. "Jason Lee."

"Martin Leigh," said Martin and laughed at Jason's surprise. "Spelled differently."

"Come in." He stepped aside. Martin walked into the cool hallway after Nina.

Jason padded behind them on bare feet. He wore old, torn jeans and a baggy white T-shirt displaying a jazz saxophonist in silhouette which couldn't disguise a well toned muscular physique. Very like Nina with a masculine version of her good looks he had dark brown rather than black hair and was taller by several inches.

"I found my cello," he said to Nina's back as she peered into a room on the left. Martin caught a glimpse of a lounge suite and a glass-fronted china cabinet.

"Was it covered in dust? Have you vacuumed recently?" She looked around critically as they walked through to the large sunny, family room at the rear of the house. Books and newspapers were scattered about along with a few items of clothing and the odd shoe but apart from that the house looked in reasonable shape to Martin.

"Last week," he answered and shot Martin a grin before asking, "Have you?"

"Where's Ringo?" Nina ignored him and opened the sliding glass door to the back garden. "Is he still alive or have you starved him to death?"

"Out there somewhere. Give me a break Nina, I've just finished my exams." Jason turned, grimacing, to Martin. The good-natured bickering reminded him of himself and his older sister, Jenny, although Nina had been uncharacteristically terse and crabby this morning, ever since they'd started on the journey across town. Regrets about their night together? He hoped not. He had none.

"How were they?" asked Martin.

"Cautiously optimistic." Jason grimaced again and then asked, "Where are you from? England?"

"Yes, London."

"Staying long?"

"I'm not sure. A few more weeks, I suppose. Then I'm going to New Orleans." Nina sat down on the lawn and patted a black cat which had strolled nonchalantly from the bushes.

Jason went into the kitchen which was separated from the family room by a counter and four bar stools. "Great! I'd love to go there. They say music just falls out of every building. Want a beer?" He opened the fridge and looked questioningly at Martin.

"Thanks. I'm not used to being this warm in November. Cheers." He raised the bottle to Jason who smiled back and took a long drink from his.

"So what's this music you want me to play?"

Martin put the envelope on the counter and opened it. They looked at the handwritten sheets.

Jason said, "Weird."

"What makes you say that?" Martin's heart skipped a beat.

"I don't know," Jason said uncertainly. "Handwritten I guess. Or…I don't know. It doesn't look very hard. Where did you get it?"

"In a secondhand music shop in London."

Nina came back in, went to the fridge and poured herself a glass of orange juice.

"What do you think?" she asked Jason. "Can you play it?"

"Of course I can. Let me finish my beer first."

"I thought you had to be somewhere soon. Hadn't we better get on with it?"

Jason looked at Nina curiously. "Why? What's up with you?"

"Nothing I just thought…" She glanced at Martin for assistance.

He shrugged. "I'm not in a hurry."

Why was Nina so edgy today? He was fairly sure she wasn't regretting last night. Particularly after that strange dream and the way she'd clung to him afterward, needing comfort and reassurance. She'd been a willing participant this morning too, when they woke up and then again when they'd showered together. It had taken ages to get themselves organised and dressed.

Now she was fidgety and snappy with Jason, although that could be their normal pattern, like him and Jenny. Nervous maybe, worried about exposing Jason to the music? He'd reassured her as well as he could on the way, on the bus and then the train, whispering so as not to freak out the other passengers and he thought she agreed they'd taken as many precautions as possible. He'd outlined the points to her counting them off on his fingers.

They weren't going to play the other parts at the same time, they weren't even taking them along so as not to be tempted.

They would only get him to play it through once or twice at the most.

They wouldn't let him touch the music but they'd try not to let him realise that that's what they were doing.

They wouldn't under any circumstances tell him anything about the music other than the bare essentials and only if he asked.

As far as Nina knew he didn't meditate and that seemed to be a common link. Martin thought he'd be safe.

Jason and Nina had been discussing their parents while Martin cogitated and surmised, now they both slid off their stools, startling Martin out of his reverie. Nina clutched his hand surreptitiously as Jason disappeared to get his cello and Martin gave her a quick kiss.

"It'll be all right."

"I'd never forgive myself if anything happened to him," she whispered fiercely.

"It won't."

"Easy for you to say. He's not your brother," she snapped.

Her words cut him deeper than he was prepared to let her see. She gazed at him in dismay and opened her mouth to say something but Jason came back in. Martin managed a brief smile and she touched his arm lightly.

Jason handed Nina his music stand and she set it up while he unpacked his cello and Martin fiddled with the cassette recorder. It had an inbuilt microphone but the sound would be reasonable if they got it close enough as he played. Martin experimented as Jason warmed up and eventually decided on a satisfactory position.

"Can I have a look at the part, Nina?"

She placed the music carefully on the stand and he looked at it for a few minutes.

"How fast does that first bit go?"

Martin clicked his fingers at the correct tempo. "About that. And the second section goes faster. About here." He clicked his fingers again.

"That last part is quite free, actually," put in Nina. "We thought I could conduct you through that."

"Why didn't you bring your violin and play it?" asked Jason

"It's too hard for me. I can't play it but I know how it should go."

"So tell me again why you want me to do this?" Jason frowned at her.

"Jason it doesn't matter, does it? Just shut up and play it, for heaven's sake."

"Got any sisters, Martin?" asked Jason in a resigned voice. Nina glanced at him. She hadn't ever asked about his family. But then hers had only come up because Jason played cello.

"An older one called Jenny and you two sound just like us when we get together." Martin gave Jason a sympathetic grin.

"I've got two. Have you met Lucy yet?"

"No." Martin hadn't heard about her either. He was just as interested as Nina seemed to be in his family but he caught a warning look on Nina's face and said hurriedly, "I'm ready when you are."

"Don't I get to practise it?" asked Jason.

"You don't need to, you're too good," Nina said.

Jason rolled his eyes and nodded at Martin. "Okay. Go. Give me a bar in. I'll count the rests out, right?"

Nina nodded and counted him in. Despite Jason's being out of practice he hadn't lost the rich vibrant sound and musicianship which Nina had first mentioned. Martin agreed with her. He could have been very good if he'd stuck at it.

Jason worked his way through the bass line, concentrating hard on his bowing and fingering, phrasing the notes perfectly even though he'd never heard the melody which went on top. *Was that a faint voice with a lilting Irish accent accompanying him as he played?* When he reached the second section he stopped, lowered his bow and shook his head, blinking as though he'd just emerged from under water.

"That was weird," he murmured. Martin stopped recording.

"What was?" asked Nina in an unnaturally calm voice.

"I thought...I thought I heard a voice when I played. Did you?" He looked from one to the other in bewilderment.

"Someone went past outside. Down the lane," improvised Nina. Martin didn't even know there was a laneway next to the house but there must have been because Jason didn't comment.

"It didn't sound like that. I want to play it again." Still vaguely perturbed. He frowned at them with the beginnings of annoyance on his initially cheerful face. The signs were all there. The someone-in-the-lane explanation hadn't convinced him, and he thought they were hiding something about the music. He was no dope and he'd start asking questions soon.

"Do the second part for us first, so that we get it continuously right through," suggested Martin quickly.

"Nina? Are you ready to conduct him."

"Yep. Okay, Jase?" She smiled. He nodded, the fascination on his face unpleasantly familiar as he turned to the music.

Nina gave him clear downbeats and held her hand steady when he should pause. Piers' violin raced through the intricate runs and cadenza-like improvisations. Both violin and flute sounded strong and clear to Martin. Nina heard them too, because she followed the ebb and flow of the music as she indicated to Jason where he should speed up and slow down, linger or play steadily. Did he hear the other instruments? It was hard to believe he didn't, they were so loud.

Nina cut the last note off and exhaled a deep rush of air. His gaze locked with hers. It was done. Jason had played perfectly. One take was enough; they couldn't, wouldn't risk more.

Martin clicked Off with a shaky finger.

"Well done, Jason." Would Jason notice the tremor in his voice? He cleared his throat and pretended to check the tape player while he regrouped.

He'd had to struggle not to succumb to the voices clamouring to be heard over the music. It was like having the whole group in the room with them. Nina was still immersed, she stood blank-faced, hands hanging by her sides. Jason *must* have heard the voice again, perhaps more than one—how could he not? Although maybe not. He'd only heard the one part and the least melodic at that. He'd never heard the violin. He knew nothing about the Shadow Music.

"Thanks for doing that," he said.

"I want to play it again." Jason raised his bow and

stared intently at the first page.

"No, you don't need to, that was perfect." Martin whipped the music from the stand and slipped it safely back into the envelope.

"It might not have recorded." Jason's voice had gained an edge. An angry edge.

"Better check," said Nina quietly, alert now. She caught Martin's eye. "We don't want to have to come back and do it again."

Martin pressed play. Jason's cello poured into the room. He hit stop.

"See, it's fine."

"Sounds good." Jason smirked. The anger melted from his face replaced by the cheeky boyish grin.

"You should practise more," said Nina.

"That's what Mum says. I don't get much time, you know. I work pretty hard at Uni." He laid his cello carefully on the floor and stood up. "What is that piece anyway?"

"We don't know," said Nina. "Thanks for playing, Jason." She stepped across and gave him a hug and kiss which he received with an embarrassed laugh.

"Calm down. You owe me one, just remember that."

"If I can help any time, I will."

"Come over and help me clean the house before Mum and Dad get back."

Nina glanced at Martin. "I might not be around. I'm thinking about going to New Orleans with Martin."

"When?" The surprise turned to suspicion. "How long have you two known each other?"

Nina sidestepped the question. "We're not sure. It won't be for at least a few weeks. I haven't got a passport or anything yet. Maybe after Christmas."

"Great stuff! Fantastic. Can I come?"

Nina burst out laughing. She'd been sure he was about to start in on all the questions she'd be asking him if the situation were reversed.

"I'd love you to," she said. "But you've got no money and I can't see the parents funding you."

"I've got a job this summer, so I can't go anywhere, anyway."

"Where?"

"Local bottle shop."

"Oh, perfect."

"Yeah, it's okay. I do afternoon shifts and sometimes night."

"Well, we should go. Thanks. I'll let you know our plans when we've got them."

He saw them to the door and stood on the front step as they walked down the path between Dad's roses just coming into bloom. Nina turned and waved and he waved back then went inside.

She took Martin's hand as they hurried toward the train station but he gradually slowed his pace so that the rush became a leisurely stroll. Suburban Chatswood's streets were leafy and green with older redbrick Sydney houses nestled into gardens filled with trees and shrubs and colourful displays of flowering plants surrounding well tended lawns.

"Come on." She tugged at his hand to keep him moving.

"No rush, is there?" He stopped to smell a flowering vine trailing over the fence.

"Don't you want to get home and try it out?" What was he doing, dawdling along like this? The whole point was to have the three parts. Now they did.

"I'm not sure I do."

"You heard Michael, didn't you? All three of them? Even Jason heard him. That was freaky." She added, "How can you not want to try it? Now, when we've finally got the parts together."

Martin stopped in the shade of a large plane tree overhanging the footpath. He looked around vaguely, then studied the ground at his feet before meeting her intent gaze.

"Do you want to know the truth? I'm frightened. Ever since Piers appeared to me. It's scary. We don't know what we're dealing with."

"But we have to. We can't not, can we? We've decided it's not going to go away, ever, unless we do something about it. The compulsion is still there. Jason felt it, I feel it, and I'm going to play my part with the tape as soon as we get home." Nina set off walking again and Martin had no choice but to follow. She was right. They had to end it somehow.

Chapter Eight

Cutting Marsh, England, August 1892

Miranda pushed annoyingly wayward strands of hair into place and secured them with a determined shove of the pin. She studied her reflection for a critical moment then pressed a damp cloth against her cheeks and neck, hoping to reduce the flush. This heat was unusually excessive. Despite the drawn curtains her bedroom was hotter than she could ever remember.

But more than the temperature of the day warmed her skin—excitement, anticipation sent surges of hot blood coursing through her veins. Hopeless to try cooling such passion. Smiling, she exchanged the now warm cloth for her hairbrush and gently coaxed the curls on her neck to sit in obedient order.

Piers loved her hair. He loved to pull it free of the restraining pins and combs and see it tumble around her face. "A silken waterfall," he said once, his rich deep voice gentle in admiration.

He would run his hands gently around her neck, lifting the hair from her shoulders and letting it slip through his fingers, cascading in a curtain of black strands. She watched his eyes as he did this, those dark fiery eyes burning with such passion and intensity she was sometimes afraid of the fierceness of his love. But his lips would close on hers, erasing doubt, erasing fear, erasing everything except her insides melting like liquid fire, her breasts straining for his touch, breath coming in short, hot gasps, wanting him…

Shameless. She giggled to herself. Mrs. Bowden would be scandalised, so would Annie the kitchen maid despite her having a suitor of her own, so would everyone else in the village. And her father and brother. They'd have Piers before the magistrate if they knew of the liaison. Tyler may even shoot him.

Her mother would have understood, though. If she had lived through childbirth. Miranda sighed, the smile faded. Her mother would have forgiven all manner of things which made her father and Tyler furious, she was positive of it. Mama wouldn't have minded Miranda climbing trees when she was ten with a group of small boys from the village. Nor would she have minded her stripping off her shoes and stockings and splashing in the river when she was eleven. Or, for a dare, riding bareback and astride on the horses in the field behind the orchard. Her mother was different. She wasn't from the village. She was foreign and in Miranda's eyes that made her special and wonderfully exotic. Piers had taught her that.

She put the brush down, cocked her head from side to side to view the effect and then, satisfied, stood up and smoothed her summer dress over her hips and narrow waist. He hadn't seen this new outfit in the modern style, the two-piece hem line higher at the front and back and the overlaid skirt dropped at the sides. It flattered her figure. Three-quarter length sleeves were so much cooler and the pattern of tiny blue flowers sprinkled over the white cotton made the whole ensemble fresh and appealing. And her new straw hat with the trailing blue ribbons she had attached herself.

Meeting Piers was far more exciting than climbing trees.

Miranda opened her door a crack and peered down the passage toward her father's study. All quiet. He was almost certainly dozing in his favourite armchair, the heat of the day and the Sunday roast Mrs. Bowden had prepared for them combining happily with the fact he'd been called out last night to attend a child with fever.

No sign of Tyler either. Probably calling on dainty Laura Jenkins at the farm.

She slipped down the passage, passed the closed study door, passed the front room reserved for visitors and entertaining, stealthily opened the front door and breathed a sigh of relief as she closed it with a soft click. The heat hit like an open furnace, the street deserted. Too hot for most people, sensible people. The sun hammered on her head from a brassy blue sky, mocking the lightness of her new dress and the meagre shade afforded by the brim of her hat.

Dust sprang up with every footfall. The grass verges had withered to brown, trees hung their leaves, listless and still. They'd had no rain for weeks. Just this scorching heat. "The hottest weather for years," people kept saying as they chatted over garden fences and after church, or when they passed the time of day in the street. "It can't last," they said.

"Not a patch on the weather in India. Drove people stark raving mad," rumbled old Major Forbes who'd served bringing proper British civilisation and order to the distant land. Piers said it was nothing compared to the heat in Jamaica where he had spent the best part of his youth.

Piers! Miranda hurried her step at the thought of him waiting impatiently for her in their secret spot. Their love nest in the cool grove of trees a scarce half mile from her home. He insisted on their meeting away from prying eyes and it had been easy so far for her to sneak away unnoticed.

Two weeks. Fourteen days since she saw him at the Summer Ball at the Hall. How could such passion come so quickly?

She reached the cluster of ancient oaks and birches growing thick and secretive in a grove a few hundred yards across the fields from the road leading to Plymouth. A quick glance around ensured no eyes observed her save for a group of cows grazing heedlessly in the far corner by the hedgerow. She entered the cool greenness and threaded her way deeper into the copse to the small grassed clearing Piers had discovered. The hot sun was completely stifled by the canopy of thickly leafed branches, the outside world ceased to exist. He was there, leaning against a tree, his jacket thrown carelessly on the thick soft grass at his feet, his grey horse tethered a short distance away. She ran into his arms.

His lips were hot, his passion irresistible. Even as his mouth devoured hers he was pulling her down to lie on the grass, his fingers teasing her breasts so they ached to be free of the restraining cotton and laces of her garments. Her own hands roamed, feeling his hardness and drawing a groan of desire as she pressed her body into his. How did he make her feel so wild and abandoned so easily? She'd surrendered her virginity to him with nary a thought, would follow him to the city if he asked, follow him anywhere…he made her crazy with desire. And she did the same to him.

"You're a wanton," he murmured in her ear as he nibbled and kissed her neck.

"Only with you." She arched her back as he undid the buttons of her dress to reveal her breasts, the nipples hard with longing. He ran his thumb over the tender tips and she sucked in air as sensation rocketed to her groin in swelling moist heat.

"Piers," she gasped.

Later, sated, drowsy, her head resting on his chest, his arm holding her close Miranda said, "Tell me about yourself. I want to know about you."

"You know all about me." His finger traced a soft pattern on her cheek. "You know me most intimately, in the only way that matters. You have always known me just as I have always known you."

She slapped his arm softly. "No. Tell me about your parents, your family, your brothers and sisters. How you came to be here in England. Jamaica is such an exotic place."

"My family owns a coffee plantation. I have one brother—Ambrose. My parents both died of typhoid fever ten years ago and I inherited the business, but my brother is running it because he loves it. I only want to be a musician. To compose." He paused and she raised her head to look at him. He was staring up into the canopy of branches, lost in thoughts she couldn't begin to guess at. Such a deep thinking man, her Piers. What did he find attractive about her, a simple country girl?

"Go on," she prompted.

"That's all."

"No. You were going to say something else."

"You'll think I'm touched in the head."

Miranda had never heard him sound doubtful. She sat up and held his face between her hands.

"No. Nothing you could do would ever make me think that, Piers. I love you. You are my life."

Piers regarded for several long moments then said, "When I arrived in England last year, I had a few names to contact, friends of my parents, distant relatives and they invited me to dine with them several times. At one gathering I met a woman who was a member of a group called the Golden Dawn. What she told me was absolutely fascinating." He eased Miranda away from his body and sat up, lost in the memory. "That was my first initiation into the mysteries of the mind, the tentative reaching toward the very soul of a man. They were investigating the possibilities of contacting the spirit world, foreseeing the future and even travelling outside one's own body."

"You mean ghosts and such? Like the ghost at the Hall?"

"Is there one?"

"So they say. And then there's Maggie Blackstone who can mix potions for various things. They say she's a witch but a good one. A lot of people still visit her rather than my father for their medicine. Even my father calls upon her for assistance at some births."

Piers said, "In Jamaica the occult is an accepted part of life and I see here in the countryside it is too, but in London and in more highly educated society they are saying it is all nonsense." He added as an afterthought. "Have you heard of Dr Freud?"

Miranda shook her head. "Father may know of him. Tell me about your music."

Piers leaned forward eagerly. "I want to write

music that is connected to the essence of life. I think, from my association with the Golden Dawn that there is a common thread running through all beings and that this is somehow attuned to the cosmic spheres, our spirituality. I want to tap into this cosmic life force with music. I feel there is a key of life, if you like—a cosmic vibration which is tuned to our souls—and that perhaps if I can get it right it will be the path to eternal life. You and I could be together for eternity."

"And have you begun to write this music?" The concept was beyond her imagination but Piers was so intense, so serious she believed him.

"Yes, I have, but it is very difficult. I think we need to use some other medium to gain strength and power to achieve the goal. Maybe meditation. Maybe opiates. It's fascinating and I'm sure at some time it will be possible. The mind of man is extraordinarily powerful. I have read of amazing things from the East. From China and India."

Miranda smiled and touched his cheek gently. He turned his head and captured her fingers with his lips.

"My mother's mother was from China," she whispered. "Some people think that is…to be ashamed of."

"I know," he said. "But I don't. You are perfect, almost too unbearably perfect. Every moment apart from you hurts me physically, causes a deep ache in my soul."

Miranda frowned. The things he said were extraordinary and sometimes she barely understood what he was telling her. But he loved her, that much she knew. And she adored him more than life itself.

"What were you doing playing music for dancing,

Piers? Surely you would rather give concert performances? You are too accomplished to play in a dance orchestra."

Piers gazed at her taking in every detail of her face, dark brown eyes, clear, slightly olive toned skin, jet black hair, full red lips—a face with the hint of something exotic, something mysterious, foreign. So familiar.

"It was destined that I should come here," he said.

"I think so too. I think…I feel I know you already, knew you before. But I didn't, did I? We'd never met?" The smooth brow creased as she wrestled with such a thought, sought a reason for the strength and immediacy of the bond between them.

"Not in the flesh but we met on a different plane. Spiritually." How could he explain? She'd never understand his attempt, he hardly understood the force that had brought them together himself.

Miranda smiled slowly and touched his cheek again with featherlight fingers. "My ghost man. But you will play music for me to dance to, won't you?"

"Your wish is my desire. You are my desire." He grabbed her and rolled her over on the grass to make love once more.

Miranda left the trees as the afternoon wore on. Twilight lasted hours in midsummer and it was difficult to judge the time when she was with Piers. She mustn't be late for supper. She cut across the fields this time taking a more meandering path home away from the dust of the main road. Clouds were building up on the horizon but the storm if it ever arrived was still a long way off. Similar clouds had appeared yesterday afternoon as well but nothing had happened. The heat had continued relentless as ever. She reached the old, weathered stone church and went through the lych gate to visit her mother's grave briefly.

In loving memory of
Amelia Miranda Sung Templeton
Born May 29th 1852
Died in childbirth October 15th 1874
Always loved, never forgotten.

"Hello Mama." She knelt before the tombstone heedless of the dry grass and dust clinging to her skirt.

Hoof beats on the road made her turn her head. Tyler sat on his tall bay gelding watching her over the low stone cemetery wall. She stood up and walked slowly across to him, closing the lych gate carefully.

"Hello." She rubbed Captain's soft, brown, velvety nose. "Have you been visiting Laura?"

"Earlier, yes. And you? Where have you been? Your dress is stained with grass and dirt." Tyler looked down at her suspiciously, his heavy brows even more threatening as he frowned. Captain fidgeted at the harsh tone of his voice.

"I went for a walk and sat down in the shade to rest and fell asleep," she lied smoothly. "The road is so dusty I walked across the fields."

"Were you alone?"

"Of course. Who would I be with?"

"Ethan called for you. He expected you to visit his mother this afternoon."

"Oh. I completely forgot." Miranda put both hands to her mouth in horror. Tea with Mrs. Broome and the neighbouring ladies. She liked Ethan's mother very much, had known her all her life. "This heat has addled my brains," she said weakly.

"You shouldn't go walking out in the heat of the day. Of course you'll addle your brains. Those you have." Tyler pulled Captain's head around. "Go straight home and write an apology to Mrs. Broome. I'll ride up and tell them you're found."

"Was there a search party?" She prayed no. Someone may have seen Piers.

"No. Only me," said Tyler. "And I've better things to do than run around the countryside after a silly young girl."

Thank goodness.

Her brother delivered his parting shot. "You need to learn some decorum, Miranda, if ever you want to be a married woman."

Tyler was only three years older than she but sounded like a crotchety grandfather. Miranda bent her head and said nothing. Tyler's words resonated in her brain. Time was she thought she'd be married to Ethan. Dependable, good-natured, kindly Ethan. The man she had loved since she turned thirteen and he was seventeen. The reason she had stopped being a tomboy and started taking pains with her dress and hair because she wanted him to notice her and instinctively knew he would disapprove of her wild, abandoned side.

The side that rendezvoused and came alive with Piers.

Miranda continued home alone, lost in her thoughts. Her future had changed irrevocably that night, the night of the Summer Ball. Ethan had proved not to be the man she thought he was and she'd changed, grown suddenly into a woman from the naïve girl she'd been until that night. Her position had become suddenly very clear. And then there was Piers.

When she was with him she forgot everything. Nothing mattered save for the love and the pleasure they gave each other. She would die for him. Would follow him anywhere if he asked. If he asked…But he didn't ask, instead he talked about eternity and strange cosmic music.

And who was he, this man of whom she knew very little except he loved her and that he held very strange ideas? Though bold enough to sneak out to meet her lover, was she brave enough to throw her future into his hands? Brave enough to face her father and brother, the scorn of the Squire and Mrs. Broome, of Ethan, the local gentry, the disgust of the whole village? Did her midsummer madness stretch so far?

Would Piers even offer marriage? Why did he insist on such secrecy? Why could he not come to the house and meet her father? He had every right. He was from a prosperous landowning family; he wasn't a penniless itinerant musician. Why? Was he married? Was he toying with her? It would answer many questions if that were his purpose.

Was he using her as men did any obliging girl? Was she a giddy fool in love and blinded by it? Perhaps she should salvage some remnants of decorum and cut the liaison. Save herself before the affair became known.

Though it broke her heart Miranda missed the next meeting with Piers. And the next although by then she had succumbed to her burning desire to see him once more, had told herself she owed it to him to explain in person, tell him face to face she expected marriage to come from their affair.

But the risk was far too great to continue the

rendezvous. Tyler watched her too closely. She knew he suspected her of something but had no proof of deceit or wrongdoing. He was an exceedingly irritating watch dog. If only he were back at University where he belonged but his summer holidays had weeks left to run.

She had no address for Piers, couldn't contact him. Her heart yearned to reassure him of her love. He must understand it was impossible for her to continue with him the way they were. After all he had offered nothing more than love. She had given him her innocence. Ruined herself.

She assisted her father with his surgery and helped Mrs. Bowden with some of the household chores her head filled with Piers, his voice, his touch, his scent. Her moods changed daily, hourly. She sang as she polished the dining table lost in the memory of their last meeting and then as she sat at table and ate with her father and Tyler, she looked at their beloved familiar faces and wondered how she could possibly think of defying them to run off with a stranger.

A week after her abandonment of Piers, Miranda dreamed of him. He stood before her playing his violin exactly as he had when she first saw him except the music was strange and haunting. Tears sprang to her eyes. She called his name but he ignored her and continued playing. The scent of roses filled the air.

She woke to find her pillow and cheeks wet with tears and a lingering perfume in the room.

He came to her every night while she slept. The dreams were eerily familiar as though she'd dreamed them before but had no recollection of them prior to this time. She began to dread going to her bed, wishing to avoid the heartbreak and longing he renewed. Every time it was the same dream. Piers playing that melody on his violin, making it sob and sigh, pouring out his heartbreak and sorrow, ignoring her, even though she called his name with ever increasing despair.

Then one night as she lay wide-eyed and exhausted, Piers stood by her bed looking down at her with an expression of such love, she held out her arms to him knocking a book from her bedside table in the haste of movement. He disappeared.

The clunk of the book on the floor shocked her. Had Piers been real? Was she dreaming? Heart pounding, hands clammy with fright she retrieved the book. It couldn't have been him, couldn't have been his ghost, he was still alive. Surely they would have heard if he had been killed somehow. What was it?

Next morning she went to see Maggie Blackstone. The old witch lady would know. Maggie lived in a cottage just outside the village, on the far side from the church and the direction Miranda took to meet Piers. Like all the other gardens hers was tinder dry as they still had had no rain apart from a few miserable drops one night after another massive buildup of storm clouds. Miranda tapped on the door and heard Maggie shuffling about inside.

The door creaked open.

"Come in, young missy. What took you so long?" Maggie peered out with bright, startlingly blue eyes part obscured by wispy grey hair escaping from a loosely pinned roll. Her grey dress had a stained and dirty hem, sleeves partially rolled up showing pale but sinewy strong forearms.

"What do you mean?" Miranda hesitated but

reassured by the old lady's sudden smile stooped to enter the dim, shadowy room cluttered with all manner of furniture and bric-a-brac. A strange, pungent smell almost made her gag.

"Everybody comes to Maggie when they're in trouble." A bony finger pointed to a chair at the small wooden dining table. "Sit ye down, missy."

Miranda perched on the edge of the chair. "I'm not in trouble." Perspiration prickled her skin, her stomach turned over, uncomfortable and queasy in the cloying air.

"Why are ye here, then, eh?" Maggie chuckled softly. She sat opposite and laid a surprisingly well shaped hand on Miranda's arm. " 'Tis a lover." She nodded confidently. "And not Mister Ethan Broome."

Miranda gasped. "Why do you say that?"

"Why?" chortled Maggie. "Because it's the truth. No use to deny the truth. No use denying the future. Or the past."

"Is the future already written?"

"Maybe the map is there. Maybe folks don't always follow it." She peered into Miranda's eyes then shook her head. "Be careful. The one you love is very powerful. He can be dangerous."

She took Miranda's hands and studied the palms, gently rubbing her thumb across the soft mounds below the fingers. She pursed her mouth but said nothing, released her grip.

"I have dreams," said Miranda softly. "The same dream every night. He plays his violin. The same melody. So sad I wake up crying. He ignores me."

Maggie nodded. "He loves you."

"Yes." Miranda hesitated. "He came to me last

night but not in a dream. He stood by my bed and watched me."

"A ghost?"

"No, he's not dead. At least I don't think he is. No, I know he's not," she said firmly.

Maggie fixed Miranda with two penetrating blue eyes. "He is a very powerful magician. He can change his shape. He can dissolve his body and fly through the vapours to another place."

Miranda stood up on legs gone shaky. "That's impossible!"

"He has done it."

"Can I stop him?"

"Go to him. He wants you to be with him. You want to be with him. You belong together. Perhaps you have always been together. To go against this is to go against your destiny."

"But I can't do that," cried Miranda.

"You will go against your destiny. You will be tempting fate."

"What should I do?"

"You must decide."

Maggie held out her hand.

Miranda fumbled in her pocket for a few coins and pressed them into the old woman's palm. She stumbled into the glare of daylight, breathing deeply of the hot air which now seemed refreshing after the suffocating atmosphere of the cottage. Maggie's black and white cat rubbed against her ankles leaving hairs on the bottom of her skirt. She looked down at it, then quickly bent and ran her hand over its head and down its back.

The perfume from Maggie's blood-red roses sat heavy in the air as she walked down the brick path to the cottage gate. A vivid image of her first meeting with Piers sprang to mind. That shock of recognition. Could Maggie be right? Could it be that they had always known each other, were destined to be together? How was it then, that Piers knew it so clearly and she didn't?

Miranda walked on slowly, absorbed in her thoughts, bewildered by the talk of changing shape and flying through the vapours. Maggie said Piers was a magician. Perhaps he was. He'd told her strange things certainly enough, about his music and wanting to tap into some sort of cosmic power.

One thing alone had become clear. She loved him to distraction and the decision to part from him was like trying to build a straw house in the wind. Hopeless and impossible.

Maggie said it would be going against destiny. What were the opinions of her father and Tyler and society against one's destiny? This was her life, not theirs. Miranda stuck her chin in the air defiantly and marched on with a firm tread.

The rattle of carriage wheels and horses' hooves sounded behind her. Miranda stepped aside to allow the driver room to pass. Instead, the carriage slowed and Mrs. Broome leant out. "Miranda, my dear. Whatever are you doing, walking in this heat? Let me drive you home."

Miranda stood mute, her mind scrambling for something to say. Her two worlds jarred together.

"Help Miss Templeton up, please, Joseph," Mrs. Broome said and Miranda gathered her wits and smiled as Joseph jumped down and opened the carriage door, offering his hand.

Chapter Nine

Sydney, 1998

As soon as they arrived home Nina dumped her bag and strode away to fetch her violin and move the music stand into the living room the better to hear the recorded cello part. Martin slumped on the couch and watched her silently as she set up and prepared her violin. Why wasn't he getting his flute ready? She placed the music on the stand without a word then turned to him. "Are you going to help with this or not?"

"All right." A deeply reluctant, deeply infuriating sigh. What was his problem?

He disappeared into the spare room, emerging a few minutes later with the flute case in his hand. He dropped back down on the couch and slowly assembled the silver instrument bit by bit. Nina waited, slapping her bow against her leg. His whole body yelled reluctance. Why couldn't he understand how important it was that they follow through on this? Piers was desperate for their help and he'd chosen them, specifically. They were honour-bound to do as he wished.

Martin had come halfway around the world in pursuit of this phantom thing how could he even consider dropping it all now? Had he forgotten already the compulsion which had consumed his life for eight months? Didn't he want it to end?

To her fury he placed his flute on the coffee table, stood up and headed into the kitchen.

"What are you doing?" she demanded.

A tap ran. He reappeared with a glass in his hand, eyes narrowed, jaw set. "Drink of water. That all right?"

The cassette was ready in the stereo system. He pressed "Play."

"Tune up," he said and switched the recording off after a couple of notes. Nina made a couple of adjustments to the strings and waited while he wandered about the room with his flute to his lips blowing single long tones.

"That's enough," she snapped. "Come on."

Martin shot her a thunderous look but she clenched her jaw and tucked her violin under her chin. Her count in sounded on the recording and eyes closed, she stroked the first note. The effect was immediate and electrifying.

The voices poured into the room, flooding her like the sea over a drowning swimmer but strangely one who is content to let herself be submerged by the tide. Her molten anger melted to nothing. She surfed on a wave of sound and exhilarating emotion, aware of nothing physical or concrete around her. Martin and the room faded away. There was only music—and the voices.

Words were indistinguishable. They were chanting in a tongue completely foreign to her. The cadence followed the pulse of their playing in an eerie way growing in strength with hypnotic force. Suddenly the voices stopped when they still had half a page of the slow section to go. Piers spoke, his voice soft and seductive in her ear, and an immense surge of the yearning she had experienced in her dreams overcame her.

"It's nearly complete. One more piece and it will be ready. You have done well, my darling, very well. Do this for me. For us. I will come to you. Tonight. Wait for me. The usual place. Our place." Piers spoke alone, to her. The others were silent but she sensed their presence and the tension surrounding them, a palpable force. They listened. And disapproved.

Piers voice grew stronger. "You cannot stop now. You must complete the circle. The harmony is crucial, the harmony of the spheres and the universe. It must be complete. We are so close."

Then Jasper's voice crashed in—angry and fearful. "We can't do this, Piers! I can't continue. It's madness, man. It's too dangerous."

"Again. We must try again." Piers, no longer addressing her, speaking to his friends desperately determined, ignoring Jasper as thought he hadn't spoken.

Then Michael's gentle Irish voice cut in, "Piers man, Miranda has gone. You can't do anything now. Let the poor child rest in peace."

"Try again, again. Mira…" Piers voice trailed off in a cry of anguish so heartfelt and despairing that tears coursed down Nina's cheeks and the music blurred so that she couldn't read the notes. Dimly she realised Martin had stopped playing, and the room was silent. She lowered her violin, stunned and speechless while tears splashed unchecked down her face.

"Nina?"

Piers had gone. She sank back into darkness. Nothing.

Martin took the violin and bow from her nerveless fingers and laid them on the dining table, as a silent scream resounded in his head. They shouldn't have played. He should have stopped her, should have refused point blank and risked her anger. But he didn't, and if she was harmed it was his fault. He knew it was dangerous, he was supposed to be protecting her.

He wrapped his arms around her and hugged her, stiff and unresponsive—not repelling him but as if she wasn't there. As though her body was, but her soul had gone. Where? That bastard Piers!

He ground his teeth then released his grip and peered into her sightless eyes.

"Nina, darling? Come back. Nina." He kissed her wet cheeks then carefully wiped her face with his fingers, fought a rising tide of panic. What if she had gone permanently? What could he do?

"Nina." He spoke louder. "Wake up."

She stirred and a ripple ran down from her head to her feet. A tremor as if…what? Her soul had re-entered her body?

"Piers," she murmured. "Oh, Piers."

"What happened? Tell me what you heard." His voice shook with the relief. He sat her down on the couch and almost collapsed beside her. But she met his anxious gaze with a terrifyingly blank look.

"Nina." He snapped his fingers in her face. She blinked several times then her eyes focussed. She was back.

"Martin?" A shaky smile hovered on her lips. He pulled her into his arms, unmanly tears threatening to spill over.

"My God, Nina. We can't do that again. It's too dangerous. I thought I'd lost you."

"We must." Her voice startled him with its strength. She wrenched herself away and went to the shelf where her stereo was set up and began scrabbling about in one of the drawers holding old cassette tapes.

"What are you doing?" The abrupt recovery was almost as shocking as the zombie-like state.

"We need a blank tape. Damn! Damn, damn, damn. I thought had some." She stared at Martin. "We have to record us as well."

"No!" The idea shocked him beyond belief.

"Yes! We do, Martin. We have to help Piers."

"The man's a lunatic. Didn't you hear him?" His voice rose in a shout of desperation. "He turned you into a zombie, for God's sake. What if you hadn't come back? What would I do then?"

"Yes, I know. But he's not a lunatic. He's just desperate, frantic with grief. He loves her. We have to help."

Nothing he could say would sway that iron-willed determination. Piers had captivated her, ensnared her. Piers, the monster.

"We have to find the other part. Did you hear him say that?" Her voice was cold as a tomb.

"Oh, yes," said Martin with equal chill. "He made that very clear."

"How do you mean?"

"He sounds like Hitler, Nina. Jasper and Michael are very reluctant, understandably I would think, they think he's crazy. So do I. And bloody Piers gets really stuck into them. Calls them all sorts of things. I'd punch him…"

Nina's face darkened, her breath hissed in and out. She was barely controlling her anger but he didn't care. Not after what just happened.

"He's not like that at all, Martin. He's…" She hesitated, chose her words carefully. "He's in love with Mira and he can't bear to lose her." She slipped her arms around him. "Can't you relate to that?" The tone was honey sweet, cajoling. Playing on his attraction to her.

"Yes, of course." He kissed her upturned lips but something wasn't right in the way she kissed him back. An uneasy feeling of dread hovered like a black cloud. He couldn't, mustn't, let her talk him into playing it again.

Nina drew away. "Did you hear the chanting?" she asked. "It fit what we played." She spoke normally now, the Nina he was used to. She picked up his glass of water and drank.

"Yes. I couldn't understand any of it. Must be one of their weird rituals." He stood up, to distance himself physically, remove himself from the distraction of her kisses. "Maybe we need help with this."

"Like who? Serena?" Nina laughed scornfully. "I don't think so. It's out of her league. Anyway, we're doing all right."

"I think it's out of our league too." Martin's voice rose as he paced about the room. "What's happening to you? I don't understand."

He looked at her and Nina shrugged, an infuriating gesture, full of innocent denial. "Look, all I'm trying to do is finish this as fast as possible. We have to go to New Orleans to find the other parts. After that? Who knows? I'll do it by myself if you're wimping out." She stood up.

"I'm not wimping out, as you put it. I'm trying to protect you—us—from whatever is happening. Piers seems to be getting some sort of hold over you. Don't you see that? He's like a Jim Jones or David Koresh. Charles Manson. And you're not helping at all." Martin realised he was shouting. Nina turned her back on him and went to the kitchen.

"Stirfry vegetables for dinner, okay?" she said stiffly. Martin flung his arms in the air and slumped back onto the couch.

"Fine," he said.

The evening passed in a polite chill. They cleared the table, did the dishes, watched TV and then at ten, Nina got up.

"I'm going to bed. I've got work tomorrow."

"Good night. I'll stay up a while."

Nina went to the bathroom, pausing on her way back to say quietly, "I'd like to sleep alone tonight, Martin."

"I thought you would." He turned back to the TV.

Nina watched for a moment then hurried to her room and her double bed. Piers was waiting. She closed the door and leaned against it, safe from Martin's angry disapproval and his hurt disappointment.

Meditation was the best means of contacting Piers, now. She couldn't play for him. Not with Martin in the next room. If Martin could do it with meditation, so could she, and she doubted if she would be capable of sleep and thus dreaming to reach him, in the state she was in. She had the opposite problem to Lady Macbeth who didn't want to sleep for fear of dreaming.

Nina cleared some clothes off a straight-backed chair and settled herself comfortably, seated this time with her feet on the floor, back straight and hands resting on her lap. She closed her eyes and forced herself to go through the familiar relaxation sequences. Gradually her muscles relaxed, her breathing slowed. Her mind calmed and the thoughts passing through decreased in number and speed. She sank deeper into stillness and quiet.

"Open your eyes and look at me." His voice was soft and caressing. Nina's eyelids fluttered open. He stood in the room with her just as Martin had reported. She gasped but strangely, felt no fear. She'd summoned him, he'd invited her. She'd expected him.

He raised his hand slowly. "Be calm. Relax and concentrate on my voice." He continued chanting in the tongue Nina recognised from earlier. She focussed on the cadence. It flowed through her mind like honey, thick, rich and invasive, smoothing out the questions, seducing her soul. She devoured every inch of him with her eyes as he intoned the strange words in his dark, resonant voice. A white collarless shirt open at the neck and black trousers with shoes dusty and worn. The handsome face was gaunt and lined with fatigue, but the dark eyes glowed with unearthly intensity and passion. His dark hair brushed his collar, his hands were long fingered and unmarked by physical labour, his body was well defined under the shirt and trousers. She knew exactly how exciting and sensual it was to touch, knew exactly how his hot skin felt against hers, longed to reach out her hands and touch him, ached to feel his fingers play her, bring her to fever pitch. The yearning in her body became unbearable. She wanted him, desperately, but the chant dulled her physical movements so she sat drugged but with all her senses on fire.

"Who are you?" she managed to whisper when the chant eventually died away.

"You know who I am. I am Piers. I am the one you have been waiting for. I have waited for you."

Hypnotised by his voice and his glowing eyes, she yearned for him to come to her and kiss her as he had in her dream, make love to her. Her body throbbed with longing. She tried to raise her hand to reach out to him but couldn't move.

"What do you want me to do?" His eyes locked on hers, a snake charmer and she was the snake, powerless in his thrall.

"You know I want you. I want you and you want me. I need you, my darling."

Nina barely breathed as he came toward her. His arms slid around her and his breath fell lightly on her cheek as he lifted her off the chair and held her tightly clasped against him. She wrapped her arms around him and buried her face in his neck as he carried her to the bed and laid her down gently. Then he began to kiss her and transported her to places she never dreamed existed…

She woke early, before dawn, lying alone in the bed. She stretched out an arm gingerly and felt about but she was definitely alone. Piers had gone but he'd left behind the vague memory of his presence and the overwhelming desire to do whatever he asked. He wanted them to go to New Orleans. He wanted them to find the music and he wanted them to go to England. How did she know that with such certainty? After he'd begun to kiss her he hadn't said anything about the music, had he?

The details of the night, his passion and his lovemaking had become a jumble of impressions and emotions. She remembered his first explosive kiss and the anticipation of indescribable rapture but after that—nothing. Until now. Was it real? Had she dreamed it? Him? All of it?

She turned over and pulled up the tangled sheet. Had she and Piers done that or had she, alone in her dreams? Whatever had happened, the fact remained that the path ahead was clear. They had to go to New Orleans and then England.

England? They'd never discussed going to England, she and Martin.

Martin. With a pang of remorse she remembered the fight she'd engineered. Why had she done that? She'd set out deliberately to push him away, which was the last thing she wanted to do. She didn't want to fight with him. He didn't deserve the way she'd spoken to him. He wasn't a wimp, far from it. He was her anchor and she needed him to help her get through this.

A cold shiver ran down her spine. If he left her...she couldn't begin to imagine what she would do if she was on her own again. They needed each other. Besides he loved her and she...Nina threw back the covers and sat up in the darkened room. Had he left?

What if he was so angry he'd packed up while she was in bed...with Piers? If he'd had enough of her anger and her insults and disappeared? He was capable of spontaneous action based on strong emotion. Look at the way he'd come to Australia. He was the type who would pack and go without a farewell scene.

A rush of intense fear that he may have deserted her made her stumble to the door in the dark, grope her way to the spare room and switch on the light. Martin groaned and buried his face in the pillow. A sob of relief burst from her throat. She turned off the light, leaning weakly on the doorjamb for support.

"Nina?" Martin's groggy voice came through the blackness.

"I thought you might have gone." Nina sniffed back her tears.

"Come here." She made her way across to the dim outline of the bed. His hands grasped her and pulled her in, cuddling her and soothing as she clung to him and cried against his chest.

"I'm sorry I was so mean," she whispered.

He kissed the top of her head. "Sshh. Don't say anything, sweetheart."

****

Martin slept as Nina lay watching the dawn light gradually increase. His arm lay across her, leaden now, but protective and comforting. They hadn't made love when they switched to her bigger bed, just lay wrapped in each other's arms whispering reassurances and forgiveness until sleep came.

Piers—words couldn't describe Piers and the effect he had on her. Lying here now next to warm, loving, flesh and blood Martin, it seemed impossible, unreal. It must have been a dream. Except that Martin had seen him too. Nina turned over, shifting the heavy arm in the process. Martin stirred.

"Sweetheart?"

"I saw Piers last night."

He opened both eyes. "How? I mean, how did you

see him? In a dream?"

"No. He was here in the room." She couldn't tell him how desperately she'd craved his embrace, how he'd made love to her. *If* he'd made love to her…She wouldn't able to hide the effect Piers had on her.

"What happened?" Martin, wide wake now, propped himself on one elbow, studying her face. "You must have been terrified. Poor darling. No wonder you were in such a state." He touched her cheek softly.

"No, it wasn't scary at all." She smiled. "I'm getting used to him. He doesn't want to hurt me, he needs our help. He needs us. He wants us to find the other part then go to England."

"Did he tell you that?"

"Sort of. I know that's what he wants." Nina held Martin's face between her hands and searched his eyes. "We have to do it, Martin. We have to."

"Where in England does he want us to go? Was he a bit more specific?"

He had that sceptical expression again. She lay back on her pillow. "I don't know. Perhaps he'll tell us later."

"Good God. This is too…weird, bizarre, crazy." Martin rolled onto his back and spoke to the ceiling.

Nina sat up. "I have to go to work. I'll find out about getting a passport today. I think I can do it through the post office."

"I'll check out flights. When do you think we can leave? January?"

"Probably not before Christmas. I want you to meet my Mum and Dad." She leaned over and kissed him on the lips. "Thank you, Martin."

"What for?"

"Staying with me."

"I'm not going to leave you alone in this. Piers might need us but we need each other."

She smiled and kissed him again before heading off to the bathroom. She knew he wouldn't desert her. So did Piers. He wanted them both, together.

Martin lay on his back and stared at the ceiling trying to make sense of Nina's increasingly frightening behaviour. Some weird new thing was happening. He knew Piers acted differently with her but it wasn't that she just felt sorry for him and wanted to help, she was totally enthralled by the man. He clenched his fists and slammed them impotently on the bed. The bastard had her hypnotised. Christ, he wasn't even real. He was long gone. Must have been dead for at least sixty or seventy years. He couldn't be seducing a living, breathing girl in the present.

But all indications were that Piers was, or had done, exactly that. And Martin was powerless against the force of that attraction.

After Nina had gone he showered, dressed, did yoga stretches and had a leisurely breakfast in the back garden. He loved the fact he could sit outside at Nina's small, outdoor table, reading the paper with Soda at his feet, the morning air fresh with just the hint of the warmth to come later in the day. He could very happily live in Sydney—with Nina. There must be freelance work for a highly experienced flute player, and he could always teach.

Dream on, there were things to be done first. His girlfriend had to be freed from the seductive clutches of a ghost, for starters.

He took his plate and mug to the kitchen, washed

them, put them away, went to the bathroom and brushed his teeth, staring at himself in the mirror.

"Get on with it, you coward," he growled at his reflection. "Stop dithering about. You wimp."

He went to the spare room, sat cross-legged on the floor, closed his eyes and began to slow his breathing in preparation for meditation. He deliberately thought of the melody and as he sank deeper into the relaxation Piers voice sounded faintly, as if from a vast distance.

"You mustn't hinder me. I am the leader, I have the power and the knowledge. I will succeed in this and you must help me in every way. I'm stronger than you know. I possess the knowledge of the universe."

He didn't sound desperate as before. The tone rang with confidence and certainty as if he had achieved what he had set out to do, things were going his way. He was pleased. Martin concentrated on the voice and willed himself to stay calm, allow the voice to flow over him.

"The music must be complete. You will do this for me. She's already mine. You will do what I ask. For her, for me. Look at me."

The voice was close, in the room, and Martin's eyes flicked open as he sensed another presence. Piers stood before him once more, clearer and more solid and substantial than the first appearance. His handsome face was stern and the eyes glared out with obsessive passion, boring into Martin's, forcing him to meet the gaze and hold it. "I need you to help her. You will help her. Promise me this."

"Yes, I will," Martin fought down the panic rising in his chest, threatening to choke him. He had to control himself. He had to do what he planned. "What's your name?"

"You know who I am. I am Piers. I am the leader. I control you." The expression didn't relax in the slightest, the penetrating eyes held him captive.

Martin struggled against the searing force to ask his next question. "What is your full name? Where are you from?"

"I am Piers de Crespigny. I am from…nowhere." He lost his certainty, sounded weaker and trailed away to silence. The intensity of the gaze wavered, the bedroom wall appeared through his body.

Martin asked quickly, "What do you want?"

He closed his eyes and tried to regain the concentration but it was gone. Piers cried in one last wail of despair, "I want…Mira."

Martin opened his eyes again but the vision had gone. He closed his eyes, remained motionless breathing deeply for several minutes, regaining his equilibrium. His mind settled, his focus deepened.

Piers spoke again. "The music must be complete. The music of the spheres, the Shadow Music. Music is the key and you must find it."

"Where?" asked Martin.

"Search. It has a place. It will find you when you are near. The Shadow Music."

"Why is the music the key?" asked Martin.

"It is linked to the powers and to the universal force of life. We can do this. We can make her live again."

"How? I don't understand how."

"Find the music." Piers' voice held such chilling intensity Martin's eyes flew open, convinced he'd reappeared, but the room was empty, normal in the

morning light. He got up on shaky legs and collapsed onto the bed with the information reeling through his head.

Piers had a full name—de Crespigny. Shadow Music was written in some cosmic combination of melody and harmony devised by that madman with the help of his Golden Dawn dabblings. The music had to be performed in its complete form and the missing part was waiting for them somewhere. Piers was using them both, in fact in his words, "controlling" them.

That remark about "she" already being his. Did he mean Mira? Or Nina?

An overwhelming urge rushed through his body like a floodtide. He had to see Nina and reassure himself she was all right. He darted about locking doors, grabbed his wallet and hurried to the ferry wharf where he had to sit cooling his heels for twenty-five minutes until the little boat appeared. By the time he'd walked the blocks to the CD store he'd calmed down enough to laugh at himself but not enough to stop himself going straight upstairs to see her.

Rolly tossed him a smile from behind the counter but Nina was serving someone so he had a chance to observe her before she noticed him. In an embroidered red sleeveless Chinese style blouse with a short slim black skirt, she looked demure, serene and indescribably beautiful as she chatted with the elderly male customer who obviously enjoyed her attention. What a fool he was, rushing so precipitously to save her from nothing.

Nina glanced up and her face broke into a smile of such total delight that his heart glowed with love and pride. How could he doubt her? She didn't know it yet with all the confusion and emotional chaos but she had fallen for him. All he needed to do was stick by her until she realised.

The customer left and Nina came around the counter. She held Martin's arm, standing close, smiling up into his eyes.

"Hello. What are you doing here?"

"I had an uncontrollable urge to see you." He grinned and had to restrain himself from kissing her. Her boss was watching from his office doorway.

"Hang around for thirty minutes and I'll take lunch," she whispered. "Meet you outside?"

"Our spot." Martin smiled—the place on the footpath where she'd met him the first evening. He squeezed her hand and went down the stairs, ready to spend an agreeable half hour browsing in the jazz and blues section. But New Orleans would be the place for that so instead, he went outside and walked to the travel agent a few doors along the street. Fifteen minutes later he came out. The friendly, efficient woman had just punched a gigantic hole in their plans.

At lunch time Nina took him to the post office and collected a passport application form.

"I'll need photos. Any photo shop will do them."

"Let's get some food. I need to talk to you."

Ten minutes later, armed with sandwiches and drinks, sitting next to Nina on a park bench, he said, "Piers spoke to me again. I asked him some questions."

"Did you? Did he answer?"

"His name is Piers de Crespigny but he couldn't say where he was from. It confused him."

"Piers de Crespigny. Wow," said Nina. "That sounds French or something, doesn't it? It suits him."

"His accent is definitely English. From the south of England I'd say with an overlay of something else. Sounds almost…West Indian." He frowned. "The name could be Belgian or even Swiss but that doesn't really mean anything. Depends who his father was."

"Martin," Nina interrupted breathlessly. "We know his name. We can find out who he was, is. No—was."

"You mean birth and death records? You're right. We have to go to England."

"Is that why he wants us to go to England?"

"Maybe…but he could tell us those dates. He's got something else planned far more important. It's to do with Mira and us and the Shadow Music. He said the music was the key and the link to the universal life force or something. He was adamant that we find the other part. He said…" Martin paused. Should he reiterate his fears to Nina given the effect that had had last time?

"What?"

"That he controlled us." A compromise half-truth.

"He does," she said calmly. "Doesn't he? Listen to us. Look at us. Our whole lives revolve around this thing now. But I don't mind any more. I'm not frightened. I want to help him. He needs us."

"Nina, I went to the travel agent while I was waiting for you. There's no way I can afford to go to the US. It'll add on thousands of dollars which I just don't have."

"But we have to. Piers wants us to." Her calm shattered in an instant.

"I thought about it and we don't really need to. We can ring the Post Office from here and ask them. It's a long shot anyway. I think going back to England is more important."

The logic, or perhaps the financial implications and the fact he wasn't pulling the plug completely, drained the fire from her expression. She gave a brief nod.

"Okay. Phone them tonight."

"I'll have to check the time there. You could try to find this Yorke person or a relative online," he said in a further effort to minimise her displeasure.

Nina spent the afternoon, in between serving customers, in a fruitless online search for the right Xavier Yorke. By the end of the day the few replies she'd had to her messages were negative. She returned home despondent but hopeful Martin might have more luck that evening but he said, "It's the middle of last night there now. I'll have to call in the morning."

"Before I go to work," she said.

"Fine. At least I found the number to call." He sounded annoyingly defensive. Surely he wanted answers as much she did?

The next morning Nina made tea and brought it to him. Yawning, he dialled the number.

"Put it on speaker," she said

"Luella speaking. How may I help you?" she asked in a soft melodious voice.

"My name is Martin and I have a friend Nina here, too. We're calling from Australia and we have you on speaker phone if that's all right. We're trying to track down the person who had a specific PO Box."

"That's all right, sir. What is the box number and post office, please?"

He read it out. "But it's about twenty years ago."

"That post office burned down. It was real bad—someone died in the fire."

"When exactly? Do you know?"

"It was 1982 on March 5[th.] I remember 'cos I knew the man was killed. Used to work there myself but got a transfer three months before. Lucky. The good Lord was watching over me that time. Everything went up in that fire. Folks never got their mail. Birthday cards, money, greetings, thank you's, invitations. Parcels. Nothing saved. It was real sad."

"How terrible," said Martin. "So no records survived either?"

"Not a thing."

After he'd thanked her and finished the call, he said to Nina, "Do you think we should give this American thing up? I mean you haven't had any luck online, either."

She stared at him in disbelief

"Do you?" insisted Martin.

A red, blinding rage frighteningly unfamiliar in its strength and force gathered inside her. The intensity was terrifying, greater than anything she'd experienced before, a gigantic impending explosion fuelled by Piers' fury. She clenched her teeth, fingers cramped into claws until she forced control and the rage subsided enough for her to speak rationally.

"I feel…that we've started this so we should keep on. What's the point of spending all this money and travelling half way round the world? We can't give up. We mustn't." She glared at him, breathing hard with the effort of stopping herself flying at him with pummelling fists and scratching nails.

"But Nina…" He spoke as if she were a child—an out of control child having a tantrum. "All I'm saying is we forget about trying to track down the part that was sent to New Orleans. It's a waste of time and energy. Don't you think?" He sounded so reasonable, so calm while she…she…

"No," she said in a voice she barely recognised as her own. "If you want to stop, why don't you destroy the music?"

Martin sat with a face like a stunned mullet. "Destroy it?"

"Yes." She waved a dismissive hand. "Now's your chance. Go on. It's right there in your room. Rip it up. Flush it down the loo. Burn it." He couldn't, she knew that as surely as she knew she couldn't do it either.

Martin's cheeks turned a dull red, his mouth firmed to a tight line. He went to his room and looked at the suitcase, lying open and half unpacked on the floor. She followed. They'd put the parts in an envelope together with a tape recording of the violin and cello, having debated whether to lug her violin with them and deciding not to burden themselves with the extra awkward baggage. As Martin pointed out they could always borrow a violin from one of his musician friends in England if necessary.

If he destroyed the music now that would be the end of it forever. There would be nothing keeping them together.

He squatted down and pulled the envelope out of the pocket inside the lid of the suitcase. His expression changed, softened as if a sudden reluctance to bother going on with the argument overcame him. She knew he hated fighting. She knew she'd won.

He said, "We won't find Xavier Yorke, I'm positive. The man's either dead or untraceable and who knows where that envelope ended up? We have to go to

England."

He pushed the envelope back into the bag. Nina smiled. The rage settled as abruptly as it was born.

Martin, stood up, back to her. "I'm not giving up I just don't think there's any point trying to trace the guy." He turned slowly and held Nina's hands tightly in his. "We mustn't ever fight again about this. We have to tell each other everything that happens and stick together. That's our strength."

Nina gripped his hands just as tightly. "Yes. No more fighting. I hated that."

"And tell each other everything?"

"Yes."

Martin stared into her eyes, then kissed her, hoping and praying but wondering. Was she telling him the truth? Something had just happened but he didn't know what. That exchange had been more frightening than any of the previous arguments about Piers. This Nina was foreign and totally unnerving, speaking in a way he'd never heard from her before.

His thoughts gathered and focussed, and his breath caught as pieces fell into place. He had heard that tone of voice before but not from Nina. She sounded exactly like Piers when he berated the other musicians. That bastard was consuming her and he wasn't getting weaker—he was getting stronger.

****

Nina loved travelling. She loved the excitement of the international terminal and boarding the plane in Sydney, the stopover in Singapore and exploring the airport but Martin didn't. He had the beginnings of a headache, was dead tired and increasingly worried about the responsibility of looking after her. She left him slumped in a seat guarding their carry on bags and went to the bookstore.

On his own, the lunacy and dangers of his actions hadn't been an issue. Now they were. The rules had changed dramatically since he and Nina had come together. To make things worse, her parents had taken him aside at the family Christmas dinner and told him how much they liked and trusted him. That they'd been initially concerned but now having met him, were quite at ease.

But her father added, in a voice incongruous given his mild-mannered professor appearance and fixing Martin with a steely eye, "If you hurt or abandon my girl, you'll have to answer to me. And don't think I won't find you."

He was left with no doubts as to where Nina had inherited her determination.

"Here, have two of these," she said. Martin opened one eye suspiciously. She stood in front of him holding out a sheaf of pills

"What are they?"

"Headache pills."

"Thanks." He swallowed two and drank from the bottle of water she offered.

Nina sat down and watched him for a moment after he closed his eyes. She was lucky he'd found her, so lucky she could barely believe it sometimes, but he was taking the responsibility of looking after her far too seriously. That was mainly because Dad had really put the wind up him at Christmas. There was no need for any of them to worry. Piers was here with her. Piers was with her constantly.

After that one extraordinary night when he'd

entered her room and her bed she hadn't meditated again. She wouldn't be able to keep the truth from Martin if Piers continued to appear to her that way. Instead he spoke to her in her dreams, wooing her, urging her to continue with their plans. She told Martin most of what Piers said. There was no point telling all of it because he'd be hurt and she didn't want that, and ultimately she couldn't bring herself to utter the truth out loud. "I've fallen in love with a spirit."

Martin detested Piers and knowing the full extent of her relationship with him would be cataclysmic in terms of her relationship with Martin.

Chapter Ten

Cutting Marsh, September 1892

Ethan called to see Miranda several days after her visit to Maggie Blackstone. She was surprised to see him in the parlour, she'd assumed he was busy entertaining his new American friend in London and far too busy to bother with her.

"I thought you were in town," she said.

"I was but it's too noisy and crowded for me. I like the peace of the country."

Miranda smiled. What did he want? He kept gazing at her as if he'd never seen her before and he was doing those fidgety things with his hands he did when he was nervous.

"Are you engaged to Miss McCusker?" she asked.

"No," Ethan blurted. "I love you, Miranda. I always have and I always will. I don't care what my parents think. I want to marry you. I don't want to spend my life with anyone else." He rushed on before she could overcome her astonishment. "We've always known we would be wed, haven't we?" He grabbed her hands in his and gazed earnestly into her face. "You will marry me, won't you?"

His features were so familiar. She'd loved him for so long but now…She smiled at the irony of it. Time was she'd longed for this moment, had lain awake at night thinking of his words, how she would respond, how his lips would feel on hers. He smiled back, mistaking her silence for an abundance of emotion. Now was her chance. If she was to change her life it would start right here with Ethan. She owed him of all people, the truth about her feelings. He bent forward and kissed her gently then with more passion. His moustache prickled her mouth.

"I love you, Miranda." He held her tight against his body. Her cheek was pressed against his linen jacket. She could hear his heart beating in her left ear. He smelled of tobacco smoke. "I want to spend my whole life with you."

"Oh, Ethan." Several tears escaped and ran down her cheeks. He held her away to lift her chin with his fingers. Guilt and doubt choked the words in her throat.

"No need to cry, my darling." He laughed. "We've a lifetime to be together in. Nothing to be sad about."

"No." She managed to turn her lips up in a smile. A lifetime with Ethan? Piers offered eternity. "But Ethan I don't know whether we can do this, I mean…aren't you already promised to Miss McCusker?"

"Not officially. I haven't asked her. It's more or less assumed." The way she'd assumed he would marry her? Poor Miss McCusker.

"Won't your parents be very angry?"

"Maybe at first but they love you Miranda. You know that. And your father is a good friend. They can't object for long."

Could he tell? Did her deceit show as a mark on her forehead, a black sign of her evil nature? But was loving Piers evil? How could it be? Was loving two men evil?

She had a decision to make, a choice, and she'd just made it. She wasn't betrothed when she met Piers. Now she was an engaged woman she would definitely forgo her trysts. He would soon move on and forget her. A pain sharp as a knife stabbed at her heart. Piers with another girl. Impossible. But she was with another man. But this was Ethan…Piers knew her situation in regard to Ethan and never said a word about it. He wasn't jealous. Strangely not so. If he truly loved her would he not be eaten with jealousy?

He could have proposed at any time but he didn't. He offered her a cosmic life together for eternity when she would settle for an earthly one. But he didn't ask her.

"Let's tell your father first then drive home to tell mother." Ethan squeezed her hand.

"Maybe you should have spoken to my father first."

"He's expected us to marry for years. He'll be delighted."

****

London, 1999

The plane shuddered and twisted as the violent, icy blasts tried to drag it from the sky and unnaturally hasten touchdown. Nina gripped Martin's hand tightly and held her breath until the thud of wheels on runway jarred the travellers and huge jet engines shrieked in reverse thrust as the pilots slowed the giant plane.

England in January. Wet, freezing, bleak. Nina's immediate and lasting impression was of smallness. Closed in, cramped, crowded—even the sky seemed smaller although that could have been due to the low grey cloud cover enveloping the city, merging with the rain and exhaust fumes into a dismal smog.

"Remember Bondi," she said wistfully as they rode in the taxi from the station to Martin's basement flat.

"I'll never forget it." He looked out at the familiar streets and the scurrying pedestrians, heads bowed against the rain, umbrellas bobbing, coats and scarves buttoned and tucked securely.

Martin clenched his fists nervously in his coat pockets. Now they were in his territory Nina would see how he lived in the dreadful, pokey, damp basement flat. After her lovely little house in Balmain she'd hate it and eventually by extension, him. If only he'd been able to keep his previous two bedroom flat. Blame Piers for that, losing his job and his regular income.

He'd called Sven from Sydney to tell him they were returning and to clean the place up, get in some food, wash the sheets, kick out any friends he may have collected in the couple of months Martin had been away. Sven had listened and boomed cheerfully, "Ja, ja, ja. Leave it by me, man. No worries," which generally was a sign to begin worrying immediately.

Nina sat beside Martin, quiet, tired, and disappointed at being unable to catch glimpses of famous London landmarks through the traffic and the rain. The trip from Singapore had been exhausting after a delayed departure, and the last part, when their destination appeared finally within reach, had been particularly bumpy and nerve-wracking as they flew into the atrocious London weather. She yawned so widely her eyes watered.

She wanted to lie down and sleep for hours in a warm comfortable bed. Sleep and dream. A tingle of excitement penetrated the mist of weariness. Piers waited here for her, aware of their proximity, encouraged and pleased they were in England.

But Piers didn't like Martin's insistence on knowing what she was thinking. She didn't like it. But she needed Martin still, needed him to help her help Piers. Nina caught herself at that thought, frowning. Where had that come from? Needed Martin still? As if she were using him. Thoughts like that flew into her head at random as if someone else was thinking for her.

She glanced at Martin and smiled as he turned his head. His mouth curved in that familiar, special way, his eyes were loving and kind, albeit surrounded by fatigue lines. He stretched out his hand and touched her cheek and she tilted her head to rest it on his open palm. He leaned over and kissed her gently, letting his lips linger on hers softly.

"I love you," he whispered.

She smiled. She would be safe with Martin.

The taxi pulled up with a jerk and they bundled out into the sleet and wind. Martin's flat was down a flight of steps behind iron railings in a typical row of English terrace houses. The dark green front door flew open as they staggered down the steep, rain-slick steps with their luggage.

A large, red-haired Viking boomed, "Welcome to civilisation. Man, you've got a tan."

He grabbed Martin in a rough bear hug then took Nina's suitcase and kissed her warmly on both cheeks, his whiskers tickling her face. She caught a glimpse of a poky cream-painted room with a dull red sofa, a table and chairs and a blue curtain across one corner.

"Hello Sven. This is Nina," said Martin.

"Man, I thought you'd turned into an Aussie by

now. A kangaroo." Sven dumped Nina's bag through a door which must be to the only bedroom. "So." He spread his arms wide. "Is it clean enough for you?" He winked at Nina who managed a feeble smile, too tired to do much else. "I make tea." He pulled the blue curtain aside to reveal a tiny kitchenette.

"Where's the bathroom, Martin?"

He indicated the bedroom. "Through there. It's not much, Nina. Nothing like your place." He yawned and blinked his eyes open. "Sorry."

"Stop worrying." She went to investigate the facilities.

Martin hadn't exaggerated. The toilet and a half size bath only just fitted into the miniscule space. Sven had cleaned as well as he could but Nina suspected the brown stains on the porcelain of both were permanent. And like the other two rooms it was cold. Not just the normal chill but a bone freezing, damp coldness that oozed from the walls. Like a tomb.

When she re-entered the living room Sven and Martin sat at the table drinking tea and talking. Sven poured her a mug from a brown china pot and Nina took it gratefully, cupping her hands around the warmth.

"Cold?" asked Martin.

Nina nodded. "It's freezing."

"Sven doesn't feel the cold. He's from Sweden and he thinks this is balmy and warm. If the sun shines he puts shorts on." Martin stood up. "I'll light the gas fire."

Sven took a noisy slurp from his mug. "How is it in Sydney? Goot? You get plenty sun there, I bet."

"It was stinking hot," said Martin, sitting again. He

218

looked at Nina. "Sven said Jessica called me."

"Ja. An old lady. She sounded like my Oma."

"When? Recently?" asked Nina.

"Two weeks ago, maybe. You call her she said."

"I will," said Martin. "First thing tomorrow. We need sleep now."

"And I go. I have a gig tonight." Sven standing up towered over them both. "I have a regular gig now. Two nights at a restaurant. Piano trio. Is goot."

"Excellent. Thanks for house-sitting, Sven. Where are you living now?" Martin opened the door to let Sven out. A blast of icy damp air rushed in.

"Upstairs. Top floor. I move from the cellar to the attic." He laughed. "Franz begged me to move in when that weird guy moved out."

Martin rolled his eyes. "I bet. What weird guy? Jeffrey isn't weird. He's an accountant."

"Weird, man. Wore a suit and carried a brief case. Nice to meet you, Nina." Sven waved through the window as he went up the steps.

Martin went back to sit opposite Nina at the table.

"Warmer now?" he asked. "We'll have to get you a better coat." Nervous now that they were alone and Nina could see the true squalor of his living conditions.

The little gas heater gave out a pitiful glow, struggling against the arctic chill of the basement. She nodded and kept her fingers curved around the mug of tea. She yawned. She hadn't commented at all. He had no idea what she was thinking.

"I think Sven made the bed with clean sheets. I'll check. I think I've a hot water bottle somewhere. Don't know why but I'm pretty sure there's one in a cupboard in the bedroom."

He got up and hurried through the inner door. After a rummage about in the bottom of the wardrobe he came up with a green rubber hot water bottle.

"Would you like a bath?" he asked. "No shower I'm afraid. I'll just fill this and stick it in the bed then it'll be nice and warm when you get in."

Nina stood up and walked over to Martin. She took the floppy green bottle out of his hands, tossed it onto the table and put her arms around him, holding him tight and resting her head on his chest.

"Shut up, Martin." She stretched up to kiss him. "Let's go to bed and keep each other warm. I could sleep for a week."

They snuggled together in the warmth of Martin's bed with Nina wearing woollen socks and an extra t-shirt under her warmest pyjamas.

"Why do you think Jessica called you?" she murmured, eyes closed, mind drifting into sleep.

He didn't reply and she thought he was asleep, but he said, "Maybe she found those missing parts."

"Call her tomorrow." Her words faded and she wasn't sure she'd spoken aloud or in her sleep.

"You are here. You're close to me. You have come to me."

"Yes," breathed Nina.

Piers stood before her, dark eyes glittering and those sensual lips inviting passion and seduction. His habitual loose white shirt was carelessly open at the throat, revealing the tight curled dark hair covering his chest. Dark pants belted with a thick leather strap and a distinctive silver buckle she hadn't noticed before. He held out his hand.

Nina took it, moving straight into his arms, into his

embrace, his lips on hers, her body pressed against his, feeling his desire hard against her, senses reeling, overwhelmed.

"You're mine," he murmured. "Mine."

"Yes, yes."

"You must do what I want. You must follow the path. Follow the music. The Shadow Music. The key of life. For me."

He kissed her again and she was falling out of control, spinning and whirling into an abyss. She flung out her arms to clutch onto him as she fell, to grasp Piers to save herself from the blackness.

"Piers," she screamed. "Save me! Save me!"

The pitch black was cold. Deathly cold. Arms encircled her. Piers' arms, holding her, comforting her, his voice whispering words of love. She sobbed. Great heaving, gasping sobs of relief. She clung to him as he lay her down, felt the warmth as he pulled covers over her, felt his body lying next to hers, his arms around her, his lips on her face, his lips on hers. The sobs died away as she succumbed to his love and her body responded to his touch.

Martin woke first the next day. Nina slept on, her face childlike and innocent on the pillow. He watched her as she lay beside him. He wondered. Wondered what had happened last night. Wondered if she would remember. Wondered if she would tell him. Wondered if she knew she had made love not to him last night but to Piers.

And he was afraid with bone-chilling fear. Afraid for them both.

Her abrupt mood changes in Australia had seemed unconscious, as if she wasn't aware it was happening.

221

Then today, in the taxi, when he'd told her he loved her, she'd offered a mysterious smile, but didn't reply in kind. That was unsettling in its own way. But it was the other times that truly frightened him. The times when he questioned the value of continuing their bizarre mission. Then she clearly changed, or was taken over. If he was to protect her as he had promised himself and her father, he would have to stay close by her side.

But how could he protect her if Piers came to her in her dreams? Dreams which had been strong in Sydney but which now if last night was any indication came with more strength and power. He knew she hadn't meditated; neither of them had since they'd left Sydney and they literally hadn't been apart, but Piers didn't need that assistance to make contact with Nina anymore. Nor did he need the music.

He shuddered to think what effect meditation and the Shadow Music combined would have now, here in England. They were clinging to a raft in a swollen river, powerless to change course, unable to get off, at the mercy of the torrent. They had to stick together or they'd be swept away. Nina must understand that. But how could he warn her without triggering that explosion of fury? Not her fury but Piers' fury channelled through her.

Martin eased out of bed slowly, pulled on socks and a pullover and went into the bathroom. Now more than ever he missed the luxury of a shower but he stuck the plug in the bath and turned the hot tap on full blast. Then to the kitchen to boil the jug for tea and light the gas fire. He squinted out the window and up the steps to the little patch of sky visible between the railings and the footpath overhead. Grey and dismal. Depressing in its rain-soaked dullness. Oh, for Sydney and the sun, sitting in Nina's small back garden with Soda curled at his feet and a cold beer on the table.

He padded back to check the bath water, turned off the hot tap, added cold water and then stripped and hopped in quickly before the cold air penetrated his skin. Neither the size of the tub nor the temperature of the bathroom was conducive to lying and soaking, so he soaped up vigorously and washed the travel staleness from his body, concentrating on the task at hand, trying not to think. Unsuccessfully.

The big question kept circling like an eagle waiting for its prey to make a dash for safety, ready to pounce. What to say to Nina? She was increasingly touchy. Like a lover not wanting to hear anything against the beloved. What could he say to her? How could he voice his fear without getting his head snapped off. How could he make her see Piers was using her, manipulating her in the cruellest most callous way possible?

He reached no conclusion and towelled himself briskly before piling on layers of warm clothes and thick woollen socks. They needed to go shopping today for a weather proof coat for Nina and some boots. She'd only brought sneakers, totally inadequate for London in midwinter. Then he'd call Jessica.

When Nina blearily wandered into the kitchen, Martin had the gas fire glowing hot and was sitting at the table going through two months worth of mail.

"Got a cup of tea going?" She hugged her arms around herself, moving to crouch in front of the little heater.

"Certainly." Martin jumped up to refill the electric

jug. "Would you like a bath?"

"Yes, please. I must smell terrible." She grimaced. "Sorry."

"No worse than I did. Hell of a trip we had."

He disappeared into the bathroom and Nina heard the splash of water as he turned on the taps. She remained huddled by the heater, her head filled with muddled and disturbing memories of last night. Piers had spoken to her again and started to make love to her but something odd happened, something frightening, then he had come to her again and held her warm and safe and they made love and the images after that were quite different.

She was in a small copse of trees, shaded from the hot sun by their arching, leafy green branches. It was private, a secret trysting place and she was waiting impatiently for someone. She leaned against a tree trunk as she waited, the rough bark poking through her thin white cotton shirt into her back. She looked down. A dark brown jacket lay on the grass at her feet. She wore boots—dusty brown leather boots. Man's boots.

Someone was coming and she peered anxiously, excited through the trees. A flash of white, a light step and then she could see a girl. A long white dress with small blue flowers, a straw summer hat with trailing blue ribbons, dark hair, brown eyes, a familiar face…her own! Love and desire swept over her as the girl ran into her open arms.

Then it was night. Warm summer night with a full moon and she was waiting again in the same place made silver and enchanted by the moon light but this time she was angry. Seething with rage, pacing restlessly.

Chanting. She could hear voices chanting and then she heard the violin. She was playing the melody, the Shadow Music. Playing brilliantly the way Piers himself played. She could see her fingers on the fingerboard and the hand holding the bow. They were strong, large fingers with dark hair on the wrist. Piers' hands. Tears fell from her eyes and she had awoken with an utterable sense of desolation and loss.

Nina stared at the flickering gas flame. If the room wasn't so cold she would have doubted the reality of her present state and whereabouts. Just like the quote of the ancient Chinese Taoist writer Chuang Tzu on awakening from a dream.

"He didn't know whether he was Chuang Tzu who dreamt he was a butterfly or a butterfly who dreamt he was Chuang Tzu."

Nobody could deny the fact, however, that her toes were like ice blocks and that when she had woken in Martin's bed her breath had steamed in the chill air of the bedroom.

But her dreams last night had seemed more real than ever. She had been Piers. And then Piers had been with her. She could touch him and hear him, feel the strength of his arms and the roughness of his stubbly cheek as he kissed her, taste his kisses on her lips, feel his body desiring hers as she desired him, as she gave herself to him completely and utterly.

Martin said, "Bath's ready," and startled her.

She rose slowly and went into the bathroom where she scrubbed away the travel grime. Dressed, wide awake and acclimatised to her position in time again, Nina joined Martin at the table. She picked up the mug of tea he'd poured.

"Thanks." Here was a caring, reliable and truly wonderful man. A man who loved her. She smiled. "Anything interesting in that lot?" She nodded at the pile of discarded envelopes and neat stack of papers he'd accumulated while she bathed.

"There's a letter from Jessica. Listen to this." He picked up a piece of blue notepaper and read:

"Dear Martin,

I wonder how you got on in your search for the music we discussed. Your visit and our conversation got me thinking and I decided to do a bit of sleuthing on my own. I started back in George's things and found a whole suitcase full of photographs collected over many years. Mostly of people long gone and forgotten but I did find some pictures of his grandfather Stanley West and Stanley's father, Michael. You may be interested in seeing them. One is of a group of musicians. Perhaps they were playing your music!

I'm going away over Christmas and shan't be back until early January. I'll telephone when I return and perhaps we can get together again. If you would be interested, of course. I must admit to a degree of curiosity about that music. I remember the fascination of that melody very clearly.

Yours sincerely,
Jessica Harrow"

"Call her," said Nina. "Have you already?"

"No. I was waiting for you to wake up."

Martin fingered the letter, licked his lips and pursed them. What he was going to say? Surely not backing off again? Hadn't they had that conversation already? She sipped her tea, face and body flushed warm from the bath, mind alive with the excitement of

Jessica's find. "Nina?"

"What?"

"You had a nightmare last night. Do you remember it?" he asked, almost cautious, afraid of her reaction.

"I didn't wake up," she said obliquely. What had so frightened him about a nightmare of hers? One she didn't even remember?

"You screamed out 'Save me'."

"And did you?" she asked mildly but her heart thumped a wild beat. A flash of memory, Piers, whirling blackness, terror…

"You didn't cry out to me. You wanted Piers."

Hot blood rose in her body but she said nothing. Martin pinioned her with those hazel eyes that usually regarded her with gentle love.

"What's going on?"

"How do I know?" she snapped. "You know as much if not more about this than I do." Her mouth finished in a firm straight line. Topic closed.

"Do I? I'm not sure about that." He stood up. "We need to buy you a coat."

"Aren't you going to call Jessica?" Nina stayed seated at the red Formica topped table scratching her finger over a chip on the surface. "I'm hungry. Call her while I have some toast."

She looked at him with an expression of such hard, calculating determination he hardly recognised the girl he'd fallen in love with. She got up and pulled the blue curtain aside, grabbed the packet of bread and shoved two slices into the toaster. Arms folded she leaned against the narrow bench and regarded him through impassive dark eyes. Martin held her gaze and they stared at each other like two wary dogs weighing up each other's capabilities.

"Nina, you made love to Piers last night. Not me." The hurt seeped into his voice.

"That's ridiculous," she said loudly.

"I don't think so. It's no more ridiculous than any of the other things that have happened. And it's happened before. In Sydney." The flicker of fear in her eyes as his words registered, was unmistakable. Her expression changed. She was his Nina again. He walked across and put his arms around her. She rested her head on his shoulder and clung to him like a child.

"I'm frightened," she whispered.

"So am I. We'd be crazy not to be."

"He comes to me when I sleep." She paused. "He's so attractive. That's such an inadequate word. He's unbelievable. I can't resist him. He's in my head. He controls me completely."

"We have to work out how to stop him." Martin swallowed a surge of jealous, bile filled rage. He gripped her tightly.

"And last night something different happened." Nina looked up at him, confusion and fear twisting her features. "I was Piers, waiting for Mira in a grove of trees. It was hot. Daytime."

"You were Piers? Has that happened before?"

"No, but that's not the weirdest thing. I saw Mira and she was me."

"What do you mean, you?"

"She had my face but I was Piers waiting for her. And I absolutely adored her. More than anything. It was the fiercest most consuming passion…"

She stopped as a realisation hit her. "Do you think he did that deliberately so that we'd, I'd, know? How he feels, felt? To keep us going?"

"He hasn't done it to me. I don't dream about him, thank God," said Martin. "He just wants to use me."

"And don't you think he's using me?" she asked incredulously. "You think I'm enjoying this?"

"Of course not! But you must stay with me, Nina. We have to do this together. Separately we don't have a hope."

She clung to him, closer now than she'd been last night when they made love.

****

Jessica invited them to her house this time. They went that same afternoon travelling by Underground and briskly walking the last few blocks fighting an icy wind direct from the Arctic. Nina, huddled into her thick new navy blue parka was grateful Martin had ignored her protests and insisted on shopping first. Her feet were warm for the first time since their arrival, in stout laced ankle boots and thick socks.

Jessica greeted Martin like an old friend. Nina hadn't known what to expect from his vague description but the woman who ushered them into her home reminded her of a bird—a diminutive grey-haired bright-eyed finch dressed in smart charcoal wool slacks, a slim-fitting green sweater with a casually knotted scarf in shades of reds and greens and gypsy-style gold hoop earrings.

Her skin had a rosy glow and the welcoming smile never wavered as she darted about taking their coats and hanging them in the hall cupboard.

"Come in, come in. You must be frozen," she said to Nina. "Coming from Sydney in the summer. This weather is hopeless. I don't know why I don't pack up and move to Barbados."

She herded them through to the living room. Nina sat on the cream-covered couch. Martin waited for Jessica to take her seat opposite then sat beside Nina.

"Now, let's get straight to the point," Jessica said. "That's what we all want, don't we?" She cocked an inquiring eye at Martin and he nodded.

"Before we see your photos, though," he said. "We'd like you to look at something and tell us what you think."

Nina opened her bag and pulled out the precious envelope containing the Shadow Music. She carefully placed the violin part on the low table in front of her.

"Can you tell us if that is George's handwriting?" She pointed to the words scrawled across the top.

Jessica picked a pair of gold rimmed half moon glasses off the coffee table and perched them on her nose. She peered at the inscription.

"Oh my, oh my," she said. "Well I never." She unconsciously clutched her hands together, fingers intertwined, knuckles white under the pressure.

"What is it?" asked Nina softly.

"That's George's writing but I've never seen that before. I mean, when he showed me the parts all those years ago he hadn't written on it."

She raised a worried face and looked from one to the other. "That would mean he played the music himself. Before he sent the parts away. I was so sure he never..." She closed her mouth firmly, obviously unwilling to admit he might have deceived her.

Martin said, "We wondered why he didn't play himself. Why he gave the violin part to the other violinist who, incidentally, detested it."

"He did play it," said Nina. "Otherwise he wouldn't have written what he did. I wonder if…" She stopped and looked at Martin. "Should we?"

"I think we should. Jessica may know more than she thinks about it."

"About what?" demanded Jessica.

"The Shadow Music," said Martin and between them they gave her a relatively concise rundown of their experiences to date. Jessica sat silent throughout, her grey eyes giving nothing away, her face alert and interested as she listened.

When Martin finished with their surprise at reading her letter that morning she didn't utter a word for several long moments. Nina met Martin's eye. Was she about to make a frantic dash for the telephone and call the police or the lunatic asylum?

Jessica cleared her throat, swallowed and said, "If I hadn't heard that melody myself I would think you two were completely and utterly barking mad. As it is, I believe every word you've told me."

A collective relieved exhalation whooshed through the room. Jessica stood up and went across to a small antique writing desk. She returned with a bundle of photographs and spread them on the coffee table. Nina and Martin leaned forward eagerly.

"These are the photos I found in that suitcase in the attic." She picked one up. "This is George's mother, Anne, as a baby. His grandmother is holding her and standing beside them is his grandfather."

"Stanley West." Nina gazed at the man whose initials appeared on the music. In the manner of all early photographs the subjects posed stiffly, staring at the camera as though at a firing squad. "When was she born?"

"October,1903. All the men wore those dreadful mutton chop whiskers. The height of fashion." She gave a little titter of laughter. "And the women all looked terribly fierce. Probably from wearing those shocking corsets."

"So this must have been taken in 1903 or at latest, early 1904. Anne's only a few months old." Nina studied the faded sepia toned figures.

"This is another of Stanley and his bride on their wedding day. Her name was Elizabeth."

"What a lovely wedding dress. Look at that veil."

"Yes that would have been in 1902. April, I think."

"How do you know the dates of these things?" asked Martin.

"I told you I've been doing a bit of sleuthing," Jessica said proudly. "Family records, Births, Deaths, Marriages, that sort of thing. The internet is very useful."

She picked up another photo. "This is the one I thought might be most interesting, and since you've filled me in, I know it is."

Six faces gazed solemnly out from the past. They held musical instruments and one sat at an upright piano. The shot had been taken in a living room, complete with potted plants and heavy velvet curtains. Nina scanned it eagerly then relaxed. Piers wasn't there. Someone else held the violin, a nondescript thin-faced man.

"This one is Michael, Stanley's father." Jessica pointed.

"He's Irish," said Martin. "Has a lilting accent and a soft, gentle voice."

"However do you know that?" Jessica exclaimed. Then she remembered. "Oh."

Martin nodded. "I heard him."

"I don't know any other names except this one, his cousin Arthur." She indicated the pianist. "I'm sorry."

"That's all right," said Nina. "We do."

Martin said, "That's Jasper with the flute."

Nina gazed at the pale, earnest-looking man trying to reconcile the flat, two-dimensional image with the voice and flute playing she had heard for months.

"But Piers isn't there." Nina looked at Martin. "We don't know any of the others, do we?"

"When was this taken?" he asked Jessica.

"Probably early 1900's. Michael was born in 1848 and Stanley in 1872. I'd guess Michael to be around fifty-five, wouldn't you?"

Martin sighed, as disappointed as Nina. "That makes this photo well past the time we're dealing with. They all sound young, don't you think, Nina? Jasper looks about fifty as well and I think he's only in his late twenties or even younger."

"It's hard to tell from voices though," objected Jessica.

"True. But we know they were involved with the Golden Dawn group and they fizzled out early in the 1900's."

Why were they gasbagging about what was so obvious? "We both know Piers is young. He's no more than thirty."

Jessica gave Nina a startled almost hurt look. A frown chased across Martin's face. She must have sounded as annoyed as she was. She modified her tone as she went on. "It's obviously a different group to ours. There are too many of them for starters. And I've never heard a piano. Ever." She slumped back into the couch. "What a fizzer."

"I'll bring the tea, shall I?" Jessica got up hurriedly and darted out of the room before either could say a word.

"Well, now what?" asked Nina.

"We stay and have tea and we'll be polite to Jessica," said Martin abruptly. "She could help us a lot. Don't you see?"

"No."

"She has access to all sorts of information and she doesn't think we're crazy."

Nina scowled but Piers said, *"The music is here. You are close to the music. I feel it."*

His voice ran through her brain like an electric shock, jolting her upright, too surprised to hide her reaction from Martin. His eyes narrowed.

"What happened?"

"Piers just told me the music is here. He can feel we're close to the music." Wide-eyed she stared at him. He reached out and clutched her fingers in his.

Jessica re-entered the room holding a tray laden with cups, plates, fruitcake and a teapot in a brightly coloured, knitted cosy. She put it down carefully on the table and began setting out cups and saucers.

"Milk, sugar?" she asked, teapot held at the ready.

"Just milk for both of us," said Martin. He took the rose patterned cup and saucer Jessica offered him. "Thank you."

"Jessica, I'm sorry if I sounded rude just now." Nina took her cup. Martin was right. They needed Jessica. Piers needed her.

"You were disappointed. That's understandable." The cheerful smile reappeared. "I should apologise for building up your hopes."

"*Find the music,*" said Piers.

"No, no, not at all." Nina took a deep breath. "Do you think George may have kept some of the music instead of sending it away? I mean, he obviously got rid of the parts we've found but what if he kept the score, for example? Is that possible?"

"I suppose so. But he was adamant about getting rid of it." Jessica frowned into her tea. "If he did it can't have been put with the other music or Martin would have found it at the shop."

"*Find the violin. Find the instrument,*" Piers insisted.

"Did you keep his violin?" asked Nina.

"Yes, I did. He loved it so much I was reluctant to part with it." She smiled sadly. "It's a little reminder of him for me when I go into the room he used as a practice room. I have my computer in there now."

"Maybe he put the music with his violin and the pieces he was playing regularly."

"Oh, he never played that piece again. I would've heard it," said Jessica quite definitely. "It frightened him too much, I think."

"It's very, very difficult—impossible—to destroy it," Martin reminded her gently. "We were amazed that he could have even managed to post the parts away and not be forced to keep playing. Especially as he had the violin music. Piers' part is the main one, the most powerful."

"Perhaps he didn't," said Nina. Piers knew he hadn't. That was why they were here. "Perhaps he kept the score and it's still here."

Jessica bounced to her feet with surprising energy for her age. "Why are we sitting here then? Let's look."

As they mounted the stairs to the first floor, excitement built with each step. Piers was almost a tangible presence by her side as Jessica opened the door to a room she called "George's study." She snapped on the light before darting across to drag apart the heavy forest green drapes and let in some feeble winter light.

Nina had already spied the violin case on a shelf of the bookcase which took up one whole wall of the room, floor to ceiling. Piers breathed hard in her ear. She glanced over her shoulder expecting to catch a glimpse of him but there was nothing.

"There! There!" he whispered hoarsely.

"May I?" she asked, barely waiting for Jessica's nod before lifting the instrument down and placing it on the desk. Piers fingers wrestled with hers as she unzipped the blue outer covering but he paused before opening the case itself. Nina slid her hand between the cover and the hard case and smiled triumphantly as she pulled out a sheaf of music.

Piers gave a shout of triumph and cried, *"There it is. You have it! Play! You must play. Now!"*

Surely they heard him? How could they not? But both Martin and Jessica were transfixed by the music in her hand. They hadn't heard a thing.

"We have to play it, Martin," she said.

Jessica clutched her hands together. She opened her mouth but words failed to emerge. She sat down hurriedly on the leather swivel chair behind George's desk. Nina spread the sheets of music before them on the polished wood of the desk.

It was a score. Six staves of music joined by a thick bar line at the beginning and end of each line. Ten unbound handwritten pages. Across the top was written in the same familiar elegant script as on their own parts, "Shadow Music." The initials P de C were printed neatly in the top right-hand corner.

"Piers wrote it." exclaimed Martin.

"Of course. Who else?" Nina scoffed. "We knew that already."

Martin frowned and shot her a suspicious look. Her voice had changed—firmer, harsher, the tone of a leader.

"We have to play it," she said again.

"How can we play it? We don't have the instruments. And you can't play the violin part properly." Piers had somehow invaded Nina once more. The selfish, obsessed lunatic. He had to fight the maniac, keep control of Nina.

"Piers will play it," she said.

Jessica gasped. "Oh, my goodness."

"Nina. We don't have the instruments. We can't."

"Sven can play the bass. Look there's a double bass line as well as a cello." She stabbed a finger at the relevant part.

"No, I won't ask him again. And we can't ask a guitarist to play. You know we can't." He barely recognised the girl behind the ferocious grimace and the raging fire in her eyes. Going head to head and arguing with her was pointless. Arguing with Piers, in other words. He changed tack. "Fine. Calm down. We'll have to think about it very carefully."

He sat down on a straight-backed chair, legs stuck out in front of him. Nina remained standing, chest rising and falling with each furious breath but the anger slowly subsided. Jessica, white-faced, swivelled her head from one to the other.

"Do you know Piers' other name?" she asked eventually.

"Piers de Crespigny," said Nina shortly. "He told Martin. If you're wondering how we know."

"Perhaps I can track him down on the internet." She sat up straighter. "Well, relatives at least. I'll give it a try tonight." She smiled at them both, colour returning to her cheeks. "You gave me quite a turn then, Nina."

Nina looked at Jessica blankly for several long moments, then her face softened and her lips curved in the smile Martin loved.

"I'm sorry, Jessica." The smile faded and her voice shook slightly as she continued, "Piers...sometimes he talks for me. I don't know how to stop him."

"Can't you just not have anything to do with the music?"

"No," they said simultaneously. Nina walked across to Martin and took his hand. He returned the pressure, trying to send comfort and reassuring strength through his touch.

"George couldn't either, could he? And he was stronger than either of us because he managed at least to separate the parts," he said.

"Piers is the key to this. We must find out about Piers," announced Jessica firmly. "He wrote the thing. There must be something about him somewhere."

"I suppose," said Martin slowly. "We could ask him."

Nina turned to Jessica. "That's how Martin found out his full name. I can't do it. I'm not strong enough to resist him. You'll have to," she said, looking Martin directly in the eye.

No one spoke until he said, "What will I ask him?"

"What the date is and where he is. No, where he was at the time—you know?" suggested Jessica. "Also find out Mira's full name, then I can do a search on her." She laughed. "I can't believe we're having such a discussion, seriously, about talking to a ghost."

Nina nodded. "I know. But we're long past thinking we're mad. Look at what George wrote. He knew, too."

"That's true. What shall we do now?" asked Jessica. "This looks like a lengthy process. I think dinner might be a good idea. You'll stay with me, of course?" Before they could reply she'd bustled across and drawn the curtains against the winter darkness which had fallen stealthy and unnoticed as they talked. "I've a good thick hotpot ready to heat up. All we need do is add some extra vegetables. After dinner we can decide on a plan of attack."

She stood with her hand on the study door handle, her eyes betraying her anxiety that they stay and not leave her alone with the realisation her husband had been haunted by a spectre from the past. And that her beloved George had deceived her, however well intentioned that deception may have been.

"Thank you very much. That sounds perfect," said Martin.

Nina said at the same time, "Lovely. Thank you."

By common unspoken consent they didn't mention the Shadow Music, Piers, or Mira while peeling potatoes and scraping carrots. Jessica poured them all generous glasses of sherry.

"To warm us up," she said and shooed them out of the kitchen so that she could tidy up.

The heavy sweet wine went straight to Nina's head. She sagged onto the living room couch in front of the gas fire, leaning back into the soft cushions. Martin sat beside her.

"She's fantastic, isn't she?"

"Mmm," murmured Nina. Her eyes drooped shut. The room was warm and cosy. She was dimly aware Martin took the glass from her fingers and kissed her cheek.

"Come to me," said Piers. "Come to me."

"Where?" she cried.

"We must be together."

"Where are you?" she cried again frantically. "Piers? Where are you?"

Her eyes flew open. Martin and Jessica leant over her both with anxious faces. Martin held her hand tightly. Warm, comforting, and above all, real.

"Did he tell you?" asked Jessica.

"Tell me what?" she asked, blinking at the light.

"Where he was. You cried out, 'Piers, where are you?' " said Martin.

"No. It was dark." Nina frowned. "I was in bed. And hot. A hot night."

"Summertime," said Jessica with great satisfaction. "He must have wanted her to meet him somewhere. Maybe they were having an illicit affair. How romantic."

"But where and when and who is Mira?" asked Martin.

"After dinner we shall combine our formidable collective brain power and find out," said Jessica.

Chapter Eleven

"What if I play the melody while you meditate?" suggested Nina. They were in George's study again. Nina had unpacked the violin and stood fiddling with the tuning pegs and plucking strings. Jessica sat at her computer already typing in Piers' name to find family details.

"I suppose that would give us the most power," said Martin dubiously. "Just keep playing the first bit but go into the second part if things get too hairy. Right?"

"All right," said Nina. "Jessica's here. She'll grab the violin if I can't stop playing."

Jessica smiled weakly at Nina's attempt at a joke.

"This terrifies me," she said.

"Me too," said Martin with a grimace riding on a deeply drawn breath.

"Ready?" Nina tucked George's violin under her chin. It was a lovely instrument, better than hers back in Sydney.

Martin sat comfortably cross-legged on the floor on a small cushion and closed his eyes. His breathing slowed. Nina began to play. The effect was instantaneous. Piers was furious.

"*Why aren't you playing all the parts?*" he demanded. "*Where are the other parts?*" Nina played on with shaking fingers, tears trembling on her lids.

She'd never heard him speak like that. He loved her, he said so.

"Why? Why? Why? Don't you care?" he ranted. *"You're pitiful, I thought you were different. I trusted you to help me."*

Tears streamed down her cheeks but she kept her eyes fixed on Martin sitting so relaxed and composed on the floor in front of her. She played the melody through three times. Piers' abuse was unbearable, his escalating rage unbearable. At the end of the third repeat she couldn't continue, shaking uncontrollably from head to toe whispering, "I'm sorry, I'm sorry," through her tears.

Martin stayed seated, eyes closed. Nina met Jessica's equally tear-stained gaze. Her sweet cheerful face wore an expression of grief so profound Nina moved quickly across and wrapped her arms around the small body. At her touch Jessica broke free from the spell. She took a tissue from her pocket and dabbed at her eyes and nose. She patted Nina's arm and smiled.

"Goodness me," she murmured and sniffed.

Martin stirred. His eyes opened and he stretched his arms over his head.

"Wow." He stood up and opened his arms to Nina who rushed across to clutch him to her.

"What did he say to you? He was furious with me. He was horrible." More tears trickled down her cheeks.

Martin hugged her close. "It's okay. I talked to him. I found out some things. Her name is Miranda Templeton and she lived in a village called Cutting Marsh."

"I know Cutting Marsh. It's near Plymouth," Jessica interrupted, clapping her hands together.

"Anything else?"

He shook his head. "He faded out. He was disturbed. More so than usual, that is."

"He was really angry that I was playing by myself," said Nina. "He kept asking why? Didn't I care? Things like that. I couldn't bear it." She sniffed and swiped fingers across her eyes. "Why did we hear him differently?"

"I've no idea. Did you hear anything, Jessica?" he asked.

"No voices. But that melody is filled with the most profound sadness it made me cry. It's absolutely the saddest music I've ever heard. It's exactly the melody George played to me." Her eyes misted over again and she wielded her sodden tissue vigorously.

"Did you discover anything online?" Martin asked.

"Yes, I did." She instantly became businesslike and brusque, sat up straight, took a piece from the desk, stuffed her tissue into her pocket and read aloud.

"Piers de Crespigny came from Jamaica. His family had a coffee plantation there. There is a bit of information about his brother who ran the business. Ambrose, the brother, went into politics so he features in that respect. Piers seems to have been the black sheep of the family. He was born in 1859 in London but grew up in Jamaica and returned to England in about 1885. He died in 1892."

"Black sheep?" said Martin.

"Because he was a violinist. An extraordinarily good one. We may find more about him if we look at newspaper archives for concert details and reviews of that period. Now." Jessica looked at them solemnly. "Piers was murdered."

Nina wailed in shock. "Murdered? How do you know?"

"It caused a scandal at the time for his political brother."

"Who murdered him?" asked Martin.

"I don't know. It doesn't go into details about Piers. The implication is that he met a fitting end."

"Poor Piers," Nina said. "No wonder he's so sad. Wandering in torment for eternity. His soul can't rest."

"Can you find out about Miranda Templeton?" asked Martin.

Jessica typed and they all stared at the screen waiting for the search results to appear.

"She must have died before Piers," said Martin. "Before 1892."

"Or at the same time," said Nina.

"No, it'd have to be before or he wouldn't be trying to revive her."

"Two Miranda Templetons. One Amelia Miranda Templeton. Three Miranda Temples. Cross out those and that one. Let's try these two," muttered Jessica and hit more keys. They all three craned forward eagerly.

One was too young, born in 1947. The other was too old, born 1826.

Jessica brought up Amelia Templeton with similar results. The fully displayed name caught Nina's eye. Amelia Miranda Sung Templeton.

"That's unusual, isn't it?" she asked. "Sung was my Chinese grandfather's family name."

"She was born in 1852. Could be our girl's mother." Jessica added as an afterthought, "Unless Piers preferred older women."

Martin, excited, said. "Remember how we

wondered why Piers chose us, Nina? What if you are related to Mira? Way, way back. If you both have a Chinese ancestor in common?"

"Amelia Templeton married Daniel Templeton in 1870 but there's no further information except that she had two children. She must have died in childbirth if she's Miranda's mother because she died in 1874. Not much time to have two children, poor thing," observed Jessica.

"If that's the case then Mira must have been only a girl when she died. If she died before Piers in 1892. She couldn't have been more than twenty-two at most, younger if she was the second child," said Martin thoughtfully.

"It's so sad," sobbed Nina, turning away to wipe her eyes furiously. "Piers loved her beyond everything. He wants her so desperately. We have to help him. We must do as he asks, Martin."

"Not tonight. It's late and we have to get home."

"But Martin!"

"He's waited over a hundred years Nina. He can wait another few days. Anyway what can we possibly do? I don't know how to set a soul to rest, do you?"

Nina set her mouth in a stubborn line. She couldn't answer those questions and at that moment she hated Martin for pointing them out. A hot surge of familiar rage flowed through her body but she bit her tongue and said nothing.

"Would you like to spend the night here?" asked Jessica. "It's very late and probably freezing out."

Martin looked at Nina and received no response other than a shrug and a turned cheek as she began to pack away George's violin.

"I think we would like to stay. Thank you, Jessica."

"I'll get the spare room ready then." She touched Martin reassuringly on the arm as she passed and whispered, "I understand now, Martin. Don't worry."

Martin smiled bleakly at Jessica and turned back to Nina.

"Nina," he said firmly. "We'll work this out together. We need sleep now."

"We have to put it on the tape. All of it."

Nina's eyes shone unnaturally bright, her face set and determined when she faced him. "Now," she said with exactly the tone of authority. Piers' tone.

Martin hesitated, calculated swiftly. "I don't have my flute with me," he said.

Nina seemed to deflate before his eyes and regain her normal self. She wrinkled her brow as she stared at him.

"No, no, that's right, you don't," she said vaguely as she walked across and wrapped her arms around him.

"Nina darling, we have to stick together," whispered Martin into her hair as he hugged her tight. So tight he could keep Piers out, keep him from invading her mind, her body, her sanity.

"Piers is so powerful, I don't think I can resist him."

"Just keep remembering you love me." He held her away to gaze into her flooded, luminous eyes. "You do, don't you?"

She touched his cheek gently and smiled. "Come on, let's go to bed."

They met Jessica on the landing outside the study, arms loaded with towels and pillow cases. Nina hastily took them from her.

"I'm sorry. I can make up the bed."

"It's already done. I've put on an extra quilt but I suspect you'll keep each other warm, won't you?" Grey eyes twinkled cheekily as she looked from one to the other.

Martin flushed. Nina laughed.

"Martin embarrasses easily," she confided to Jessica as they followed her up the stairs to the top floor. "It's his English reserve."

"Yes, I know all about English reserve." Jessica opened the door to their room. "Dear George was very proper. Mind you, he had his moments."

Nina giggled and dumped the towels on the bed. "Yes, I know what you mean." She began putting a slip on one of the pillows.

"Excuse me ladies, but would you mind continuing this conversation without me." Martin picked up a towel. "I'm going to the bathroom."

Laughter followed him out the door but he smiled to hear Nina's happy voice as she joked and chatted with Jessica, telling her about Florence back in Sydney. He'd cheerfully be the butt of any joke if he could hear that laughter. He'd been wrong about Jessica. She wasn't nearly as proper or as elderly as he'd thought. She'd get on with Florence like a house on fire.

****

She ran constantly. Terrified. Hot. Cold.

A field of grass stretched endlessly into the distance whichever way she turned. The sun beat down on her head searing into her brain. A man on a big brown horse galloped across the field toward her and she veered away toward a grove of thick, cool, green trees but her skirts tangled around her legs and she fell with the thunder of hooves loud in her ears, drumming closer and closer.

The scent of roses wafted in the air and she lifted her head to see where the scent was coming from but all around were thick tufts of grass. The hoof beats were upon her and she covered her head with her arms, sobbing in terror.

Then it was pitch black. Was she dead? Trampled by the horse?

Rain pelted down. Her dress clung to her legs like clawing fingers, chill water soaked her to the skin. Something lay on her, crushing her chest so she couldn't breathe through the pain and the fear.

Then she was running again in the darkness. Terrified. Sobbing. Wanting only to reach Piers. But she didn't know where he was, just that she had to reach him. Piers was waiting. Somewhere.

Trees. Stately ancient oaks, dark, green and cool in their silence. Terrifying.

Nina woke with a cry on her lips, heart pounding in fear. She lay panting and exhausted in the bed, watching as the feeble winter morning sun struggled through a gap in the curtains. Martin slept beside her. He had such certainty and strength. If only she had the same but she didn't and she needed him to give her an anchor, a safe harbour.

In the months since they'd met he'd gained weight, his skin had tanned and his face no longer had that gaunt, haunted look. She trusted him to keep her sane through this torment. He and Jessica. Without them she'd be lost to Piers and his dark, forceful, hypnotic attraction, living in a twilight world of fantasy and dreams which became increasingly frightening.

He was stronger than ever now. When he spoke to her as a lover she was completely powerless to resist, wanting to do exactly as he asked heedless of consequence. How could he be stopped? How could they lay his soul to rest? Who had murdered him and why? Was his murderer brought to justice? Did Mira have anything to do with it or was her death earlier and unrelated to his? And why had she died so young?

At breakfast Nina related her nightmarish dreams and voiced those questions which tormented her.

"Piers doesn't seem to be bothered about being murdered," said Martin thoughtfully as he sprinkled brown sugar onto the steaming bowl of porridge Jessica had placed in front of him. "He only talks about Mira and the Shadow Music."

"She was his great passion. She and his music." Jessica gazed at nothing, porridge ladle held poised over the saucepan. "Terribly romantic."

"Terribly terrifying," said Nina wryly.

"I'm sorry. Of course it is." Jessica plonked the ladle into the porridge and doled out another bowlful for herself. Nina had opted for toast and marmalade which she picked at listlessly.

"You'd think the ghost or spirit of a murdered man would only be interested in revenge," continued Martin. "But he's not. I wonder what happened. Where exactly is Cutting Marsh?"

"Close to Plymouth. Only ten miles or so to the northeast. Some very dear friends of mine live there. They bought the old manor house in the 1960's. Broome Hall. We used to laugh and call it the Broome Cupboard although it's large and rambling, hardly a cupboard." She paused. "We should go there, shouldn't we?"

Martin nodded meeting her bright excited eyes.

Nina said in a strained voice. "How will we get there?"

"Go to Cutting Marsh!" Piers urged her but she fought hard to make him recede. She poured herself more tea and concentrated on Jessica's reply. The thought of going to that place frightened her in a way she couldn't articulate even in her mind. An uneasy, fearful, heavy dread that had nothing directly to do with her doubts about Piers.

"We could go by train to Plymouth, and then take a bus or taxi but probably the quickest and most convenient way is to drive," Jessica said.

"We'd have to hire a car," said Martin.

"I can borrow mine back from my nephew, I'm sure. I gave it to him when I stopped driving a year ago. The traffic is horrendous in London so I gave up. I'll call him right now. Can you drive, Martin?"

"Yes. While you're organising that, Nina and I should go home and pack a few things." He took a deep breath. "I have the feeling we're finally going to sort this out."

Piers said, *"Soon. Soon we will be together. Play the music and you will be mine forever as we were meant to be."*

Nina gripped Martin's hand. She screwed her eyes tight shut. Her heart skipped a beat and then resumed at a breathless gallop.

Martin said hoarsely, "Nina? Is he there?"

Nina opened terrified eyes and her voice shook so much she could hardly speak. She opened and closed her mouth, swallowed and said, "He said, 'Play the music and you will be mine forever as we were meant to be'."

Martin and Jessica froze as the change in words registered exactly as they had with her.

Nina whispered, "Did you notice? He said 'you' not Mira and 'we'. Does that mean he thinks I'm Mira, that he's reincarnated her as me?"

****

Cutting Marsh, September 1892

That night Piers stood in her room again. Miranda expected him this time but he still shocked her, appearing so suddenly. She sat up, wide-eyed.

"Piers," she whispered. "Piers, speak to me."

"Mira. You can see me, hear me?"

"Yes. How is it so?" Her voice trembled with excitement and fear. He looked so real, standing beside the bed in shirtsleeves and grey trousers, dark eyes shining, face tense and pale.

"Come to me Mira. Don't desert me. We belong together."

That's what Maggie said. Could it be true? Or was she losing her mind?

"Where shall I come, Piers?"

"Come to me." He was fading, the curtains visible through his body.

"How? Where? Where are you?"

He disappeared completely. She lay on the bed, waiting, watching eagerly and suddenly he was there again.

"Mira. You must come to me. Come now."

"Where?" Almost sobbing in frustration.

"Come." He faded and although she waited he didn't reappear. She sat up and tossed the covers away.

There was only one place he could mean. Their secret place in the oak grove.

Miranda flung off her night gown and dragged on a skirt and blouse. She listened at the bedroom door and heard the murmur of voices as Tyler and her father sat smoking in his study. The door was open. She'd never sneak passed unobserved. Out the window. It wouldn't be the first time although on the other occasions she'd been quite a bit smaller.

She clambered through, hitching her skirt up unceremoniously. Something ripped as she slid across the sill, then she was slipping along the side of the house hoping Tyler's dog wouldn't catch her scent, out through the kitchen garden to the lane at the back of the house and away down the road toward the churchyard.

The sky was pitch black, covered in cloud and with the distant growl of thunder. The storm was approaching and this time might make good its promise. She paused briefly considering whether to run back for a coat. No. Too risky. Miranda hurried on, finding her way by instinct. The road shone paler than the darker grassed verges and she followed it rather than cut across the fields. There would be too many ditches and fences to navigate.

The heavy bulk of the stone church loomed on her left and she quickened her pace as she caught glimpses of pale tombstones rising out of the blackness. A wind sprang up, hot and restless, rustling the leaves in the trees overhanging the church, scraping branches, disturbing the dead. It tugged at her skirt and whipped her loose hair around her cheeks so that she felt the bony skeletal fingers scraping and pawing, clutching and clinging.

Miranda ran, panting and sobbing with fear until the church receded behind her and she caught the familiar, earthy, agricultural smell of cows coming from the fields beside the road. Jenkins's dairy farm. She slowed to a walk and wiped her face with shaking hands. Two large drops of rain plopped onto her sleeve. Then another and another thudded into the dust at her feet and brought welcome coolness. She lifted her face to the black sky. The drops increased in number. Soon she would be soaked to the skin.

A crack of lightning split the night around her. She shrieked and scampered through the gap in the hedge as a gigantic thunder clap deafened her ears. The storm was upon her and she ran in sodden skirts, stumbling and falling as she struggled toward the shelter of the oak grove. And Piers. Her hair hung limp, plastered over her head, blinding her in the driving rain. She slipped and fell again, lying breathless and exhausted in the soaked grass, the stinging rain pelting down on her back, a million tiny hammer blows.

"Piers." Her voice was weak in the cacophony around her. She clutched at tufts of grass to pull herself up. Her long skirt tangled itself around her leg, she fell again after two steps but rose and staggered on toward the dark mass of trees, only twenty or thirty yards away. The wind was furious now. The giant trees groaned and creaked. Tall branches whipped and twisted in agony tortured by the relentless wind and the torrential force of the rain.

She slipped again as she reached the first trees and crawled on hands and knees into the blackness of their shelter. All sense of where she met Piers on those idyllic, hot summer afternoons had fled. Unfriendly and alien now, the oaks, unwilling to accept her, to allow her to witness their torture by the elements. She clung to the nearest trunk. It shuddered under her cold wet hands as she pulled herself up to stand, dragging in heavy, gasping breaths of air, staring with fearful eyes wide against the darkness. In Hell. All around the wind screamed against the roar of the rain and the crash of thunder. Occasional flashes of lightning shocked the darkness and the grove glimmered in shades of black and grey, contorted and unrecognisable. Tears streamed down her face mingling with the rain which still soaked her to the skin despite the relative shelter of the trees.

"Piers," she screamed. "Piers."

She barely heard her own voice. He would never hear her. She had to go deeper into the grove. Miranda let go the gnarled trunk and with arms outstretched stepped tentatively forward.

She grasped another tree and fumbled her way around it with numb fingers. As she moved further from the edge the force of the rain diminished although she knew the storm raged just as strongly outside.

A branch crashed down somewhere to her right. Miranda clung to her tree as a new fear assailed her.

"Piers," she cried again. "Piers, where are you?"

Another branch hurtled down. Miranda sobbed in terror. Her tree shuddered and twisted as if to release itself from her grasp. She let go and ran blindly, panic-stricken, her one thought to get out away from the trees, out into the open where at most she would be soaked with rain. A low flailing branch struck her a numbing blow and she felt warmth on her cheek as blood flowed. Dazed she stumbled on, deafened by the roar of the storm and the shrieks of the trees, her sense of direction completely gone.

****

England, 1999

Martin drove Jessica's silver-grey Saab confidently and well. They left the city early after lunch, hoping to reach Cutting Marsh by nightfall. Drizzly grey rain fell in London but as they left the outer suburbs it stopped, giving way to an icy wind which bowled vast boulders of grey-black cloud across the sky.

"Where will we stay?" asked Nina from the backseat as they sped along the highway southwest toward Dartmoor and Plymouth.

"I rang Rupert and Georgina but they're away in Greece for the winter. We can visit Broome Hall, though. Mrs. Turner, the housekeeper said we should stay at Blackstone Cottage. It's a B&B. She said she would arrange it."

"That's very helpful of her," said Martin.

"Her sister runs it."

"Even more helpful."

"A lot of the villagers have ancestry going back centuries in the area. A visit to the churchyard could be informative," said Jessica.

"Miranda could be buried there," said Nina.

"She probably is," Jessica replied calmly. "Poor soul."

"This weather's atrocious," interrupted Martin, peering out through the windscreen at the lowering grey-black clouds ahead. The wind had picked up since they left the city, buffeting the car. Trees whipped wildly in a tormented dance by the roadside and visibility decreased rapidly as the storm clouds approached. Even as he spoke the first drops of icy rain splashed onto the windscreen. The headlights of oncoming cars shone bravely through the misty gloom.

"Would you like to stop?" asked Jessica.

"No. We should go as far as we can, I think." Martin clutched the steering wheel as an extra strong blast threatened to pluck the car from the roadway. They and their fellow travellers slowed to a crawl as the rain hit, each relying on the small red pinpoints from the tail lights of the car in front.

Nina shivered inadvertently even though the Saab's heater worked extremely well. The closer they got to Cutting Marsh, the less comfortable she felt. The uneasy threatening dread had coalesced into a sick lump of fear sitting heavy in her belly.

"How much further?" she asked.

"We're about half way," answered Jessica.

"With any luck we'll drive through this," said Martin. The rain thundered onto the roof of the car, deafening them so they had to shout to be heard. Several more timid travellers had pulled to the roadside to wait out the cloudburst but Martin battled on, straining to peer through the curtain of water revealed by the straining wipers. Visibility was reduced to mere feet. It seemed to go on forever.

Then suddenly it was over. The drumming on the roof eased to a more normal patter and they could see the car in front clearly again. A farmhouse appeared across the fields on the left and a road speed sign loomed before them, then a large sign with destinations and distances.

"Plymouth 47 miles," read Martin. "Nearly there."

"I could do with a strong cup of tea," said Jessica. "How about you, Nina?" She looked over into the back seat. "Nina, what's the matter? Pull over, Martin."

Martin screeched to a halt on the safety strip, lights flashing and leapt out of the car to wrench open the back door and clutch Nina in his arms.

"Nina! What is it?" Eyes closed she lay in his arms, face pale, completely unresponsive.

Jessica pressed fingers to Nina's wrist. "Her pulse is strong."

"Piers, you bastard," hissed Martin.

"Do you think it's Piers?" Her surprised face turned to him, damp hair wisping into her eyes, drops of rain on her eyelashes.

"Yes. It's Piers all right." Martin lay Nina across the seat and pulled her coat over her. "Come on. Let's get to Cutting Marsh. I want to settle this." He closed the door with a gentle click and got back into the driving seat. Jessica scrambled in and fastened her seat belt.

An hour later they drove into the village of Cutting Marsh.

Chapter Twelve

Rain pelted down, stinging her skin with tiny darts, blinding her, forcing her to her knees in the mud of the field. She clutched at the grassy tussocks and hung her head, shielding her face from the onslaught, gasping for breath.

Piers voice was in her ears urging her on, calling to her, "Come. Come to me."

"I can't," she whimpered and fell full length on the rain-sodden grass as a blast of wind knocked her sideways. She struggled to stand and staggered a few steps before the wind and rain caught her again to hurl her mercilessly to the ground once more. The noise of the storm deafened her. The wind shrieked and howled like a living thing and thunder roared and ranted all around. A shaft of lightning cracked the darkness apart and she caught a glimpse of a grove of dark forbidding trees looming through the rain and mist.

Nina stared in horror.

"No," she screamed, "No," and turned desperately to flee. Away from the trees, away from the darkness and the unnamed terror she knew lurked within.

"Mira, Come to me. Mira," cried Piers.

"Piers," she screamed. "Piers, save me. Where are you?"

Again she fell and the rain drove relentlessly down. Nina closed her eyes and wept, her tears mingling with the rain to wash the mud from her face as she lay sprawled, helpless and weak in the midst of the pasture. Her fingers clutched feebly at the sodden grass under her hands, her cheek fell in despair on the comfortless tussocks.

"Nina?"

Warmth. A gentle featherlight touch of fingers on her cheek. Dry softness beneath her body.

"Nina?"

Her eyes flickered open. Soft yellow light. Warm, cosy something covering her. A man's voice, loving and concerned. Nina? Who was Nina? He was…Piers? No.

"Martin?" she whispered. Tentative, trying out the name.

"Nina, thank God!"

She was scooped up into an embrace so tight she had to struggle to loosen the grip so she could breathe. He let her down gently onto the pillow. Nina. She was Nina.

"Where are we?" Her eyes wouldn't leave his face, the relief was so strong. Martin, her Martin sitting on the bed holding both her hands tightly in his. She smiled weakly and he leant forward and kissed her. A hint of moisture glistened in his eyes as he sat back.

"We're in Blackstone Cottage, Cutting Marsh," he said. "What happened?"

She frowned, thought hard. "I was in a field in the rain. A storm like today except it wasn't a winter storm, I don't think. It wasn't icy cold just soaking wet. Drenching rain." She closed her eyes. A tremor shuddered through her body. "I was terrified. There were trees. I was looking for Piers."

259

"Did you find him?"

Nina opened her eyes and stared around the room. "No. He kept calling me."

"Is he still with you?"

She shook her head. "This cottage is ancient." The walls were made of lumpy white painted plaster with dark wood beams in the low ceiling and a door which didn't quite fit the frame. "It's lovely."

She sat up and swung her legs over the side of the bed, a small double one covered with a patchwork quilt in triangles of pinks and reds. A posy of dried flowers stood on a plain wooden cabinet by the bed, and a chest of drawers against the opposite wall was adorned with a large china dish and jug. Bright floral curtains were drawn across the window. The wind buffeted the outside of the cottage. Trying to get in?

"Where's Jessica?"

"Downstairs talking to the landlady, Mrs. Wookey."

"What on earth did she think when you had to carry me in?"

"We told her you've been ill and fell asleep in the car."

"What's the time? How long was I..." Gone? Dreaming? Lost? It wasn't any of those things.

"A couple of hours."

"Oh. Martin," Nina whispered. A ground swell of fear built up instead, choking her, crushing her. "What's happening to me?"

He held her hand tightly. "I think you were right this morning," he said slowly. "I think Piers thinks you are Mira, and that he's succeeded in reincarnating her as you. Don't ask me how it works. It's crazy but..."

"It's happening," she finished. She pulled her fingers free and lifted both hands to examine them. Both dry and clean, no mud or grass stains. Her body was warm. "It was so real," she whispered. "The trees. They were terrifying. I thought—I knew—I would die there."

Martin pulled her close and she rested her head on his shoulder. A steely core of determination formed inside his belly as he held her. Piers would not take her away from him. He would protect Nina with his life if necessary. He heard Piers' voice suddenly—not in reality, a memory—saying "*Mira, my life, my love*." Piers' love for Miranda had endured beyond the grave, had turned from something beautiful to something obsessive, destructive and dangerous growing ever stronger.

Martin gritted his teeth. Piers had to be stopped, laid to rest, banished, exorcised, killed again or whatever it took. And they had to find a way of destroying the music.

"Are you hungry?" He loosened his grasp slightly. Nina straightened up.

"Starving."

"Mrs. Wookey doesn't do dinners but there's a pub just down the road, she said."

"Sounds good. My first English pub." She gave him a shaky smile.

Martin grabbed her again and held her tight. "I don't know what I'd do without you," he whispered, his cheek on her hair. "I thought I'd lost you. You've no idea how…when you opened your eyes…"

"I know. You've no idea how I felt when I realised it was you and I was back."

Nina responded fervently to his kiss but Jessica tapped tentatively on the door and called softly, "Martin?"

"Hold that thought," he whispered.

****

The storm had passed next morning but heavy, grey clouds hung threatening and gloomy with rain not far away. At breakfast in the tiny dining area Jessica suggested they walk to the churchyard first and then, if the rain held off, walk up to Broome Hall.

Mrs. Wookey provided two large golf umbrellas for Nina and Martin, and with Jessica clutching her bright yellow one they set off. The churchyard was on the far side of the village, a ten-minute walk through chill, damp air with their breath steaming. Ancient trees, skeletal in their winter bareness, stood like sentinels beside the path leading to the main entrance of the squat grey building.

The church faced away from them on this road so they entered the small graveyard surrounding the church, from the side. Martin opened the old wooden lych gate in the low stone wall.

Nina stopped, breathing hard.

"What is it?" He and Jessica immediately closed in, peering anxiously at her face.

"Nothing. I had déjà vu. Just a bit unnerving." She tried a feeble smile to reassure them. Martin took her hand and they moved on.

The ground was soggy. He had to let go her hand because if anyone stepped off the narrow path their boots sank into the spongy grass. Cold drops of water spattered from the overhanging branches as the wind tugged and teased.

Nina's feet took her to the left along an overgrown narrow gravelled path toward a small cross-shaped tombstone leaning at an angle, moss-covered and stained with age. Jessica and Martin followed wordlessly. She stopped and looked down knowing with a chill of foreboding what the words would be before she read them aloud.

"In loving memory of Amelia Miranda Sung Templeton. Born May 29th 1852. Died in childbirth October 15th,1874. Always loved, never forgotten."

Suddenly she was kneeling beside the neatly kept grave with the sun beating hot on her head. "Hello Mama," she whispered, then turned her head to see a man on a tall, bay horse watching her over the stone wall.

"Miranda's mother." Jessica's voice cut in softly. Nina blinked—wet, cold, grey day, neglected grave at her feet, Jessica beside her saying, "I wonder if…" and then, "Here's her father."

She indicated the next tombstone, a rectangular stone standing firmly in the damp grass. "Daniel Alfred Templeton, born 1842, died 1911. How sad for him to bury first his wife and then his daughter so young."

Nina shook her head as the brief images faded. Neither Martin nor Jessica appeared to have noticed anything odd in her manner. She stared at the place by the wall where the man had been, and shivered. His appearance frightened her. The eyes narrowed with suspicion, and the relentless heat contributed frustration and anger but it wasn't just that—he looked merciless. Nina knew she knew him well but his name escaped her. The horse too was familiar, big and brown, broad-chested and strong…

She looked down at Miranda's father's grave. An overwhelming and profound sense of sorrow swamped her but, curiously, she had absolutely no prior knowledge of the inscription. She was positive of that, whereas Amelia's grave was familiar.

"But where's Miranda?" The question burst out. "Wouldn't they bury families close together? And wasn't there another child?"

She began walking slowly along the overgrown path, peering intently at the inscriptions. Martin had wandered further through the rows of dismal stone crosses and memorials. The grass grew long and ill-kempt in this corner of the graveyard. Three large pine trees along the wall gave an even more gloomy aspect.

"Here are some Broomes," he called. "Lots of them. There's an Eleanor who would have been around at the time and a Joseph. And here's an Ethan. He died youngish too. In 1900. He was only thirty, poor man."

They stood staring at the sad reminders of people long gone and mostly forgotten. Reading the names carved on the stones elicited not the slightest flicker of recognition or emotion apart from the natural sombreness always associated with such places. And there was something else. Something missing.

"Piers isn't here," she said.

"Perhaps it's to do with the churchyard, the proximity to the church?" suggested Jessica. "He may not be in a state of grace."

"I think we can safely assume that," said Martin. "He dabbled in all sorts of things the church would have frowned upon. And we don't know he died near here. He certainly wasn't from the village."

"Should we talk to the vicar?" asked Nina. "He

might know something about what happened to these people."

"He'd have to be about a hundred and thirty to remember them." Jessica chuckled. "The parish records might be interesting. I'm quite happy to do that part, if you like."

Martin nodded. "Let's see if we can find him."

The church was locked which Nina found unaccountably disturbing and sad.

"An indication of the times we live in," commented Jessica. "It would never have been locked in Miranda's time. A church was regarded as a sanctuary. No one would've dreamed of vandalising one or stealing the Poor Box."

A note on the door recommended that visitors seek out the Reverend Giles Peabody at the vicarage. An arrow indicated the way. They trooped round the far side of the church and along a more well worn path to a rambling building adjoining the churchyard. A small ship's bell hung by the front door. Martin gave a hefty pull on the bell rope.

"Let me do the talking," said Jessica firmly. The bell tolled through the house. No one came. Rain began tumbling from the leaden sky and they stood under the shelter of the little porch debating what to do next.

"I'll run back and get the car," said Martin. "Then we can drive up to Broome Hall. No sense all of us getting our feet wet."

He dashed down the path jumping puddles as he went, umbrella bobbing. Soon after he left, a small white car pulled up in the driveway, the door slammed and a plump young man scuttled toward them holding his coat over his head in a hopeless attempt to keep himself dry. The ends of a red woollen scarf flapped behind him.

"Good morning, good morning." He fumbled wet keys in his hand searching for the right one. "Are you here to see me? Or perhaps you're just seeking shelter from the storm?" His round face split into a grin as he flung the door open. "Either way, do please come in. It's a stinker of a day." He removed the drenched coat and hung it on one of a row of hooks just inside the front door. His scarf fell to the floor and he fussed about picking it up.

"Reverend Peabody? We did want to speak to you." Jessica followed in his wake as he surged on down the long hallway. Nina closed the front door behind them, a detail he seemed to have forgotten.

His voice came floating back, "Call me Giles. I don't stand on ceremony. Tea? Mrs. Webb usually manages the kitchen for me but she's away visiting her sister this morning. I know there's some of her super fruitcake, and I can come up with a decent brew."

Jessica threw Nina an amused glance over her shoulder. Nina grinned back and shrugged.

"That would be lovely, thank you, Giles," said Jessica.

"Just make yourselves at home, there on your right." He reappeared briefly and waved an arm toward a door next to them. "Shan't be a moment."

Nina and Jessica sat down in the comfortably furnished living room. A log fire burned brightly in a large fireplace but Nina suspected it was more for show than warmth. The vicarage looked too big to be heated solely by wood fires and she couldn't imagine Giles chopping wood. Perhaps Mrs. Webb was a dab hand with an axe as well as in the kitchen.

"Lovely fire," she said to Jessica.

"Yes, it always gives such a homey glow to a room."

Nina giggled suddenly. "I don't think Giles is a hundred and thirty, do you?"

"Not unless he's found the elixir of eternal youth." Jessica smiled, eyes twinkling. She craned her neck to peer out through the window between heavy, red brocade curtains. "We must keep an eye out for Martin."

"Surely he'll see the car and come in," said Nina.

"Tea's up." Giles bustled in with a laden tray. "Are you expecting someone else?"

"Our friend went to get the car. We're staying at Blackstone Cottage," explained Nina. "I'm Nina Lee and this is Jessica Harrow. We did want to see you."

Giles shook their hands in a firm, warm clasp. "I'm glad I came home when I did, then. How can I help?" He poured tea and handed them cups. Rich, dark slices of Mrs. Webb's fruit cake sat temptingly on a plate.

Jessica said, "We're trying to find information about a family who lived here in the 1880's and early1890's. Templeton. Miranda Templeton, to be exact. She died in 1892."

Giles frowned. "May I ask why?" He sipped his tea and peered at them over the rim of the cup looking exactly like Humpty Dumpty peeking over his wall.

Puzzled by his reaction Nina said, "It's a long story. Do you know something about them?"

"You're not reporters of some kind are you?" he asked.

"Hardly," said Jessica as Nina said, "No, no. It's

personal."

Giles looked from one to the other as if assessing their veracity. They must have passed muster because he said, "I imagine you saw the tombstones in the churchyard?" They nodded in unison. "Her parents. He was the doctor in Cutting Marsh for nearly forty years. I've only been vicar here for two years so I don't know all the details but some people still talk about the Templeton scandal. More a tragedy really, by today's standards. Moral standards were rather rigid in Victorian England, especially in the country."

Nina put her cup down before her shaking hand spilled the lot.

"Perhaps we should wait for Martin," suggested Jessica. "So he hears it firsthand too."

"Are you related to the Templetons?" Giles asked Nina, surprising her. Would they have been of Chinese ancestry? Unlikely.

"Me? No, I don't think so. Although Sung was my Chinese grandfather's family name on my mother's side."

"Really?" The interest on his face was unmistakable. "I ask because you resemble a painting of Miranda hanging in Broome Hall. It was done when she was about eighteen. Quite extraordinary."

"I've never seen that," exclaimed Jessica. "Rupert and Georgina are old friends and we used to visit quite a lot when my husband was alive," she explained.

"Rupert found it in a storeroom last year. He was quite taken with it. Her looks were remarkably striking. Very exotic features."

"Do you believe in spirits?" Nina asked. Two startled faces turned abruptly toward her. She must have spoken louder than she thought, or more harshly.

"Well, the Holy Spirit, obviously," Giles said. "But I'm assuming you mean the ghostly type, apparitions and clanking chains, midnight moaning and so on?"

"Along those lines, yes," interrupted Jessica before Nina could follow up her question.

"I also assume you mean in relation to Cutting Marsh and in particular the Templeton's?" asked Giles slowly. He looked directly at Nina and she nodded once. "There is a local tale about a ghost which haunts the area but I can't say I subscribe to the belief."

"Whose ghost?" asked Nina. Surely she wasn't a ghost. Not Miranda.

"The story goes that it's a man, a grief-stricken man searching for his love. Some say it's Miranda Templeton's lover, others that it dates from much longer ago, well before the Templeton scandal." He shrugged. "Who can say? I've never seen him—or rather, it—myself."

There was a brisk ring from the ship's bell and Giles excused himself to answer it. Nina peered through the window.

"It's Martin." The Saab was parked behind Giles' little runabout. Voices echoed down the hall then Martin appeared, smiling and rubbing his hands together against the cold. Giles darted back in with another teacup.

"We've been discussing ghosts," he said cheerfully. "Not that I subscribe to any other than the Holy kind." He chortled and the others joined in with dutiful little chuckles.

Jessica said, "Giles tells us there are stories of a ghost in the area. A grief-stricken man searching for his lost love."

"He also tells us there was a scandal about the Templeton's concerning Miranda. We were waiting for you to come back before Giles told us." Nina glanced at Giles.

"Go ahead." Martin settled himself beside Nina and took her hand securely in his.

"Well." Giles pursed his lips. He frowned and seemed to order his thoughts before beginning his tale. "The Templeton's were well known and respected in the village. Daniel Templeton was the doctor. He had a young wife and that fact itself caused rather a stir in the village. Not that she was younger," he hastened to say, "but that she had foreign blood. Chinese to be exact."

"How on earth did that come about in those days?" asked Jessica. "I can imagine the fuss it would have caused!"

"Yes indeed. Daniel travelled extensively as a young man. Remember, England had a vast Empire, and I can only assume they met somewhere overseas. Hong Kong or even Shanghai, perhaps? Amelia was only part Chinese apparently, and was extremely beautiful, but it says a great deal about their love for each other and of Daniel, that they were prepared to defy convention. Anyway he brought her back here and set up as the local doctor when the old one died. They had two children. First Tyler and then Miranda. Tragically Amelia died in childbirth. Miranda grew up in the care of her father, who never remarried, and a housekeeper. She was rather wild and independent, spoiled by a doting, grieving father and fiercely protected by the older brother. When she was eighteen Miranda was engaged to the local squire's son Ethan

Broome."

"We saw his tombstone," interrupted Martin.

"Yes. The Broomes didn't have a family crypt. They are all buried in the churchyard."

"Is it Ethan's ghost?" asked Jessica.

"No, it's supposed to be Miranda's illicit lover." Giles smiled, obviously a man who loved an audience and relished the telling of a good tale. "Now—the squire held a summer ball every year. That year, 1892, it was scorchingly hot—they were in drought conditions—and Miranda met and fell in love with one of the musicians in the orchestra the squire had hired to play for the festivities. This was scandalous of course, and Miranda and her lover must have known full well the impossibility of their affair."

Nina gasped. Martin gripped her hand tightly. Jessica sat forward anxious not to miss one word. Giles scanned their faces obviously delighted with the rapt attention of his audience.

"But Miranda being the sort of girl she was, didn't care, and her lover would have been more than happy to take advantage of a beautiful and innocent young girl. There was no question of their marrying." Nina stiffened and made to object but Martin squeezed her hand and she bit her lip even though the rage was building. "He had her absolutely besotted and they met secretly in a grove of oaks a mile or so out along the Plymouth road. As I said the weather had been absurdly hot and it finally broke in a cataclysmic storm. Miranda was waiting for her lover in their meeting place and was caught outside. He stayed safely back at his rooms in Plymouth until the storm passed and then ventured out in case she decided to go after all. He found her crushed under a tree branch in the grove. She died."

Again the annihilating weight crushed down on Nina's chest as she gasped for breath. Martin held her tightly, both frantic hands on her upper arms. Their faces swam before her as if through a mist. Martin the closest, intent, his mouth opening and closing as he spoke to her, Giles staring in horrified concern, Jessica pale and anxious clutching her hands together as if in prayer. The roaring in her ears subsided and her breath flowed freely once more. Martin's voice sounded as if the volume had been restored suddenly to a video picture.

"Nina. Are you all right?"

"It's never affected anyone like that before," Giles said. His worried gaze flew from one face to the other.

"Nina is very responsive to this sort of thing, very sensitive," Jessica said. She made it sound perfectly natural.

"Psychic?" asked Giles.

"In a way, yes."

Nina lay back against the cushions of the couch, incapable of sitting upright, the strength sucked from her body. She fixed anxious eyes on Giles. Martin held her hand tightly.

"What happened to P...her lover?" she whispered hoarsely. "Afterward?"

Giles looked at Martin. "Should I continue?"

"Yes, please go on."

"Please," croaked Nina.

"He was blamed for her death," said Giles, although his previous delight in the retelling of a juicy story had gone. "Of course everyone was horrified at what had been going on. The man wasn't even properly

English. He came from somewhere else, a foreigner, one of the colonies. The West Indies, or Australia maybe?" He smiled tentatively at Nina. "And it was rumoured he'd entranced her somehow, had her under his spell. Witchcraft. Voodoo." He chuckled and then stifled it quickly. "He certainly did, poor dear, misguided girl. The brother was furious, her father heartbroken and the fiancé devastated. What a tragedy all round." The round face took on an unaccustomed gloom.

"Where is she buried?" Nina sat forward. Giles glanced warily at Jessica but she was regarding him as intently as was Nina.

"The minister at the time refused her burial in the churchyard." He spread his hands and grimaced. "I must say I'm not proud of the attitude of my predecessor. Very harsh. The Broome family made a plot available on the estate. At the insistence of her fiancé. He must have loved her dearly and shown a truly Christian spirit of forgiveness."

"And her lover?" asked Martin.

"I'm sorry to say he was hunted down and murdered by the brother. He held the poor man responsible for his sister's death, you see? Tyler. The brother's name was Tyler," he finished. "Oh, my dear girl!"

Nina slipped gently from the couch to the floor, powerless to prevent the collapse, surrendering to a total and overwhelming nothingness.

Chapter Thirteen

"You are with me now, my dearest, my only love."

Strong arms held her close, warm breath tickled her ear, her cheek and then insistent lips found hers in a crushing kiss. Nina opened her mouth and responded to the passion, desire leaping like a flame making her body weak and fluid, ready to do anything he asked, go anywhere so long as she could stay with this man, be his, forever.

He lifted her in his arms, her body feather light as he swung her upward. A sharp pain stabbed in her chest but then she was floating and the pain had gone. All around was music, Piers' music, entrancing and beautiful.

"Piers," she murmured. His face swam toward her on waves of sound. His eyes held her in their dark intensity. She felt the love and the passion pouring from him to her, saw the emotion crackling and dancing between them in golden beams of light. And all around sang the Shadow Music, Piers' music, Piers' violin sobbing and sighing, calling to her, loving her, calling, pleading...

"Mira. You will live. You are my life. My love. Mira, Mira." And his face appeared again, his unutterably handsome, beloved face contorted by grief and tears, his hands reaching for her but she was slipping away.

"Piers," she breathed, "Piers, hold me, hold me." And then the pain pierced her chest again, tearing her in two, but the pain of grief combined with the physical agony and she couldn't escape.

Nina floated. She felt no pain. She saw Piers and he was kneeling in their spot under the giant oaks in the grove. His head was bowed and his shoulders heaved with the violence of his sobbing. She longed to reach for him, to comfort and hold him and lay his dark head against her breast but she was powerless, could only watch helpless and detached.

The music overwhelmed her, voices chanting and Piers' voice clearly intoning a phrase of some sort over and over. The sound drew her inexorably. Piers stood before her smiling, arms outstretched and she fell into his embrace. Into blackness.

****

Piers was winning, he was taking Nina away and Martin didn't have the faintest idea how to fight him. How to fight a man dead for a hundred years or more? Tyler had it easy, all he had to do was put a bullet in him. Martin was powerless and with that came a deep bone chilling fear he'd never experienced before in his life.

Nina was completely adrift this time. Nothing they did roused her. Giles helped lift her to the couch and then scurried off to fetch a blanket. Fortunately he was completely unaware of what they were dealing with. Jessica and Martin had a frantic whispered conversation while he was out of the room.

"I think we should tell him everything," she said.

"Why?"

"He may be able to help with the spiritual thing.

Do an exorcism or something," she replied but her voice was unusually feeble and shaky, her eyes reflecting his own fear. "It might help. Mightn't it?"

He didn't have Jessica's faith in the Christian church and its rituals. This was outside the realms of mainstream religious practice. Piers wouldn't be abiding by any rules. He'd circumvented everything.

Giles bustled back in at that point with a red checked rug which he carefully placed over Nina. Her breathing was steady and her pulse strong but her face had a deathlike pallor. She was much deeper into the trancelike state than yesterday. He looked at Jessica with a raised eyebrow. A small frown appeared but she nodded. He turned to Giles.

"We have a story to tell, too," he said. "You'd better sit down. It's going to take a while."

Between them they told him everything they knew and to his credit he sat and listened intently, asking for clarification now and again but taking it all in, in silence. Perhaps as a minister he was used to nutters unburdening themselves. When they finally stopped talking there was a long pause. Martin glanced at the window. The rain had ceased and a watery sun was trying to break through the clouds in feeble little fits and starts. Nina lay pale and still under the blanket.

"So," said Giles. "If I understand it correctly, Piers was experimenting with astral travel fuelled by meditation and chant. He must have attempted to reach Miranda this way after her death. He must have tried crossing into the spirit world. He also had the notion of using his music, the Shadow Music, as a means of passing said boundary and actually reviving the woman he loved. Something went wrong and he was left to wander eternity as a displaced spirit constantly trying to reach his beloved Miranda."

"Perhaps," said Jessica, voice and face taut. "Piers' body was physically killed while he was astral travelling. His spirit wasn't able to return to its home."

"Maybe. Or maybe it just doesn't work. Goes against all the natural laws of life and death," suggested Giles.

Martin leapt to his feet. "Piers is evil. He sounds romantic and tragic the way you put it and I know that's how Nina sees him, too. He's seduced her, mentally and physically. You don't know how powerful he is. He's dangerous and he's ruthless and we have to stop him! Look what he's done to her." He finished pacing about the room yelling the last words at their concerned faces.

"Martin." Jessica rose and took his tense hands in hers. She held tight and forced him to meet her earnest gaze. "It's not Nina he's seducing, it's Miranda. He thinks Nina is Miranda." She emphasised the last words.

"But they're rapidly becoming the same." He closed his eyes and tried to calm the seething mass in his mind into coherent thought. "What can we do?" She patted his arm and sat down. He slumped into the nearest chair as despair robbed him of strength. "What can *I* do?"

"Love is a very strong emotion," said Giles after a moment. "I've read that these physical manifestations by spirits need to be fuelled by a strong emotion. In this case it's love, I don't think we can doubt that. It's not hate or revenge making Piers seek out Miranda—it's love."

"If it is, it's been hideously distorted by time and

grief," Martin said. "He wants Nina. He can't have her."

"You have to destroy the music first," said Giles. "From what you've told me it's the key to the whole thing."

"We can't. Lots of people have tried and failed."

"Perhaps I could try?" Giles' voice quivered with suppressed excitement.

Martin looked at Jessica. She pulled a face and shrugged.

"No harm in trying."

So Martin reluctantly left them watching over Nina's motionless form and drove back to Blackstone Cottage. When he returned with the music Giles had prepared soup for lunch and they sat at the dining room table to eat.

"I play the organ, you know," said Giles in an attempt to lighten the mood. "The church has a wonderful pipe organ. The donation of a generous, rich member of the congregation."

"Yes, I've heard it," said Jessica brightly. "Such a special, glorious sound, a pipe organ. It must go straight to God's ears."

Giles beamed at her. Martin managed a tiny smile. He'd never been one for organised religion but it obviously brought comfort and strength to many people.

"I know what you'll probably say," Giles went on, "but I'm rather curious. I mean what you've told me is so extraordinary. Very intriguing."

Jessica and Martin exchanged glances then turned to Giles and waited. He was going to suggest he play the music and Martin was going to say, "No." An emphatic and decisive "No."

"I wonder could I hear the melody? I mean it's not likely to have any effect on me, is it? Piers would hardly be interested in me."

"We can't play it to you," Martin snapped.

Giles's round face flushed pink. His plump fingers slid up and down the silver handle of his soup spoon. "I thought perhaps I might be able to have a quick run through on the organ. And then destroy it. Throw it in there." He indicated the open fire burning vigorously in the fireplace, his cheeks creased in an apprehensive smile but upon Martin's implacably opposed expression said, with a cunning Martin never suspected, "It would certainly make it easier for me to believe what you say."

"Why not, Martin?" murmured Jessica. "He's right, Piers won't be interested in him."

"All right," Martin said. "But against all my better judgement. You stay here with Nina, Jessica. Giles and I will go to the church."

He stood and picked up his empty bowl and spoon but Jessica took them from him and moved around the table collecting the rest. Giles threw another log onto the fire then left the room. Martin knelt beside Nina and stroked her cheek gently.

"Nina, darling," he whispered. "I'll be back shortly." He kissed her forehead and as he sat back gazing at her, her eyelids flickered and her lovely, dark eyes opened. They focussed slowly on his face. Recognition dawned.

"Martin," she sighed. Her lips curved slightly. "Martin."

He gathered her into his arms and squeezed her

against his chest. Tears pricked at his eyelids. "I thought he'd taken you. I was so frightened. Nina, you must fight him. Stay with me."

"Martin," she breathed again. "I want to sleep. I'm so tired."

Her eyes closed gently but this time she was sleeping. Her face had resumed its normal colour. He kissed her lips and drew the blanket up over her body. Jessica stood beside him, fingers twisting together.

"Is she asleep?"

Martin nodded, throat too choked to speak. She reached out and gripped his hand tightly as he stood up. "I'll sit with her. You two go—but hurry back."

He bent down and kissed Jessica's soft cheek. "Thanks. I really don't think this is a good idea," he whispered.

"What can happen?" she replied equally softly. "And if it makes him believe us, so much the better. He could prove very useful, Martin. This sort of thing is much more his field of expertise than ours. And he's already told us things we didn't know."

Martin nodded, still unconvinced. The whole thing smacked of disaster. Giles was really an unknown entity. "I suppose."

"And he may act as some sort of spiritual deterrent for evil." Jessica gave a little laugh but Martin didn't doubt that on some level she wanted the sanctity of the church as embodied by Giles, to give her support and backing. He couldn't blame her for that and he also couldn't deny it to her.

Giles came in, buttoning up his coat. "Better put your coat on. The church has no heating. Well, it does but it's too expensive to run outside of services."

Martin and Giles walked along the path between the churchyard and the vicarage. The rain still held off but the weak sunshine had been smothered by further looming clouds of the dark and threatening variety. The gravel walkway was flooded in places and they had to step carefully around pools of muddy brown slush. Drops of ice-cold water fell from the heavily laden bushes lining the path.

"Looks like snow on the way," commented Giles cheerfully. "It's been relatively warm this winter. Not so much icy as wet and windy. But summer is a long way off."

"You wouldn't believe it," said Martin, "But we were in shorts drinking cold beer a few weeks ago in Sydney. We went paddling at Bondi Beach."

The longing for that sun-warmed patio and the little outdoor table under the tree in Nina's special garden slammed in so hard it was almost a physical ache. He wanted to be there with Nina again, laughing over lunch with Florence, cooking dinner together in Nina's little kitchen, making love in Nina's big bed. He desperately wanted this endless nightmare to be over. He had to end it.

"Australia is one place I would really love to visit," said Giles.

"You can stay with us."

Giles gave him a penetrating look. "Will you be going back there?"

"Oh, yes, definitely. I don't think Nina wants to live anywhere else."

"True love."

"I think so." Martin nodded.

"That could be the deciding factor in all this," said

Giles. "Love is certainly the common element binding the main players together. You must remain steadfast in your love for Nina and trust that she loves you just as much despite your fears regarding this spirit. This Piers."

But did she love him as much as he loved her or was it only because of Piers they were together?

They reached the church and Giles produced a key to unlock the door. The ancient wood had swollen in the damp. Martin had to help shove as it stuck on the doorjamb but it swung open with a complaining squawk. As Giles had warned, the inside was bitterly cold, making their breath rise in steamy wafts as they exhaled. Giles switched on lights and the dim interior took on a friendlier less sepulchral air. St Bede's wasn't a large church but it was of a solid design dating from Norman times with its square tower and thick stone walls.

Brightly coloured crocheted kneelers hung from hooks on the backs of the pews, the work, no doubt, of an enthusiastic church ladies' guild. Stained glass windows depicting various apostles and Bible stories let in faint red and blue light, but apart from the altar the main feature was the array of magnificent silver and brass organ pipes. They covered the wall above the main entrance and the organ keyboard itself was situated in a small wooden choir loft also above the entrance. They had to ascend a tiny, cramped, curved stairway which wound its way up the tower with narrow high steps carved into the stone. Martin followed Giles as he squeezed his bulk around the tight twists, wondering what he would do if the vicar became wedged.

Breathing heavily, Giles emerged in the loft and by the time Martin arrived beside him, stepping gingerly on the creaking wooden floor, had already opened the keyboard and begun fiddling with the stops.

"Violin and flute, you mentioned," he muttered and made the appropriate adjustments. Suddenly the opening bars of a hymn banished the brooding silence of the church with a blast of full, warm-blooded sound. After a verse and chorus he swung into a Bach chorale.

"*Sleeper's Wake*" resonated gloriously, bouncing from the arched roof beams to the grey stone walls to the stained glass of the windows filling the air with rejoicing and hope.

Martin suddenly wished he'd brought his flute from the cottage as well. The acoustics were marvellous even though his fingers were frozen and would probably barely move.

"You play well," he said when Giles stopped.

"I get in here and practise quite a bit. It's such a magnificent beast. I've organised a few recitals too, with singers and other instrumentalists. I've got a very nice choir as well now. We did the *Fauré Requiem* one year. Wonderful work."

"Yes, it's beautiful."

"Now then." Giles looked hopefully at Martin and then at the bag which held the music. Martin reluctantly drew out the score and placed it on the music stand. Giles studied it for a few moments then reached out to turn the page but Martin quickly whipped out a hand to stop him.

"It's probably better not to touch it yet," he said.

Giles didn't argue despite a brief flicker of annoyance. He nodded and allowed Martin to complete the page turn.

"Interesting harmony," he said. "Shall I try the guitar line with the chords? Perhaps you could play the melody line on the keyboard."

Martin shook his head. "I can't. I mean it won't let me. I tried to play the cello part on my flute once and couldn't. It resisted." A thought occurred to him which gave him partial relief from the intense anxiety about this whole venture with Giles. "Maybe it won't let you play either. It's not written for organ."

"We'll see, shall we? Giles splayed his fingers dramatically over the keys. "I can try the bass part with my feet." He felt for the correct pedals with his feet and began.

The Shadow Music sounded quite different on organ used as Martin was to hearing the sobbing and soaring of the violin and his own silvery flute sound. He held his breath as Giles played the opening bars.

Nothing happened. The voices remained silent. The music had no effect beyond inducing a peculiar deflation of spirit. Such an extraordinary contrast to the heartache and anguish that beautiful slow melody usually produced. Giles would never believe them after this. He'd think they were loonies.

Martin released the pent-up breath slowly. He rose, ready to make some excuse, some feeble sounding explanation as to why the spirits weren't reacting. Tell him the organ wasn't the right instrument to re-create the spiritual vibrations. Sound a complete lunatic and accept Giles' kind reassurances and denials.

But Giles strained forward intent on the page before him. It wasn't just the focus of sight reading a new piece of music or the difficulty of deciphering the handwritten notes. Martin pursed his mouth. Here were the frightening beginnings of the obsession which had gripped Nina and himself. Giles was a believer just as they were.

He had to be protected.

Martin stood up and whipped the music from the stand.

"Hey, don't!" Giles attempted to snatch it back but expecting the reaction Martin stepped out of reach.

"You see?" The music quivered in his hand but he steeled himself against its anger. He slid it into the bag with the other parts. Giles flushed and rubbed his hands over his face.

"I'm sorry, Martin. It's quite extraordinary. I didn't want to stop." He looked up with a bewildered expression. "I don't think I could've stopped if you hadn't…Quite extraordinary."

"I know exactly," said Martin.

Giles smiled feebly. "Of course you do."

"Did you hear him?"

"No. It just gave me the most unutterable sense of sorrow, great and overwhelming grief. I wanted to keep playing."

"That's what Jessica felt, too. The sorrow."

Giles closed and locked the organ keyboard and Martin followed him down the spiral staircase. When they reached the bottom Giles said, "I think I'd like to stay awhile. Ask for guidance, you know?" His normally ruddy, cheerful face was pale, his expression bewildered, confused.

Martin nodded. "Of course. Is it all right if we stay a little longer in the vicarage? Until Nina wakes up?"

"Yes, yes by all means." Giles gripped Martin's

arm. "We have to get to the bottom of this. I'd be most upset if you continued on the quest without me." His eyes searched Martin's face.

"Thank you very much. You've no idea how comforting your support is. For all of us but especially Jessica." Martin held out his hand and Giles clutched it firmly with both of his. "We'll have a brainstorming session later. You'll stay for dinner?"

"I'll talk to the others but I'm sure they'd love to. Thank you."

"Give me half an hour or so," said Giles.

Martin turned to drag open the heavy wooden door and step out into the gloomy afternoon. The clouds had settled even lower and more rain was imminent. A restless wind had sprung up, icy and biting, tearing at his hair and coat as he followed the muddy path through the graveyard. The big, dark pines down one side wall waved and moaned overhead. Martin shivered involuntarily, nothing to do with the chill. What did they say? Someone stepped on your grave. Big drops began to fall and he sprinted the last few yards to the shelter of the vicarage, shoulders hunched against the cold of the rain and the ruthless attack of the wind.

He entered by the back door, the way he and Giles had left, calling out to Jessica so that she would know who it was and not be alarmed. He went through the kitchen, removing his coat, welcoming the warmth of indoors filtering through the layers of clothing. Giles surely had more heating than that open fire. Martin hung his coat in the hallway and cautiously stuck his head around the door to the living room. Jessica sat in one of Giles' big armchairs with the wingbacks, head back, eyes closed, fast asleep. Martin smiled.

What a remarkable woman she was. He watched her for a moment or two then walked further into the room to where he could see the couch. The red blanket lay bundled on the floor in an untidy heap. The couch was empty. Nina had gone.

"Nina," he shouted. "Nina." He rushed from the room and down the corridor searching for the bathroom in case she'd gone to the loo. "Nina."

His frantic voice roused Jessica.

"Martin? What's happening?" She sounded feeble, suddenly old and frightened. He ran up the stairs calling Nina, louder, more urgently when there was no response. He threw open doors and peered into bedrooms, a storeroom, a spare room filled with extra furniture and boxes. Jessica stood at the foot of the stairs peering up white-faced as he came running back down.

"Where is she?" he shouted, gripping her arms tightly. "Where's Nina?"

Jessica shrank from his rage. Martin realised with a shock how frail and small she was and how harshly he was acting. He released his grip and she rubbed the place where he'd held her. Tears gathered in the grey eyes.

"I'm sorry, Jessica, sorry," he said. "She's gone. I can't find her." He rubbed a hand over his face, dashing away the hint of tears which sprang into his own eyes.

"It's my fault. I went to sleep. So stupid of me." She clenched a soft hand into a fist and thumped it into her open palm.

"We have to find her," said Martin. "Perhaps if you stay here and tell Giles when he comes back I can go to the cottage and see if she went there."

Jessica darted toward the front door. "Her coat," she said. "It's still here." She held out Nina's new navy blue parka Martin had insisted she buy in London just a few days ago. "She'll freeze out there without it."

"Giles thought it might snow." He stared at her, fear coiling in his belly like a snake. He sprang into action, grabbed his own coat still damp from the rain which was now falling in earnest, and flung the door open.

Blackstone Cottage sat squat and solid in its winter garb. He had the sudden strong impression that the cottage was a living thing, hibernating in its garden of bare rose bushes and leafless shrubs, waiting for the sun to bring it to life again. It seemed to be settling deeper into the cold earth. He jumped from the car and ran down the narrow path to the green front door.

Mrs. Wookey greeted him cheerfully and said, no, the young lady hadn't been back and would he like a cup of tea?

"No, thanks. If Nina turns up, please call the vicarage. We'll be having dinner there."

"All right. So you've met Giles, then? Made such a difference to the parish he has. Started a wonderful choir. Very musical. Did you know that? He's organised all sorts of things, concerts and shows..."

Martin nodded and thanked and edged toward the door. "I really must try to catch up with Nina, Mrs. Wookey." He opened the door. "Thank you." A black and white cat darted in as he closed it behind him, nearly tripping him.

"There you are, Maggie," she said as the door closed. Martin sat in the car and tried to think. Where would she go? Rain drummed on the roof and ran down the windows in a waterfall. He switched on the engine and the wipers began their tireless swish, swish. The Hall? Would she go there? Think! Was she acting as Nina or Miranda?

Nina might go to the Hall but she wouldn't go without him and Jessica. She must be acting as Miranda and where would she go? Not to the Hall. It had nothing she wanted. Miranda wanted Piers. Where would Miranda go to meet Piers? Martin heard Giles' voice in his head as he related the story of the doomed lovers. "They used to meet in a grove of oaks along the Plymouth road."

Mud and gravel spurted from under the wheels as he wrenched the Saab around in a tight u-turn and roared back along the road to the vicarage.

Giles had returned from his commune with God and sat in the living room with Jessica when Martin burst in.

"The oak grove. Where's the oak grove?" he demanded.

"About a mile away in a field." Giles leapt to his feet. "Do you think she's gone there?"

"To meet Piers." Jessica pressed her hand against her breast. She stared at Martin, horror etched into her features. "That's where she died. Oh, Martin, save her, save her." Tears streamed down her face. Giles put a solid arm around her.

"We'll bring her back safe and sound, don't you worry," he said. "Wait here by the fire, in case she's simply gone for a stroll and comes back cheery as can be." He gave her an encouraging minister's smile. "Don't forget. God's on our side."

Jessica raised a weak smile in return and settled

back into her chair but her fingers twisted tightly around each other.

"Come on." Martin was already heading for the door.

Wind and rain lashed the car as they drove in silence along the road to Plymouth. Martin peered through the watery windscreen hoping for a glimpse of Nina's little figure taking shelter under one of the occasional trees along the route or perhaps huddled under the hedgerow on the side of the road. He saw no one.

"She may have gone across the fields. It's more direct." Giles thought a moment. "But Nina wouldn't know that, would she?"

"No," said Martin. "But we're talking about Miranda."

"Miranda?"

"She's going to meet Piers, the way she always did," replied Martin grimly, daring Giles to object. But Giles didn't, he accepted the explanation without further comment.

"See. Over there." He pointed at a dark, forbidding patch of giant trees across the barren field on the left.

Giles parked the car off the road by a farm gate. He buttoned his coat tight round his neck and pulled up the collar before clambering out into the drenching rain. Martin opened the gate with stiff cold fingers and pushed it open. Giles followed clumsily, floundering and sliding on the muddy ground but Martin didn't wait; he forged ahead as fast as the driving wind and rain would allow, head down fighting against the elements trying to prevent his approach. The wind howled through the treetops. Nina's words pounded in his head.

"The trees. They were terrifying. I thought—I knew—I would die there."

He struggled on. Twice he slipped and fell to his knees but dragged himself up. The rain soaked through to his skin, his coat hung heavy as lead from his body dragging him down, slowing him, pulling him back. But he fought on.

"Nina," he shouted. "Nina." But his words were carried away on the wind and drowned by the torrents of water pouring from the sky. Sobbing with fear and exhaustion he staggered between the first of the trees. They resented his presence, whipped their bare branches toward him with animal malevolence. He ducked his head and leaned against a damp knobbly trunk to catch his breath. Giles blundered to his side, gasping and shaking. He gripped Martin's arm.

"The centre," he shouted. "There's a clearing in the centre." He ploughed away between the trees, shielding his head from the fury of the branches. Other smaller evergreen varieties had sprung up at random, making visibility even worse. Martin followed as best he could. The pounding of the rain and the howling wind in the trees deafened him still, even though they were partially sheltered from the worst of it.

He shouted again, "Nina. Nina."

Ahead of him Giles did the same but their voices were lost. She'd never hear them. They burst through into a small cleared area. A branch from a huge tree had fallen a long time ago and lay moss-covered and decaying across the middle. Martin struggled around the edge of the clearing calling Nina's name frantically. If she wasn't here where would she be?

Giles circled in the other direction so they reached the opposite side at same time. Nina lay right against the trunk of the fallen branch, face up, eyes closed, features composed in the still mask of death, rain dripping like tears from her face.

"Nina," wailed Martin. He flung himself forward to scoop her into his arms and hold her against his breast. "We're too late. Too late."

"Martin. Martin." Slowly he became aware of Giles kneeling in the mud at his side, trying to prise Nina's body from his grasp with clawing fingers.

"No," he shouted. "Don't touch her." He buried his face in her neck and cried tears of misery and despair. Piers had won. He'd taken Nina just as he said he would. Martin had lost, he'd failed Nina. He'd sworn to protect her and he'd failed. He'd promised her father. He'd lost her.

"Martin!" Giles spoke sharply. "She's alive. Get up. We have to take her home."

"Alive?" Martin stared at Giles uncomprehending, then looked down at the pale face.

"She's breathing. Come on, we have to warm her. Put this on her." Giles had stripped off his coat and together they wrapped it around her lifeless body. Martin rose and carried her like a sleeping baby in his arms through the trees and the driving rain and the wind, stumbling across the tussocky bare field to the gate which Giles unlatched and swung open to allow him to pass through with his precious cargo.

Chapter Fourteen

Martin sat in the backseat cradling Nina in his arms, crooning to her as Giles drove fast along the slick and winding road to the shelter and haven of the vicarage. She wasn't alive. Giles was wrong. Piers had killed his Nina the way he'd killed Miranda all those years ago. Now perhaps he would be satisfied, he would leave them alone. Now Martin would suffer the way Piers had suffered, the difference being Martin was not vindictive like Piers and wouldn't seek to visit his anguish and grief on an innocent party. The way Piers had. For over a hundred years. What a malevolent, vicious, cruel bastard the man was.

Martin hugged Nina to him and kissed her lifeless cheeks and then her cold mouth. He gently stroked a wet strand of hair from her forehead and whispered, "I love you, Nina."

Giles swung the car too fast around a corner and slewed into a skid. He corrected frantically, called "Sorry" as he straightened. Martin glanced up as he braced himself and Nina against the momentum of being hurled across the car. He looked down at Nina. Her eyelids flickered. Two deep dark pools of life stared at him for an instant, then the lids fluttered closed.

The breath stalled in his lungs. "Nina?" he whispered through a throat gone hoarse.

Her eyes opened again and this time she shifted slightly in his arms.

"Cold," she murmured.

"You'll be warm soon, my darling. You're safe now."

The wisp of a smile flickered. "Piers," she murmured. "My love."

"We'll take her to the doctor," yelled Giles over his shoulder.

Martin couldn't reply. He gazed at the girl in his arms. Who was she? Nina or Miranda? He didn't know anymore and neither did she. Every inch of her face was familiar and dear to him, every line, every hair on her head. He loved her as he had loved no other. But so did Piers.

"We have to make Piers understand that Miranda is dead," he muttered to himself, and then louder, "How much longer?"

"We're here." Giles jammed on the brakes. The car skated across the shiny tarmac and narrowly avoided crushing the doctor's garden gate. He bundled out and opened the door for Martin.

Gruff, grey-haired Doctor Krupp listened to Giles' necessarily partial explanation, took one look at Nina and said, "Bring her through. She needs warmth."

He led the way to a small clinic style room with two empty beds. Martin stripped off Nina's soaked boots and socks while the doctor removed Giles' coat and her wet sweater. "Take off her other wet things and put her into bed and rub her all over with this." He handed Martin a towel. "I'll get some hot water bottles under way."

"I'd better tell Jessica," said Giles.

Martin nodded absently concentrating on his task. He grasped Nina's frozen right foot and began rubbing as vigorously as he could. When the skin felt more pliable he moved to the left one, then her hands and arms and torso, her pale body fragile and lifeless under his hands as he worked. The doctor returned with a night gown, thick socks and three hot water bottles. Together they dressed her and tucked her in.

"Her colour's a little better. I'll give her a check up, temperature, pulse etcetera. Perhaps you could fill me in on what happened? Has she been ill? Any medical conditions I should know about?"

Martin sat on the end of the bed with his hand resting on the quilt covering Nina's legs.

"No, no. She's been having…we've both been under an emotional strain lately. Nina's from Sydney, Australia. We're trying to trace someone and it's been traumatic for her. For both of us." Martin looked at the doctor hopefully. It didn't sound at all convincing to him but if Doctor Krupp thought his explanation odd he didn't comment. He nodded and stuck a thermometer in Nina's mouth while he held her wrist.

"Pulse is racing. Temperature's up a bit. Nothing too alarming," he reported. "Emotional strain." He cocked a bushy, grey eyebrow at Martin. "Had a fight, did you? She ran off?"

"Not exactly," said Martin. "It's complicated."

"Friends of Giles, are you?"

"More or less. We're staying at the B&B with Mrs. Wookey."

"I see. Leave her here tonight. I'd like to keep an eye on her."

"Tonight?" Martin looked up sharply. "No, no. I'd

feel better if she were with me."

Doctor Krupp studied him from under hedge-like eyebrows.

"My dear young man," he said. "Your Nina is severely chilled and in a state of nervous shock. I think it would be best if she remained under my care until she recovers enough to walk out herself. We don't want to risk pneumonia."

"But she mustn't be left alone," insisted Martin. "Can I stay? In the other bed?"

"I'm not running a hotel."

"Please. I need to be close to her. If she wakes up she won't know where she is."

The doctor stared at Martin, then at Nina. "All right. But you'll need to get some things for her."

"I'll send a friend. Thank you, doctor." Martin grabbed the him by the hand and pumped it up and down. "She'll be all right, won't she? She won't die or anything?"

"If she'd stayed out much longer it'd be a different story. My wife's just come in. I'll tell her we've a patient and a guest."

"Please. I don't want to be any trouble. I can eat at the pub but Nina hasn't eaten since breakfast."

"She'll be hungry when she wakes up then, won't she?" said the doctor and left the room.

Martin lay down next to Nina and put his arms around her.

****

Cutting Marsh, 1892

People were whispering nearby. The low hisses and murmurings turned themselves into words but she couldn't sort out what they meant. Miranda's eyes flickered open and her father's face swam into view then receded. Something deliciously cool was pressed against her forehead. Her skin was burning up. Fingers pressed against her wrist.

She was cold. Unbearably so. Cold and wet, frozen to the very bone. So cold she wanted to die, couldn't move, couldn't make the effort to force the air in and out of her lungs. Frozen.

Her eyes opened. She was in her bedroom but somehow it was different. The walls had changed colour, the curtains…strange furnishings…of metal?

A strange face appeared, clean shaven, young and kind with gentle eyes and a sad, worried expression. He loved her. She knew that without his saying a word. She tried to smile at him. He lay beside her and put his arms around her and held her. She was safe and warm in his embrace.

Music poured into the room and enveloped her, taking with it the bone-chilling cold, tearing her from the arms that held her—a soaring, passionate violin, the like of which she'd never heard before. The melody called to her, wakened something in the depths of her soul so that she wanted to follow and give herself up to the very essence of it. It was part of her, it was part of her destiny and her life. The throbbing violin became louder, closer. Miranda strained for a glimpse of the player.

She was in a garden, a rose garden, heavy with scent from the rich, sensuous blooms lining the pathway, velvet petals fallen like blood red drops on the gravel beneath her feet. She walked and all around her the music sang and caressed and seduced her senses. The she saw him. A tall, dark-haired figure standing, waiting. He turned as she approached. His eyes burned into hers. She knew him. She'd always known him. He was her destiny. He was Piers. He held out his arms and she ran to him.

"At last I have found you," he whispered. He kissed her and his mouth was urgent, his body hard, filled with desire. He drew back from the embrace and gripped her arms tightly with strong fingers. "I will come for you, Mira," he said. "Soon. Very soon."

He left her then and she was unable to follow as he disappeared between the arching boughs of a willow growing by the ornamental pond. The music faded and she was alone with just the perfume of the roses.

"Miranda?" Her father's voice came to her through a fog. He must be very far away. She struggled to open her eyes. His dear face appeared with the wrinkles around the pale blue eyes and the tufts of greying hair springing from his head. But his face was shiny with perspiration and he was in shirt sleeves.

"Is it raining yet?" she murmured.

"No, my dear, not yet. How do you feel?"

"Tired."

"You've been ill with a fever for several days. Sleep now. The worst has passed." He laid a cool hand on her brow. Miranda closed her eyes and smiling, slipped into sleep.

****

Nina's eyes flicked open. Her right arm was pinioned beneath her and she shifted to free it. Pins and needles made her grit her teeth and grimace. She sat up and stared around, rubbing her arm vigorously. This wasn't their bedroom at Blackstone Cottage. It was a newer building and had the feel of a hospital. The bed and the small grey cabinet by the window were clinical and sterile looking. A second bed in the room had been slept in but there was no sign of its occupant.

Where on earth was she? And where was Martin? And Jessica? She threw back the covers and swung her legs over the side of the bed, heart thudding. An unfamiliar pair of thick, red, woolly socks adorned her feet and not only that, she had on someone else's pink nightie. Nina padded across to the door and carefully eased it open. Voices came from farther down the passage to the right. She listened, straining her ears to hear, trying to ascertain the source. Martin? Jessica? No, not Jessica. The woman's voice was younger. A chair rasped on a tiled floor.

Nina fled back into her room and jumped into bed, heart pounding. She dragged the covers up to her chin and sat fearfully watching the door as two sets of footsteps clumped along the passage.

"Martin?" she called, her voice wavering.

The door flew open and he rushed in. "Nina. Thank God."

His body trembled in her arms as he hugged her so tightly she could barely breathe.

"What happened Where are we?" she asked when he released his grip enough for her to speak.

"Martin and the Vicar brought you here last night, half frozen," said a deep, gruff voice. "I'm Dr Krupp. Would you mind telling us what you were doing running about in a storm in the dead of winter with no coat, getting drenched and scaring your friend here half to death? Not to mention our Vicar and the other poor lady."

Nina stiffened in Martin's arms as the implications

of the Doctor's summation sank in. He held her away
and looked deep into her eyes.

"Where was I?" she whispered.

"In the grove of trees. The oaks we passed on the
way in."

He didn't need to add "where you passed out
yesterday". Nina shuddered and closed her eyes as a
memory flitted through her mind. A sharp chill of pain,
darkness and despair, an overwhelming crippling fear.

"That's where she died," she said softly.

"Miranda?"

Nina nodded and rested her cheek against his
shoulder as he drew her into his arms again.

"I gather you're not going to share your secrets
with me," said the doctor.

Martin turned. "Thank you for your help, Doctor.
Please give me your account. Nina will be fine now."

The doctor gave them both a penetrating stare and
withdrew without another word.

"Wasn't that a bit rude?" asked Nina.

"Do you want to explain it to him?"

"No," she admitted.

"Come on, let's get you dressed. Jessica brought
over some more clothes."

Ten minutes later they thanked the doctor, paid his
bill and stepped out into the bleak morning.

"Where are we going?"

"To the vicarage," said Martin. "We're staying
there with Giles until this is sorted out."

****

The vicarage teapot squatted solidly in the centre
of mugs and plates and the remains of breakfast. Nina
pushed a crust of toast around the rim of her plate. A

tide of frustration and exasperation had built slowly since she'd finished eating. Relief at feeling something as normal as being hungry had worn off as her body regained its energy from the pile of scrambled eggs, toast, and bacon Giles had virtually shovelled into her.

The longer they sat, the stronger the annoyance grew. They'd been talking for an hour and got nowhere. They had to do something positive soon or she'd get up and…No!

Nina dropped the piece of toast onto the plate and balled her fingers into fists. That was Piers talking, Piers' frustration and anger, Piers' selfish manipulation. She had to regain control of her mind or she'd never function as Nina again. Already the demarcation was blurred, frighteningly blurred between her reality and the tragic nineteenth century girl.

She had to fight Piers with every last ounce of strength she had. She'd never tried to deny him before but yesterday's experience was too terrifying, filling her with a deep and nameless dread which chilled her soul. She not only felt Miranda's love and pain and fear but when she travelled to that other world she *was* Miranda with all Miranda's heightened emotions and desires. But most terrifying of all she was still Nina when she returned, with all Nina's knowledge of Miranda's life and Miranda's hideous and painful death. And that far outweighed the love she felt for Piers. It had to or Nina would be consumed. Her rational mind told her this.

Her rational Nina mind therefore told her to resist Piers, to save herself, salvage her own identity. Her irrational Nina emotions told her to love him and help him every way she could. Rational Nina was in danger of being swamped by both irrational Nina and innocent, lovelorn Miranda.

"This is how I see it," said Giles. "We can't destroy the music so we have to make this Piers character realise that Miranda is dead and that he is as well. He must realise that Nina is not Miranda. The only problem is how do we do that?"

"I think I'm becoming Miranda," blurted Nina. "Or Miranda is becoming me." She couldn't prevent the tremor of fear in her voice.

"Rubbish!"

"Nonsense!"

Both Giles and Jessica burst out so vehemently in denial Nina was astonished.

"I can't tell anymore," she wailed and covered her face with both hands.

"We can and you're Nina," said Giles so firmly Nina was almost reassured. She lowered her trembling hands and looked at Martin who'd remained silent. He knew Piers' strength. He knew far better than Giles or even Jessica, what they were attempting to overcome. The slight reassurance Giles had provided trickled out like air from a leaking balloon.

"Can you do an exorcism?" asked Jessica.

"I can, but of what? He doesn't inhabit a particular place, does he?"

"Our heads," offered Nina glumly. "My head in particular."

Martin reached out and squeezed her fingers. "And mine sometimes."

"If we knew where he died it might help. Or where he's buried," said Jessica.

"I don't think it will," said Martin. "And I don't think an exorcism will help either. We're not dealing with a normal ghost."

"He's a lost soul," said Giles. "A wandering soul."

"What's a normal ghost?" asked Jessica. "I thought they were all supposed to be lost wandering souls."

"We have to go to the Hall." Nina pushed back her chair and stood up. "I want this to finish. I want it stopped now. I can't stand to be like this anymore." A wave of panic crashed through her body. "Are you coming? We have to do it now before he comes to get me again. I'm scared." She stopped, struggled, failed to prevent the tears which broke through in a flood and poured down her cheeks as she gripped the back of the chair.

Martin sprang to his feet. "We will stop him. I promise. We will." Gentle firm fingers stroked her hair and held her tightly until she drew a couple of deep shuddering breaths and said in a voice muffled by his woollen sweater clad shoulder, "I'm sorry, everyone."

"No need to be sorry," said Jessica. "I'm terrified too. For you. But we won't give up, Nina. We won't desert you. Be strong."

"We'll drive shall we?" said Giles briskly. His chair scraped on the tiled floor as he stood up.

Jessica held out Nina's blue coat. "Put this on. It's freezing out."

Nina managed a watery smile and released her hold on Martin. Jessica slid the coat onto her outstretched arms like a mother with a child. She fussed with one of her tissues and wiped Nina's cheeks.

"Don't worry, we'll fix his wagon," she said firmly. Nina gave a little spurt of laughter.

****

Broome Hall was a medium-sized country house,

Jessica told them. Two stone gate posts and a small lodge marked the entrance and they drove between towering oaks, bare and gaunt in their winter hibernation, along a gently curved drive to reach the rambling three-storey building. A rounded portico with Roman style columns protected the front door and gravel crunched under the tyres of the Saab as Martin drew up and pulled on the brake in the sweeping circular driveway.

Lawns stretched away in front of the house down to the trees lining the driveway. The rain had held off so far but a stiff breeze whipped the clouds about the sky and darker masses loomed in the distance. Shrubs and greenery still dripping from yesterday's downpour grew close to the grey stone walls of the house and ivy climbed up toward the second floor windows along one corner. The gravel drive continued around to the rear where, presumably, lay garages, stables, and other outbuildings.

Nina stood in the biting winter wind and gazed at the house. She knew the others were watching her closely for any sign of distress or recognition but there was nothing. She smiled at their worried faces.

"Nothing," she said in relief. "I feel nothing at all. He's not here. What a beautiful old house."

"Yes, wait till you see the interior," said Jessica. "Costs an absolute fortune to maintain, of course. The roof alone put Rupert back as much as some folk earn in a lifetime." She pulled her pale blue woollen cap further down over her ears.

"What does he do that he can afford to live here?" asked Martin.

"He owns a bank. International. Very high power.

Rupert and Georgina have an apartment in Manhattan as well."

"Owns a bank?" repeated Nina incredulously.

"Well, not exactly owns it but he's a director. George always used to joke that Rupert owned a bank."

Jessica strode to the imposing front door and gave the bellpull a vigorous tug. A faint jangling sounded from the depths of the house. They waited, shivering in the wind, shuffling their feet about and rubbing their hands against the iciness.

"Hard to imagine a heat wave," said Giles. The ends of his permanently escaping scarf flapped over his shoulders and his nose had turned rosy pink.

"Hard to imagine summer in Sydney." Martin smiled at Nina. She smiled back.

The door opened suddenly and a grim-faced woman in a dark blue dress regarded them sternly.

"Hello, Mrs. Turner," said Jessica. "How lovely to see you again. Thank you for allowing us to visit."

"Mrs. Harrow, Vicar." She inclined her head in greeting. Tight little rows of grey ripples on a springy mat of hair, thin angular face with a prominent nose. She studied first Nina then Martin but her unnerving gaze returned to Nina. Her brow creased in a frown.

"This is Nina and Martin, visiting from Australia," said Giles.

"How do you do," said Martin. "Actually, I'm English. Nina's Australian."

"Hello," said Nina.

"Good morning." Mrs. Turner stepped back to allow them access.

They crowded into a vestibule with a checkerboard marble floor and continued on through a doorway to an open hall area. On the right a broad polished wood staircase rose gracefully to the floors above and closed doors indicated rooms leading farther into the house. Double doors, also closed, were to the right of the stairs and a corridor went off to the left. A magnificent chandelier hung above their heads and a couple of small hallstands furnished the area holding either potted plants or ornamental vases.

Nina shivered involuntarily and Mrs. Turner, whose disconcerting grey gaze had focussed itself on her face again, said, "It's a bit chilly. I don't heat the whole place when the master's away."

"No, I can understand why," said Jessica.

"What was it you were wanting to see?" asked Mrs. Turner.

"Well, we were wondering could we..." began Jessica.

"The garden," interrupted Nina. The thought sprang into her mind from nowhere. "The rose garden."

"The rose garden," repeated Mrs. Turner. "Not much of a rose garden now. Used to be more. In the old days. No roses, of course. It's winter." In case they hadn't noticed. "This way, please."

She turned and strode to the closed double doors, Nina and the others following like an untidy flock of sheep. Mrs. Turner stood aside holding the door to let her little tour group pass.

"Straight on to the windows," she said.

Jessica led the way across the vast empty room with its polished wood floor and wood panelled walls. Heavy curtains of a deep red fabric were pulled back from a set of three French doors in the far wall letting in the weak winter light.

"This is the main hall," Jessica told them. "Where the Summer Ball would have been held."

Nina gazed around trying to imagine the cavernous room filled with happy, laughing people dancing to Piers' musicians. Miranda dancing with her fiancé Ethan and seeing Piers for the first time. She couldn't. The whole place felt cold and lifeless as if it harboured a deep and implacable sorrow.

Martin touched her arm and she turned to him.

"Do you feel it? The sadness?" she murmured.

He nodded. "There's no energy left. It's completely empty—drained. Weird."

"This must have been where Piers and his friends played." Giles came across to where they stood in the centre of the room. "Amazing."

He stared around with his head cocked slightly to one side as if straining to hear some faint refrain still echoing in the air.

"I feel nothing in here except sadness. Not the extreme grief of Piers, though, it's duller and emptier," said Nina. "Strange isn't it? You'd think Piers would be at his strongest."

"Perhaps because this wasn't his house," suggested Giles. "His influence is diluted by the family who lived here perhaps. And they would have been very antagonistic after Miranda's death. His spirit is not welcome here. He doesn't belong."

"Anything wrong?" Mrs. Turner was watching them speak quietly to each other, her eyes narrowed in suspicion, one hand resting on the handle of the central of the three French doors.

"No. We were just saying what a big room it is," said Martin.

Nina exclaimed brightly. "It's enormous. I can't imagine cleaning this place."

"They used to have an army of servants in the old days, these houses," said Jessica. Mrs. Turner sniffed but offered no comment.

"You must have help, surely?" said Nina as the housekeeper opened the door.

"Mr. Turner does the grounds," she answered. "And a girl comes in from the village to help clean. Not much to do when they're away on their holidays or in America."

The cold wind bit again as Nina stepped outside onto a long stone terrace which followed the wall to the right and then did a ninety degree turn on the inside of an L-shaped corner in the building. The garden was thus partially enclosed by the house.

"The rose garden is to the left," said Mrs. Turner. "You can come back into the house through the drawing room. You know your way, Mrs. Harrow?" She looked at Jessica who nodded.

"Yes, thank you Mrs. Turner."

"I've a few things to do indoors. Just ring the bell when you come back in and I'll show you the upstairs if you like. You mentioned a painting?"

"Splendid, thank you very much," boomed Giles.

She turned and went back inside. The glass door closed firmly behind her.

"Down here." Jessica stepped down the flight of shallow steps leading to the garden.

Even in winter bareness it was plain the garden had been beautifully designed and laid out. Two paths curved gracefully away through flower beds now dormant but evergreen shrubs gave colour to the otherwise bleak vista. A fountain rose from the centre of a small ornamental pool but it too was lifeless. The rose bushes were in abundance despite Mrs. Turner's remarks to the contrary about neglect. Reduced to leafless branches and waiting for the annual pruning, they filled the garden beds on either side of the path leading to the left.

Nina took Martin by the hand and walked amongst the roses. They passed under an arching trellis. The path continued on between taller evergreen shrubs which screened the house from view. Giles and Jessica had taken the path which curved right and their voices carried on the cold, blustery wind.

She stopped and gazed around. There was something vaguely familiar about this spot—a quivering in the air, tension. Martin waited, watching her face, she knew for any sign of a relapse.

"I think…" she murmured.

A burst of music and laughter rang out from the direction of the house. Bright lights shone through the branches of the trees, soft night air caressed her cheek. The wind was warm and gentle suddenly and the scent of roses hung heavy on the air. Excitement surged through her veins. He would come to her, here. Piers would come, she knew it."

Nina gasped and shivered as the chill of winter daylight crashed in.

"Did you hear that?"

"What did you hear?"

"Music. And people laughing. It sounded like a party."

"Anything else?"

Nina closed her eyes and remembered. "It was hot

again. Night time. And the roses were in bloom, all around. They smell wonderful."

"Was he there?" His voice was harsh with loathing.

Nina shook her head and opened her eyes.

"No, he wasn't but I think this is where she waited for him. The first time."

Feet crunched on the gravel. Nina and Martin both spun about in shocked anticipation then relaxed as Giles and Jessica joined them.

"There aren't any roses around the other side," said Jessica. "It's wonderful in spring and summer, this garden."

"It doesn't matter," said Martin. "Nina just heard music and people having a party. She thinks this is the spot where Miranda first spoke to Piers."

"I don't think, I know, Martin," snapped Nina. "I was there. I mean I was here. Right here."

Piers' rage grew inside her like a thundercloud making her body tremble with the violence of his anger. She glared at Martin and the almost overwhelming desire to strike him made her fingers clench into fists. She stepped forward with her arm raised, her gaze fixed on a face which wasn't Martin's but was for an instant, a familiar, square face with a bewildered expression under a thatch of blond hair—a moustache.

Martin shouted, "Nina. Stay with us. You're Nina not Miranda. Fight him!"

Nina blinked. Fight Piers? But Piers was…She was Nina. She had to resist. He must not be allowed to act for her. No! She was Nina. The anger subsided leaving her with ragged breath and a faint residue of his passion, like a stain after a spill has been wiped away, and mild surprise at how easily it had been quelled.

310

Something about this place—Broome Hall. Ethan. The name popped into her head.

"Yes," she said vacantly and then stronger, "Yes. Martin, there was another man. I think it may have been Ethan. He loved me too. I wanted to kill him." She put her hands over her face and pressed the fingers tightly against her eyes. "I really wanted to kill him. Or Miranda did. Just for an instant."

Martin flung his arm around her shoulders and peered into her face as she clung to him. "You didn't. Miranda didn't. Ethan was her fiancé. It was Piers. I hate that evil bastard."

"Let's go inside," suggested Giles. "And have a look at that painting I mentioned. I'm sure Mrs. Turner noticed the resemblance to Nina. Did you see how she looked at her?"

"I sure did. Her hair is like one of those steel wool pads." Nina gave Martin a tiny smile and tucked her hand into his arm as they walked toward the house. "She's just like that housekeeper in that book. You know, Mrs. Something in *Rebecca*."

"Mrs. Danvers," said Jessica and then added reprovingly, "Mrs. Turner is an absolute treasure even though her manner is a little stern."

"Wonder what Mr. Turner's like?" murmured Martin in Nina's ear so his warm breath tickled her cheek.

"Terrified," she replied softly. He gave a little spurt of relieved laughter and intertwined their fingers. And the image flitted across her mind that it was just the way she'd done all those years ago at the Summer Ball with Ethan by her side.

Chapter Fifteen

The two paths converged at a set of steps further along the terrace on the longer side of the L. More French doors led to different rooms. Jessica pulled one open and ushered them inside.

"The drawing room," she announced. This room was a comfortably furnished, modern, sitting room complete with sofas, a couple of armchairs, TV, lamps, and coffee tables. A large fireplace dominated one wall. Family photos crowded onto the mantelpiece.

"Do they ever use that big hall for dances?" asked Martin.

"Occasionally, I think. Wonderful for parties. They throw open the doors in summer and the guests can wander out onto the terrace and into the garden. I spent my last New Year's Eve with George here," said Jessica wistfully. "Although we didn't wander outside then except to watch the fireworks, too cold. I'll summons Mrs. Turner, shall I, and she can show us the painting?" Jessica strode across and yanked at an old-fashioned tasselled bellpull hanging by the door. "Do we want to see anything else?"

"No," said Nina. Indoors she felt curiously flat and disappointed. The house had an aura quite different to outside in the garden. The all-pervading air of sorrow even extended into this bright and cheerful room. "I don't know what I expected but I thought there might be more somehow, inside."

"Some stronger force," agreed Martin. "I know. It's odd."

He put his arm around her shoulders and hugged her quickly.

"What do we know about the Broome's?" asked Giles suddenly. "We know Ethan was supposed to marry Miranda but what happened to him after she died? Perhaps Mrs. Turner knows. She's been in this area her whole life and her family before her. She'll probably know a great deal about the whole thing. All the local gossip."

Mrs. Turner said nothing at first when Giles posed the question about the Miranda Templeton scandal. She indicated they should follow her from the drawing room and led them along more corridors to a back staircase. Nina lost all sense of direction by the time they'd made their way up to the broad first floor landing.

Mrs. Turner stopped before a closed door, turned to them, gathered expectantly before her and said in her dry voice, "Some folk say the young girl was seduced by the devil. My Gran told me it was her foreign blood made her susceptible. Different beliefs." She stared hard at Nina again but still made no comment. "Gran was only small at the time, about eight or nine but she remembered."

"What about Miranda's fiancé? Ethan Broome?" asked Giles.

Mrs. Turner folded her arms and drew a deep breath. She pursed thin lips. "Gran said he near went mad from grief. He had no idea, of course, that she was having an affair, until later but it wasn't her betrayal that upset him so much as that she died. And in such a

313

horrible way. He locked himself away and wouldn't mix or speak with anyone outside of his immediate family. Shame, some people said. The dishonour of it. That's when he painted this."

She opened the door and stood aside for them to enter a sitting room furnished with a couple of easy chairs grouped by the empty fireplace, a table with a lamp, a bookcase and a writing desk on the far wall beside the window, but it was the life-size portrait of a girl hung on the side wall which commanded immediate attention.

A beautiful girl with black hair and olive-toned skin, dark almond-shaped eyes and a faintly exotic curve to the cheeks and full red lips. She carried a bonnet in her hands, dangling it by a blue ribbon in front of her and she wore a light cotton print dress of tiny blue flowers on a white background. Behind her was the rose garden they had just visited but it was in full bloom and the sunlight slanted across catching the highlights in her glossy hair and illuminating the blood-red petals of the blooms.

The sadness in the room was suffocating, as if all the pent-up grief of the house had coalesced here.

"Miranda," Nina whispered. Her throat tightened as tears rushed to her eyes and her breathing faltered. "She's beautiful."

"She's the image of you," Martin said.

"She's so sad," murmured Jessica.

They gazed in silence until Mrs. Turner said in an oddly subdued tone, "Ethan Broome painted this after she died—from his memories. The strange thing was no one knew he could paint at all. He'd never shown any artistic talent in any form. He just shut himself up and this is what he produced."

"He was a remarkable man," said Giles solemnly. "He also insisted that Miranda be buried here in the grounds."

"Where?" Nina's voice erupted so harshly it startled not just her but the others as well.

"No one knows anymore." Mrs. Turner turned her curious gaze on Nina once more. "The headstone has been lost and there's no way of knowing where she lies."

"How could that have happened?" asked Jessica.

Mrs. Turner pursed her lips again and took another of her deep, considering breaths. "They said the grave was robbed by that devil."

"By her lover?" asked Martin as Nina gave an incredulous gasp, half laugh, half shocked choking.

"So the story goes. Took all trace of her."

Giles shook his head. "I think you'll find there's a much more prosaic explanation. If they used a wooden cross it has probably rotted away or been destroyed. Don't forget also, this area had an airfield close by during the war and it came in for some bombing attacks. Defensive fortifications were erected all over the shop. They could easily have demolished a grave site by accident or built over it without even realising."

"That's right. The house itself was nearly hit several times by bombs. They lost the stables and a plane crashed in the grounds once unable to make it back to the airfield," put in Jessica.

"Wouldn't her family have looked after her grave?" asked Nina.

"She was in disgrace, remember," said Giles. "Morals were very strict in those days."

"And remember what her brother did to her lover?" said Jessica.

Mrs. Turner sniffed. "I'm just telling you what the story says."

"What happened to Ethan in the end?" asked Martin.

"He was killed in the war."

"Which war?"

"Africa. The Boer War. He was killed there and his body shipped home."

"That was what? Six or seven years later?" said Giles. "1899 I think it started."

"He never married?" asked Nina

"No."

"The poor, poor man. What a complete tragedy." Jessica wielded her hanky.

"And it was all her fault." Mrs. Turner cast a disparaging look at Miranda's picture. "Don't know why Mr. Evans insisted on putting the thing in this room. Should have left it in the attic where he found it."

"He was quite taken with her, wasn't he?" asked Giles. "I remember him dragging me up here to have a look just after he discovered it."

"Irresponsible little witch! Some say she cast a spell on poor Ethan. Having that other foreign blood in her veins. She was different, not like proper folk."

Martin gripped Nina's arm hard as she made a sudden movement in the direction of the housekeeper but this time it wasn't Piers who was furious, it was Nina herself.

Jessica said diplomatically, "I suppose she was just a young girl who fell in love with the wrong man at the wrong time. If they'd met in another era they wouldn't have had such a problem. Nowadays for example, anything goes, as far as I can see."

"That's certainly true," said Mrs. Turner.

"Thank you very much for showing us around, Mrs. Turner," said Giles at his most vicarly. "We won't keep you any longer."

"Glad to have been of help though you haven't seen much of the place. Perhaps Mrs. Harrow can bring you back when Mr. and Mrs. Evans are here."

"I think we've seen what we wanted," said Martin. "Thank you."

"Yes, thanks," muttered Nina. She took one last lingering look at Miranda and made a silent promise to unite her with her love.

"I promise," she vowed. "You will be together again. I promise on my life."

She turned abruptly and stepped back out into the corridor filled with a new determination.

"Well," said Giles from the back seat when they were in the car and heading for the village once more. "What do you think about that?"

Nina twisted around from her place in the front next to Martin who was driving. "I think Mrs. Turner is singlehandedly responsible for every cliché about crabby housekeepers," she said. "She hates Miranda."

"She seems to inspire very strong emotions, our Miranda," commented Jessica. She tucked a wisp of hair back under her beanie.

"Yes, she had two men desperately in love with her and a brother who killed to avenge her honour," said Martin. "I wonder how Ethan managed to paint that portrait. It was very good, wasn't it?"

"Love," said Giles. "People can do extraordinary

things in the name of love be it earthly or spiritual. They can rise above themselves. The great artists often say some other force guides their hand when they are creating. They are simply conduits for a higher consciousness."

"Do you think," said Nina slowly in a tight voice, "Do you think maybe Piers guided Ethan's hand?"

"Piers wasn't an artist," objected Jessica.

"We don't know that," said Martin. "He was a very talented man. We don't know much about him at all."

"We know he didn't live long enough to fulfil his potential. And that Miranda's brother shot him," said Nina. "We have to help them. Did you feel the sadness in that place?"

"No, I didn't," said Giles in a surprised tone. "I felt coldness. The whole house was freezing."

"Nor me, although I thought Miranda looked sad. Something about her eyes," said Jessica. She lapsed into a pensive silence.

Nina looked at Martin sitting next to her. "You felt it, didn't you? In the room?" she murmured so the two in the back wouldn't hear.

He nodded, not taking his eyes from the narrow road as it wound between waterlogged cow pastures. They reached the first of the village cottages and he slowed the Saab when the swinging *Rose and Crown* pub sign came into view. A few slanting rays of the sun pierced weakly through the massed clouds and drops of water glittered brightly in the sudden spotlight. The yellow crown on the green background glowed gold briefly then faded to dull mustard as the sun disappeared again.

"Anyone for a pre-lunch pint?" Martin asked.

"Not for me thanks. I'd better take care of a few parish duties this afternoon," said Giles. "Wouldn't do for the vicar to go about smelling of beer."

"I'm ready for a rest. You two go," said Jessica. "Have some time alone together."

"We'll walk back from the vicarage then," said Martin. "All right, Nina?"

"Mmm." The crushing sense of that room of sorrow weighed heavy in her mind. What could they do to solve such an insurmountable problem? How could they, modern people, deal with a tragedy over a hundred years old, heal pain and suffering long since inflicted and constantly endured? Was it simply an echo from the past? Were they, as Martin had once surmised, picking up long gone psychic emissions?

Nina didn't think so. Her experiences were too terrifying and too real and very much in the present. Piers proved it.

When they retraced their route through the village on foot, hand in hand, Nina said softly, "I've never felt such sorrow in my life as in that room."

"Me neither. It was heartbreaking."

"I could barely breathe. But why didn't I hear Piers, Martin? He wasn't there at all except in the rose garden. And he was so angry. I've never felt such an all-consuming rage." Nina swallowed and clenched her free hand in her pocket at the memory.

Martin walked on slowly, considering his reply. "Giles might be right. It's not his place. It's Ethan's and Ethan was his rival. She was engaged to the man and maybe she refused to run off with Piers. It would have been a mighty brave thing to do, leave her family and the security of her future as mistress of Broome Hall.

Piers could see Ethan as a permanent obstacle. His was an obsessive, possessive passion whereas Ethan was devoted to her but expressed his love in a different way."

"You mean it's Ethan's grief we're feeling?"

"Yes. He was shattered by her death, too, but he wasn't such a passionate, emotional man as Piers and he was also able to live on past the immediate shock. Piers died in the midst of it all or pretty close to. His grief is unresolved. Ethan died years later."

"But his grief lives on in that painting he did." Nina stopped and wiped her hand over her eyes. She sniffed. "Not just his though, Martin. I think it's Miranda's sorrow too. Her yearning and loss is in that room as well. Did you see her eyes, her whole expression?"

"He captured it all in that painting, you think?"

"Yes, I think so. Maybe Piers had a hand in it somehow. Maybe Ethan painted it before Piers died. It was Piers who dabbled in the supernatural, after all, not Miranda like Mrs. Bigot Turner said. We'll probably never know."

"The others felt nothing. That's strange isn't it?" said Martin.

"They aren't as involved as we are," said Nina. She started walking again and Martin slipped his arm over her shoulders and hugged her close to him. The wind had lost none of its chill despite the brief bursts of sunshine. "Is it going to snow?" she asked hopefully. "I've never seen snow."

"Never?"

"It doesn't snow in Sydney, Martin, and I've never been to the snowfields."

"It might snow." He studied the heavy grey clouds being blasted across the sky like giant boulders. "I wish it was summer again. I've had enough of the cold and damp."

"Do you want to come back to Sydney?" What would she do if he preferred to remain in London? She squinted up at him as they walked. She hadn't thought much past the moment they were in since she'd left home. The post-Shadow Music future seemed too far away to contemplate but somehow she hadn't doubted Martin would be in that future with her. But they hadn't ever discussed it.

"I want to be where you are."

The rush of relief saturated her whole body. "Good."

"Did you think I'd let you go back to Sydney alone?" he asked. "I think we belong together and it's the only good thing about this whole mess."

"Piers brought us together," said Nina. "He wanted us to be together."

"But only to help him," said Martin. "I'll always be grateful to him for that if nothing else. The bastard."

They reached the pub and Martin pushed open the door. Inside, wood panelling and a low ceiling gave the room a warmth and cosiness exaggerated by the gruesome weather outdoors. A roaring log fire at one end of the room gave off a blast of heat. They were the only customers and the man behind the bar bade them a cheery welcome as he polished glasses and lined them up on the counter.

Martin gave their order while Nina moved across and stretched her hands toward the fire. A mantelpiece over the fireplace held an array of sporting cups and trophies and one or two photographs of cricket and football teams. Various paintings of hunting dogs and horses decorated the walls. Nina gave them all a cursory glance then stared into the leaping flames. Warmth began to creep back into her extremities and she peeled off her thick coat and slung it over the back of the nearest chair. Martin placed two brimming half pints of beer on the table.

"We can have lunch here if you like," he said.

"Fine." Nina sat down. Martin took a deep draught of his beer.

"What can we do?" she asked. "I don't want to go through that again, what happened yesterday. And today."

"I know but I don't know how to stop it happening." He was as bewildered as she beneath the relatively calm face he showed her.

But he wasn't cracking under the strain. If he collapsed the way she sometimes felt like doing there was no telling what would happen to her. Martin was her touchstone of sanity, had been from the moment she'd set eyes on him. She loved him, she realised with a sudden burst of clear thinking. Martin was her partner, her lover, her friend, that elusive being everyone searched for but few found in their short allotted time on earth.

Piers and Miranda had found each other. Briefly. Piers knew the importance of the find, Piers knew how rare it was but Piers could not be allowed to usurp her soul to replace what he had lost, that love that shone and glowed white hot then was brutally ripped from his grasp by fate. It wasn't his to take from her and Martin the way he had torn happiness from Ethan.

"I'm trying to fight him now," she admitted. She raised her eyes to his face. "I didn't at first. He's so strong and so…I couldn't resist him, Martin. He told me what he wanted and I tried to do it for him." Her voice trailed off.

"I know. I was as just as hooked as you by the music, remember."

"But you didn't fall in love with him," she cried and then quickly dropped her voice as the publican shot her a startled look. "I did."

"You or Miranda?" Martin asked softly.

"I don't know but after that last time I can't do it anymore. I have to resist him. Why has he picked me?"

Martin gazed at her. "She is amazingly similar," he murmured. "I wonder. Could you really be related? Remember we wondered before but we hadn't seen her? You have the same name in your family. What do you know about your Chinese grandparent's families?"

"Hardly anything. The Sung family came to Australia in the gold rush—the 1850's. I have no idea about any other relatives, or who might have married who and travelled abroad."

"So there is a possibility that Miranda's mother's family is connected with yours way back in China or even since they moved to Australia. Miranda's father did travel and brought his wife back from overseas, we know that much. He could have gone to Australia."

"I suppose so."

"I thought so, remember? It would explain why Piers chose you," said Martin. "He's had to wait a long time for the circumstances to be right and now he's not going to give up."

"But he thinks he's resurrecting her," she objected.

"He's confusing her with me. I'm confusing her with me." A small strangled laugh emerged which nearly turned to a sob.

"We have to prove to him that he's not and that you're a different person."

"But that won't help them be together," she said.

"They can't be, Nina. It's impossible!"

She firmed her mouth into a flat line. "If we don't get them together we won't achieve anything. This will go on and on forever just as it has been and I can't guarantee he won't absorb me completely even if I do try to resist him."

"What do you suggest we do then?" Martin leaned back in his chair and studied her as if to say the problem was hers to solve. "Giles has ruled out exorcism so we can't get rid of the damned man that way. We can't destroy the music. We don't know where either of them is buried. We've achieved absolutely nothing by coming here," he finished in disgust.

"But we have achieved something. We've found Miranda and we know where she died." Her voice faltered and she stared at Martin as the memories of that nightmarish hallucination flooded her mind.

"Nina," he said sharply. He grabbed her hand and squeezed her fingers so hard she cried out in pain.

"Stop it. I'm here with you. I was just remembering. She wanted to be with him so much." Her eyes filled with tears. "There must be a way."

"When you think of it, tell me because I haven't a clue." He picked up his beer glass. "Let's order lunch."

Jessica joined them a short while later. She came in with her cheeks pink and her nose red, an excited light in her eyes, pushing through the lunchtime drinkers who had slowly gathered in the bar.

"May I?" She indicated the spare chair at their table. She pulled off her coat and Martin hung it up for her as she sat down.

"We've ordered soup," he said. "Like some?"

"Lovely. Thank you."

He went to order for her.

"I'm sorry to barge in on you two but I've been thinking," she announced when he sat down again.

The crowded room, full of chatter and laughter effectively screened their conversation but Nina and Martin instinctively leaned closer to hear what she'd come up with.

"We've been trying to think of a way to prove to Piers that Miranda is dead, haven't we?" she asked. "Trying to stop him manipulating you. Now, I asked myself, what is it he wants?"

"To be with Miranda," answered Nina promptly.

"Exactly."

"But we were just discussing that and it's impossible." Not impressed by Jessica's brainwork so far.

"But he can be," she said triumphantly. "We've got Piers whenever we want him or at least you can summon him up Martin, can't you, like you did in London?" She was almost breathless with excitement.

"But we don't have Miranda," said Nina slowly.

"We do now. We have the painting of the real Miranda, and we have you." Jessica eyes were wide, her face flushed from the fire and her own animation. "You can play the Shadow Music just as he wants. We can bring them together. We can bring Piers to life in front of the painting and he'll see her and recognise her, here in the village where they met."

"And then what?" asked Martin.

"Don't you think if we play the music and Nina allows Piers to come through and speak to her and she speaks for Miranda and we control it they'll be together and maybe he'll be satisfied?"

"No," said Martin. "I think he'll want more. And what makes you think we can control it? Look what happened last time."

Nina said suddenly, "What if we marry them? If we get Giles to bless them and marry them?"

"Yes," breathed Jessica. "Oh, yes. Lay them both to rest as a married couple."

"What do you think?" Nina turned to Martin expectantly. He screwed up his brow and cocked his head to one side sceptically.

"Maybe. It'd be dangerous though, for you. Very dangerous." He leaned forward and grabbed her hands. "Could you do it?"

Nina swallowed. "I think so. We have to try, don't we? But…" she gave a tiny ghost of a laugh, "There's always the danger I'll end up married to Piers instead of Miranda."

Martin smiled. "There is one other problem of course. We have to get the painting out of Broome Hall, and do you think Mrs. Turner will let us take it? We can't possibly do it there."

"No problem," said Jessica fiercely. "We'll get her to call Rupert, or I will, and ask his permission. But why do we need to move it?"

"Because that place is grief stricken and Piers can't go there. It's Ethan's grief, we think," said Nina. "We both felt it. It's oppressive. Like a shroud."

"Goodness. I've never felt anything remotely like that there," said Jessica in amazement. "But if you say so. Perhaps the church is the best place then."

"Would Piers approve?" asked Martin.

"I think he would for Miranda's sake," Nina said after a moment. "I think he would want whatever she wanted and she would want to be married in church, her own church."

"And she'd be forgiven at the same time," said Jessica. "If Giles blessed her. Nina's right, a girl of Miranda's time and place in society would want to be married in church with the blessing of her family and her community."

"Poor girl won't have the blessing of her family," said Martin.

"Unless you count me," offered Nina.

Their soup arrived and as soon as the waitress had gone Jessica said, "That must be so, mustn't it? Why did we never think of it before?"

"We did," said Martin, "but we hadn't seen how much alike they are. That painting really clinches it, doesn't it?"

"Do you think Giles will be in it?" asked Nina. "Marrying a ghost to a painting?"

"Why ever not?" Jessica gazed at them both with her soup spoon suspended above her bowl.

Nina and Martin stared back at her and then all three burst out laughing at the same moment. Nina had to put her spoon down she was laughing so much and they cackled and wheezed at their table until exhaustion and sore stomach muscles made them stop.

"Bags you ask him," gasped Nina to Jessica.

"It was your idea," she retorted.

"Do you think it will work?" Nina looked at Martin, serious now.

He picked up his spoon and took a mouthful of soup. Nina did the same. Leek and potato soup, hot, thick and hearty with chunks of brown bread to go with it.

"Good soup," he said.

"Martin?" Nina swallowed the mouthful and watched him intently. "Do you?"

He raised his eyes to hers and said softly, "I absolutely couldn't bear it if anything happened to you, Nina. I'd never forgive myself, I couldn't live with myself." He paused, moisture in his eyes as he gazed at her. She stretched her arm out and gripped his hand in hers. He smiled. "And your Dad would have my guts for garters."

"What could happen, really?" asked Jessica.

"I've no idea," said Martin. "That's the trouble. We just don't know. I suppose the worst that could happen is Nina actually becomes Miranda or Miranda takes over Nina's spirit or whatever, and we lose her to the past."

"But I can fight him now," said Nina. "I know he wants Miranda not me."

"But can you really?" asked Jessica. "Look what happened yesterday. You had no control over that."

"But I went willingly. Now—now, I don't want to go through that again. Anyway you'll all be there, and we'll be in the church. It'll be different." To Nina herself that sounded forlorn and by his expression Martin was far from convinced. "We should see what Giles thinks. If he won't be in it we can't try it anyway."

"I'll contact Rupert this afternoon and see if we can get Miranda out of that room," said Jessica in a stronger more purposeful tone. "Now, eat up. We'll need our strength to face Giles."

Chapter Sixteen

Giles didn't return to the vicarage until the evening. The light faded rapidly as the afternoon wore on and although it wasn't late, Jessica turned on the lights and drew the curtains against the cold and encroaching darkness. Martin managed to keep the wood fire going in the living room and even brought in another basket of logs from the wood shed outside.

"Wood fires are all very well," he grumbled as he dumped the basket on the hearth. "But they're bloody hard work."

"Very romantic, though." Staring into the flames, Nina sat snug and warm in one of the armchairs, her feet tucked under her and a glass of wine in her hand.

"You can bring in the next load of wood then." He bent to kiss her. Nina slid her hand around the back of his neck and pulled him closer. The urgency in her kiss told him she was frightened, wanted reassurance despite her apparent calm. He squatted down beside the chair.

"Are you sure you want to try this?" He held her face gently in his hands and kissed her again. Nina nodded.

"We have to," she said firmly.

"Okay." He stood up and went to the kitchen where Jessica was assisting Mrs. Webb, Giles' cook and housekeeper. If Mrs. Turner was the epitome of a nasty housekeeper Mrs. Webb was the opposite—nonstop talk and spent most of her time sitting down as he far as he could gather from their short acquaintance.

"It's my legs you know," she said to Jessica as Martin entered the kitchen. "They go right up to my knees."

"Goodness gracious," exclaimed Jessica and shot Martin a look fraught with suppressed laughter. He looked away quickly and went to the cupboard for a glass.

"You don't have to stay, Mrs. Webb, we can manage very well, thank you, now that you've got the dinner under way," said Jessica. "It's so nasty out tonight you'd best get home early. Don't want to be running about in the cold late at night. With your legs."

Mrs. Webb hauled herself up off the chair her face wreathed in smiles.

"That's very kind of you, Mrs. Harrow. I would like to get off home. Sid worries when I'm out late this weather. I tell him it's only a skip and a hop to the vicarage from home but you know what men are like, think we women are helpless. Little do they know, eh?" She gave Jessica a conspiratorial wink and nodded in the direction of Martin who was pretending not to listen while he poured himself a glass of red wine. "Let them think it, I say. The dinner's in the oven and should be ready in an hour and a half. Just check occasionally that it hasn't started to dry out. The flame can go under the potatoes and other veggies about twenty minutes before you want to eat.

"Thank you very much," said Jessica. "It'll be wonderful and we'll manage."

"Leave the dishes and I'll clear up in the morning." Mrs. Webb struggled into her coat and pulled a yellow and purple knitted hat down over her ears. "Night all. Here I go off into the wild, black yonder." She gave a raucous shout of laughter.

"Take care," called Martin. "Good night."

"Thank you, good night." Jessica closed the kitchen door firmly as Mrs. Webb's bulky figure disappeared into the night. "What an exhausting woman. Excellent cook though, I think."

"Smells good. When will Giles be home?"

"She thought about five-thirty. It's after that now."

"Glass of red?" Martin held the bottle up invitingly.

"Yes, please. I think we all need fortification. This is the most extraordinary thing I've ever come across, Martin. I hope I'm strong enough to be of some help to you."

"Jessica, you're marvellous." Martin reached down another wine glass from the cupboard and filled it. "You've no idea how we felt when we met you and you believed us. And you have helped, enormously. We didn't know about Cutting Marsh or Broome Hall—you did. And how would we have found the painting without you?"

Jessica smiled and touched Martin's arm. "Thank you. My worst fear is becoming a silly, useless old woman. I tell my children to knock me on the head if I get like that."

Martin kissed her soft cheek. "You've a long way to go yet, Jessica Harrow."

"So. Can't leave you two alone for a minute and you're canoodling in the kitchen." Nina's amused voice made Martin smile. She held out her empty glass and he poured her another.

The front door crashed open and a blast of cold air rushed down the hall and into the kitchen.

"Good heavens, it's cold. Snow on the way, I'll wager," came Giles voice booming around the vicarage. "Anybody here?"

"In the kitchen," called Jessica. Martin got out another glass in readiness.

Giles came in, rubbing his hands, a wide smile splitting his face, pudgy cheeks glowing red, hair wispy and wet against his forehead.

"How are we all?" he boomed. "I must say it's lovely to have company when I come home, especially on a foul and desperate night like this."

"Here." Martin thrust the glass of red into his hand.

"Oh, I say, what service, thank you indeed, Martin." He beamed around at them all and raised his glass. "Cheers."

"Cheers," they chorused.

"Dinner will be about an hour and a half," said Jessica. "I sent Mrs. Webb home."

"Marvellous."

"Come and sit by the fire, Giles, we have something to ask you," said Nina.

They waited while Giles went upstairs for a moment and then returned in woollen sweater and slippers to settle himself with his wine in the armchair next to Jessica's. Nina and Martin sat facing them on the couch.

"Fire away," said Giles.

Martin exchanged a glance with Nina. It was her crazy idea. He'd support her in it but he wouldn't promote it.

"We've decided we should change our approach,"

said Nina. "The whole time we've been trying to think of ways to prove to Piers that Miranda is dead and that he can't resurrect her."

"We should help them be together," burst in Jessica eagerly. "Don't you agree, Giles? Reunite them. That's what Piers really wants."

"Yes, I do agree," Giles said slowly. "How?"

"Marry them," announced Jessica.

Giles absorbed this dramatic statement and then the realities and ramifications began to manifest themselves. His cherubic face froze in an expression of bewilderment while Jessica's words hung in the air. Then he opened and closed his mouth twice and looked desperately at first Martin and then Nina as if seeking reassurance that he'd heard correctly.

"Who exactly?" he asked.

"Piers and Miranda," said Nina.

"Who else?" asked Jessica.

"Indeed." Giles picked up his wine glass, drank, and replaced it on its coaster on the coffee table. "They don't exist," he said. "Anymore."

"But they do," exclaimed Jessica. "Piers can be summoned at will. Both these two have seen him and spoken to him."

She leaned forward, fingers gripping each other so hard the knuckles were white. Giles stared at her. He might suddenly decide he was hosting a group of lunatics and throw them all out. Martin glanced at Nina and she too was gazing at Giles with an eager, apprehensive expression.

"We have to do something, Giles. I know this sounds insane but this has to be stopped before Nina is permanently harmed. We're getting desperate," Martin said in as rational a voice as he could muster. "We think that painting of Miranda that Ethan did, holds her spirit. She's waiting there in deep sorrow."

"Waiting for Piers," interrupted Nina. "She's devastated. The sadness in that room is unbearable. If we take that painting to the church we thought we could summon Piers with the music and then I may be able to summon Miranda's spirit or allow her to appear through me and then…"

"You want me to marry them," finished Giles.

Nina nodded. Martin held his breath as the silence stretched. Jessica still clutched her hands together. Giles closed his eyes. His lips moved in prayer then his eyes popped open. He looked at Jessica.

"Can we get the painting?"

"I'll ring Rupert and ask him to speak to the housekeeper."

"If I hadn't experienced that music…I suppose it's no more insane than anything else we've been up to lately." Giles laughed a strained-sounding laugh quite unlike his usual boisterous chuckle. Then his face clouded. "Won't it be dangerous for you, Nina?"

"Yes," she said. "It might be but if we don't try it what else will we do? Go on like this forever? Time has no meaning for Piers. And we're so close to resolving it."

"True." Giles nodded. "I take it you'll be using the music to summon Piers?"

"Yes," said Martin. "Perhaps we can record the parts and play it that way. I can use meditation as well. That seems to be the most effective combination. We need Nina to represent Miranda. At first, at least. We want Piers to see the painting and then, who knows?"

"I'll be in charge of the tape player," said Jessica. "I can turn it off if things get too out of control."

"So you want me to perform the marriage service when he appears and Nina will make the responses for Miranda?"

"Yes," said Martin and Nina together.

"At worst I'll be married to Piers," added Nina with a weak little smile.

"Piers didn't appear to be a believer, a Christian," said Giles.

"Does that matter?" asked Jessica. "Miranda was. Anyway we don't really know that about him. Many people dabble in alternative beliefs and still cling to a belief in God and the church when it comes to the important events in their lives."

"Hatch, match, and dispatch," agreed Giles. "Sadly yes, you're right. Even less so now than back then, I would surmise."

"So you're saying that even if Piers did experiment with the Golden Dawn thing he would have been brought up in the Christian tradition?" asked Nina. "And still basically follow the church teachings?"

"I would say so, yes," said Giles. "Given the era and his family background and social standing.

"Miranda most certainly would have been a faithful churchgoer," said Jessica. "She deserves to be given eternal rest and happiness."

"So does Piers," said Nina. "His only crime was to fall in love."

"A crime of which we're all guilty at some time in our lives," said Giles. He raised his glass. "To Piers and Miranda, may our plan succeed and grant them eternal rest in each other's arms."

"Piers and Miranda," chorused Martin, Nina, and Jessica. "Here's to this one final and irrevocable step," added Martin. Glasses clinked. For better or for worse. Till death us do part.

****

Nina peered through the trees. The sunlight slanted between the branches of the oaks in shafts of hot silver. She lifted the heavy hair from the back of her neck. Twigs had caught in her bonnet and pulled it off as she walked along the narrow track to the clearing. Her hair had come loose and tumbled down, hot in the stifling afternoon.

"Piers," she whispered. "Where are you?"

She sat down on the cool grass under one of the trees and plucked some small yellow flowers. The jingle of his horse's bridle sounded and the thud of its hooves on the hard earth. His voice spoke soothing words to the horse and then she caught sight of his tall frame moving between the tree trunks, hurrying to meet her, his love. She jumped to her feet and ran across the clearing to throw herself into his arms.

"My darling," he said.

His lips moved against hers, his arms held her tightly against his body. This was where she was meant to be, here in his arms. Forever.

"Mira, my life, my love," he whispered.

Nina pulled away. "I'm Nina," she said. "Not Miranda, I'm Nina."

Piers dragged her back into his embrace and kissed her again so her body melted boneless against his. He began to undo the small buttons on her dress and slide the light cotton from her shoulders. He kissed the bare skin, heated now with desire. His lips caressed her neck and her throat and searched lower to her breasts where his gentle fingers were sending ripples of desire cascading through her body.

"Piers, I love you," she whispered.

"You're mine. I want you to come away with me. Be mine. We should be together. Mira, my darling,"

"Nina!" The word shot from her lips like a whip crack. "I'm Nina."

She pushed Piers away but he smiled. "You're Miranda and you're mine. You love me with all your heart and with your soul and I love you. I won't let you go. You belong with me. You know that. You feel it the way I do. You come to me." He stepped closer and gazed into her eyes. Nina's resolve faltered as a tidal wave of desire swept through her body. He slid his arms around her waist and kissed her gently, letting his lips toy with hers, gradually increasing the pressure as he felt her ardour grow and her resistance fade.

Nina came awake with a start. The room was pitch black. She groped frantically with her left hand and felt Martin's solid bulk beside her. He stirred and rolled over toward her to pull her against him. Nina snuggled into his chest with his arms wrapped securely around her body. Martin, not Piers. Martin was the man she loved.

She had to fight. She was Nina. Piers knew she was Nina but he didn't care. But she'd been dreaming and odd things happen in dreams. It was a dream. Wasn't it? Nina lay awake until she heard Giles lumbering to the bathroom and then downstairs to get the breakfast tea underway. Then she slid out of bed.

****

Jessica joined Nina and Giles in the kitchen.

"It's all fixed," she said. "Rupert called Mrs. Turner and we can collect the painting whenever we like. He just wants us to take care of it and return it in one piece. He's very attached to it he said."

"Miranda makes another conquest," remarked Giles. "More tea, Nina?"

"Thanks. What did you tell him we wanted it for?" she asked.

"I'm afraid I told a little fib. I said I had a friend who thought she might be related to Miranda and wanted to take the painting to Plymouth to be professionally photographed for her family back in Australia. I told him you were researching your family history."

"And he didn't mind?"

"No. He thought it was fascinating that you were so similar in appearance, and Mrs. Turner will certainly back us up there. It's not a valuable work at all. Only to us. So. When do we do the deed?" asked Jessica.

"Wait till Martin gets back," said Nina. "He's gone for a walk. He's worried about this. He doesn't think it'll work."

"He's frightened for you but he'll go through with it, I think," said Jessica.

"Yes, he will."

"He loves you. Love gives people amazing strength," said Giles. "That and faith."

"I don't have religious faith as such," said Nina. "Will that matter?"

"You might not have faith in the God Jessica and I have faith in but you have a good heart and you know what is the right thing to do. God rewards those things."

"Does that mean Piers will be damned for

eternity?"

"I think his soul has lost its way. If he has led a good life and his heart is true he will be given salvation."

"We don't know what sort of life he led," said Jessica. "But he loved truly and passionately. Love certainly gave him strength."

"I just want them to be together," said Nina. "Then they will both be happy, regardless."

"Whatever happened to Tyler?" asked Jessica suddenly. "Do we know?"

"Her brother?" said Giles. "He was arrested for the murder and convicted. He went to gaol but was released before he'd completed his sentence. He died as well, in Africa."

"In the Boer War?"

"No, later. He left England as a migrant. Went to Kenya and died of some disease. Never married, poor man."

"So the Templeton family died out?" said Nina.

"That branch did. Whether there were relatives or not I don't know."

"What a sad, sad saga. And the poor father outlived them all," said Jessica. "Such irony, his being a doctor and dedicating his life to helping others."

The back door opened and closed with a bang. A rush of cold air preceded Martin as he entered the kitchen. His nose and cheeks were red and he rubbed his hands together before pulling out a chair beside Nina.

"What did you decide?" asked Jessica.

Martin drew a deep breath. "I think we have to try. We have to make it as safe as we can but we have to give it a go. I can't think of anything else even remotely likely to work, let alone better."

Nina sighed. Another voice breathed in her ear. "Yes."

"Piers wants us to do it," she said softly.

"Did he say so?" asked Martin. His eyes narrowed under a frowning brow. "Is he talking to you, now?"

"No, not really. He's pleased. I can tell."

"Only because we're finally doing what he wants," said Martin. "He's a bully."

"Or it might be because he thinks it will be a solution," said Giles.

"How can he possibly know what we intend to do?" asked Nina. "He's never suggested he wanted to marry Miranda. He's never mentioned the word at all. He wants her to go away with him but he's never said marry me."

"That's because he was taking advantage of her, the poor innocent girl."

"Maybe he feels the change in attitude. That we're not fighting against him anymore," suggested Jessica.

"Possibly," admitted Martin. "I'm sorry. I'm just so sick of that bloody man and his broken heart running my life. It's been nearly a year. I want it ended. I want my life back."

"It's been well over a hundred years for him," said Nina tartly.

"Other people lose loved ones. Other people deal with it and keep going without creating chaos through the ages. He'd have no notion of time anyway. He's got eternity to mess around in people's heads."

"That's why we have to do something. Now." Why was he being so damned belligerent? This was their best chance. "They have to be brought together. I want him out of my head too, Martin." And her bed and her body.

"Won't we need rings?" asked Jessica into the tense silence.

"One should be enough. Just one for Miranda," said Giles calmly. How could he miss the force field crackling like lightning between herself and Martin?

"I don't have anything suitable," she muttered.

"We can use my wedding ring," said Jessica.

"Are you sure you want to take it off?" Martin's voice was quieter, accepting of a decision taken.

"I think it may be in a good cause." Jessica smiled. "It slips off my finger so easily in this cold weather." She stared at the slim gold band gleaming dully against her pale skin.

"Thank you," said Nina.

"Anyway, it's not as if I'm going to lose it, am I? It'll be on your finger, won't it?"

"Will it? I suppose so."

"It can't go on Miranda's," Jessica pointed out. "Here, see if it fits."

She slid the ring off and offered it across the table to Nina who studied it in her palm for a moment.

"It's rose gold," said Jessica.

"It's lovely." It went on to her third finger easily. "This is so weird," murmured Nina. She handed the ring back to Jessica. "How exactly will we organise this wedding ceremony?"

They sat and discussed and argued on and off for most of the morning. Giles eventually announced he had to prepare his sermon for Sunday.

Nina asked, "What day is it, today?"

"Friday."

"I had no idea. I've completely lost track."

"When will we do it?" asked Jessica. "I could collect Miranda this afternoon."

"I'll drive you," said Martin. "And you should come with us," he said to Nina.

"I don't want to go into that house again."

"Wait in the car then or walk in the garden. I'm not leaving you here alone. Giles will be busy and I don't expect him to keep an eye on you."

"We could do that and then spend the afternoon in Plymouth," said Jessica.

"We can take Miranda to Plymouth," said Nina. "She might like an outing."

"I don't think so," said Martin. "It's a large painting. I'm wondering if it will even fit in the car."

"I think it will although Nina may not fit in the backseat as well," said Giles.

"I'll stay here with Giles. I'll sit quietly in the corner of his study and read a book until you get back," said Nina. "I promise."

"We won't be long, Martin," said Jessica. "Half an hour and then we can pop in to Plymouth for a late lunch and leave Giles in peace for the rest of the afternoon. There are some wonderful historical sites."

"Sir Francis Drake," exclaimed Nina. "The Mayflower."

"Yes and lots of other things besides."

****

Martin and Jessica carefully stowed the painting of Miranda in the backseat of the Saab. Mrs. Turner had draped a large cloth over it and propped it against a wall in the foyer, waiting.

"I won't be sorry to see the back of that," she said. "Mr. Turner said it gave him the creeps just touching it to bring it downstairs."

"We'll bring it back safe and sound in a day or two," said Jessica. "Thank you, Mrs. Turner."

"Thank you, Mrs. Harrow." She closed the door, not even waiting to see them to the car.

Martin carried Miranda in to the vicarage and propped her against the dining room table. Jessica carefully removed the cloth.

"She looks happier already," said Giles.

"Is Piers here?" asked Jessica.

Nina frowned. "No. It's funny, I thought he'd be terribly excited to see her. He may not have known there was a portrait of her and now she's out of Broome Hall you'd think he'd be here."

"It's just a painting," said Martin. "It probably holds no spiritual link to the real Miranda."

"Well, if that's the case what we want to do won't work." Nina's heart plummeted.

"No, but you do, you feel the link," said Jessica and placed a reassuring hand on her arm. "And you both felt the sorrow emanating from it, so there is something there."

"Let's go to Plymouth," said Martin. "I'm hungry and I want to think about other, normal things for an afternoon."

When they returned to the vicarage after eating and sightseeing and generally trying to behave like tourists despite the miserable weather, Giles was out. He'd moved the painting to a place against the wall in the dining room.

Nina stood in front of Miranda and studied her

carefully. She recognised elements of her own face—the rounded cheeks and hint of Asian ancestry in the eyes and full-lipped mouth. But where they differed apart from the obviousness of clothing and hair style, was in the expression. Ethan had captured a certain light in her eyes and a downturn of the lips which, while not making Miranda actually frown or grimace, exuded a deep sorrow, a soul sickness, as if great sobbing, shattering tears might break free and flow down the painted cheeks.

Martin came and stood beside her.

"Her heart is broken," Nina said softly.

"Poor girl. She was beautiful. Just like you. No wonder he adored her. What a horrible way to go. I wonder if Piers found her before she died."

Nina paused before she answered. An image flashed before her mind's eye.

"Yes, he did. I saw it once. I was looking down at them. I think I was Miranda's spirit leaving her body." Nina shuddered and whispered, "Piers was kneeling in the mud and the rain, holding her in his arms and crying." A tear trickled down her cheek.

Soft music began floating about the room. The Shadow Music.

"Martin? Do you hear it?" She gripped his fingers and looked around quickly, fearfully. The sounds faded. Mrs. Webb laughed in the kitchen.

Martin said, "I think so. It was it, wasn't it?" His voice was hoarse. "My hair's standing on end."

"He's here. Piers is here, waiting for her."

"Is he speaking to you?"

"No, but I can feel him. He's watching. Waiting."

The music came again, stronger this time. The

violin soared above the other instruments; the temperature in the room rose. Voices chanted.

The outer door slammed. Giles called, "Hello all, how was Plymouth?"

The music and voices stopped instantly. Giles appeared in the doorway with a wide smile which faded immediately when he saw their faces. His gaze flicked behind them to the painting.

"Good heavens."

Nina and Martin spun around. Miranda was glowing. Faint and rapidly dimming but a definite glow emanated from her skin. Her eyes almost sparkled with life.

"It'll work," exclaimed Nina. "Martin, see? We must do it. Right now."

"What's happened?" asked Giles.

Nina gabbled, "We were looking at the painting and discussing Piers. I could feel his presence but he wasn't talking to me."

Martin broke in. "And then the Shadow Music started playing. With all the instruments, and voices chanting."

Nina interrupted again. "Then you came home and it stopped. But it works."

Giles stared from one to the other. "Extraordinary," he murmured. He rubbed his chin and studied the painting. "But what about the chant? That could be a crucial part. None of us know that."

"We could re-create it and you could listen and write down the words. It's sure to be in Latin. You do speak Latin, don't you?" demanded Nina.

"It wasn't my best subject at Theological College but yes, I do."

"It didn't sound like Latin to me," said Martin. "Isn't it more likely to be an eastern chant?"

"Om mani padme om?" suggested Giles.

"Yes, but it's not that."

Jessica came in carrying a tray with nuts, cheese and crackers. "Hello, Giles." She placed the tray on the coffee table. "What's going on?"

"Did you hear the music just now?" asked Martin.

"Which music?"

"The Shadow Music," said Nina. "Piers played it to us a few minutes ago. With chanting. It made Miranda glow."

Jessica sat down abruptly. Her face went pale and she pressed a shaky hand to her mouth. "So that means he's here? With us?"

Nina nodded. "He's waiting."

"Did you hear it in the kitchen?" asked Martin.

Jessica shook her head. "Not a thing, although Mrs. Webb was going on about her son. He lives in Canada."

"We have to do the wedding tonight," said Nina. "Giles? Can we?"

"I have a meeting first. I have to go in to Plymouth."

"How long will it take?"

Giles frowned, disconcerted by Nina's peremptory manner. "I should be home by eleven."

"We'll do it then," she replied. "We can add the flute part to the tape tonight while you're out."

"I'd better put the heating on in the church or we'll freeze to death. It's very hot in here, by the way."

Martin looked at Nina. "The temperature rose when the music played, I think."

She nodded. "Maybe we won't need heating in the

347

church after all."

"I need a sherry," announced Jessica. "This is all getting to be rather disturbing."

****

Giles returned at eleven fifteen. Rain poured down again.

"Are you sure you want to go ahead with it tonight?" His hair dripped onto his collar and his damp face shone like a rising moon in the mist. He came farther into the room. The bottoms of his trousers were soaked, and his shoes left dark footprints on the carpet.

"Yes," said Nina firmly. "Yes, definitely."

"We can't stand anymore," said Martin quietly.

"Not much point my changing then." Giles smiled then straightened his lips into a thin line and raised his eyebrows. "We'd better cover Miranda. Don't want her to run."

"We've done that already," said Martin. "I'm afraid we raided your coat closet."

"In that case, let's get on then, shall we?"

Nina clutched the handle of George's violin case and tried not to let the insanity of what they were about to do take over her mind. Martin's flute, in its case, was tucked inside her parka and Jessica splashed behind her carrying a tape player wrapped in plastic bags, and a large umbrella which she held partially over Nina as well as herself. Giles and Martin went ahead with the painting, their two umbrellas waving wildly about as they struggled between the branches hanging low and heavy with rain, over the path. Were the ancient pines trying to prevent them entering the church? The building loomed above them, dark and forbidding, darker and more threatening than the wretched night itself. Disapproving. Were they about to commit a sin against God? Against nature?

But Giles was with them. He was the custodian. Surely he gave sanctity to the whole affair?

He ushered them into the comparative warmth, turned on the lights and closed the solid old wooden door against the clawing wind. He'd turned the heating on before leaving for his meeting but their breath still rose in steamy vapours in the chill air. Martin carefully removed the sodden overcoats and carried Miranda to the altar rail where he removed her coverings and propped her facing the body of the church.

"Shouldn't she face the altar?" asked Jessica.

"I don't know."

"Yes," said Nina. "She should."

****

Cutting Marsh, 1892

Hurrying to wait for Miranda in their special place, Piers was hampered by a sudden storm on the road from Plymouth where he had stayed for the weeks since the Summer Ball. Rain had fallen lightly in the town but passed on earlier, so the onslaught of drenching rain surprised him as he approached the village, the storm shocking in its violence. He sheltered in a barn in a fever of impatience, waiting for the worst to pass.

Then he was away, galloping in panic-stricken flight, urging his horse faster over the slippery, treacherous ground. Knowing deep in his soul something was wrong, something had happened to send a deathly chill through his body.

He reached the grove an hour after the passing of the storm. The clouds had parted and stars twinkled brightly, the fresh scent of moist grass and thirst-quenching rain taunted him as he rode toward the glowering trees. They huddled dark and mysterious, secretive, hiding he knew not what.

He tethered his panting, steaming horse and pushed through the trees, stumbled in the darkness over tree roots and fallen branches. The grove had suffered severely in the storm.

His heart rose into his mouth and he shouted, "Mira. Are you here?" He prayed that his desperate attempt to contact her by thought had failed and she had once more stayed home. He would rather she shunned meeting him yet again than venture out this foul night. He could never forgive himself if she were harmed.

The wind stirred the high branches overhead. Cold drops of water splashed onto his face and coat. The ground squelched soft underfoot and he forced his way forward until his path was blocked by a large fallen branch; a giant limb from one of the oaks sprawled wide and heavy. He picked his way around it, shaking with trepidation.

A pale patch amongst the dark caught his eye and he cried out in fear as he darted forward to find Miranda lying trapped, her beautiful body bloodied and crushed.

He knelt on the sodden damaged ground, cradled her head in his arms and her eyes opened. Her lips formed the word "Piers". She smiled weakly as he pressed his lips on hers. He laid her down then set about freeing her broken body from the massive weight of the branch. She whimpered with pain as he struggled with all his might to drag the limb off her chest. Slowly, carefully, gently he pulled her clear and held her once more in his arms.

Then he sat crooning and whispering to her, sobbing as her life ebbed away.

Piers watched Mira die in his arms and as the last fluttering breath left her body he lifted his tear-stained face to the star-studded black velvet of the sky and vowed they would be together again. They would be together always. He would find a way, no matter how long it took, how far he travelled, what sacrifices needed to be made.

"I will be with you, my darling, my love, my life," he cried to the wind and the stars and the moon shining swollen and full through the trees. "You will live again. We will be together."

He bent and kissed her lips, those lips once so full of laughter and love now pale and chill in death. He stroked her silken locks and folded her soft white hands across her shattered breast. The breast upon which he had laid his head so many times and the hands whose fingers had caressed him so tenderly, now stiffening in the harshness of death.

"I will find you Mira. We will be together. I will find a way."

****

Cutting Marsh, 1999

"How will we do this?" asked Martin. "Should we play the tape and see what happens, or should Giles begin the marriage service?" His voice sounded small and feeble in the cold, empty space.

"There's not much point starting the service without the bride and groom," pointed out Giles.

"I think we should play the tape and if that's not strong enough you and I can play as well," said Nina.

"I should meditate. That's what summoned him up

before. Physically."

"He actually appeared? Oh, dear." Jessica's hand flew to her lips.

"I hope I can focus deeply enough." Martin took a kneeler from a pew and sat on the far side of the altar next to the portrait, facing it. "The conditions aren't ideal."

Nina shivered. The heating didn't have much effect on the cold air inside the church. Any warmth rose into the icy darkness of the vaulted ceiling and disappeared amongst the heavy wooden beams supporting the roof. The lights barely reached the far corners draped in mysterious shadow.

"I'll stand on her other side, have her in the centre," she said. "And I'll make her responses for her."

"Are we ready?" Giles took his place, bible in hand. "I've chosen the old traditional version they would have been familiar with but cut bits out to streamline the proceedings."

Martin looked up at Nina. She smiled and bent to press a kiss on his mouth. "This is it," she whispered then, "Ready," to Giles.

She glanced down at her heavy winter clothing. She should have worn something more bridal—a skirt at least rather than thick woollen slacks. Would that make a difference? Would Piers care? Miranda would have been so excited to marry her man, she'd have dressed for the occasion. Too late now.

A sharp click broke the deep silence, a hiss of tape followed and then the sound of Nina's violin poured into the still, cold air. The other instruments joined in. Martin's eyes were closed, his face relaxed. How could he possibly meditate? Her own mind was a seething mass of questions and doubts and worries.

But the music surrounded her and invaded her body, poured into every cell, filled her soul, grew in volume and intensity. The violinist wasn't Nina, he was far, far better and other musicians played the missing parts. Piers was playing. Piers and his group. Chanting began but so distant she wasn't sure she heard it or imagined it. The voices grew stronger, much stronger. So loud and close they could have been in the church.

Suddenly he was there before her. Not completely solid, the image shimmered slightly, but dark eyes fixed on Nina with an intensity born of deep and endless passion. Jessica gasped behind her but stayed silent.

All the love she'd carried for this extraordinary man suffused her very being. His features were achingly familiar, the straight firm nose, full lips, dark hair. She knew his touch, his kiss, the feel of his body…honeyed warmth spread outward from her centre. She smiled. The image firmed.

Giles erupted into speech.

"Dearly beloved, we are gathered together here in the sight of God, and in the face of this congregation, to join together this Man and this Woman in holy Matrimony." Giles usual booming voice had faded to something barely audible, just above a whisper.

Miranda's portrait began to glow with a subtle inner light. Her skin took on a richer hue, her eyes came alive. The music filled the church now, rebounding from the ancient stones, echoing from the highest points, soaring heavenward.

Giles continued bravely with the service.

"I require and charge you both, as ye will answer at the dreadful day of judgement when the secrets of all

353

hearts shall be disclosed, that if either of you know any impediment, why ye may not be lawfully joined together in Matrimony, ye do now confess it. For be ye well assured, that so many as are coupled together otherwise than God's Word doth allow are not joined together by God; neither is their Matrimony lawful."

Piers stepped closer. "Is it you?" he whispered. "Is it really you?"

"Yes, my love." Nina held out her hand, Miranda a palpable force urging her on. "Marry me, Piers." He extended his hand and her fingers were enclosed by a strong warm grip. An electric pulse shot up her arm and she almost cried out. But Giles had forged ahead, his voice stronger now, anxious to get the service finished.

"Wilt thou have this Woman to thy wedded Wife, to live together after God's ordinance in the holy estate of Matrimony? Wilt thou love her, comfort her, honour, and keep her in sickness and in health; and, forsaking all other, keep thee only unto her, so long as ye both shall live?"

She held Piers' gaze for an eternity, waiting, praying he would respond. He'd never said he would marry her but she wanted more than anything in the world to be his wife. He must know that. He had to marry her, she'd given herself to him freely and never doubted his trustworthiness. If he didn't, her future was ruined. Ethan would shun her and so would his family and friends. If Piers loved her as much as he said, how could he not?

"I will." It came on a sigh, floating into the air and echoing around the stone walls.

Giles turned to her, his face an impervious mask although drops of perspiration beaded on his brow. The temperature had soared with the music.

"Wilt thou have this Man to thy wedded Husband, to live together after God's ordinance in the holy estate of Matrimony? Wilt thou obey him, and serve him, love, honour, and keep him in sickness and in health; and, forsaking all other, keep thee only unto him, so long as ye both shall live?"

"I will." Her voice rang out strong and proud.

"Who giveth this Woman to be married to this Man?"

Giles paused.

"I do." Jessica stepped forward.

Piers didn't take his eyes from hers.

Giles nodded.

"Repeat after me. I, Piers de Crespigny take thee Miranda Templeton to my wedded Wife, to have and to hold from this day forward, for better or for worse, for richer, for poorer, in sickness and in health, to love and to cherish, till death us do part, according to God's holy ordinance; and thereto I plight thee my troth."

He repeated the vow with Miranda then nodded to Jessica who pulled her wedding ring off and handed it to Piers with a shaking hand. He stared at the ring then he took it and slid it onto Nina's finger.

Giles addressed Piers. "Repeat after me. With this Ring I thee wed, with my Body I thee worship, and with all my worldly Goods I thee endow: In the Name of the Father, and of the Son, and of the Holy Ghost. Amen."

Piers repeated every word.

"Let us pray."

She sank to her knees and bowed her head, eyes closed, tears pricking at her lids. It was done. At last they were man and wife.

"Those whom God hath joined together let no man put asunder.

"For as much as Piers and Miranda have consented together in holy Wedlock, and have witnessed the same before God and this company, and thereto have given and pledged their troth either to other, and have declared the same by giving and receiving of a Ring, and by joining of hands; I pronounce that they be Man and Wife together, In the Name of the Father, and of the Son, and of the Holy Ghost. Amen."

Giles raised his hands.

"God the Father, God the Son, God the Holy Ghost, bless, preserve, and keep you; the Lord mercifully with his favour look upon you; and so fill you with all spiritual benediction and grace, that ye may so live together in this life, that in the world to come ye may have life everlasting. Amen."

The thick intense music gradually faded until the only sound was the original recording, the instruments thin and toneless, the melody unremarkable.

Nina's eyes opened slowly. She was Nina, not Miranda, the intense spirit of the other girl had left her. She wiped shaky fingers across cheeks wet with tears. Piers had gone. She stood on shaky legs and turned, searching the dim recesses of the church for a final glimpse of his dark and tragic figure, straining her ears for the sound of his voice. He was gone. Completely and utterly.

Jessica stopped the tape and the silence was complete. Martin opened his arms to Nina and she walked into his embrace.

"It's over," he whispered. "It's finally over."

She nodded, unable to speak, unable to express not only the relief but also the inexplicable sadness that went with it. Piers had been the most extraordinary man she would ever meet in her life. She would miss him and she would never ever forget him. Or Miranda. Both had become a part of her and always would be. On some level Piers was her husband.

"My goodness," Giles declared.

"She's changed completely," Jessica said.

Nina spun about to look at Miranda. The supernatural glow suffused the whole painting and spilled over to the surroundings. Then, as they watched, it gradually dimmed. Miranda's skin and clothing returned to the painted colour but it was her expression that commanded attention. Her eyes sparkled, a smile played on her lips—she was a carefree, happy girl.

"She looks like a girl on her wedding day," said Jessica. "So very happy." Tears rolled down her cheeks. "Isn't she beautiful."

"It *is* her wedding day," said Giles.

"Look at her hand," whispered Nina. A gold wedding band gleamed on the third finger left hand.

"Extraordinary," said Giles. "Absolutely extraordinary."

"I can't believe we've done it. At last, we can have our lives back," said Martin.

"I'll miss Piers," said Nina.

"No, you won't." Martin grabbed her and swung her off the ground. He put her down and kissed her soundly. "I'll see to that."

"Did you hear how the music had changed?" Nina asked.

Martin nodded. "Pretty ordinary piece really.

Lovely melody but…"

"Nothing more," Nina finished.

"I think it's time for bed." Jessica picked up the tape player. "I'm exhausted."

Martin and Giles covered the painting with the coats while Nina collected the instruments and umbrellas. She followed the others as they went down the aisle, slowing her pace for a last silent farewell to the man who'd loved so much and been loved so much. She paused at the last row of pews ready to walk out into the night and into her future with the real man she loved with all her heart.

"Goodbye, Piers. May you rest in peace, now."

She stepped through the door and as she did she heard what might have been the winter wind sighing in the trees but could have been Piers' voice one last time.

"Thank you. My love. My life."

Thank you for purchasing
this publication of The Wild Rose Press, Inc.

For questions or more information
contact us at
info@thewildrosepress.com.

The Wild Rose Press, Inc.
www.thewildrosepress.com

To visit with authors of
The Wild Rose Press, Inc.
join our yahoo loop at
http://groups.yahoo.com/group/thewildrosepress/